Whispering Winds

THE MÊLA
BOOK ONE

CASSIDY STEPHENS

Copyright © 2023 by Cassidy Stephens

All rights reserved.

No part of this book may be reproduced in any form or by any electronic or mechanical means, including information storage and retrieval systems, without written permission from the author, except for the use of brief quotations in a book review.

❦ Created with Vellum

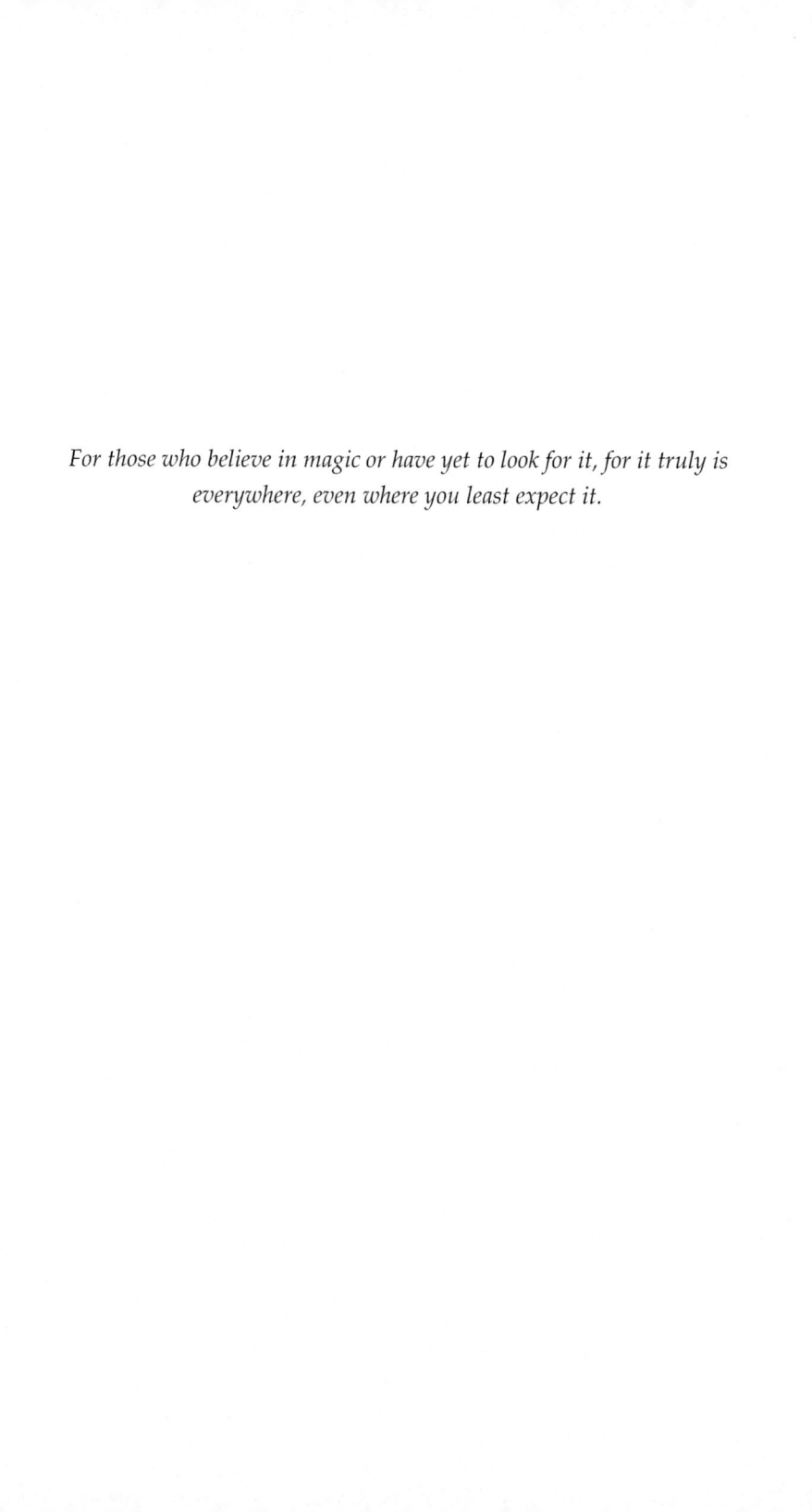

For those who believe in magic or have yet to look for it, for it truly is everywhere, even where you least expect it.

"All that is gold does not glitter,
  Not all those who wander are lost;
  The old that is strong does not wither,
  Deep roots are not reached by the frost.

From the ashes a fire shall be woken,
  A light from the shadows shall spring;
  Renewed shall be blade that was broken,
  The crownless again shall be king."

J.R.R. TOLKIEN, *LORD OF THE RINGS: THE FELLOWSHIP OF THE RING*

Preface

We tend to live in a world of realism. Everything is created through a logical standpoint. Jobs. Education. Technology. Even family. All that we know has been formed to create an easier experience for everyone on Earth. Science is the leading factor to most's worldview. Sure, there is religion. There is a God who sees over us from the Heavens. It seems like He isn't there sometimes, as if His miracles and presence are mere fairytales. But what if there is so much more beyond that?

For the longest time, I have doubted my faith in Christ. I was raised in a Christian household, going to church every Sunday and praying before every meal and before I go to bed. It was routine for me, a Science that I had learned over the years. For a while, it was nothing more than that. Then, a recent tragedy among my inner circle opened my eyes to who God really is. I started studying the Bible on a daily basis. I began to pray more often than when I simply needed something. I started receiving answers to the questions I've asked for my entire life. I started to believe again.

What once was a lonely girl became one of great faith and a love for sharing her journey. That girl was me. God's presence in my life is certainly something to behold. I hope to share my story through the protagonist of this series. Ophelia "Lia" Sage Hart is a woman of Science. She never believed in magic but only logic that stemmed from her extraordinary academic talent. Before she knew it, she was whisked into a situation she never would've expected. Now, she's searching the world - and herself - for a hint of this magic that she did not even know existed. I hope that you can see yourself in Lia's shoes as she embarks on her journey of faith just like I have. Along with Lia's kindness, witty remarks, and an odd obsession with J.R.R. Tolkien's *Lord of the Rings* trilogy, there is a burning desire to discover the truth...no matter what.

Prologue

Realms exist beyond our own…realms that involve unique qualities from our own…realms possessing significantly elevated nature and life. These realms are not like our own, but instead much different. Rather than falling apart and dying, these domains are instead filled with life at every corner, from the cornerstone seeping through the edges. This realm in particular was not like the others. Oh, no, how it differed greatly. You could feel it in the breeze, through their sun's rays ebbing on the land. You could feel it through the raindrops cascading down the leaves of the trees, soaking up the jade stalks of grass. You could smell it in the air. It was obvious by now.

Kythaela was filled with magic. No, not the enchantments and charms of a jester or another of the liking, but instead in the world all around us. Societal norms contradicted the lifestyle of our own realm. Instead, conflicts were resolved in a reasonable, heartfelt manner. Mother Nature administered to the troubles at hand. Human muddles of any sort were diffused before a wildfire ravaged the land. This was how it used to be…how Kythaela was a realm of peace and harmony that the environment held loosely by the reins.

That was before the flame of discord grew too large to be extinguished.

It began with the Twelve. Three were of the Earth: grounded, stable, and physical embodiments of Mother Nature Herself. Three were the Air: flaccid as the wind, illuding the world around us. Three rippled as Water: empathetic and all-knowing. Finally, three were the Fire itself: passionate, strong-willed, altering the trajectory of Kythaela as it was once known. The Twelve maintained Mother Nature's duty of euphony throughout the land from the Myrlyl to the Lumena. While the sacred Mother Nature ruled over her domain of the weather and the ever-changing seasons, these Twelve committed to their own responsibilities: keeping Kythaela in a state of grace.

The Earth, Air, and Water representatives performed their area of expertise with outstretched arms and open minds. The Fire Wing, one fourth of the Twelve, did not. As time passed on, the Three grew increasingly distant from the rest of the Twelve–beckoning themselves into the shadows that they believed were their calling. They grew hasty and felt that their importance for the realm was in jeopardy. They ventured into the Northeastern land that they called Sundikar–a volcanic wasteland filled with nothing but ash and soot.

Not one Kythaelan resident would ever forget the night the Fire descended into madness.

It was a night like any other. The breeze whispered daintily between the trees making up the forest of Myrlyl that surrounded the Kingdom of Luthyia. This Kingdom, perching on the edge of the Vonvlees Mountains, was where the Twelve took residence. After the Sun set and the Moon took its place in the night sky, Mother Nature took watch over the darkness and it was time for the Twelve to rest in their own quarters. Day in and day out, this was a routine for the four Wings, but on this night in particular, the Fire Wing proclaimed their separation.

Below, Luthyia Village awoke from the abrupt increase in temperature on that very night. From the Castle to the outskirts of Myrlyl, lanterns were lit and illuminated the cobblestone streets that soon filled with the concerned residents. Soon did they learn that gathering in the paths at night was a monumental mistake. Lanterns burst from the sheer pressure of an expanding flame. Wildfire spread from lamps and candlelight, beginning to devour whatever structure was in its way. Soon enough, one wooden house was consumed by the flames, followed by another, and then a third. One by one, they all were consumed agonizingly slow by the tongues of fire.

The villagers lost count after that. Screams and desperate cries ripped through the alleyways and intersections, bewitching the Castle overhead. The attention of the other Three Wings was grabbed by the eerie luminescent glow quickly spreading. Once the Three Wings checked the Fire Wing's quarters, they knew the source of the issue.

They were gone, resulting in the catastrophic destruction lying below. The Nine peered down at the Village in horror, knowing there was nothing they could do to prevent Luthyia's ultimate demise. The greed and distance they put between themselves had grown too far gone to repair, so in order to fulfill their "destiny" as they called it, the Fire Wing took it out on the others. If there was no one to stop them, there was nothing in their way.

Beyond the jurisdiction of the Village laid a house, or a hut, more like. Shrouded by the canopy of the thick greenery lived a Woman who once crossed paths with Luthyia, but instead took to Herself in restful solitude. She believed the Twelve had Kythaela under control, but the very argument, the shadows disregarding all morale, a sickening howl, wrenched Her from Her slumber that night. The Woman, whose hair was paler than Her skin, grew white as a ghost. She knew the inevitable had come. It had been under Luthyia's nose the whole time.

The Woman gaped out of the only window in Her hut and did not hesitate to climb through. Her bare toes seeped into the moist soil below, contrasting the unusually escalated humidity.

Her white nightgown stretched down to her ankles. As She ran towards the source of the heat, dirt flicked its way onto the pearly fabric. She did not care enough to look down, but instead lurched forward, snaking through each tree as if She knew the unmarked route by heart. Branches flicked past Her face and pebbles flew from under Her feet. In one foul swoop, the Woman leapt from one side of the Lumena's temporarily tame rapids to the other. Sweat dripped down Her heart-shaped face as She bolted to the Village She knew and loved dearer than Her own relatives, which were scarce.

Her pupils dilated when they locked on the torched town laid out in front of Her. She fought the urge to sink to the ground in horror as Her homeland, the place She treasured more than anything in this realm…faded away into ashes.

"No…"

The single word etched itself on Her chapped lips. A lone tear escaped from Her gaze, cascaded down Her cheek, and wetted a petite patch of soil below. It was perhaps the only source of extinguishment Luthyia would endure until the Eternal Winter began. Villagers filling buckets to the brim from the Lumena and dumping them on the ever-growing flames did nothing to douse them. Instead, another patch grew from any source of life and began engulfing another.

A monumental rumble clapped from the sky sheerer than cobalt overhead. The Woman's sapphire eyes snapped up to meet several of the Vonvlees beginning to crack and depart. She, unlike the Village, buried a shriek of horror as the mountains collapsed and showered Luthyia in an avalanche only Mother Nature Herself could stop; without the Twelve, though, such a miracle was far from occurring. When one Wing would be corrupted, the rest would follow. She knew the remaining Nine were long gone, dispersed from Kythaela without a second thought.

The Woman knew what She had to do. Once more, She Weaved her way through the dense Myrlyl, ignoring the scrapes and scratches the trees were bestowing upon Her in Her haste. She leapt through Her window and scrambled to gather Her most important, prized possessions. From books to ingredients to rare plants to Her favorite clothes, She piled them all in the quilted blanket atop Her bed and tied it tightly shut amongst one end of Her pure white staff. She hoisted the heavy load atop Her shoulder and passed through the door this time. She took one last look at the hut She called her home for years upon years, before the Lumena was abundant as it now was.

Luthyia, followed by Kythaela itself was left behind in the flames bringing it to an end. No more was the harmony that once encased its very essence from dawn to dusk. Long gone was the balance the Twelve provided for over a millennia. Instead, only destruction in the form of embers lapping up the remnants the flames left to die. Luthyia was nothing but ruins after that fateful night. Ash turned to snow as the heat from the Fire Wing left along with them subsequent to their prior attack. In the morning, the Sun would hesitate to inevitably rise to give way to a new day that was no longer promised. No more was the guaranteed peace the Twelve brought forth and maintained through their abilities. The Woman clothed in white and despair knew it was meant to be. She had seen it all along in Her mind's eye. The prophecy was written a thousand times over, page after page in Her treasured books. It was as plain as day. No matter how hard She tried to keep the prophecy from fulfilling itself, fate stood in the way. There was no going back now.

Together, there is harmony. Divided, only chaos remains.

One

Despite being a realm of normality, magic existed on Earth. From the hilltops to the valleys to the whispers in the breeze, there was something unique about it all. Raindrops glistened on the pavement outside, creating puddles that the neighborhood children adored to splash into with their rubber boots. The pitter-patter of the rain splashed onto the windows of every house of the Elwood Manor district. Even with the Sun behind the ominous clouds, the municipality of Oakbrooke was a mesmerizing place.

Tucked on the outskirts of Atlanta, Oakbrooke was a much quieter town than the metropolis to the northwest that dwarfed it. On occasion, tourists would bleed through the city's borders and vacate into hotels just outside the perimeter for half the price. The residents of Oakbrooke simply had to get used to snarky, less than pleasant tourists bombarding their suburban paradise. What Oakbrooke was already accustomed to were the roaring of jet engines overhead, rushing passengers to and fro the International Airport just miles away.

In the long run, none of those inconveniences mattered to the residents of the hidden treasure. Instead of relishing in the negative aspects, the suburbanites lived their own lives amongst themselves, paying no mind to the absurdly ginormous neighbor to the north. Most were satisfied with their picture-perfect homes concealed from the public. That was exactly how the Oakbrookians liked it; each and every one of them ventured down their own path that frequently crossed with other locals. This was most definitely the case with one specific resident.

In a house in Elwood Manor lived a girl. No, just a moment... that sounded too much like another tale such as this. Elwood Manor was a neighborhood like the others–containing middle class households. Most homes in said complex sheltered a family of some sort, meaning several school-age children were present. One of these "school-age children" on eighty-eight Magnolia Terrace, was just peering up at the showerhead as the droplets cascaded down her face and washed the lavender soap from her body down through the drain peeping through the tiled glass stall. The humidity fogged up the glass as she rinsed off her pale, but rosy skin.

The environment around her instantaneously became cold when the spout of water was switched off, leaving small remnants of water streaming down her body. The girl's blurry hand in front of her reached out of the opening in the cubicle and grasped onto a black towel, tugging it into the shower with her. A miniature rainstorm ensued when a waterfall released from long strands of hair; it splattered on the off-white tiles and then the black rug she stepped onto. She scrubbed the water off every inch and crevice in her petite, still-developing frame. The young girl reached for her wire-rimmed glasses she had set down on the edge of the sink and unfolded them just before sliding them on her face. She grimaced as the lenses fogged up and she had to remove them, wipe them off, and repeat the process all over again.

As she passed by the mirror mounted on the gray walls, her reflection paused to assess itself. Looking back at her was a girl who could not have been older than sixteen. Freckles dotted her nose and cheeks where her round chocolate eyes blinked the remaining droplets off her short eyelashes. Her chestnut eyebrows were a shade darker than her damp waves falling down her back a few inches below her shoulders. She was well-aware that when her hair was completely dry at least an hour later, the strands would curl into an unruly mess unless she brushed it out.

A chill rushed through her body, so she decided to get moving. The young girl padded up the stairs into her bedroom which was directly through the door at the top, her bare feet treading amongst the gray carpet as she entered. She shut the door behind her and let the towel escape her grasp as she ventured towards her dresser which was on the same wall as the door. She dug through her drawers for a shirt, pants, underwear, and even a bra that would somehow come together to create an outfit. Eventually, she stood in front of her full-length mirror - fully clothed and with deodorant *surprisingly* on - in a black *Pink Floyd "Dark Side of the Moon"* shirt, ripped light-washed jeans, and a red and black flannel...complete with pink *Hello Kitty* socks.

Even though she was fully dressed, she believed there was something missing. Her glasses nearly flew off her face as her gaze snapped towards the tall glass cage at the foot of her bed and next to a large spruce bookshelf. She dashed over to the vivarium filled with a soil base, greenery stretching to the top of the enclosure, and several rocks and branches and peered through the glass walls until she found what she was looking for. An orange and tan sunkissed corn snake awoke from her slumber and slithered towards its best friend of sorts. The girl did not hesitate to open a small hatch in the side of the vivarium, stick her hand in, and watch as her pet snaked - literally - onto her arm before pulling it out and letting the little lady claim her as her own. She stepped back into the range of the mirror and nodded this time. An internal stamp of approval was enough to propel herself forward - almost slamming into the closed door prior to opening it - and dash down the stairs.

The pair of Hello Kitty sock-clad feet thumped onto the dark wooden floor and darted towards the pantry past the foyer in the kitchen on the right. A creaking sound made it evident that the once empty kitchen was now populated with at least one inhabitant with a grumbling stomach. The teenager fished through the pantry until she emerged with a chocolate dipped granola bar–one of her favorites. She closed the pantry door to reveal her mother, Cheyenne Hart, on the other side.

Mrs. Hart was one of the kindest, but busiest women her daughter had ever known. Working two jobs - one in-person and one remote - meant not much free time for the woman in her forties. From all of the stress piled on her shoulders over the years, it was a wonder that she had not one gray hair in her scalp filled with otherwise dark brown hair tied in a bun. That reminded her daughter of the hair tie she left on her wrist–hence making an attempt to pull her hair back into a low ponytail with one hand. Eventually, she gave up and stuffed the partially unwrapped granola bar in her mouth.

"Morning, Lia!" Cheyenne's smile lit up the entire kitchen more than the LED lights in the ceiling. "How are you–oh, my goodness!" She cut herself off and pointed to what she referred to as the "nope rope" sliding her way around her daughter's neck and draping like a loose scarf. "Ophelia Sage, be careful with that snake–that looks dangerous."

Respecting her mother's wishes with a sigh, Lia lifted her hand to cautiously remove the reptile from her shoulders and allowed her to coil around her arm. "But Mom," she whined with a full mouth, resorting to biting half the granola bar between her teeth and chewing hastily. "We've had Noodle for almost a year now. She'd never do anything to hurt me."

"Remind me why your father and I let you get that anaconda-looking thing," she grimaced.

Lia just sighed, swallowing her food. "She's a *corn snake*," she retorted as if it was a mundane routine. "She's harmless, and besides, she was all I wanted for my birthday."

"I still think Noodle is a–"

"Nope rope?" the teenager smirked teasingly. Her mother nodded. "Noodle wouldn't hurt a fly...well, unless she wanted to eat it."

Cheyenne's round eyes that looked identical to her daughter's widened, but she exhaled a long breath and instead plastered on a grin. "I'll trust you on that, Sweetie. I'm sorry–I'm still getting used to having a pet without fur...or legs. You know her best."

"Just...don't go in my room when she's feeding if it frightens you that much."

"Oh, Honey, I've already learned that the hard way."

"What?"

"Nothing!" Cheyenne opened the pantry and picked up a granola bar for herself. "So, Lia, your birthday's tomorrow. Are you excited?"

Lia took another bite out of her own bar and nodded, ignoring the fact her mother changed the subject so quickly. "Mhm," she mumbled heartily.

"What's the plan? The usual?"

"Yep!" Lia crumpled up the wrapper and tossed it in the nearby trash can. "Us three, Nana and Papa, Maylene, her sister, and Noodle, of course, will be here."

"What kind of cake?"

"You know my favorite."

"Vanilla with green frosting and rainbow sprinkles–got it. Decorations?"

"Whatever you can find at Wally-Mart is fine."

"Perfect," Cheyenne declared, checking off an invisible list. "Are you sure you don't want to do anything else? It's your day, Lia–seize it!"

Lia pulled a couple of loose tendrils from her ponytail and let them frame her face. "I like how we do it every year. Being with the family is the most important thing to me."

"Even on your Sweet Sixteen?"

Cheyenne was caught by pleasant surprise when her daughter stood on her tiptoes and wrapped her arms around her in a hug.

"*Especially* my Sweet Sixteen."

There was nothing like a mother's hug. Pure love and affection seeped from one older body to the younger one. It was as if any situation, no matter how tragic, was turned to nothingness manipulated in size from a mountain to a speck of dust blown under a chair never to be seen again. That was exactly how Cheyenne embraced Lia–with the intent to make all of her problems go away in a heartbeat. At least, that was the case until the poor woman realized a certain corn snake was beginning to crawl onto her shoulder. Cheyenne flinched away from her daughter and Lia caught her pet before she dangled and fell.

"Eek! Get it off! Get it off!"

"What was that, Mom?!" Lia lovingly poked Noodle's snout while a laugh bubbled up in her throat. "She's not going to hurt you."

"Praise Jesus she has a cage," her mother sighed in relief.

"Vivarium," she corrected.

"Right."

Being in a typical suburban household was not very exciting, but somehow, the Harts made it entertaining. The first - and most obvious - aspect that made their little corner of Elwood Manor unique was Noodle the corn snake, whom Lia did not want to return to her vivarium before leaving for the day. Before being returned to her habitat, Noodle aided her in packing her lunch, which consisted of a peanut butter and jelly - minus the jelly - sandwich along with a bag of pretzel sticks, a cut-up green apple, another of the chocolate-dipped granola bars, and a few double-stuffed Oreo cookies. As she zipped up her maroon lunch box, Lia could not comprehend how Noodle would last a week or even two without being fed a meal; she was a foodie at heart. To put it plainly, she would not cherish life as much as she

CHAPTER ONE 13

already did. One of her mottos was "Why have food if you cannot enjoy it?" and she lived by that.

Lia stuffed her fern green canteen - would you look at that–a rhyme - into the suffering cup holder on the right-hand side of her beige backpack. She hoisted the heavy bag onto her shoulders and nearly fell right back down on her backside from the weight. Nevertheless, Lia trotted out the door and pulled the hood of her flannel jacket over her head once it made contact with the delicate rain outside. Her mother was not far behind, fishing the keys to her black Honda Civic out of the bottomless pit she called her mahogany purse and slinging it over her right shoulder. Cheyenne shut the dark green front door behind her and unlocked her fairly new vehicle with a spritely beep. Lia hopped into the driver's seat while her mother got into the passenger's seat.

"Ready, Mom?" Lia buckled her seat belt and then inserted the key in the ignition, turning it sideways and listening to the engine purr to life.

Cheyenne swallowed down a lump of anxiety and smiled instead. "I'm ready."

No matter how often Lia drove her mother's vehicle, Cheyenne never got used to it. Ever since her daughter got her learner's permit just about three months ago, Cheyenne did her best to be supportive, but, needless to say, her heart nearly leapt out of her throat every time Lia's foot pressed the gas pedal. Lia was an exceptional driver, nevertheless. Taught mostly by her father, she knew most of the ins and outs of Oakbrooke. She was not brave enough to venture into Atlanta just yet; in fact, almost nobody in town was to begin with. Cheyenne's main dilemma was failing to believe her only daughter was growing up so fast. Just yesterday, she was a toddler bursting into tears over a daffodil stem she accidentally snapped in the front yard.

Windshield wipers flicked the drizzling drops from above off the front window at an intermittent setting. Rubber rolled against the familiar asphalt it had trod a thousand times, but maybe eighty with Lia behind the wheel. She steered the car towards the entrance of the neighborhood, which took a couple of minutes, but at the final turn before the exit, she made a right. This led the black sedan down a side street until it reached a cul-de-sac, which she turned right once more to enter. Lia steered the vehicle into the driveway straight ahead leading to a single-storied home, or a cottage, more like, where the exterior siding was made of stone. Rain bounced off the dark, gray-shingled roof and slid down the matching shutters surrounding the dark oak-framed windows. Once she switched the vehicle's gear into "Park," Lia removed her phone from her flannel's pocket and typed out a message labeled to two recipients.

"I'm outside! :)"

Lia could not decide for the life of her if she was feeling lazy or blatantly did not want to walk up to the front porch in the rain, but nevertheless, the dark oak front door opened and two identical girls stumbled out. From straight-as-a-pin black hair and bangs atop their heads, almond-shaped brown eyes, and milky pale skin, these girls were mirror images of each other. The only difference was how they chose to style themselves. The first girl that rushed through the quickly intensifying rain wore a pair of pastel pink overalls over a white long-sleeved shirt. A matching pink headband adorned her head but neglected to pull back her bangs while brown birkenstocks adorned her bare feet. The second possessed a massive faded blue hoodie stretching down to mid-thigh, black leggings that complimented her slender legs, and black converse with white laces that she wore every day. The twins opened the back door on either side and shut it behind them in unison as if they had rehearsed. Both buckled their seat belts and set their backpacks at their feet.

"Good morning." Lia's greeting rippled from the front seat.

"Hiya!" the twin on the right exclaimed.

"Morning!" the twin on the left chimed in.

The Zuíhuí twins, Maylene and Yasmin, were something to behold. While both of them looked the same, their personalities were like Yin and Yang. While Yasmin was the more sociable type and spoke to everything that had a pulse, Maylene was quiet and reserved, focusing on the one friend she cherished more than anyone else outside her household: Lia. Ever since the two of them were little, Lia and Maylene were attached at the hip–sometimes more often than the latter with her twin sister. The two sisters from different families were like two peas in a pod, never leaving each other's side. Both of them tried doing as many classes together as they could, which often did not end well, but it was worth a shot.

Lia put the vehicle in reverse and checked both sides of the road behind her prior to resorting to the backup camera for the rest of her ordeal. "How are you guys?"

"Good!" both twins chorused. Yasmin - the girl behind the driver's seat - began a conversation. "You would not *believe* the Mahjong battle we had last night."

"Oh, really?" A smile blossomed its way onto Lia's face while she drove. "Tell me about it."

That was exactly what Yasmin - and occasionally, Maylene - did. Cheyenne shook her head lovingly at one of the twins she considered her "second" and "third" daughters. Lia was much accustomed to the game of Mahjong; she had been playing it with Maylene and Yasmin ever since the very first time they invited her over to their home. The one hundred and forty-four tiles consisted of five types: Bamboo, Characters, Dots, Honours, and Bonus. All of the tiles were shuffled and each of the four players drew thirteen tiles from the bunch. A die was rolled to determine who would go first and that player would draw an extra tile to begin the game. Throughout the game, players take turns drawing and discarding tiles to make four suits and a pair. When the winning hand is made, the player exclaims: "Sik wu!" and then the game is over. It had become a favorite of Lia's over the years.

After about ten minutes of a nearly torrential downpour, Lia's unwavering concentration despite the constant giggles and exclamations from the back seat, and Cheyenne resisting the urge to clasp onto the "uh oh" handle above her door, the black sedan miraculously made it to Oakbrooke High School in one piece. Once Lia steered the vehicle into the closest available spot in the drastically bustling parking lot, she adjusted the gear into "Park" for a second time and leaned over to wrap her arms around her mother just like every day.

"Have a great day at school, you three," Cheyenne wished her girls well and then beamed at her biological daughter. "Nice driving, Honey."

"*As if,*" Lia chuckled to herself. "Thanks, Mom. I love you."

"I love you too."

Lia, Maylene, and Yasmin took Mrs. Hart's parting words as their cue. In a matter of five seconds, three doors were opened and closed, three backpacks were upon backs with lunch boxes in hand, and the trio of teenagers walked side by side towards the intimidating building they inhabited as their second home for five days a week. Oakbrooke High School was massive, having two floors, dozens of classrooms, a gymnasium, an auditorium, several faculty offices, and a courtyard that also acted as the cafeteria all under one roof. The most notable feature of the building was the monumental oak tree sticking straight through the roof of the domed courtyard. In fact, that same tree was what Oakbrooke was named after and what the city itself - and quite literally the school - was built around much before Atlanta became such a metropolis.

The glass double doors opened to reveal what appeared to be a miniature community. Especially beyond the foyer and the welcome desk, past another set of doors was what could only be defined as pure chaos. Everywhere that met the eye, there were at least five people per three square feet. The vast walls of lockers that would normally take up space had been removed as of the previous year to make way for more online learning, yet still, the entire student body made the hallways their stomping grounds. At once, numerous conversations from every direction meshed together into a chromatic disaster, leaving utterly no room for silence. Maylene flinched closer to Lia while Yasmin did quite the opposite. It seemed as if as soon as the trio walked through the doors, she found a small group of people she knew as at least acquaintances.

Before she left for good, though, Yasmin hurtled to her left and barreled into her two sisters - one biological and one not - with a strong embrace. "I'll see you at lunch!" she promised them. "What class do you have first again?"

"Ceramics," Lia and Maylene replied. It definitely was not the first time they had spoken in unison.

Yasmin's nose scrunched up, however a smile was still on her face as she let go. "Have fun with that," she offered encouragement anyway. "See you later!"

"You too." Maylene's farewell was less than a whisper compared to the crowd.

Lia shrugged and nudged her friend in the upper arm. "Yeah, right," she chided to just the two of them.

Maylene smiled, knowing that her sister would indeed not come back. It was never truly intentional. Yasmin was too much of a social butterfly for her own good. One minute, she was completely enamored by Maylene and Lia, and the next, one of her countless friends from any rung of the social ladder would be shouting to her from across the hall. Neither Lia nor Maylene minded, though; they were more than content with each other's company. That was why the former's spring in her step grew larger as the two pairs of eyes watched the storm of students parading every which way. Lia turned to her left.

"Ceramics?"

The ebony-haired beauty grinned. "Ceramics."

So, that was exactly where Lia and Maylene headed. While still in the open lobby area of the massive building, Lia grasped loosely onto Maylene's wrist and guided her towards the propped open door leading to the stairwell. Thankfully, most of the flock was walking in the same direction, it being the beginning of the school day and several classrooms being upstairs rather than on the ground floor. Maylene subconsciously walked directly behind the brunette who made it her life mission to reach the second floor, even if it meant pushing past people and muttering an apology every five seconds. Despite the struggle, the two friends made it to the top of both flights in one piece. This time, Maylene took the lead. She knew the Ceramics classroom by heart. It never changed from semester to semester and Maylene never failed to enroll for said class whenever it was available–usually in the first semester of every school year.

"I still don't know what I should do for my final project," Lia admitted as they passed through the door leading into Room 208: the fourth door on the right-hand side of the hallway.

This semester was Lia's first in Ceramics, meaning it was automatically the hardest. Maylene, on the other hand, thrived in such a creative environment. While Lia struggled to keep a mound of clay steady on the potter's wheel, Maylene was on her third or fourth by the time her best friend figured it out. More often than not, Maylene would drop whatever she was working on, whether it be a vase, bowl, or even a small sculpture of an animal, and aid her friend whose talents lay elsewhere. Lia's projects were nowhere close to perfect, but Maylene pitched in and offered assistance when requested.

"Whatever you want," Maylene reiterated what their teacher said just earlier that week. "That's the fun part!"

Lia sat down at the table both of them shared. "What are you making again? I know what it is, but I can't remember what it's called."

"An ocarina," the girl next to her beamed. "I'm still working on the base, but I started it Monday and it should be nearly ready to have the decorative assets added."

"How are you so talented? I don't understand."

Maylene flushed red due to the compliment. "How are you so good with music?" she answered Lia's question with one of her own. "You can play pretty much anything in the music store when we visit."

"...Because I had years of practice." It was Lia's turn to pinken.

"Exactly. What is it you wanted for your birthday from your mom and dad? A mandolin?"

Lia shrugged yet smiled anyway. "Yeah."

"And how long did it take you to teach yourself how to play one of them at Ear Candy? Ten minutes?" Maylene pressed gleefully.

"The internet was helpful."

"Sure, but not everybody can do that."

Lia appeared as if she was going to disagree, but the accidental slam of the door closing followed by a pair of black heels clicking against the off-white tiles laid out through the entire school–minus the gym, cafeteria, and auditorium. All eyes in the packed classroom gave their attention to whom everyone referred to as Miss K. She was a young woman in her mid to late twenties who always had a unique outfit to display. Today, she was wearing a black dress with multicolored paint brushes all over it along with rainbow paint palette earrings. Her light blonde hair was tied up in a messy bun much like Lia's mother's was that morning. The only difference was the red bow atop her head. Just one glance at Miss K brightened her students' day.

"Good morning, class, and happy Friday!" she chirped just like every time she began a class period. "Let's make it a good one. How is everybody doing today?"

Murmurs of "I'm good," "I'm tired," or "I'm ready for the weekend" filled the classroom. Miss K smiled and set the manilla folder she walked into the room with down on her desk. "Well, the weekend is upon us–one more day to go!" she noted to lift their spirits. "Today, we're going to have a free period. Everybody please pick up your projects from the back counter and continue working on them. If you decide you're finished for the day, and after I take a look at them, you're more than welcome to either work on homework, listen to music, or talk amongst yourselves as long as it is not disturbing to the others."

The class seemed to be very happy about that. Once more, Miss K's lips quirked upwards. "Alright, then! Since everyone is on board, let's get to work."

The class was instantaneously a herd of elephants attempting to get to their stomping grounds. Lia and Maylene remained at their seats until the room cleared out enough for them to retrieve their projects. Maylene cradled her ocarina that actually looked like it was supposed to in her arms. Lia looked down at her warped vase that she claimed had character, but deep down, she was disappointed in her work, especially after eyeing Maylene's. Lia kept her negative thoughts to herself; she knew the first thing Maylene would do would be to shut it down and compliment her project to her heart's content. Lia knew it was not perfect, but she brought it back to her desk with a smile and mustered up as much confidence as she could.

Both of their projects had already been sculpted and shaped throughout the week which meant they were ready to paint. Miss K had a plethora of paint colors to choose from on her desk, so that was Lia and Maylene's next stop. Lia chose her usual favorite colors of forest green, maroon, brown, and pastel yellow. Maylene, on the other hand, chose three or four shades of pink, three shades of green, a couple shades of tan, and some of the same pastel yellow that Lia retrieved; she said that they could share. Miss K aided them in putting each color on a white plastic palette to take back to their table. When they returned, both girls set their palettes, several brushes, and a cup of water along with paper towels to wash them in the center so they could share. Each picked up a paint brush, dipped it in their base colors - brown and tan - and gave each other a knowing expression.

Lia was the first to break the ice and splash some color onto her project. "Let's get to work!"

Two

As said in the previous chapter, magic truly existed in our realm. It was interpreted by some as the weather–the sunshine beaming overhead drying the raindrops formerly coating the asphalt streets, mossy grass, and the pavement that flowed through it all. Magic was the occasional squirrel climbing up into a tree across the way or even an acorn on the ground symbolizing life as it was supposed to be lived. Magic was the chiding of good spirits and authentic compliments between strangers on a street corner. Magic was the fact that those who worked nine-to-five jobs safely returned home to their families for a ravishing dinner and precious quality time under one roof. All throughout Oakbrooke, magic was in the air. This was even the case for the mainstream high school that nearly every child of age attended unless they decided on enrolling in a private school or resorting to homeschooling. Magic was in the students' passions, their positive friend groups that thankfully did not become cliques, the kindness of the teachers, and the unique levels of encouragement each student gave one another.

That was why Lia snuck a peek at her best friend's work

before she concealed it by her side. "Wow, that looks gorgeous," she could not help but gush.

Maylene set her ocarina down on the table, her face nearly as pink as the rosy paint she was beginning to outline certain parts of the object with. "Oh, thank you, but I'd love for it to be a surprise, if you don't mind," she replied politely.

"Oh!" Lia blinked away the confusion from before. "My bad. I'll just keep working on my pot…thing."

"Your vase?"

"Right. It looks more like a bowl to me, though."

Maylene giggled at Lia's deadpanned expression. "Either way, it looks lovely."

"Thank you for your pity," chortled the brunette as she continued to paint.

Maylene's ocarina was truly stunning; even she knew it. After years of doing everything she possibly could in the art field, she had become very talented with almost every form of art–from sketching to painting to sculpting to even origami. As long as she had her imaginative mind and a couple of MyTube videos on her side, Maylene could create practically anything. It was a talent that Lia was often jealous of. Despite being aware of her own abilities, she somehow caught herself wishing she was something more. Her parents, Cheyenne and Lucas Hart, would always be proud of their lone daughter no matter how she performed as long as she tried her absolute best. That was all that mattered to them. Lia knew deep down that no matter what she brought home from Ceramics that semester, it would be proudly displayed somewhere in the house for everyone to see on a daily basis.

When class ended and each project was summoned back to the shelf at the rear of the classroom, Lia fought the urge to sneak a peek at Maylene's. Instead, she tugged at the straps of her backpack and ensured their security prior to picking up her lunch box as well. She then lingered by the wide desk for two as Maylene continued gathering her things, making sure that she had all of her belongings with her. Black hair was brushed away from her face as Maylene noticed there was a particular reason she was not being left behind. Her cheeks rosened when she came to the realization that the classroom was empty besides the two of them and one more student who was speaking to the teacher. Lia allowed Maylene to take the lead.

As the two of them floated past the desk, Lia offered the blonde woman a cheeky farewell. "See you tomorrow, Miss K– thank you!"

"You too, Darlings," the Ceramics teacher crooned.

It was safe to say that Miss K was Maylene and Lia's favorite teacher in all of Oakbrooke High. There were only a few "duds" as they called them in the vast faculty, but both Lia and Maylene drew the lucky cards in the deck and ended up with a good hand for the Fall semester. Miss K taught the majority of the Art classes, so Maylene often registered in one of her classes since she took Art every semester for her elective. Ceramics was normally offered every Fall while Drawing & Painting was available in the Spring. On the contrary, Lia liked to mix up her electives, such as taking Ceramics one semester and then Photography the next. During her freshman year, Lia even took a Personal Finance course. Lia relished the fact that she could enroll in a plethora of electives; she had the concept of testing out of certain classes to thank. She believed that dabbling in a little bit of everything was the prime route to take for a high school student whose mind was endlessly developing.

"You have Geometry as your next class, right?" Lia asked Maylene while their two pairs of shoes squeaked against the hallway tiles towards yet another classroom.

Her slightly shorter friend merely exhaled in defeat. "Yeah."

"I'm sorry," she sympathized with her. "Is there anything I can do to help?"

"I'll be okay." Maylene smiled, but Lia could tell it was forced by the way her brows tightened.

"Are you sure?"

"Positive."

Before both of them knew it, they had made it to Maylene's classroom on the opposite side of the second floor. Lia especially adored the way the school was wrapped around the courtyard in a sense, which was in the very heart of the building. She wrapped her arms tightly around Maylene's petite frame, assured her that she would see her at lunch, and stood vigil as she ventured into the depths of her horrid Mathematics classroom. She was well aware of Maylene's hatred for the subject–she had endured it for years. Despite finishing Algebra II at the end of her freshman year, Lia continued on in her studies to see how far she could get in such a field. She considered herself quite lucky that her middle school offered Algebra I even though the eighth grade class only consisted of three people. Most grade-schoolers began such a journey once they walked through the doors of Oakbrooke High for the first time, but not Lia. Whether she knew it or not, she was an intelligent overachiever.

Lia sat down at her usual desk at the front of her Advanced Placement Chemistry class. This was yet another of her countless endeavors. Since she had no idea where exactly her goal lay in her high school career, she decided to try a little bit of everything. If she did not enjoy said class, then she would merely test out of it and earn the credits for her record. Choosing a poor course or being stuck with an unenjoyable teacher was not a make-it or break-it moment for her. Instead, she would pick and choose her priorities. If said situation did not align with her mindset or caused more stress than necessary, then she would solve the problem, set it aside, and then search for a new–*better* opportunity for her.

Mr. Wilson, her balding, gray-haired Chemistry who always wore some sort of plaid shirt was not quite dull enough for Lia to find atrocious, but he was still annoying. "Morning, class," his borderline monotonous tone filled the already-sleepy classroom. "Today, we will be concluding our discussion on Thermodynamics to prepare for our test next week. Everyone please open your books to Chapter Thirteen."

Lia did as requested and opened the thickest textbook she had in her backpack this semester. The hardcover's pages flopped to and fro until the header, "Chapter Thirteen: Thermodynamics," was displayed at the top. Lia removed a pencil from her pouch within her fern green three-ringed binder that consisted of most of her notes. In high-density classes such as Chemistry, however, she chose to write important tidbits of information within the margins of the textbook - in pencil due to the fact she rented all of her books - and copy down the necessities later. While other students in the classroom preferred to use laptops or even tablets with stylus pens, Lia went the old-fashioned route of a pencil and paper. Writing things down helped her to retain information with an accelerated confidence.

AP Chemistry came and went, or at least the seventy-five minutes appeared to tick by quicker for Lia than some other students. At one point, a snore from the fatigued senior in the back rattled her senses and caught the attention of the rest of the class. Mr. Wilson could not find it in himself to care, though. Everyone was exhausted by that point, so he just let them sleep. Lia did not quite understand why some people fell asleep in classes when there was so much information dished out at every turn. She was not enchanted to educate herself on certain topics, but what was the harm in trying something new? The Fall semester only had about six weeks excluding Christmas break to go, after all.

Lia's next class was one that she did not appreciate as much as the others: Physical Education, or PE as the majority of the school population called it. For once, PE was the single class that Lia could not test out of, but instead was required until the end of her sophomore year of high school, which meant after the Fall semester and the Spring semester, the dreadful subject would be concluded. One aspect that she could be thankful for was the fact this course ensued before lunch so she would not be developing nausea after a hearty meal in the cafeteria. Lia was lucky enough to pick the PE time slot prior to her break. The main thing about PE that she did not appreciate was the fact she needed to change into the t-shirt and exercise shorts she stuffed in her backpack. When Lia first discovered the gymnasium showers, she made the intelligent decision not to use them. Instead, she would freshen up with deodorant and body spray she kept in her backpack and tie her usual ponytail up higher.

 That was exactly what she did following the dreadful class that would never end despite being just as long as the others. Coach Jenkins, a petite brunette woman in a tracksuit who was much scarier than she appeared, made the whole ordeal seem like a military regime. By the time their twenty-five pushups, fifteen sit ups, suicide sprints, a few laps around one of the two basketball courts in the gymnasium, and a couple games of dodgeball had commenced, Lia was out of breath. She had gone through an entire canteen of water by the time her laps were finished. Dodgeball, to say the very least, was miserable. Usually, Lia was up for a challenge, but when all of the "doofy" teenage boys ganged up on the girls who did not want to play, the game did not seem as fun anymore. The breaking point eventually was when one of the taller, more cocky boys with black hair that she was not particularly fond of, cannoned a ball that hurtled directly into the side of her face–nearly breaking her glasses in the process. Oh, no, Lia was not going to have that. In one foul swoop of retaliation, she fixed her crooked glasses, tightened her ponytail, and picked up the ball on her way off the court. She took a split second to aim and then fired it directly at his head. It ricocheted off his perfect hair and caused the tall, even muscular, boy to stumble backwards. Before he could regain his posture, Lia was long on the bench with the other girls slapping her on the back and cheering her on.

 Lia did not care much for bullies or those who made poor decisions on a whim. In fact, she did not have enough room in her heart to see the other side of things, sometimes. What happened next in her school day was one of those instances. At that moment, she did not need to see the other side. In fact, the scene unfolded directly in front of her. Lia was making her way from the gymnasium, which was on the left-hand wing of the school towards the cafeteria, where near the doors, she would meet Maylene and join her for lunch. On the regular, Maylene would wait by the propped open doors, leaning against the wall closest to where her friend would approach, but when Lia neglected to spot her, her heart dropped to her stomach. Usually, Maylene was quick to exit her third class of the morning, which was Biology. To put it plainly, she despised said lesson and would sneak out the door as soon as her teacher dismissed the class. Not being present like she was every day was concerning.

That was when Lia made the decision to investigate. Maylene's Biology course took place in a classroom on the second floor of the left wing. Lia had already come from the first floor, so she opened the doorway leading to the left-hand stairwell and trotted her way up. Footsteps of several students trekking the opposite way towards the cafeteria echoed off the walls and bounced through her ear canals. One of Lia's useless expertises happened to consist of darting around and dodging those who might not be paying attention. Lia would not consider herself as invisible as a wallflower, but her hearing was keen and she often knew much of the gossip floating around the brick walls and tiled floors. Lia shoved open the door at the very top of the stairwell and continued to search for her friend. Eventually, one voice stood out from the others being mixed together.

"...Stop."

Lia's breath hitched in her throat as she rounded the corner and watched the scene unfold. She had located Maylene, but not in the scenario she had hoped for. Originally, she thought her friend might have lingered to speak to her teacher about certain assignments, or maybe she was finishing her notes. Maybe she had stopped by the bathroom, but no. None of those suggestions were applicable; the truth was much worse. Maylene's already-tiny frame appeared to be even smaller due to the boy towering over her that had not yet grown into his height. His cacao brown hair dipped into his dark, menacing eyes. Lia wanted to rip the stupid red varsity jacket right off his shoulders. She knew his face all too well. This had happened many times before.

"You're the one asking for it." The boy's snarky remark dripped from his tongue as bitter as citric acid. "Are you serious? *Pink* overalls? What are you, five? This is high school, you twit. Did you get your outfit from the kids' section?"

As much as Lia wished Maylene would stick up for herself, her lips were wired shut. Rivers of black hair fell over her face that acted as some sort of shield to guard away from the unnecessary criticisms. Lia's face fell when she realized that was not going to happen. She was well aware of Maylene's shyness and knew the last thing she wanted to do was provoke the predator looming over her like a mossy gargoyle. Lia could not stand there any longer and let the problem fix itself. Instead, she was going to do something about it.

"If you're going to go out in that, then you should expect people to give you crap," the atrocious bully continued. "Next time, don't shop at the thrift store."

"Actually, the thrift store has lots of quality clothing if you look hard enough," Lia butted in before he could say anything else.

At once, the boy's head snapped to the side to view a furious brunette stomping towards him in her favorite shoes. She might not have looked intimidating, but Lia's normally warm brown irises were glazed over with fury. Her fists opened and closed in an attempt to calm herself or to prevent her from doing something she would regret later. Lia was better than that.

"Look who we have here," he spat cockily. "It's the fearless leader herself. Here to pick up your sidekick?"

"Oh, lookie here," Lia mocked his attempt to emotionally harm her. "It's the big bad bully whose teeth are brighter than his future. What do you want this time, Declan?"

Declan turned the rest of his body towards the sophomore about half his size. "Aw, are you trying to hurt my feelings?" he pouted with sarcasm lacing his tone. "Nice try, Hart."

"Oh, are we using last names now?" Lia took another step forward and craned her chin up to look him in the eye. "Alright, Abner." It did not take her long to conjure up a clapback. "Just because you haven't hit puberty yet at seventeen doesn't mean you have the right to pick on my friend for doing nothing but expressing herself. Now, take your nose out of our business and go put it in towards someone who actually cares."

That got Declan Abner quiet. It did not take the faint of heart to stand up to someone who was twice her size. Unfortunately, though, Lia was used to these circumstances. Every now and then, she needed to shield Maylene from Declan's mindless antics. She figured that he had low self-esteem. Sure, she was far from pitying him, especially since he clearly had nothing else to do with his life than pick on others along with playing on the Oakbrooke Mustangs basketball team. It seemed as if the giant with spaghetti noodles for arms did not have anything else up the sleeves of his varsity jacket to dish out. Instead, he straightened the collar of said coat, blew his fringe out of his chiseled face, and backed off while he had the chance.

"I'll let you have this one," he gritted out when he realized Lia would not step down. Declan then eyed Maylene up and down, which provoked her to shrink down into her pink overalls, and bit one last comment: "No wonder you only have one friend."

Lia promptly slammed her foot down on Declan's high tops.

"Ow!" he whimpered out of surprise. His eyes landed vigorously on Lia's snarling face. "Listen here, you little bi-"

"What?" she innocently interrupted him. "Are you really going to call me that? Looks like you've run out of insults."

Declan's jaw tightened. "Just shut up."

Lia made the wise decision to ignore him. She instead looped her right arm around Maylene's left and declared, "Come on, May–let's scoot."

Maylene was more than happy to oblige. She dashed after Lia to keep up, whose strides were larger than hers. When a pair of compassionate chocolate eyes rested on her as the two of them entered the stairwell, Maylene's complexion became pinker than her overalls. Her pupils dilated with emotion rather than constricting with fear from just moments prior. For a second, she swallowed down a lump in her throat. Tears pricked the backs of Maylene's glistening windows to the soul, which Lia could tell was in agony. Without giving it another moment's thought, between the two flights of stairs, Lia wrapped her arms around Maylene's timid figure. Her reserved friend - her *sister* in a sense - which she gratefully returned. Lia always ended up as Maylene's shoulder to cry on if she ever needed it. This was a role she took on for several years, but it was not manipulative in any way. Instead, Lia offered herself as a steady rock for her best friend to lean on. This time, though, Maylene fought back her tears and simply rested in Lia's embrace for a while. That was exactly what she needed when she needed it.

"Are you okay?" Lia inquired when they began walking down the stairs again.

Maylene nodded and tightened the straps of her backpack. "Yeah. Thank you."

"It's what friends are for."

This was a fact that Maylene had known since the beginning. No matter how often she got stuck in a game of tug-of-war between Lia and some sort of antagonist, Maylene was always just as fearful as before. Every instance was different. Only one thing was constant, though: many of these verbal and emotional attacks came from no one but Declan Abner. After every circumstance of this, Lia asked herself why in the world someone would take time and effort out of their limited days just to bring down someone else's? At the very beginning, Lia pitied the boy. Maybe he had self-esteem dilemmas, or had a constant war within his mind. Such instances ensued, and Lia's compassion dwindled like a flame on a cold night. Eventually, the fuse froze over and had yet to melt. Declan was a fly that Lia and Maylene thought they had shooed away but kept coming back for more, buzzing mindless nothings into their ears.

Neither Lia nor Maylene desired to dwell on the past and, on the contrary, looked forward to the future. Both of them slunk through the propped-open doors towards the very center of Oakbrooke High. To put it quite plainly, the courtyard doubling as a cafeteria was magnificent. In a way, the outdoors was brought indoors. The only thing separating it from such were the walls surrounding the spherical room and the glass dome acting as skylights to allow the sun to soak into the artificial grass that replaced the tile lining the rest of the building. A flat cobblestone pathway weaved through the courtyard and branched out into four directions leading towards the north, south, east, and west portions of the building wrapping around it. Countless picnic tables took up the four quadrants of the courtyard, leaving room for half of the school population. That was why there were two lunch sessions for thirty minutes each, but the whole population of the school received fifty-five minutes of break they could use to study or talk elsewhere.

The very heart of the courtyard was the most noticeable aspect. There in the center was the oldest oak tree in the city. Poking through the top of the glass skylights was the epitome of life and flourishing. No matter the season, the symbol of Oakbrooke itself thrived. In this case, it was nearly winter, which meant most leaves had changed from green to maroon, amber, and gold and fallen onto the windows overhead. Since then, they had blown off, leaving the majority of the branches bare, but still regally pointing to the cloudy azure sky overhead.

"I wanted to thank you again for stopping Declan...again," Maylene cringed as the two of them sat down across from each other at an empty picnic table for two.

Lia was already biting into her peanut butter sandwich at

that point. "I don't mind," she replied, mouth partially full, but somewhat closed. "What else was I going to do–just stand there? I mean, I did, but I told him to knock it off too."

"Well, you did step on his foot."

"That's true."

Maylene used a pair of wooden chopsticks to pick up a small bite of her vegan poke rice bowl, which was a regular of hers to bring. In this case, her bowl consisted of watermelon radish, cucumber, red cabbage, edamame, carrot, and avocado: the usual. "So, you're still having your party tomorrow night, right?" she hastily changed the subject.

"Yep," Lia confirmed, breaking open her bag of stick pretzels. "You and Yasmin are invited."

Two pairs of eyes darted over towards the tree in the middle of the courtyard where a circular bench sat surrounding it. There was Yasmin in her ginormous faded blue hoodie and leggings topped with a messy bun looking as talkative as ever. She was seated on said bench with a group of at least ten people. Lia recognized one of them as the boy with black hair who hit her in the face with a dodgeball in PE. If this was a year ago, she would have been offended, but now, she sat in front of one of her favorite people who had a wide smile on her face. Lia smiled back and offered her full attention.

"Oh, good!" Maylene cheered, swallowing down her first bite of her rice bowl. "I have your gift wrapped and ready for you to open."

Lia's cheeks grew scarlet. "You know you don't have to get me anything."

"I wanted to. You're a great friend to me."

"Same for you."

Maylene's smile grew as she shifted the conversation for a second time. "So, what kind of cake are you having? The usual?"

"The usual."

Both girls burst into a fit of laughter for one another. It was true: Lia had the same type of party every year, but that was why she loved it so much. Her whole family was involved, including her two "sisters" from closer to the front of the neighborhood. Later that afternoon, Lia would aid her mother in making the cake and assist her father with setting up the regular birthday decorations. Of course, her family purchased new ones every year, but she always told them to surprise her with the theme. Last year, Cheyenne picked rainbow unicorn decorations because she thought they were "fun." Lia agreed and gladly set them up despite the fact she was turning a decade and a half–not seven. She smiled at the thought and let the anticipation of her Sweet Sixteen follow her for the rest of the day.

She was very much looking forward to it.

Three

The day of the party arrived. Lia awoke that morning with an elevated serotonin level. Sunbeams from overhead peeped through the window blinds and summoned stripes of gold illuminating the gray carpet. All four corners of her poster bed loomed towards the ceiling where a fan spiraled overhead. It was not until the rays of the Great Star overhead delicately poked Lia between the eyes that the teenager's lids fluttered open to immediately squint. A nest of brown hair soon became upright as Lia sat against her pillow. Today was going to be a great day–she knew it already. Being a year older did not mean reminiscing on the past but instead wishing everything good over the future.

Lia kept that hopeful feeling in her mind as her morning routine ensued. She stepped in and out of the shower within a span of fifteen minutes. Her damp hair dripped against the back of her black towel. The lenses of her glasses repeatedly fogged up from the humidity following her from the bathroom she called her own and up the stairs into her room that was secluded from the rest of the house. Lia relished in claiming the loft above the one-and-a-half car garage as her own. It was given to her in a heartbeat–once she opened her eyes to the world around her for the very first time. Her eyes drifted to Noodle, who was inquisitively watching her every movement from behind the glass in her vivarium. Noodle's eyes never left Lia as she threw on a pair of fluffy red plaid pajama pants and an oversized *Rolling Stones* tee and brushed through the tangled bush upon her head. Eventually, the branches were untied and instead hanging loosely past her shoulders. She straightened her glasses and then opened Noodle's vivarium to retrieve her beloved pet, who was more than happy to oblige.

Noodle draped over her shoulders as Lia's bare feet skipped down the steps and eventually landed on the cold hardwood floor. Lia entered an oddly quiet remainder of the house. Suddenly, she was walking amongst ice ready to crack at any moment. The floor beneath her soles creaked with every other step as she approached the living room, which was directly to the left of the stairwell and in front of the garage where the house opened into a broader concept. Something about the whole environment seemed off. The house was silent. The only movement was from the ceiling fan blades circling overhead. Even the television was off, which her father watched cartoons on every Saturday and Sunday morning. Noodle's expression was just as puzzled as her master's. In fact, if both of them were the same species, they would be identical.

All was discovered in due time, however, when Mr. and Mrs. Hart leapt out from behind the counter that partnered as a bar perching between the living room and the kitchen. At the exclamation of "Surprise!" Lia stumbled backwards, exemplifying the meaning of the word itself. She flinched at the sudden noise and fell into the couch while keeping a steady hold on Noodle. When her body sunk into the cushions, she breathed out a hearty bout of laughter. Her parents had done it again. Without fail, Cheyenne and Lucas surprised their daughter using a different method each year. Lia smiled at the memory of her mother and father hiding sticky notes around the house - the first being on her forehead - as a scavenger hunt that eventually led her to the backyard where her parents were waiting for a picnic breakfast. This time, Cheyenne and Lucas took a simpler approach and concealed themselves behind the counter.

"Oh, good grief!" she huffed between giggles. "You got me again."

"That's the plan!" Lucas put down the party blower he was holding and dashed around the counter to hug his daughter. "Happy birthday, Kiddo."

Lia did not hesitate to hug him back. "Thanks, Dad."

"Oh, my Jesus, you have Noodle-" Cheyenne shrieked when she followed her husband and leaned forward to do the same.

"Thanks to you too, Mom," Lia teased while watching her recoil at the snake looped on her shoulders like a scarf.

Cheyenne chuckled uneasily. "I still don't know…"

"I'd say Noodle's pretty cool," Lucas commented, winking at the reptile. "It's her gotcha day today too." Then, he beckoned towards Lia. "That *is* what it's called, right?"

"Yeah, it's "gotcha day.""

"Well, happy gotcha day to you, Noodle." Lucas extended his index finger and tapped the petite snake on her nose.

Noodle seemed to like that, sticking her slotted tongue out to observe the gesture. Lia grinned and caressed her pet's scaly skin. "Are you sure you don't want to pet her?" she asked her mother with sincerity.

"No, thank you," Cheyenne replied like she always did. "If you don't mind, though, could you please put her back in her cage-"

"Vivarium."

"-yes, whatever, so we can start on your cake? I can do it myself, but I remember you saying you liked helping."

"I do." Lia was immediately on board. "Let me put Noodle back and then we can get started."

"I'll get Looney Tunes on the TV," Lucas offered and grasped the remote to do just that.

Cheyenne asked cheekily, "So you can watch it and pretend to do something productive while Lia and I do it all?"

"...Yes, Dear."

Both Lia and her mother chortled at Lucas' honesty. Lia did as she promised and returned Noodle to her habitat where the snake would get some much-needed sleep. Winter was approaching fast, which meant that the reptile would be resting for up to two hours more than the eighteen-hour average the rest of the year. Now, it was time to bake. Cheyenne had all of the supplies to make the cake out on the counter, which Lia imagined she set up at least an hour before she woke up mid-morning. Lia tended to sleep in late on weekends and especially on her birthday. No matter what day it was, she would refrain from doing any sort of schoolwork - even staying home from the building itself - so she could rest and enjoy her day off that her parents approved of every year.

Cake-baking was underway just a moment later. Cheyenne poured the vanilla cake mix from its box into a mixing bowl while Lia cracked two eggs and added them. Next, the precise measurement of powdered milk and water was dumped in the bowl. To make matters easier, Cheyenne plugged in a white mixer and placed the stirrers in the bowl. Lia switched it on and both of them took turns mixing the batter until it was smooth without any chunks in it. Next, the batter was poured into two molds that made layers which Cheyenne would later place icing in between after they were finished baking and cooled. When that moment finally arrived, Cheyenne and Lia each opened a forest of green icing and together, they iced the cake. One layer was placed on the other and icing smothered every crook and crevice. The finishing touches were a countless number of rainbow sprinkles and the two numbers "one" and "six" in candle form placed in the center. Lia and her mother stepped back and admired their work. It was never perfect, but each year was better than the last.

Lia spent the rest of the morning watching cartoons with her parents on either side of her on the couch. She and her father burst out into laughter at every possible punchline or even a lack of one. Cheyenne joined in every so often, but it was clear that she was focusing on her crocheting more than anything else. It was a favorite hobby of hers–creating her own patterns for blankets, hats, scarves, and whatnot, so Lia and Lucas left her alone to do her own thing. That was how the rest of the day ensued– exactly how Lia liked it. With every waking minute, she expressed her gratitude for her parents making today all about her. Although she was an only child and this was the normality, it meant more than anything on her birthday above all else.

Eventually, five o'clock rolled around, which was the designated time Lia chose for her party to begin. Everything was prepared, including the decorations and foil balloons tied to each of the seven chairs - three of them foldable - around the kitchen table. The green birthday cake sat in the middle of a mint green tablecloth. A colorful "Happy Birthday" banner draped over the large window behind the mahogany table in the kitchen with gray and white walls topped with white cabinets, stainless steel appliances, and marble countertops. Every nook and cranny was as neat as a pin–Cheyenne had spent a bit of the morning tidying up everything along with the help of Lucas and Lia despite telling the latter to relax and savor every moment. Instead, though, Lia desired to feel helpful instead of letting her parents do all of the work themselves.

Nana and Papa, Lia's grandparents on her father's side, were the first to arrive. She sprung out the front door as soon as their silver sedan pulled into the driveway. Papa, a tall man who her father was a spitting image of minus the gray hair atop his head, exited on the driver's side. Nana, a small blonde woman with glasses and flecks of gray in her hair - the only remnants of her age shining through - left the passenger's side door. The older couple circled their way around the hood to meet Lia in the middle, who leaped into their embrace with open arms. She had to reach up for her Papa but lean down for her Nana.

"Hi, Nana! Hi, Papa!" Lia cheered from in between them. "Thanks for coming."

"Happy birthday, Lia," Nana wished her while Papa echoed the same.

Lia did not even notice the present each of her grandparents held as she coaxed them inside, instead taking in their smiling faces. "I'm so excited you're here!" she gushed to Nana and Papa who looked upon her with nothing but love. "I have party games all planned out and Dad's making hamburgers on the grill for dinner. I hope you guys like it."

"I'm sure we will," Nana assured her. "We always do."

Papa just grinned and followed behind them. "As long as we can play-"

"Yes, we'll play Uno," replied Lia with a chortle, patting her grandpa on the shoulder.

"You two are something else," Nana joked and shook her head.

Lia and her Papa shared a fist bump as they passed through the front door. "Yoo-hoo!" Nana called into the house as she entered.

"Hi, Beth!" Cheyenne replied from the kitchen. "Hello, Clive! Welcome, welcome! We're just getting everything set up. Lucas is out back getting the burgers started."

"Where should we put your presents?" Nana asked her granddaughter.

"You didn't have to get me anything," Lia countered just like every year, "but you can put them on the coffee table, please."

"It's our job to spoil you."

Lia took after her grandpa and shook her head amusedly. "You know you don't have to."

"We want to," argued Nana, pinching her cheek.

"It's fun," Papa agreed.

Lia fought the urge to fire back a playful retort when Yasmin burst through the green front door wearing the same outfit from yesterday out of comfort. She appeared as if she was going to greet her by stepping forward, but once she realized the reason Yasmin was not joined by her twin, she backed away. Yasmin held open the door as wide as she could, squishing herself into the wall, to make way for Maylene who was carrying a thin gift that was half her height. Lia's jaw battled against the urge to shatter on the floor. When she looked closer, she realized Yasmin was holding a gift bag half the size of Maylene's gift, but she did not care. All Lia valued was the fact her two best friends - one a little more than the other - had arrived at all, just like they had done every year. Lia immediately bolted for Maylene and took a hold of half of the present so she was not struggling to carry the awkward box-like structure. Yasmin shut the door behind them. Maylene and Lia set the red present against the coffee table and Yasmin placed hers on the surface. Once everyone's hands were free, Lia captured them both in a hug.

"You made it!" she exclaimed into their ears. "Thank you for coming."

"Of course!" Yasmin cheered and happily ruffled Lia's hair that was pulled back into a braid. "It's tradition, and May and I can't turn down free food."

Maylene's brows furrowed at that. "Lia's the reason we're here."

"And the food is a bonus."

"Can you believe we're related?" Maylene whispered to Lia as Yasmin skipped into the kitchen to greet her parents and grandparents.

Lia could not conceal her smirk any longer. "Yes. Yes, I can."

"Excuse me?" giggled the girl who elbowed her. "I don't think we're *that* alike."

"I'd beg to differ."

"Watch it, *Hart*," Maylene mocked Declan Abner's method of attempting poorly to get under her best friend's skin.

Sure enough, the opposite occurred. Lia's smile was wider than ever when the realization of what Maylene was doing hit her. "Good one," she complimented, finding it more amusing than she probably should have.

Then again, this was her birthday. As her parents said, she could do whatever she wanted as long as it was within the confines of morality. Cheyenne and Lucas knew that their daughter was one of the most authentic individuals they had ever known in the past sixteen years; not because she was their blood, but since they had been her guides ever since she was a mere thought in their late twenties. Now, at sixteen, she was easily the favorite person of her parents. She became everything they had ever wanted and more. Lucas and Cheyenne were optimistic about their child's future. As long as she remained as she was in the present, the chapters that followed would likely be just as successful.

"Hi, Nana!" Yasmin endearingly used Lia's names for the older woman in the kitchen. She was quickly followed by Maylene.

Nana turned towards the twins and grinned joyfully. "How are my two favorite granddaughters doing?"

"Good," Maylene and Yasmin chorused without fail—just like every other time.

"Hey!" Lia yelped in faux offense.

Nana just chuckled and placed a hand on her shoulder. "You know I'm just picking. I love you, Sweetheart."

"I love you too, Nana."

"But we're her favorites," Yasmin interjected with a playful twinge.

"Hey!" Lia fussed for a second time.

Lia then passed through the glass door leading to the backyard deck where her father and grandfather were sitting and talking. The aroma of nearly done burgers filled the air, which Lia breathed in deeply. She hopped onto one of the benches that surrounded the deck in place of a railing - besides the stairs - and let her bare feet dangle over the grass on the other side. She listened as Lucas and his dad spoke about recent sports affairs, whether local or professional. Sports was a topic that the father and son bonded upon. Lia wanted to join in the fun, so she began watching different sports on television with her father so she would be able to discuss them with him and Papa. As said earlier, Lia indeed dabbled in a bit of everything.

Soon, everything was ready and the family put together paper plates of food for themselves and sat around the kitchen table for dinner. Lia, of course, sat in the middle closest to the window with Maylene on her right. Her parents sat at each end of the table and Yasmin squished herself between Nana and Papa since she thrived off of the attention. Today was all about Lia, though, and everyone knew that. That was how it was every year, rain or shine, school or an absence of it. Lia's brown eyes scanned the room being met with six pairs that meant the world and more to her. If magic truly existed in this realm, then it would be in the form of the people she loved, forming a lavender haze secluding her from the terrors this world was plagued with.

All things poorer than good were forgotten as the party ensued. After dinner, it came time for the promised games that Lia prepared every year. Cheyenne made a slide show trivia game featuring Lia herself for her quinceñera the previous year. This year, though, Lia took a simpler approach and grabbed a few of the board games out of the hall closet including Pictionary, Guesstures, Yahtzee, and Uno, which was what everyone decided to play. Lia plopped down next to her grandpa while the seven sat in a circle on the floor. Lia and her Papa took turns shuffling half the deck and the latter dealt out seven cards to each person. Initially, Lia frowned at her hand, especially when her grandpa passed her a yellow "plus two" card as his turn came, but when a wild card and a "plus four" card appeared in her hand from the deck in the middle of the circle. When Mrs. Hart eventually placed down a reverse card to the dismay of her husband, Lia smashed down the plus four and grinned wickedly at the older man.

CHAPTER THREE 43

"Ha!" Lia cheered and clutched the one card she had left. "Uno, and I'm changing the color to blue."

Papa just shook his head and chuckled, "Oh, good grief."

"Did someone rig the deck?" Yasmin accused the pair. "You two shuffled–what gives?"

"It's talent," Lia excused the coincidence.

"Oh, BS."

"She's the birthday girl," Maylene refuted cheekily. "After all, it's her special day, so it's even better if she wins."

Lia wrapped an arm around the girl next to her. "See? She gets it."

"I think she rigged the deck," Lucas antagonized his daughter.

"No, I didn't! It's pure talent. I win!" The brunette placed down her final card, which was a wild card. Even if the color had changed, which it did not, no one stood a chance.

"Rigged."

"Talent."

"Rigged."

"Talent."

"Rigged."

"Talent."

"Rig-"

"Okay, I think it's time for presents!" Cheyenne interrupted the playful banter and changed the subject. "Or we could do cake. Or we could play a game that doesn't wreak havoc."

"Presents sound good," Lia suggested hesitantly. "Unless you guys want to do something else."

"It's your birthday," Yasmin shot down her uncertainty, "Do whatever you want."

"I still want everyone to have a good time." Lia took one look at her family - blood or not - who offered nothing but support and then made up her mind. "Presents it is."

Lia shuffled her bum across the white and smokey gray swirled rug draping the living room floor towards the table where all of the presents sat neatly at least for a moment. That moment quickly ended when Lia picked up the first present off the pile, which was a petite box wrapped in robin egg blue paper topped with a gold bow. Immediately, Lia knew this was from her grandmother, as blue and gold were her favorite colors. She picked up a card from on top of the gift with her name written lightly in cursive on the front. Carefully, Lia tore open the flap to reveal the card, which was decorated with flowers–namely roses and violets adorned with cartoon bumblebees. Lia understood the theme once she opened the card and read what was inside.

Roses are red
You know the rest
Grandchildren are special
But you are the best.
P.S.: That's our secret!
Love,
Nana and Papa

Lia smiled and placed the card next to her on the floor. "I love the poem," she complimented them with genuinity, "but there's one problem."

"What's that?" Nana frowned.

"I'm your *only* grandchild."

"That's the point."

Papa just guffawed at the interaction. "Well, we have these two over here." He gestured to Maylene and Yasmin.

"Hey!"

"Open your gift," Nana encouraged her granddaughter. "Your Papa helped me pick it out, so we hope you like it. Sorry it's so small."

"I wouldn't care if you got me a rock from the front yard," Lia teased, but it was true.

She tenderly tore open the wrapping paper to reveal a black velvet box–no engraving or anything of the sort on the top. Lia lifted the top and choked on a gasp at the amber hue of a gold necklace with an infinity symbol as a charm in the center. At once, she knew it was fragile, so she handled it with care as she removed it from the box and struggled to undo the clasp to place it around her neck. Cheyenne darted over to her daughter and aided her by pulling her hair to the side and closing the clasp to allow the infinity symbol to dangle from her neck.

"I love it," Lia breathed, watching as the charm glistened in the light from the ceiling fan. "Thank you so much, Nana and Papa."

"You're most welcome," Nana replied for the two of them when Lia hugged them tight. "The infinity symbol is because we love you forever and want you to remember that."

Lia subconsciously glanced down at the metal around her neck. "I will–I promise. I love you both so much."

"We love you too."

Lia's grandparents' love for her was as authentic as the gold jewelry. She did not have to wonder why such a gem was the only present from the two of them.

After the shimmering chain was opened and secured loosely around her neck, there were more presents to open. Lia chose the gift bag that Yasmin brought next. It did not include a card, but she did not care–the fact that Yasmin was present at her party was more than enough. She removed the tissue paper from the bag to reveal a chestnut teddy bear surrounded by all of her favorite candies. From gummies to lollipops to spearmints, Lia was more than satisfied with what Yasmin had picked out for her. She was a lover of all things food, which especially included sweets. Food was a major staple in her life and she was not ashamed to admit that like some other girls at Oakbrooke High. She would much rather be sustained and have a couple of rolls here and there than hinder her body of its valuable nutrients and meet society's beauty standard. That was another thing wrong with the world and prevented magic from ever bleeding through. While all creatures were beautiful in their own way because of their individuality, society convinced us we were not.

Lia sometimes struggled along with the rest of them, though. She was human, after all.

The next to last present in the small pile was in the shape of a tall pyramid. From the very beginning, Lia knew what was behind the green wrapping paper, but she refused to believe it. As she set the moderately heavy gift on her lap, her eyes enlarged to an extent where she thought they would fall out of their sockets and bring her glasses crashing down with them. Her mother and father preliminarily wore knowing smiles upon their lips. Lia had opened the card from them this morning which was yet another cheesy comedy card that had some sort of fart joke on the inside. It was now sitting on the mantle below the television mounted to the wall. Nevertheless, Lia eyed her parents with scrutiny.

"You didn't have to get me this," she pleaded against their nonverbal coaxing. "It's a lot of money and I could always play the one in the store."

"Honey, we saw how much you loved it and wanted to take it home, so we made that possible," Cheyenne cooed affectionately. "Your father and I love you so much and want you to know you deserve good things. Now, go ahead and open it so we can hear you play!"

So, that was exactly what Lia did. She tore open the wrapping paper like a mouse who had just found a massive hunk of cheese. Sure enough, the Ear Candy logo with a treble clef was on the front of the oddly shaped box. Lia used a pair of scissors that her father retrieved to cut the tape and open it the rest of the way. After the insulation keeping the instrument safe was removed, Lia gawked at the flawlessly polished instrument sitting in the packaging. It was the exact one she had played in the store in the recent past. She recognized the smallest dent in the top of the mahogany sunburst body. That one small imperfection was the very thing that told the whole story of her parents' love. Right then and there, she remembered how her father had "went to the bathroom" as Lia and her mother stepped outside to prepare to leave. It hit her like a dump truck—this was planned. Needless to say, Lia flung herself into the arms of her parents and thanked them a thousand times. She vowed to the group that she would play them all something on the mandolin once she was comfortable enough.

Last, but certainly not least, was the ginormous red gift left leaning against the table. Lia eyed Maylene with suspicious brows. "You didn't have to get me anything, especially a new roof."

"It's not a roof," Maylene giggled at her friend's obvious joke. "Open it!"

Lia did not have to wait for Maylene to tell her twice. The quieter girl rocked back and forth with anticipation while sitting cross-legged on the rug. As soon as the wrapping paper was torn away, Lia was stunned silent. On her lap in the gift's place was a true masterpiece, a canvas covered with the forestry hues she loved so dear. Trees surrounded a dirt path that led in a twisting, turning direction towards a rustic village with a majestic river flowing through it. Flawless mountainscapes pointed to the dim, partly cloudy sky, but in the top right corner, the sun could barely be seen peeking through. In the distance was a stone castle perched upon one of the mountains. In the forest, a small herd of deer grazed the grass underneath their cloven hooves.

"Maylene...I-...," Lia began to stutter after a moment of nothingness. "I don't know what to say. I knew you were a phenomenal painter, but *this*..."

Maylene's smile stretched widely across her face. "Read the back."

"There's something on the back t-"

For a second time, Lia froze as she turned the painting over and read the delicate handwriting on the back in green pen.

Lia,
  I know you believe in Science more than magic, but in my life, the

latter is real. It exists through you and your friendship that I always hope will be kindled. If I can help it, that flame will forever remain lit through the wind and rain and sunny days. Keep being your magical self. I love you, my Second Sister.

Love,

Maylene

Lia tentatively placed the painting against the table and wrapped her arms around the girl who had been her friend since before their kindergarten days. Nothing had ever become quite as special as this–as how much time and love she poured into the artwork she crafted. "I love it," she choked out. "Thank you so much. I know just where to hang this so I can see it every day."

"I'm so glad you like it," Maylene gushed, almost with a sense of breathy relief. "It was so much fun to make in my free time."

"You didn't have to," she repeated a phrase that was used several times that night.

"But I *wanted* to."

Lia sat back and took in the environment around her. There she was, sitting in the middle of the living room surrounded by her six favorite people: her parents, grandparents, and two "sisters," Maylene and Yasmin. All of them had come together to celebrate her life, *her* existence, and her place in this world even though she had not found it yet. Then again, as she assessed the pure affection in the atmosphere, her chosen family around her, Lia began to realize that magic might not have been real, but this was as close as it would get. At least, that was what she thought was the truth.

Little did Lia know that was about to change.

Four

It was clear that when it came to Lia's sixteenth birthday, all of the dominos cascaded in a line. Today was perfect, from the quiet morning to the eventful evening. The final aspect of the celebration consisted of the entire house centering around the cake Lia and her mother made earlier that day. The two candles flickered until the inevitable melody concluded and the subject of said song extinguished the flames and the joy ensued. Even after Nana, Papa, Maylene, and Yasmin took their leave, Lia was already certain that her wish came true.

Lia never took off the gold necklace that her grandparents gave her. She did not plan to in the first place. The candy from Yasmin was half-opened and consumed, the rest sitting on the desk on the opposite side of the loft from her bed. Her new mandolin that she treasured so dear rested tenderly on an instrument wall holder mounted in the center of two instruments. To the left was her circular-bodied maple ukulele with stars and a crescent moon engraved on it. To the right, her white acoustic guitar was hung. A tortoise maroon pickguard painted with floral outlines and a dove - Maylene's artwork - was the finishing touch. All three of these instruments were hung where Lia could see as soon as she woke up. This was the same case with the newest edition to her wall. Maylene's masterpiece of a painting left Lia wonderstruck. Her father aided her with hanging the art upon the only free space the wall across from her four-cornered poster bed. Lia's chocolate irises were locked on the painting that now lived above her desk until she fell through a rabbit hole to Dreamland.

In a normal sense, Lia's slumber was often uneventful. She tended to not understand when Maylene or Yasmin would reminisce about their dreams from previous nights. Even her mother and father had such experiences. Lia, on the other hand, saw sleep as some sort of time travel mechanism. One minute, she was laying in bed, glasses off, hair draped down her shoulders instead of being pulled back and scrolling through endless social media portals on her phone until her eyes closed. The next, sunlight peeped through the windowblinds and welcomed her to a new day and new opportunities. There was nothing magical about it in Lia's eyes. Instead, it was normality, a routine that she had lived through her entire life.

The type of light that ebbed into her room that night was not from the Sun. No blinds secured her comfortable loft from the outside world. Instead, the outside was brought indoors with no restriction. The white, almost ghastly light growing from the center of the room eventually met the walls and, finally, Lia's sleeping form. It was the light along with an inexplicable breeze spreading from the inside out. Lia disorientedly opened her eyes to an alabaster orb in the middle of her room. One second, it was the size of a pearl, and by the time she was fully conscious, the sphere took the size of the free floor of her room. Lia screeched in fright and scrambled to the darkest corner of her bed where two perpendicular walls met. Normally, she would stand tall, grab the nearest heavy object, and fight back, but not now. This type of occurrence was...*not* normal. No one answered her desperate cry, not even her parents asleep in their room just downstairs. She did the only thing she thought of in a hazy state, which was throw the comforter of her bed overtop of her shaking body and pretend she did not exist.

The abrupt silence taking place of whatever sorcery had amassed probed Lia to peek out from under the blanket, reach towards her nightstand for her glasses, unfold them, and slide them on her face. Where the orb of light had once formed stood a tall Woman who could only be described as *white*. Everything about Her was as pale as newly fallen snow; Her skin, Her dress, Her hair, and even Her eyes, which were a crystalline blue. The only color was in the Woman's cheeks, which had the faintest tint of a rosy hue to them. Her illuminated form rid the entire room of the darkness it originally inhabited. Rather than being too stunned to make a sound, Lia's respirations became quicker and heavier. Confusion and fear mixed themselves together in her mind to create a concoction meant for nothing but disaster.

To Lia's own surprise, she spoke first. "Who are you? What's going on?" she interrogated the stranger. "What are you doing in my room? I swear if you lay a finger on me, I'll-"

"Ophelia."

A calm voice smoother than silk halted the teenager's river of censored profanities. The sound of her name - her *full* name - addressing her and no one else, stunned the poor girl into clenching her pillow so tightly that she thought it was going to snap in half, albeit impossible. Part of her wanted to chuck the feather-filled object at the Stranger, but the other part begged her to hear the Woman out. This was a once-in-a-lifetime experience! Why not take advantage of it? Plus, a Woman materializing in the middle of your room sounded like a cool idea for a song–not that Lia wrote any of that sort of thing.

"How do you know my name?" Lia inquired, remaining rooted to her spot.

"Oh, my apologies," the pale Woman smiled and corrected Herself, "it slipped my mind that you prefer a nickname. How are you faring on your birthday, Lia?"

Lia was dumbstruck by this point. "Um, it was fine, but…*who* are you?"

"You can say I'm an enchantress of some sort," She elaborated soothingly. "It's an honor to finally meet you."

"…Meet me? Enchantress? I thought that kind of stuff was for little kids. I thought it wasn't real. How…wait. I must be dreaming. Tell me I'm dreaming."

The Enchantress found Lia's doubt to be amusing. "This is all too real, my dear. Would you be willing to discuss it with me?"

"Discuss–wait. How are my parents not hearing this? We have an alarm system and everything, so how the heck did you get in?"

"That's not important, I'm afraid." Her eyes and smile softened. "But, if you must know, I've enchanted the room with a soundproof barrier. It's invisible and transparent but will fade away when I do. That is to keep our words confidential."

"Confidential?" Lia repeated once more. "Okay, *now* you're starting to freak me out. I thought I was going to before, but this is getting a little sketchy."

"If I were to make you one promise, it's this: I would never hurt you, my dear. I bring nothing but good intentions for the good of the realm beyond your own."

"Is this lady on some sort of drugs? What is she talking about?" Lia wondered prior to speaking aloud, "Realm beyond my own? You mean like another world?"

The Enchantress smiled. "Yes, Lia. Another world. That is where I'm from."

"Okay, okay. Let me get this straight." Lia finally sat up straight and removed the blanket from her plaid pajama-clad figure. "You're an Enchantress coming from another world where magic apparently exists because you used it to make my room soundproof, you know my name, and you came here to meet me?"

"Exactly."

"*Why?*" she spluttered out.

The last thing Lia was expecting was for the Woman's pale lips and blue eyes to fall from an expression of endearment to one of despair.

"Because I need your help."

Lia's breath caught in her throat. For a second time in the past couple of minutes, she thought she must have been dreaming, but all of this was too real. If she could keep track of her own emotions, Lia figured she would be screaming of fright, red with fury that this woman had interrupted her sleep, or her eyes filling with confused tears. If this was even real in the first place, how would someone - much less a mere teenager - dwindle from the confines of Earth and instead cross the barrier into a realm of magic when she did not believe in it in the first place? There was no Science to prove what she was experiencing right now. She must have been unconscious. Yes, that was it… Needless to say, Lia had been smacked with a club of reality.

"You're likely wondering why I've extended my hand to you."

Lia refrained from fiddling with the pillow in her lap, her eyes snapping up to meet the Enchantress'. *"Geez. She's good."*

"Not everything can be explained now, but it will be in due time," She coaxed the young girl. "My realm is in grave danger and you are the only one who can save it."

"Me?" Lia stumbled over her words. "Why me?"

"As I said, all will be made clear in due time."

"Oh," she sighed dejectedly.

The Enchantress extended a glowing hand towards Lia's bed, a silent request to be seated. All the girl could do was nod, and the Woman sat down. Now, Lia could tell that this Woman was wearing no shoes, Her bare feet shimmering above the carpet. For someone wearing a sparkling flowing dress, Lia expected Her to wear at least some sort of shoe. Maybe flip flops? Socks at the very least?

"Are you ready to listen?" the Enchantress asked her in a whisper.

Lia fought the nerves clawing up her throat and made herself nod. "Yes, Ma'am."

Despite the Enchantress not having any sort of wand, it was clear She was channeling Her otherworldly magic into their surroundings. What used to be Lia's room washed away into a current of nothingness. All of a sudden, a new setting materialized around them. Lia stood from her bed that was now invisible. The darkness gave way to another world, as the Enchantress put it. Rather than instruments on the wall, a desk, a bookshelf, and even Noodle's habitat, Lia and the Enchantress were surrounded by a regal stone courtyard. An enormous castle perched upon a mountain towered spires in all directions around them. She looked down to see four golden symbols that she imagined resembled a compass rose. She did not know what they meant, but each of the four circles looked a bit different from one another. Lia could not decide if the mossy exterior made the palace look older or newer. Either way, the kingdom around her - at least she thought it was some sort of kingdom… or a village - seemed to have been enduring for hundreds of years. A dominant river flowed through the center of the village houses below surrounded by lush, murky forestry as far as the eye could see.

"*What is this—Rivendell from Lord of the Rings?*" Lia gaped at her surroundings. "Uh, Miss…where are we?"

"Kythaela."

"Kai…they…what, now?" she enunciated the best she could.

The Enchantress exhaled a breathy chuckle. "Kythaela," She repeated and then gestured to the new world around them. "This is an illusion of what our vast kingdom of Luthyia once was."

"Okay, first of all, I can't pronounce either of those."

"That's okay, my dear. May I continue?"

Lia tried not to be distracted by the stone under her feet that still felt like the carpet in her room. "Yeah, yeah, sorry."

The Enchantress snapped the fingers on Her right hand. They

were not alone in the courtyard anymore but instead were surrounded by a circle of unearthly individuals. Lia identified several human traits in each one of the creatures as she did a three-hundred-and-sixty degree turn to count a total of Twelve. The diverse humanoids all had similar features–two eyes, a small nose, lips, two arms, and two legs, but their ears were pointed, and they were noticeably taller than the average human. Lia noticed how the twelve creatures seemed to be split into four groups of three. One wore green robes, one wore gray, one wore blue, and one wore amber. The closest comparison Lia could find to these Twelve were the elves from J.R.R. Tolkien's most famous works. All of them had one thing in common: those unusual, pointed ears.

Lia leaned towards the Enchantress and whispered, "Who are they?"

"The Mêla," She answered, beginning to point to each group. "The Earth Wing embodies Mother Nature: grounded and stable. The Air Wing is as free as the wind; illuding the world around us. Third is the Water, all-knowing and empathetic. Lastly is the Fire Wing, passionate, but dangerous. All Four of these Wings created harmony throughout this land while Mother Nature took the four seasons by the reins. It was their duty to fulfill their responsibilities, and for over a millennium, they did."

"So...why are you talking in past-tense?" Lia's lips curved downward. "These guys are like the "gods" of your Kingdom and, from what I'm getting, they can live forever. What happened?"

Another snap of the Enchantress' fingers and the Twelve disappeared. What was once a sturdy castle became ruins before her very eyes. Rather than the neutral temperature of her room, a gust of wind shot through Lia's frame which summoned chills from the inside out. She reached around desperately for her bed's comforter but she could not find it, instead tugging the red hoodie she wore to bed tighter around her. Before Lia could prevent it, her teeth began chattering. What once was Summer became a freezing Winter. It was not until a warm arm was put around her shoulders that her core temperature began to return to normal.

"W-...What happened?" Lia stuttered out, shuffling closer to the taller woman.

"The Fire Wing chose not to fulfill their duties after their hearts filled with greed and hunger for power," the Enchantress quite literally took Her under Her "wing" of sorts. "Instead, they claimed a portion of Kythaela as their own and named it Sundikar: a land full of ash, soot, and volcanic terrain. This left the rest of Kythaela in a bitter cold: an Eternal Winter, if you will. The remaining Nine fled once they realized there was nothing they could do to restore the land. Little did they know that this further destroyed it. If they're gone for much longer, our realm will be at a point of no return."

"I'm so sorry," the young girl breathed as if her lungs were deflating balloons. "I don't know what to say...I just...I wish there was something I could do to help."

The Enchantress tenderly patted her shoulder. "This is where you come in, Lia."

"How so?" Lia's brows furrowed, intrigued.

"The Mêla each represent one of your Earthly Zodiac signs. Have you heard of those?"

"Of course. I'm a Sagittarius."

The Enchantress laughed softly at her response, "I figured as much. Are you aware that each of the twelve Zodiac signs are sorted into one of the four elements: Earth, Air, Water, and Fire?"

"Yeah, I think so," she shrugged nonchalantly.

"So are the Mêla, as you now know." Her eyes darkened with superiority. "Lia, you do know that if you choose to accept this task that I am about to give you that it is a huge responsibility, correct?"

Lia wished she had been given more time to think, but her gut rumbled with the epiphany that this was something she was meant to do.

Or maybe she was just hungry.

"Yes, I understand," she nodded, albeit uncertain.

"Lia. The remaining Nine of the Mêla have fled into your world. I have reason to believe that the Earth Wing is inhabiting your school."

Lia was more confused than ever. "Why would a group of immortal beings choose a high school of all places?"

"Your guess is as good as mine. Can I put my faith in you to search out these Three Mêla and convince them to return to their homeland?"

"How am I supposed to do that? I can barely talk to people who *aren't* Maylene, who's my best friend," Lia protested, beginning to pace the desolate courtyard.

"There's a reason I chose you, you know," the Enchantress gently coaxed her. "I can't tell you right this minute, but I need you to trust me."

"Why can't you tell me anything?" The brunette frowned at Her confidentiality. "If I'm going to do something for you, for this *realm* that you speak of, I want to know what part I play in this and why I play it."

"I know this must be frustrating, Lia, but for your own safety, I cannot tell you. It's simply–um, there's a-"

In the midst of her pacing, Lia had forgotten that despite her surroundings seeming much more open, she was still confined to the limits of her room. She figured that out once she slammed face-first into a wall.

"Ow," Lia hissed and rubbed her forehead with her palm. "Okay, okay, I get it. You can't tell me because I need to be inconspicuous or whatnot and you're afraid that I'll blab about it to the wrong person. Is that right?"

"Precisely."

"Got it. I just have one more question, though."

"Ask away."

"How am I supposed to know when I find one of these... Mêla people? They blend in with everybody else, right?"

The Enchantress seemed to have yet another trick up Her sleeve. What Lia at first thought was an optical illusion turned out to be reality when a glimmering white spark burst into many in between the Woman's hands. Her irises, entranced by the whirlwind of sorts, locked on the Enchantress' pale, slender fingers as they molded what appeared to be a Ring from the flowing river of magic cascading from Her fingers. Lia's hunch was right; she determined that once the blinding, but somehow soothing, sparks faded into nothingness and a yellow-gold Ring was left in the Enchantress' palm. She did not move until the woman's kind eyes met hers. She reached for Lia's smaller hand and slid the Ring on the ring finger of her left hand.

"When this Ring pulses tightly, you will know you're in the presence of one of the Mêla," She elaborated. "You must keep it on at all times."

"I will," Lia promised, admiring the jewelry on her finger. "I can't wait until Maylene hears about this–she's going to be-"

"I am sorry, but you must be confined to secrecy."

The Enchantress' words made Lia's heart drop to her bare feet. "...You mean I can't tell anyone? Not even Mom and Dad? They wouldn't say anything. Neither would Maylene, or Yasmin, or Nana and Papa, or-"

She shook Her head solemnly. "You cannot risk it," She denied her request. "Kythaela is in a state of depression and must be kept hidden for our own safety. If word leaks out to the Fire Wing that we are regathering the Nine, then…"

"...Then what?"

"The repercussions are too much to bear," the Enchantress finished. "We do not know what the Fire Wing is capable of, especially when anger clouds their judgment."

"Wait, wait, wait," Lia stopped her in her tracks. "How come this Fire Wing is so powerful? Why can't the Earth, Air, or Water ones stop them? They're all equal from what I'm gathering."

The Enchantress held up Her hand to halt the teenager's

inquisitiveness. "We cannot risk one of the Wings going against another. That is not what the Mêla stands for."

"What does "Mêla" even mean?"

"Together, there is harmony. Divided, only chaos remains," the pale Woman whispered.

"Oh," Lia realized until her train of thought derailed from its tracks. "I don't get it. Wait a minute. *Oh!* When the Twelve are together, there's peace, but when they're separated, everything gets chaotic. Is that right?"

The Woman nodded. "Exactly, my dear."

"And my job is to look for the Three Earth Mêla in my school," she concluded to the Enchantress' relief. "Got it."

"I know I can count on you."

"What should I do if I need help?"

Instead of pulling her closer, the Enchantress inched Her way into the distance. "You will know what to do. I will be by your side."

"Wait!" Lia tried to chase after Her but was instead rooted in place as Kythaela started to fade away. "Don't go! I'm not sure if I'm ready for this!"

The ruined courtyard surrounding her crumbled and collapsed around her. A scream ripped through her lips when the mountains followed behind. The leaves of the trees blew off in a flurry as a whirlwind captured the reality that the Enchantress created. All of this chaos…and Lia was at the heart of it. Desperately, she cried out for any sort of aid–the Enchantress…her parents, but no one came to her side. Instead, her consciousness began to fade, dragging her back into Dreamland where she was at the beginning of all of this. Lia's body folded in on itself and curled into a small ball on the floor. The last that the teenager was aware of were the three words echoing in her ears while her pupils rolled back into her head.

"*You are ready.*"

Some time later, chirping of two birds frolicking from tree to tree before eventually settling on a power line rang through Lia's subconscious. She jolted upright to an empty room other than the red and orange Noodle slithering up a branch in her vivarium. In an attempt to zone back into reality, Lia's eyes followed Noodle's tail as it coiled around the same branch. Lia shoved the comforter off of her and extended her arms, rolled her shoulders, and cricked her neck on both sides. A pair of short legs swiveled to hover over the floor. Lia hopped off the bed and let her toes sink into the gray carpet below. For a second time, Lia stretched out the sore muscles throughout her petite figure. She determined she was still waiting on a growth spurt, but at newly sixteen, Lia guessed that was not going to happen.

Since it was a weekend, Lia made the executive decision to remain in her pajamas. It was not like she was going to leave the house anyway. Sundays were mirror images of Saturdays in the Harts' household. That was why Lia briefly ran a brush through her hair and left it down rather than yanking the strands back into a ponytail. She eyed herself in the full-length mirror next to her dresser and squinted when she realized she had apparently worn her glasses to bed. Lia removed the lenses from her face, wiped them off with her hoodie's sleeve, and slid them back on. A yawn escaped from the back of her throat. Lia made the mistake of inhaling once her mouth closed and grimaced at the morning breath. With a scrunched nose, she fanned away the abrupt smell that hit it.

A knock at the door made Lia turn around and straighten her posture just a tad. "Come in!" Lia exclaimed, knowing it was one of her parents.

The door opened to reveal Lucas Hart whose eyes were somehow brighter than his smile. He was still in his pajamas which were blue and had Batman symbols on them. He wore an old t-shirt with a miscellaneous skate shop logo on it. Even though he was carrying a thawed fuzzy, which was a small mouse that took up the majority of Noodle's diet with a pair of kitchen tongs, he seemed brighter than ever.

"Morning, Sweetheart!" Lucas grinned at her. "I figured I'd let you sleep while I got Noodle's breakfast."

Lia took the tongs holding the fuzzy from him, stood on her tiptoes, and kissed him on the cheeks. "Thanks, Dad. I know you think they're gross."

"It's my job," he chuckled warmly. Then, he pointed downwards. "Where's you get that, Lia?"

As the brunette started to turn around to feed the miniature mouse to Noodle, who was patiently awaiting in her habitat, she looked to where her father was gesturing. It took a second, but when it clicked, her vision blurred and nearly went out. Everything she had experienced, the Enchantress, the vision, Kythaela...everything...was real. There, resting snugly on her ring finger was the golden band made from Her very hands.

It was not a dream.

Five

If a list was composed of what Lia hated the most, the item at the very top would be "lying." From a very young age, she had been taught that honesty was always the best policy. When a situation became too turbulent for her shoulders to bear, Lia confided in her parents, who always had a logical solution that worked for everyone. When Lia failed her first test back in her freshman year, the first person she told was her mother, who planted a chaste kiss on her forehead, wrapped her arms around her, and exclaimed how proud of her daughter she was. Lia never had to worry about her parents' disappointment. As long as she was honest and tried her best with every scenario, that was enough for them.

Lia's heart fractured from the first splinter in the center after she released a fib as to where the Ring around her finger came from. She claimed she had found it in the junk drawer of her dresser. Since that particular area of her room was an endless void of miscellaneous belongings of hers over the years, Lucas did not ask any questions. In order for her mother not to be suspicious as well, later on that morning, Lia hopped down the stairs and exclaimed, "Look what I found in my junk drawer!." Sure enough, Cheyenne replied, "That's beautiful, Sweetheart!"

and left it at that. It was a little white lie, but still an authentic one, which consumed Lia with guilt. She knew it would go away someday - maybe not soon, but eventually - and therefore shoved it onto the back burner. She had a much larger task at hand.

The brunette had turned an otherwise mundane Monday morning into a mission. The alarm on her phone went off fifteen minutes early. Her usual twenty-minute shower was shaved down to ten. Lia took her time picking out an outfit for the unpredictable day ahead of her, which somehow turned out to be similar to her usual everyday wear. Lia nodded in approval at the black turtleneck, light-washed heavily ripped jeans - under the knee, of course, so she would not be dress-coded - under black fishnet tights, and her hair braided loosely out of her face. The golden infinity necklace given to her by her grandparents hung around her neck, unmoved since Saturday. Finally, the Ring from the Enchantress clung to her finger, Lia was afraid to pry it off, especially since it was forged from nothingness.

Before Lia knew it, she was making her way downstairs to continue her usual routine of grabbing some sort of snack food from the pantry for breakfast and then making a peanut butter and jelly - minus the jelly - sandwich along with other snacks to pack in her lunch. With a bright smile, she discovered the massive unopened box of fruit snacks. Lia made sure to pack two of them in her lunch box because the serving size of one packet was absolutely offensive. Along with a bag of pretzel sticks, a sliced up green apple, and a chocolate dipped granola bar, Lia ensured she had her canteen full of iced water that would remain cold throughout the day until she needed to fill it up again.

Lia bid Noodle farewell and ensured she had everything she needed before she was on her way. Her poor mother, once again, was terrified in the passenger's seat as Lia navigated her black sedan through Elwood Manor and retrieved her two "sisters." Maylene and Yasmin were not particularly excited about the day ahead of them, but on Lia's side of the table, she had a three-course meal on her plate. The Enchantress' words echoed in her mind like a broken record.

"*I am sorry, but you must be confined to secrecy.*"

To the best of her ability, Lia kept her eyes on the road and away from the sun, which was grueling her from just underneath the shade hung over the top of the windshield. Lia despised her "vertical challenge-ness" - if that was even a word - since her torso was just short enough for the sunshield not to do anything to help unless she lifted the faux leather seat. If she did that, then her legs would be too short to reach the pedals below the steering wheel. Nevertheless, she squinted and maneuvered her way around the familiar Oakbrookian town. Her knuckles paled as she gripped the steering wheel with all her might. Stopping at street lights was made much more difficult with the sun in her eyes. At one point, the light switched to green and Lia neglected to place her foot on the gas at the correct time since the sunshield blocked the light itself. Needless to say, the vehicle behind them was raring to go. All four occupants of the black sedan flinched in unison when a horn blared. Lia slammed her foot down on the gas and sped forward at a semi-reasonable speed.

"Sorry!" Lia grimaced once the vehicle was in the clear. "The sun was in my eyes."

"It's okay, Sweetheart. It happens to the best of us," Cheyenne trembled from the passenger's seat while clinging onto the "uh oh" handle for dear life.

"That was so cool!" Yasmin flung her hands up in the air like an ecstatic penguin. "That felt like we were in a getaway car! Hit the gas, Lia! Do it again!"

"No!" Cheyenne and Maylene yelped.

Lia's cheeks flushed red. "Sorry, everybody."

"You were driving the getaway car–we were flying, but we'd never get far," Yasmin sang the lyrics of a fitting song but in a horrifyingly wrong key.

"Don't pretend it's such a mystery," Lia continued the words as she turned into Oakbrooke High School's parking lot, "think about the place where you first met me."

"Ridin' in a getaway car."

"There were sirens in the beat of your heart," Maylene chipped in with her soft tone.

Lia was next: "Should've known we'd be the first to leave…"

"Think about the place where you first met me!" all three teenagers shouted to the dismay of poor Mrs. Hart. "In a getaway car, oh-oh-oh! No, they never get far, oh-oh-oh! No, nothin' good starts in a getaway car!"

Lia, Maylene, and Yasmin burst into laughter after singing the chorus of one of the songs that belonged to one of their favorite artists. Yasmin held out her hand for high fives. Maylene was the first to return the favor. Yasmin leaned forward and splayed her hand over the center console. Lia pulled into the drop-off line beginning at the curb and waited until the vehicle was vacant from moving before she smacked Yasmin's hand.

"Girls, you sound beautiful, but *please*," Cheyenne whined dramatically. "I forgot aspirin this morning."

This prompted more laughter and three collective "sorry's" murmured in her direction.

"Your mom's cool for putting up with us," Yasmin said to Lia once the black sedan made its way to the front and all three of them got out.

Lia just shrugged, hoisting her backpack out of the trunk and onto her shoulders. "She's pretty cool," she admitted teasingly. "I just wish she wasn't so scared of Noodle."

"Yeah, Noodle's cool," agreed the talkative twin.

"I can understand why she's a little scary," Maylene sympathized with Mrs. Hart. "I was scared of her too at first, but now we know she's a sweetie pie."

"Exactly." Lia dashed over to the driver's side of the car where her mother was now standing. She flung her arms around her frame and placed a kiss on her cheek. "Love you, Mom!

Thanks for putting up with us," she echoed Yasmin's words from before.

"It's always a pleasure," Cheyenne giggled breathily. She planted a kiss on Lia's forehead and slid into the driver's seat. "Have a great day, Sweetie."

"You too, Mom."

"Thanks for the ride!" Maylene and Yasmin chorused from the other side.

"You're welcome," Cheyenne called just prior to shutting the door behind her.

Mrs. Hart watched as the three peas in a pod walked beside each other - each twin on the outside and Lia in the middle - towards the tree-topped Oakbrooke High to begin a new week. Once the massive double doors were opened and shut behind them and Lia, Maylene, and Yasmin dispersed into the crowd safely, Cheyenne shed a bittersweet smile and moved her vehicle's gear into "Drive," leaving the parking lot and preparing to continue her work day.

Meanwhile, Lia struggled to keep her eyes on the hallway ahead of her. It did not help that the continuous swarm of students spreading every which way acted like a constant fog glazing over each pair of eyes attempting to make it to the stairwell to the second floor. Like a usual school day would begin, Yasmin bid her two "sisters" farewell and dashed towards the "popular" group that was likely on the opposite side of the school since that was where the majority of their classes were. That left Lia and Maylene to venture towards their Ceramics class together, which the two of them did not mind so much. Lia could tell that Maylene sometimes needed a break from her eccentric sister. The twins loved each other dearly, but obviously had different comfort zones. While Yasmin preferred being in large groups of people, all of whom she could consider her friends, Maylene favored Lia's company. She brunette was her best friend, after all.

Maylene watched Lia out of the corner of her almond eye.

Skepticism was written all over her face when she zoned in on Lia's demeanor. She walked brisker than normal, almost leaving Maylene in the dust while going up the stairs. Her hair was tied in a looser braid than normal, yet somehow, Lia appeared to be dressed neater than before. Her clothes did not have any sort of pocket, so Lia clasped her hands together and let her fingers writhe against each other with more force than necessary. Maylene frowned when Lia began fussing with a hangnail on her index finger. Usually, Lia left herself alone and instead prioritized her schoolwork. That was why Maylene cleared her throat to get her friend's attention.

"Lia, are you feeling okay?" she inquired softly. "You seem really stressed."

"Huh?" Lia nearly slammed into the door at the top of the stairwell; sheepishly, she pulled it open and sidestepped through with Maylene in tow. "Oh, yeah! I'm fine. I'm just stressed about...about a test for Chemistry."

Maylene cocked her head to the side. "You never said anything about a Chemistry test."

"That's why I'm stressed," Lia fibbed for the second time that morning, "because I forgot about it until just now when we walked in."

"Oh, well...I'm just about finished with my ocarina. Maybe I can help you study during this period if Miss K gives us a free day? You know she will because everybody else is far behind in their projects."

"Oh, no...how do I get out of this one?" Lia fought back an anguished groan at the thought of reading her Chemistry textbook for no reason rather than painting a vase. Instead of following her instinct of telling the truth, she smiled gratefully. "I can go over it while you work on your ocarina–thank you, though."

Maylene patted her tenderly on the shoulder. "No problem. You're going to ace that test."

"Thanks, I hope so."

Lia already knew that her lie was digging a hole deeper than she wished to fill up with anything other than dirt. She might as well have buried herself at that point since she was not looking forward to reading her Chemistry textbook chapter on Thermodynamics without a clear motive. Sure, she did have a test later in the week on Friday, but she had already prepared the necessary flash cards based on the notes she had taken for the past week on the chapter, even getting ahead of herself and reading the second half before it was time to discuss it. Now, she was mindlessly reading the material for a second time. Maybe she could quiz herself on the footnotes as well. She could get Maylene to help her with that. Then again, listening to music while she painted her lopsided vase sounded much more fun. Another idea came to her once she and Maylene sat down at their usual shared table: multitasking. Lia was certainly good at that.

Sure enough, when Miss K entered the room wearing yet another fascinating outfit - multicolored paint-stained denim overalls underneath a purple tee and the same black heels she wore the previous Friday - she announced that this period, each student would be free to either work on their project or use their time for something else. Miss K's overalls reminded Lia of Maylene's turquoise pair she wore today along with a matching headband. Once Miss K set the class loose to do their own things, Maylene eagerly tied her hair back into a ponytail and dashed up to her desk to retrieve some of the same paint colors she received the other day. Lia followed suit and picked out a couple of colors to continue working on her vase while she "studied." She did not miss the odd glance that Maylene gave her when she placed her vase and painting supplies on one side of her workspace while opening her Chemistry textbook on the other.

"Would you like some help studying?" Maylene asked while dipping her brush into her pink paint. "I can always do this another day."

Lia shook her head and did the same with her green paint. "I got it. Thanks, though."

"You're welcome."

The multitasking began without a hitch. Well...it was a feigned act to say the least. While Maylene concentrated deeply on painting intricate details on the clay instrument, Lia painted her own project. Every so often, when Maylene would look over or inquire about how the studying was going, Lia would pretend to be deeply enamored by the Chemistry textbook rather than face confrontation. In her eyes, multitasking was a "god" of some sort, sweet like honey...a relaxing thought, perhaps? It was as relaxing as it could have been anyway, with Lia doing two things at once. That was what she excelled in.

The eighty-five minutes designating the Ceramics period came and went quicker than Lia originally had thought. Maylene had asked regarding Lia's feelings about the test after the class commenced. Now, after a brief hug and Maylene's departure to her second class of the day, which was Geometry, Lia was prepared to endure a meaningless second period discussing the chapter she just "studied." All's well that ends well, supposedly, so Lia made the most of it by mentally preparing herself for PE as her third block.

Lia had promptly changed into a t-shirt and shorts for her PE class. Thankfully, the students were given a few extra minutes to do so before and after the lesson. Coach Jenkins, who was wearing a muted purple tracksuit this time, was at the front of the gymnasium standing on one of the sets of bleachers when Lia entered carrying her backpack and large canteen which she kept with her. Awkwardly, she shuffled towards the middle of the group and squeezed her way into the front to the slight frustration of a few of her classmates she had to weave around. Lia would have remained towards the back, but being as vertically challenged as she was, she decided to be just a little bit selfish and make her way to the front.

"Okay, class," Coach Jenkins announced in her explosive

voice. "Today, we're going to do the usual pushups, sit-ups, suicides, and laps. Then, we're going to play a few games of basketball. I assume everyone knows how to play?"

"I don't, Sir," one boy with a face full of zits and thick-rimmed glasses squeaked from the back. His scrawny friend elbowed him. "Er–I mean, *Ma'am*."

Coach Jenkins jumped down from her spot on the bleachers. The crowd parted like the Red Sea for the spritely woman who seemed to be more of a man, apparently, to this boy. Lia watched, fighting an amused smirk off her face as the coach marched right up to the lanky boy and delivered one of the most passionate angry face scrunches Lia had ever seen. The boy gulped and it looked as if his friend scurried away at the last second. By the way the Coach's fist was clenched at her side, Lia observed that the woman wanted to grab onto his collar…but that would end up in her getting fired.

"You have a ball and you have to get it in the hoop," she gritted out with a strained smile. "Got it?"

The poor boy nodded vigorously. "Yes, sorry, Ma'am."

"Good." Coach Jenkins strutted her way back to the bleachers. "Everyone give me twenty-five pushups *stat*!"

And the class was underway. Lia struggled under the weight of her own body due to her arms that resembled noodles more than the associated appendage. Despite this, she pushed through with sweat brimming on her forehead. The sit-ups proved to be much harder, especially after the pushups. Lia's entire frame shook with each movement. Suicide sprints were even worse. Lia was not a runner to begin with; the only thing she was thankful for was not having lunch yet or it would have been on the floor by then. Lia shoved the thought to the back of her mind and instead focused on her goal. Every couple of minutes, she would glance down at the Ring on her finger. Nothing changed despite being around at least a third of the school's population in the hallways and in her classes. Lia's eyes scanned the room for any possible subject regarding the Mêla. She had no clue in the slightest of what to look for, but then again, the Enchantress did not even give her a description. All she saw in the vision were figures in colored cloaks. Unless a few students wore cloaks to school, Lia was going to have a tough time.

Basketball was the next objective on the PE session's agenda. Since the class was substantial in size, both basketball courts were utilized. Still, several people sat on the bleachers while waiting their turn. Lia was one of these individuals, watching as the game closest to her seat went down. She had done her own research on sports to have something in common with her father, but when it came to playing them, Lia seemed to be much less than mediocre. Instead, she preferred listening on the sidelines, watching and waiting for her predictions to come true. Her mind was more practical than physical, which left her as a better referee than player.

That was the very reason why Lia shrunk down into her seat when Coach Jenkins barked, "Lia Hart–you're next up for small forward."

Lia gulped down her nerves that sprung out of sheer nothingness. She was well-aware of the fact she was needed to play at some point in the session, but the fact it happened so fast caused her anxiety to skyrocket. Now, Lia was not a severely self-conscious person. Sure, she had her own insecurities, but Lia knew she was just like everyone else when it came to bodies. She had never met someone who was not insecure about their looks or something else about their person. She had learned over the years that no matter what you look like, you will never be completely satisfied. Wise words for such a young woman.

This did not change when she slunk her way onto the court and got into position as she was shown by her father on the television last time they watched a game. Once Coach Jenkins blew the whistle, Lia stood firm in position while making sure she was open for someone to pass her the ball. She watched as members of her team dribbled the ball and passed it to each other like it was one fluid motion. Lia dashed behind one of the taller boys who ran towards the opposing team's hoop, dodged an enemy player's attack, and guided the ball into the hoop with ease. Lia then awkwardly chased after her team as their role switched to defense. She gazed at one of the girls on the opposing team who attempted to achieve a three-pointer, but the ball ricocheted off the rim and was handed to her team.

The pattern ensued and the temptation of stepping off the court plagued Lia when she realized she had not been passed the ball in the brief, but eventful game. Her mind began to shove thoughts into her head like an overused binder that could not fit any more sheets of paper inside. "Why isn't anyone passing you the ball?" was the first question her imagination asked her, followed by, "Do you not look athletic enough?" or "Maybe you're too chubby for someone to want you to be on their team." Lia fought the urge to swat away her brain's mindless chatter. She was a healthy weight regardless and even if she was not, it was just a number and it did not matter–end of discussion.

All of the banter continued until a teammate shouted in her direction. The next thing Lia knew, the ball was passed to her and she was faced with an even greater challenge. The net was at least twice her height, and she was surrounded by a bunch of taller, more intimidating people. Nevertheless, Lia began cautiously dribbling. Her awkward jog turned into a powerful sprint towards the opponents' hoop. Before she could even aim to take a shot, though, amidst her final stride, an excruciating squeezing ensued on the ring finger of her left hand. Lia recognized the fact that the Ring given to her by the Enchantress was pulsing just as She said. Lia dropped everything mid-run and mid-dribble and allowed her brown eyes to scan the room for who exactly could be triggering the ring. Alas, before the realization she was still in the middle of a basketball game hit her, something else did, quite literally. Lia yelped in surprise as she crashed into another body and flew backwards onto the ground. The back of her head hit the hard maple. Lia attempted to lift her head upright to assess the situation, but before she could, her eyes rolled into the back of her head and it flopped back down onto the ground.

The next thing she was aware of was the snapping of two fingers directly in front of her face. The blurry world opened back up to Lia when her eyelids fluttered and she straightened her glasses. With an awkward grimace, she realized she was indeed in the middle of the basketball court along with half of the class crowded around her and kneeling over her–the exception being the other half playing their own game. Lia's gaze focused on Coach Jenkins, who was the one snapping her fingers. Once Lia was conscious again, she clapped her hands.

"She's okay, class," the coach notified everyone. "Continue on with your games."

Lia wondered how exactly her team would continue on until she realized a substitute stepped on in her place. She just shrugged and decided to lay there for just a little while. That was...at least until a tall figure loomed over her. Lia thought nothing of it until her Ring began pulsating against her finger for a second time. Lia shot upright, but then clutched her forehead when a stab of pain shot through it. Lia curled into a small ball with her knees to her chest so she could retrieve her breath and not collapse again. A clearing of someone's throat briskly grabbed hold of her attention, especially when her Ring squeezed her finger tighter. Lia stuffed her left hand in her pocket and gradually lifted her gaze upward. In front of her stood a tall boy who appeared to be no older than seventeen, but the Ring definitely told her otherwise as it continued pulsing quicker than her own heart rate. Black bangs nearly reached this pale boy's brown eyes right smack in the center of his chiseled face. His muscular - but not bulky - frame was at least six inches taller than Lia, maybe even passing the six-foot range. He wore a red V-neck t-shirt and a pair of black basketball shorts. Rather than a typical smirk, this boy wore a concerned frown. When he noticed Lia's initial shock, he bent down to her height.

"Hey, are you okay?" His voice was as smooth as silk. "I'm

sorry for bumping into you—I should've watched where I was going."

At first, Lia was speechless, especially since she recognized him as the boy who had hit her in the head with a dodgeball that past Friday, but once she realized she needed to keep her cool, she offered a lopsided grin. "It's alright. It was my fault, really."

"But are you okay?"

Lia eyed his hand being held out to her as if it was some kind of foreign object. Hastily, she grabbed it and allowed him to hoist her up. "I'm fine—ow!" she squeaked when her forehead ached from the altitude.

"Are you sure?"

"...Yes, I'm sure." Lia's breath hitched in her throat. Now that she was standing up straight, she could take in the person across from her and who was subconsciously walking her off the court. "Thank you, though."

"No problem," he replied, and *gosh*, Lia could not tell if she liked or despised his smile. "Well, uh, see you around."

Lia watched numbly as the stranger dashed back to the court and left her in the dust. She was unsure of why she was staring, other than the fact that she suffered an overexaggerated "brain injury" from him chucking a dodgeball just last week. Lia thought she heard Coach Jenkins advising her to sit on the bench for the rest of the session and watch, which was what she preferred doing in the first place, but her thoughts were clouded with immense emotions she had not felt in quite a while. Maybe she did want to sit on the bench and watch the two sweaty teams battle it out for a little while longer. Was it possible that she wanted to zero in on a specific player? Lia could have smacked herself with the realization of what had just happened. The boy who had aided her was the first member of the Earth Wing she had encountered, and one thought in particular spiraled in her brain like a top:

"Oh, God... Do I seriously think he's cute?"

Six

Being a teenage girl meant processing a multitude of emotions. Lia was no exception to this unwritten rule. Hormones were hormones no matter the scenario, and unfortunately for Lia's case, they sent her into an upward spiral through the roof. She had been stiff with numbness as the strange boy with black hair and a jawline that could cut butter hoisted her up as if she was a feather and merely...left to be with his friends once again. She knew he had hit her with a dodgeball, which might have been an accident due to his antics on the court today. That was actually all she knew about this young man...or older man. She had no idea how long the Mêla were around–at least a millennia at this point, perhaps. Lia desperately wanted to avoid being the accidental victim of some sort of immortal pedophilia...or the opposite depending on what was next in store for her.

Lia did indeed sit on the bleachers for the rest of the game but kept to herself rather than trying to make awkward conversation with anyone else around her. That was something Lia tried to do in her spare time, but often, it did not end too terribly well. Instead, she pretended to text on her phone but was actually playing a multitude of trivia and word games at once to keep her mind juices flowing on something other than an attractive human...or immortal...or whatever this black-haired beauty was. She had a much bigger problem at stake.

She knew that this boy was always en route to socialize with one of the most popular groups at Oakbrooke High. Lia saw him from time to time, but having an up close and personal encounter made her emotions skyrocket. At first, she tried to shove the idea of him being just another student into her mind, but then she remembered that if her ring was correct - and there was a ninety-nine point nine percent chance it was, unless it was all some sort of joke - this boy was from another world entirely. How in the world would she be able to communicate with him, much less convince him to return to a place he fled from? Then, it hit her. One girl in particular always ensured she was with the popular crowd. This was her ticket!

Lia exited her crossword puzzle game and opened the messages app on her phone. *"Hey, do you know anything about that really tall guy with black hair, a jawline sharp enough to cut steak, and usually wears a varsity jacket? I think he hangs out with your group at lunch."* She sent it to Yasmin.

For someone who had such a vibrant social life, even Lia was surprised how quickly her friend replied. *"Do you mean Jared Huxley?"*

"Oh, no...not a "J" name..." Lia shook her head at the thought and then responded, *"Probably."*

"Why?" Yasmin's next text read. *"Is everything okay?"*

Lia was unsure of that...yet another lie contributed to clogging the drain. *"Yeah, everything's fine. Long story, but I slammed into him in PE and it got a little weird. Never got to apologize since he left so fast."*

Lia watched the flowing bubbles bounce up and down as Yasmin tentatively formed a reply on the other side. Then:

"Oh, that's weird... Maybe you and May can come sit with us for lunch. You can talk to him then and get everything cleared up."

"*Great idea,*" Lia texted without thinking through it. "*I'll ask her and see where we go from there.*"

"*Okay! I'll be looking for you! :)*"

It was too late when the realization of the fact Lia might have made a mistake hit her. Coach Jenkins had dismissed the class once everyone was finished with their games. Jared was on Lia's mind for the entire time she was in the ladies' restroom freshening up and changing back into her regular clothes. She spritzed extra of her lavender body spray on her person and then hoisted her backpack onto her back. Despite looking ready for her spontaneous decision. It might not work out—at the very least, Maylene would not want to join the more popular group like her sister. Lia could not leave her alone, though; that would be poor of her. Instead, Lia spoke encouraging thoughts under her breath as she made her way through the halls and towards the courtyard. The fact Maylene was waiting by the propped open double doors rather than being trapped against a wall face to face with a bully. When Lia caught her eye, her smile shimmered, bejeweled with optimism.

"*Okay, Lia, you can do this.*" Lia attempted to match her expression, but the grin on her face did not reach her eyes. "Hey, Maylene."

"Hi!" she chirped, lunchbox in hand. "How was PE?"

"It was…eventful to say the least. How was Geometry?"

Maylene reddened at the thought. "I might not have done too well on our pop quiz, but I tried my best."

"And that's all that matters!" Lia smacked her lightly on the back. "Great job."

"Thanks," she whispered.

"*Okay. It's now or never.*" Lia bit the bullet and spat out her question, "It's totally okay if you say no, but is it okay if we sit with Yasmin and her friends today? I need to talk to one of them and it would be easier at lunch. Yasmin already said we could but I told her I'd ask you."

"Oh, um…" Maylene dragged her sneaker-clad foot against

the tiles with uncertainty, but she did not want to disappoint her friend, so she nodded. "Sure. We can do that."

"Are you positive?" Lia tilted her head just a bit. When Maylene was nervous, it was the moon in a starless sky. "We don't have to. I'll just chat with him later."

At her compassion, she smiled. "No, we can. I'll just stick by you two."

"Are you sure?"

Maylene nodded. "Yeah."

A sliver of guilt pulled at her like a nuisance of a hangnail on her finger. Maylene had accepted her request, but Lia could tell there was something off about the entire situation. All she could do was remain loyal to the Enchantress since she was chosen for such a large task that she did not quite understand yet. One step at a time, she told herself throughout the entire morning. Now, she was going to "man up," crack her knuckles, and troop to the group that intimated her the most. As the two of them walked through the courtyard doors, Lia thought she looked a bit silly with her lunchbox in hand and a determined expression on her face. Her eyebrows lowered as she scanned the room for the boy she needed to talk to. Sure enough, right by the tree at the very center of it, Yasmin was waving both of them over. Lia glanced over at Maylene one last time, and she nodded, which gave them the go-ahead.

"Hey, guys!" she exclaimed cheerfully. "Over here! I saved a seat for you both."

Neither of them hesitated to join the group of at least twenty students. Lia sat down on the bench by Yasmin and Maylene squeezed in between both of them. Yasmin ruffled her twin's hair but somehow, it fell back into place after she adjusted her turquoise headband. Both Lia and Maylene fished through their lunchboxes for the food they had packed. Once again, Maylene brought her usual vegan poke rice bowl. Lia did not wait to begin consuming her lunch as if she was a starving woman who had not eaten in days. Her stomach was a bottomless pit and she was far from being ashamed of it right now. As she took another large bite of her peanut butter sandwich, her Ring started throbbing, and she remembered why exactly she was in the midst of all the chatter. There he was, standing across from the bench and striking conversation with two of his male friends with similar builds. Lia imagined all three of them were athletically inclined in at least some way. She needed to build up the courage to open her mouth. Once she did, though, she regretted it

"Hey!" she gushed more enthusiastically than she meant to. Lia wanted to slap herself when the boy with black hair abruptly faced her. "Uh...hi," she quieted down. "Remember me? I slammed into you in PE?"

Jared just shook his head and let himself smile. "How could I forget?"

"*Uh oh,*" she cringed at herself. Lia caught Maylene hiding her grin. "Yeah, uh...I wanted to apologize about that. I hit you pretty hard. Are you okay?"

"Oh, I'm fine." The boy's eyebrows raised. "You're the one who took most of the damage. You were out like a light for a good thirty seconds."

Maylene's eyes bulged. "You were?"

"...I guess?" Lia's complexion heated. "I didn't really notice. My fault anyways, so I'm sorry."

"That's alright," Jared shrugged and took a sip out of his orange soda can. "I could tell you were new to the sport."

"And what's *that* supposed to mean?" Lia scrunched her nose.

His head swayed from side to side. "I'm just messing with you, Hothead."

"My name's Lia," she gritted out between clenched teeth.

"Okay." Another sip from his soda. "I'm Jared. I bet you've seen me around."

Lia pretended not to admit she had. "Maybe in PE, but nowhere else," she antagonized.

"Have you ever seen a football game here? I'm the starting receiver."

"As you said, I never have been one for sports."

"...No, I just said you were new to the sport."

"Quit flirting, you chickens," Yasmin bellowed, averting from her conversation with three other girls. She turned her attention to the boy. "Jared, you loser–go on and ask her out. She's hot and smart and you like that, I think."

Both Lia and Jared blushed in sync. "I wasn't," the latter blurted out.

"Not interested," Lia lied right through her teeth.

"Yeah, right," Yasmin chortled followed by a snort of laughter. "You two have so much tension already. Just go ahead."

"No," they chorused.

"Gross–he's like a thousand years older than me," Lia thought distastefully.

Maylene sat up straighter and finally found the courage within herself to speak up, "If they said no, they mean it, Yas…"

All eyes turned to the timid girl sitting on the bench and leaning against the massive tree behind it. As if it was instinct, Maylene's shoulders slumped and she pretended that she had not said anything at all. Instead, she hunched over and seemed to be enamored by her poke bowl. She winced when a bite fell out of her chopsticks and back into the bowl. Lia completely ignored if Jared had said anything else and focused entirely on her best friend. She shuffled closer to her and remained by her side in the uncomfortable storm of people surrounding them both.

If Lia had managed to shift her attention to the reason for their seating arrangement in the first place, she would have noticed the fact that Jared's eyes were locked on both of them, but more specifically one of the two girls. Jared would never admit it, but he was caught by surprise by the encounter in PE class just about twenty minutes prior. Being around new people was not something he was particularly used to. Lia sincerely tried her best, and when she fell down, she got right back up again and wanted to give it another shot before Coach Jenkins sat her down on the bleachers to rest her head. Lia had been fine, but Maylene on the other hand, did not appear to be as such. Instead, her head was hung low as Lia consoled her through whispers and platonic sweet nothings. Lia's right arm rested amongst her shoulders.

"I was kidding, May," Yasmin assured her, then her face fell. "Are you alright?"

Maylene nodded and continued eating her lunch. "Yeah, thanks."

Lia leaned over and whispered, "Would you like to move?"

"Yeah, if you don't mind," she accepted the offer.

So, that was exactly what they did. After giving Yasmin a hug, Lia and Maylene bid farewell and awkwardly left the center of the courtyard to return to their usual table, which was vacant just like all the other times. Lia sat across from Maylene, who neglected to meet her eye. Lia, for once around her, was lost for words. Usually, Maylene did the listening and she did the talking. Now, though, the opposite occurred.

"I'm sorry," Maylene apologized to her. "I know you wanted to be over there, but I just got so overwhelmed, and…"

Lia did not hesitate to stop her. "Don't worry about it," she replied authentically. "If you're overwhelmed, you're overwhelmed. I would much rather sit with you anyway,"

Her best friend smiled a tad. "Thanks, but I know you wanted to talk to Jared or whatever his name is."

"And I did. We're all good."

"Are you sure?"

"Positive."

Maylene took another bite out of her rice bowl. "So, how did your Chemistry test go?"

"It was fine," Lia fibbed. The fact that the lie left her mouth so easily unnerved her. "I did better than I thought."

"I knew you'd do well."

"*Me too,*" the brunette frowned. "Thanks for offering to help me study. How's your Ceramics project going?"

"It's good." Maylene hid a mischievous glint in her eyes. "I think it's finally finished."

"That's so cool! Can I see it?"

"I want it to be a surprise,"

Lia nodded, slightly disappointed, but remained optimistic. "Sounds good. My poor excuse of a vase looks...special."

"You made it. Of course it's special."

Lia's cheeks inflamed. "You're too pure for this world."

It was an honest-to-God fact. Maylene was never someone to pick a fight with; throughout their countless years of friendship, Maylene never gave Lia a reason to be mad at her. She had been nothing but kind and supportive when it came to Lia's endless endeavors, spontaneous decisions, and even when the girl just refused to make any sense. She always acted as a listening ear to all of Lia's ideas and never missed an opportunity to throw a compliment her way. Lia knew deep down that there was no way to match her friend's love for her, but that did not stop her from trying...no, not one single bit. It was sort of like a friendly competition between the two. Who could be a better friend? Who could make the other smile the fastest? Oftentimes, it was things as simple as fart noises that made the other chuckle.

Mrs. Hart and Mrs. Zuíhuí found it ridiculous. Mr. Hart and Mr. Zuíhuí on the other hand...hilarious.

Embarrassment heated her cheeks continually throughout the rest of the school day. Her final two classes went by without a hitch, thankfully for her. Lia was well-accustomed to her final two subjects, which were Advanced Placement English Composition and Advanced Placement United States History. Despite being only a sophomore, Lia was granted allowance to take as many Advanced Placement classes as she could. Seeing that her intelligence was far above average, the school's faculty agreed to further her education to the maximum. It was clear that Lia had a bright future ahead of her, but the fact that she had no clue what it held frightened her.

Lia grimaced as she pressed down too hard on the page of her notebook and watched the lead from her mechanical pencil flew from the desk and disappeared on the floor. With a huff, Lia clicked a bit more lead from her pencil and continued writing her notes regarding the Civil War in the nineteenth century. She had learned about this particular point in history numerous times, therefore finding it the slightest bit boring. The only reason that this United States History course was considered Advanced Placement was because it included accelerated coverage of the history of the respective country. It was too late to switch classes now.

"Okay, students–thank you for being so diligent today," Mr. Bristol, the teacher at the front of the class, looked up from his watch and noted. "It looks like our time is up. Be sure to complete the assigned worksheets by Thursday evening at eleven fifty-nine. Participation is a crucial aspect of this class. See you all tomorrow."

Lia listened boredly. She had already done the worksheets for this week; therefore she was free to do as she pleased. The rest of the class, on the other hand, was more than eager to finish the semester and get away from the monotonous lectures that Mr. Bristol put forth. The gray-haired man was very charming and knew his history, but after a while, his voice grew to be droning and words started blending together. Despite this, Lia paid attention to the best of her ability and color-coded her History notes to entertain herself. Today's colors were lilac and pink, which Lia was more than happy with. Her favorite color was sage green, which coincidentally was her middle name, but trying new things was in her nature.

The United States History classroom consisted of students flocking out into the hallway with no regard for anyone's safety. Lia hid amongst them as the herd of elephants stampeded through the hallway and towards the stairwell to the bottom floor. Lia remained near the back to avoid getting trampled by the raging river. She clung onto the railing with one hand and cringed at the thought of the germs crawling onto her hands. Thankfully she kept lavender hand sanitizer with her, which was what she used the moment she hopped off the second flight and onto the first floor at the back of the flock. Lia straightened her glasses and let her eyes wander around the hallways that wrapped around the courtyard and made up the basic structure of the building. Lia stayed put as she waited for Yasmin and Maylene to approach on opposite sides of the building from their respective classrooms. This was a tradition of theirs: meeting at the front of the building to await Mrs. Hart's arrival. Lia's gracious mother always gave them a ride home...well, with Lia in the driver's seat.

Lia fiddled around with a game on her phone - the same word game from PE class - until Maylene and Yasmin appeared right on schedule. Lia bounded for Maylene first, giving her a hug and then lurched towards Yasmin to do the same. Unlike that morning, the bags under Yasmin's eyes were darker, much like Maylene's. Lia guessed that the former was worn out from committing so much social interaction. This was what occurred every day. Yasmin's social battery lasted a substantially long time, but once that duration was up, she needed a power nap.

"Hey, Yasmin," Lia stated with a smidge of concern, "are you okay? You look exhausted."

Yasmin shrugged, shoving her hands in the middle pouch of her blue hoodie. "Yeah, I'm all good. It was just a busy day and I'm happy I'm heading home soon."

"Speaking of home, should we head outside?" Maylene softly questioned.

It was at this time that Lia's bladder initiated war. The brunette sighed and responded, "I'll meet you there. I need to use the restroom."

"Sounds good," Yasmin replied for both of them. "See you out there."

Lia begrudgingly made her way to the nearest restrooms, which were down the hall on the right wing of Oakbrooke High's generous building. For someone with a bottomless pit of a stomach, her bladder seemed to wreak havoc on her at the worst time. She hated the way she needed to clench her legs together and waddle to the restroom. Thankfully, the surprisingly clean bathroom was nearly empty since most students were well on their way out the door. Lia shut herself in a stall and did her business before emerging once more and washing her hands thoroughly. She used one of the brown paper towels from the dispenser to open the door before throwing it away. She took extra care to dry off the Ring on her finger. Since it was made of magic, she figured a little bit of water would not hurt it, but then again, you never know.

Speaking of such jewelry, Lia's stride stuttered to a stop when it began to pulse again. She halted in the middle of the hallway, which was not such a good idea for a crowded area. A miscellaneous person collided into her body which knocked her to the ground. Lia grimaced when she hit the tiled floor and was almost expecting Jared to help her up again just like in PE, but it turned out that this person was a stranger and simply muttered a quick "Sorry" before walking away. Lia lurched to her feet and let her eyes search the endless hallways, which she quickly learned would be a lost cause. Not everyone had left yet; in fact, the school's grounds were just as populated as ever. Lia had no chance of figuring out who triggered the Ring. At first, Lia thought it was Jared, but after a once-over, there was no sign of the boy. Then, she started walking down the hall that circled the courtyard one way. Her brisk walk turned into a jog as she eventually cleared the entire first floor of the school. Then, Lia bounded up the stairs and tried the second floor. Even though it made no sense since everyone was meant to be leaving, she thought she would try anyway...but it was to no avail.

By the time Lia was done searching both floors and climbed back down the two flights of stairs, her lungs screamed for air.

Lia's respirations were labored with each step. She pushed open the front doors of Oakbrooke High and trudged her way to her mother's black sedan, where Cheyenne, Maylene, and Yasmin were all waiting. Lia meekly grinned in their direction. Once Mrs. Hart saw her daughter, she got out of the driver's seat and walked around the hood. Lia was greeted with a peck to the forehead and a warm smile.

"Hi, Honey!" she exclaimed. "How was your day?"

"It was good," Lia mustered up the best reply she could.

The brunette tossed her braid behind her left shoulder as she slid into the driver's seat with her mother to her right. Subsequent to buckling her seatbelt and prior to switching the black sedan's gear into "Drive," Lia felt the urge to turn around. When she did, both Maylene and Yasmin eyed her with identical lifted eyebrows.

"What took you so long?" Yasmin bluntly broke the ice.

Yet again, Lia was forced to come up with a lie. "Let's just say my lunch didn't agree with me today."

The poor girl tensed up at her own dishonesty. This was going to be a lot harder than she initially thought.

Seven

What are the characteristics of Earth Zodiac signs? No. It needed to be more specific.
How do Earth Zodiacs act? No. Maybe search for a specific sign.
Taurus personality traits. Much better.

Lia pressed the enter key on the keyboard below her hands. The screen in front of her was transformed into a plethora of results for her web search. Lia opened her fern green spiral notebook and wrote the word "Taurus" in sweeping cursive letters at the top of a fresh page. Lia clicked on the top website and began to read the contents, making a bulleted list of each detail that she deemed important or worthy of memorizing at least at some point.

Taurus Qualities: A Taurus' best trait is considered to be their passion for things they love. Other qualities of a Taurus include:
   -Hard-headed
   -Down-to-earth
   -Reliable
   -Loyal

-*Sensual*

-*Stubborn*

Lia scrolled down the website that she thought was much too pink and "girly" for her liking and wrote down other qualities.

Those who align with Taurus are often regarded as the most attractive of the Zodiac children. They are well-loved because of their honesty, kindness, and compassion. Tauruses are possessive, which means they need their people and their things. They will do anything that they can to get it. The Taurus have a strong will and might have a short fuse, but this is what makes them even stronger in the best way.

Lia tapped her pencil to her mouth while reading what she had written. "*How many of these traits does Jared display? Heck, is he even supposed to represent a Taurus as we understand them?*"

"Hard-headed? Maybe." Lia put a question mark by the bullet. "Down-to-earth? He was to me." She swished a checkmark. "Reliable?" Question mark. "Loyal? He hangs out with the same friends a lot, so I guess?" Checkmark. "Sensual? He was cute." Lia smirked to herself and placed a final checkmark. She had no idea about "stubborn" yet.

Okay…so what now? Lia was unsure of what to do after making a list and checking off certain bullet points that identified with Jared's character. That was the most she could do at the time, which was rather unfortunate. Lia knew she had two other Mêla to look for, much less convince to return to their home world. Lia began to resent the Enchantress for placing such a heavy burden on her where she had no clue whatsoever where to start. Her adventure began with a bang, quite literally, but would it continue as such? Lia needed to keep her eyes and ears open for *anything*.

Perhaps Lia had gone too far overboard. Today, she made the borderline reckless decision to skip her Chemistry lesson in order to do her own research. She knew the material. Even if she did not, she could read the textbook and catch up with flying colors. That would not be necessary, though, since she was already ahead in the class itself. She knew where her priorities lay. What was more important: a Chemistry participation grade or an entire realm's prosperity? Of course, Lia chose the latter and continued on with her studies.

"Okay, next step?" Lia whispered out loud as she scribbled down a message with several stars around it so it would pop out. "Ask Jared his Zodiac sign. If the Earth Wing represents a Zodiac sign, then they *must* align with it, right? I would think so."

Lia went with her gut and shut her spiral notebook. She clicked out of the embarrassingly childish website she had been using on the computer and spun around in her wheeled chair to examine her surroundings. She was so enamored by her work that she had forgotten the vast beauty and magnificence the Oakbrooke Library represented. Tall, arched windows framed the front of the two-story brick building that seemed more like a home than a place of work. Shelves of books lined every wall except for the front, which was where the checkout registration system along with a help desk resided. The interior of the library was dimmed, an extravagant golden chandelier hanging from the tallest point in the domed building. Lia would have sat on the second-floor loft containing study rooms and a seating area that overlooked the rest of the library, but alas, the computers were on the first level, so she was stuck. Lia frowned at the fact the library was hardly ever utilized by the school directly across the street. Even when Oakbrooke High issued library cards linked with every student's school identification card as well as unlimited study room access, only a few more students began trickling in.

The brunette felt the slightest bit rebellious as she packed up her things and slung her backpack over her shoulders. The clock on her phone had reminded her that PE was her third class, and attending that dreadful monstrosity was crucial to her mission. Lia waved to one of the ladies working the front desk, who returned it with a kind smile, before bursting through the doors. Lia walked over to the crosswalk and pressed the button on the streetlight that allowed her to eventually cross. Time ticked by slower than usual while she waited for the red hand on the other side of the street to turn into a green walking stick figure. When it finally did, Lia looked both ways and then bolted across. She did not mean to be in a rush, but her studies kept her longer than she thought they would.

Lia threw on her PE clothes in the nearest bathroom and tightened the drawstring of her oversized, yet comfortable black shorts. She dashed into the gymnasium and winced as her sneakers squeaked against the hard maple flooring. She despised how no one could mind their own business or even listen to Coach Jenkins as she announced the class' agenda for the day. Of course, it was the usual warm up routine, but Lia made sure to listen anyway in case anything had changed. As the class began their daily workout, Lia scanned the room for Jared. Sure enough, the very person she was looking for appeared to not have any trouble whatsoever with his pushups...or situps...or anything else. While Lia was huffing and puffing, he did push ups on two fingers of each hand. Huh...she thought only Bruce Lee could do that.

"*How strong is this guy?*" Lia envied his athletic ability. "*Definitely Taurus behavior.*"

When it came time for three laps around the entire gymnasium, which Lia dreaded since it was a bit more than normal, the brunette conjured up an idea. When the class began their jog, Lia shuffled along in an attempt to keep up with the very individual she needed to talk to in order to ensure her research was legitimate. Half a lap had passed, which jump started her adrenaline. Lia hit the gas and lengthened her strides in order to catch up to

Jared, who was at least a quarter of a lap ahead of her. Feeling her lungs constricting did not stop her. Instead, she powered forward when her Ring made itself known and eventually reached his pace. Jared was looking straight ahead with an earbud in each ear. Lia cleared her throat in an attempt to get his attention.

"Hey, Jared."

There was no answer. Lia tried again. "Jared? It's me–Lia."

Once again, there was no response. Lia exhaled a groan. With one last burst of energy, she lurched in front of him and waved her hands in front of Jared's line of sight. This finally retrieved his attention, as he slowed down his momentum to allow her to keep up. Lia fought back a relieved sigh when Jared removed one earbud and looked in her direction. An abrupt wave of self-consciousness washed over her at that very second. Did she look sweaty? Of course. Was she dressed to the best of her ability? Absolutely not–she was in her gym clothes. Great. Lia was definitely not prepared to speak to a boy she found attractive. Lia, in her mind, was screwed.

"Oh, hey...Lia," Jared fumbled to remember her name. "How's it going?"

"Good grief, that smile..." Lia shook the thought out of her head and focused on her pacing. "It's, uh...*going*, How are you?" She could have slapped herself. *"Lia, you moron."*

She despised how the boy next to her jogged and talked so easily. "I guess that's all you can say when it comes to this school year. Let me tell you...this stuff is hard."

"Academic stuff or athletic stuff? Because you appear to be doing the latter just fine."

Jared's shoulders lifted up and down rhythmically with his stride. "Academic." When he hesitated with an unreadable expression for a moment, Lia's mind began whirring. "I've never been good with this...school stuff."

"Right, because you've never been to school before," Lia wanted to say out loud, but she restrained herself. "You know, if you need

any help with your classes, I can try to contribute. I think I'm quite well-acquainted with the academic field."

"Are you serious?" Jared's eyebrows shot up. "Why would you do that?"

The brunette just smiled. "Why not? I like making new friends and helping people. School is my forté, so I don't mind sharing any of my knowledge."

"You know, I'd like that."

"Thank goodness!" Lia acknowledged his disguised acceptance with a nod. "Sounds good. Would you like to sit with Maylene and I at lunch today? You've met her, right?"

Something...different flashed in Jared's eyes. Somehow, the cacao brown hue became a couple of shades darker. "Yes, I've met her."

"Is something wrong?"

"No, of course not," he deflected the question. "I'd love to sit with you both if that's alright with her."

Lia thought the shift to Maylene was slightly unusual but decided not to question it. "Perfect. You can just join me after PE."

"Cool."

Lia surely thought it was cool. After their three laps had been run and the rest of the class ensued, which was not much of anything, actually–mainly discussions about health and a few yoga stretches. Despite the promising fact that Jared could be considered a friend, which was one step closer to completing her mission, she kept a close eye on him to ensure the safety factor, especially around Maylene. Her best friend was not the best when it came to socializing with other individuals like her sister and Lia respected that as well as her boundaries. That was why as soon as class was dismissed, she yanked her phone out of her pocket and sent a quick text.

"Hey! I was chatting with Jared in PE just now and was wondering if he could sit with us at lunch today. He mentioned having

trouble with school-related things and I offered to help. If not, I'll tell him to scoot! :P"

It did not take long at all for Maylene to reply. In fact, Lia was in the nearest restroom changing back into her clothes just after dousing herself in her deodorant and body spray. *"That's fine. If I don't talk much, I just don't know what to say."*

With one hand tugging her hoodie over her t-shirt, Lia typed back with her free appendage, *"Okay, thank you. If you're uncomfortable, I'll leave with you."*

"Got it. :)"

By the time Lia had thrown on her clothes, Jared was waiting outside of the gymnasium. He was very easy to spot, being taller than most heads on campus. Lia wondered if that was a special "Mêla" thing or not. Maybe he was merely a tall human, being almost six-foot-three. Lia looked like a gnome walking next to him, and she noticed several heads turn in their direction. Now, Jared was new to this school as of this past year. Often, individuals never tended to mind their own business, wanting to soak up every last drop of gossip regarding everyone around. Lia, though, albeit intrigued, did not do everything in her power to retrieve such information. Instead, she focused on Maylene and her homework. Speaking of Maylene, the ebony-haired girl waved cheerfully in their direction. At the sight of Jared's tall figure next to Lia, Maylene tensed up in the slightest, but resorted to being friendly nonetheless.

"Hi, gu–ah!" Maylene started to greet them, but she was halted by an extended foot shooting out to trip her.

Whoever's plan that had been sent in motion was blatantly successful. Maylene stumbled over the denim-covered leg topped with a sneaker. Her knees skidded across the tiled floor followed by her arms cushioning her fall. Within instinct, Lia rushed towards her friend, who nearly hit her face on the dirty school floor. Maylene's hair stuck to her face since her violet headband flew off from the impact. Lia's legs ached from her three laps earlier, resulting in her speed being diminished. Before she came to Maylene's aid, the latter's left arm was grabbed tightly by a strong hand. It yanked her up carelessly until she came face to face with none other than Declan Abner.

"Nice moves, Loser," the bully sneered through a smirk.

"Hey!" Lia immediately dashed towards the arising conflict and stood in between the two of them, leaving Jared to watch awkwardly. "Leave her alone."

Declan's grin became a scowl when the brunette appeared. "Oh, look…it's the loser's barking guard dog."

"Just shut up and leave her alone." Lia firmly placed a hand on her hip. "What's your problem anyway?"

"Right now, you."

"Okay, that's it, Mister–hey!"

The scene unfolded like a tarp in the wind. Where Lia was standing became empty when Declan clutched her collar, shook it around, and then shoved it aside. Lia backpedaled a few steps and hit the wall on the other side of the hallway. As soon as she regained her balance, she charged towards Declan like a raging bull at a matador with a red flag and pushed him back as hard as she could. Unfortunately for her, Declan seemed to be stronger than he looked, seeing as he stood his ground and merely laughed at Lia's futile attempt to fight back. Declan raised his fist to smack Lia with, but before it could pummel down and hit her, a veined hand clasped it. Three pairs of eyes - one angry, one determined, and one peeking through her hands - snapped over to meet Jared's tall figure looming over Declan's suddenly scrawny one.

"Hey! Who are you?" Declan pushed his fist down, but it was to no avail; his arm simply would not move, trapped in Jared's hand. "Let go!"

"Back off," the black-haired boy snarled between clenched teeth.

Declan's eyebrows shot up at his tone. "This doesn't concern you."

"The moment you touch them, it does."

"Okay, that was...oh, knock it off, hormones!" Lia struggled to keep herself afloat.

The brunet was lost for words as Jared continued glaring in his direction. Abruptly, Declan realized that he was not going to get anywhere without having to punch through Jared first. He made the wise decision to unclench his right hand and follow Jared's lead of yanking him away from both Lia and Maylene. It was Declan's turn in the rotation to stumble away. Without another look towards the two girls and the boy who was even more intimidating than Lia initially thought, Declan dashed down the hall in the opposite direction. Lia shot the back of his head a wide grin and then turned her attention to Maylene. When the frightened cowering of her stature hit her, Lia dashed over to save her tears from hitting the floor.

"Are you okay, Maylene?" Lia inquired urgently.

The poor girl sniffled and merely nodded.

Jared, who now had his hands comfortably in his pockets, strode over to both of them and eyed them with furrowed concern. "Are you both alright?"

"Yeah," Maylene squeaked.

"I'm fine." Lia could not control the grin growing on her face. "Did I mention that was so bada-"

"It was nothing," Jared interrupted before she could swear out of excitement.

"It surely seemed like it. You hardly moved–you were like a statue standing your ground while the little weasel tried to make a few cracks with a chisel. Then, I love how you practically threw him down the hall. Thanks for doing that, by the way. Declan's a big bully and needs to know when to leave people alone. I mean, you *yeeted* him."

The boy's head cocked a bit. "...Pardon, but what does "yeeted" mean?"

Lia's cheeks flushed. "Oh, uh...basically you chucked him away."

"Chucked?"

"Threw."

"Oh."

"*I need to remember that he probably doesn't know modern terminology...*" Lia briskly changed the subject. "We should probably head to lunch...if you guys still want to sit together."

"Sure," Jared agreed and then watched Maylene, who timidly nodded.

So, the courtyard was exactly where the trio headed in that same moment. By this time, it was mobbed with students at every corner. The line for the purchasable school lunches was out the door. Thankfully, Lia and Maylene always packed their lunches, but did Jared? He did not seem to have anything with him. That sent Lia's mind into a spiral. Did Mêla have to eat? If they were immortal, did they still have three meals a day? Could they starve to death? How in the world did being immortal work? Lia ever so desperately wanted to ask the man himself who could provide all of the answers, but revealing the fact she knew his identity could jeopardize everything. Lia thought Jared would be waiting in line until he simply followed both of them to their usual picnic table. Then, the brunet realized that he probably did not have any human money. Should Lia offer to buy him lunch?

No. She was just about as broke as the mythical creature.

Like normal, Lia and Maylene sat across from each other, but this time, each of them scooted over to make room for their guest. Jared appeared as if he was puzzled as to where he was supposed to sit, but it did not take him long to make a decision. Lia thought she noticed his complexion pinken, but maybe it was her imagination. Either way, Lia found it just the slightest bit odd that Jared looked at Maylene instead of her.

"Can I sit on this side?" he asked her politely.

Maylene seemed unsure of what to say, but, nevertheless, she nodded to be polite. "Yeah, go ahead," she granted him access.

"Thanks. I like your outfit."

Lia and Maylene blinked in unison. The latter looked down

at her purple overalls and then meekly smiled. "Thank you. I like your...jacket."

"I like it too. So-"

"*Okay*, so what would you like to work on first?" Lia interrupted the awkward flirting...or was it flirting? She had no idea anymore.

"Oh, um..." Jared was caught off-guard, but then pulled his Algebra textbook out of his backpack and set it down on the table. "I don't understand any of this."

Lia straightened her glasses and had to do a double take. "What part of it?"

"All of it."

"...But the semester's almost over?"

"I know." Jared sheepishly opened the book to the first chapter. "I just don't understand finding X, linear equations, the inequality stuff...what does that even mean?"

Lia and Maylene looked at each other, the former taking a deep breath - plus a bite out of her peanut butter sandwich - before coming to a conclusion: "Let's do some review, then."

"I don't get why they added letters into math. Math is math. It's numbers; not letters."

"I can concur." Lia then began to elaborate. "Letters are in math because they symbolize numbers. To solve problems, you need to know what variables and constants are. Think of them as replacements."

Jared squinted puzzledly. "Why not just use a number so there wouldn't be a problem in the first place?"

Lia flipped through Jared's textbook which she used several years ago to the first page of the first chapter. "How about we just...suck it up and try some problems?"

"I guess."

Explaining math to Jared was like trying to teach a fish how to climb a tree. There was simply no way Jared was going to pass this class, especially since he did not even know what solving for X meant in the first place. While Maylene picked at her poke rice bowl, Lia tried several different methods to try to gain Jared's understanding. Math was not Lia's favorite subject, but she had done many semesters of it, making her very well acquainted with the concept. When she recited the Quadratic Formula, she thought Jared was going to keel over. Eventually, he gave up, shut the book, and stuffed it back into his backpack.

"Thanks for trying," Jared expressed his gratitude without meeting her eye. "I guess I'm just not cut out for math. It's such a strange dialect."

"You're welcome. I'm sorry we couldn't get anywhere with it. If you want, we can try a different approach."

The boy shook his head. "No, I'll figure it out. Thanks anyway, though."

Once more, Lia took a second look at Jared's confident expression. She easily picked up the frustration in his eyes from the darker hue, clenching of his jaw, and his fists opening and closing from underneath the table. All of them were tell-tale signs of being annoyed—not necessarily at Lia personally, but at the situation. The intelligent scholar could not quite place herself into his shoes since she never had a problem with school. All she could do was imagine how difficult life would be without her trusty brain by her side. It might have been annoying, but wasn't everyone at some point in time? Speaking of which, Lia's voice had one more thing to say before the trio finished their lunch in between silence and intermittent small talk regarding athletic endeavors to make Jared feel at home.

"Stubborn? Check."

Eight

Life was full of experiments. In reality, no one knew what they were doing, what goals they were trying to achieve, or how to gain knowledge regarding the Science of happiness. Was anyone in the universe truly happy? Content, perhaps? There was no way to tell. Whenever a goal that an individual set was achieved, no matter how gradual or swift, they would only want more. It was never enough. The stakes lofted at a higher velocity, growing with each passing second. Was happiness in the world around us? Was it anywhere at all? What was happiness to begin with? The concept of happiness was melancholy taboo.

Happiness was an experiment of its own. What aspects of the solemn world around us produced happiness? Something that was pleasing to the senses, maybe? What about a small, fluffy kitten? A favorite song? A warm blanket? The alluring aroma of freshly baked cookies? What about the taste of your favorite meal? All of these things were wonderful, but material, meaning that joy would fade as soon as they did. Did it linger, though? All human beings were unique in this aspect. For all we knew, emotions were a social construct to describe our intricate brain waves seeping into the depths of our hearts and souls. Happiness is nothing without contentment. Plucking the petals of satisfaction from our favored things around us, whether material or gratified, was what kept the human mechanism going.

That was the problem from the very first instincts. As far as Lia knew, the Mêla were far from human. Yesterday's attempt to gain one of the Mêla's satisfaction was in vain. Lia had wondered why exactly Jared was having such a difficult time with his Algebra concepts, but later that evening, it hit her. How likely was it that Algebra existed in the realm of Kythaela? To dig even deeper, what were the odds that one of its caretakers would feel the need to find the value of X? The answer was simple: they did not. Despite Lia's best efforts, the much higher evolved and significantly educated brain of the boy across from her at the picnic table could not grasp it. When the moment of realization hit her, Lia's mind felt as if it was as small as a walnut shell. It might have been the size of a Stegosaurus' brain, but then again, how smart were the dinosaurs if they went extinct? Lia was well aware of the external source, but it made no sense to her. How could an entire civilization be wiped out from one small action? After a bit more consideration, Lia developed the epiphany that Kythaela was suffering the same fate, and if she could not aid them like the Enchantress requested of her, then the magical realm would fall apart.

That very thought was what kept Lia going according to plan. She spritzed her lavender body spray all over her figure. Coach Jenkins had just dismissed the PE class after a vigorous exercise that Lia disdained with fatigue. Despite her aching muscles at every corner, Lia threw on the outfit she picked out that morning. Lia took a simple approach to what she decided to wear, which was a simple pair of jeans with a hole in the right knee as well as an oversized jade green hoodie she had gotten during her freshman year. On the left breast, the words "Oakbrooke High School" were written in a white regal font while on the back, a white mural of an oak tree stretched up the spine, branching out to the shoulders. The words "Rooted in Excellence" were at the bottom written in the same font as the logo on the front. Lia rebraided her hair as she dashed out of the women's restroom just outside the gymnasium with her backpack on her back and the handles of her lunchbox looped around her non-dominant arm.

Even though she rushed through her post-PE routine, Lia was nearly left in the dust by the very person she was trying to keep up with. "Jared!" she yelled at his departing head as a last resort.

To her luck, the boy spun around and greeted her with an awkward, but seemingly genuine smile. "Oh–hey, Lia. What's up?"

"*His voice is so...stop it! You can't think like that.*" Lia knocked some sense into herself and started walking next to him towards the cafeteria. "Not much. I was wondering what you were up to."

"...Getting lunch?" Jared's brow lifted.

"You didn't get lunch yesterday," Lia commented obliviously. "Is everything okay?"

The brunet noticed a slight fumble behind the boy's eyes, but it was executed flawlessly. "Uh, yeah," he replied, his voice smooth like butter. "I just wasn't sure what to get and the line was much too long."

"How about we get there early so you can get something?" Lia suggested, fighting the urge to drag him. She remembered how strong he was yesterday; it was...almost unearthly.

Jared seemed hesitant, however, he did not object. "Lead the way."

Lia seemed to be satisfied with that. She did as he requested and led him into the courtyard just before the line to purchase food near the entrance was as monumental as the previous day. Before Lia struck up any more conversation with Jared, though, she took out her phone and sent a quick text to Maylene.

"*Hey! Jared and I are in the lunch line so he can get something to eat. Come join us if you want! :)*"

Lia clicked send and then exited out of her messages app. She then swiped through her home screen and opened up a social media app to do a brief scrolling while waiting to reach the front of the line. This was something she did upon occasion when she had nothing else to say. It did not occur to her that being on her phone would be considered rude until she remembered why exactly she was in the line in the first place. When she looked up, Jared was watching her phone as if it was some sort of foreign object. It was like he had never seen anything like it. Maybe he hadn't, in fact? Did phones exist in Kythaela? Lia wished she could ask him, but that would blow her cover and Lia could not risk something so dangerous when Jared barely knew her.

"Is everything okay?" she could not help but ask him.

Jared ran his fingers through his shaggy hair and replaced his widened eyes with cool irises that could fool anyone else. "Of course. I just zoned out. What do you think I should get?" He hastily changed the subject.

Lia looked at the menu hung over the counter that each of the students could choose from. "Um, I haven't gotten anything here in a while, but if I remember correctly, their chicken sandwiches and fries are quite good."

"Chicken sandwich and fries?" Lia nodded at his question. "Got it. There's just one thing, though…"

"What's that?"

"I don't…," Jared trailed off in defeat, "really have any money to pay for it. I don't know if you've noticed, but I'm new to the area and don't have a job to pay for things."

To his surprise, the girl smiled and removed one backpack strap from her shoulders to fish through it. "Honestly, I haven't noticed since so many people go to this school, but don't worry about it." Lia revealed her small leather wallet from the outermost pocket. "Lunch is on me."

"Are you serious?"

Lia nodded, perhaps a bit too enthusiastically. "Yeah–it's what friends are for, right?"

"...I guess? Why would you consider us friends, though?"

"Uh oh..."

"I mean, we barely know each other. I'm just surprised, is all. I'm all for making new friends," he clarified to Lia's relief.

"*Phew.*" Lia opened her wallet and removed her red debit card. "Me too. So, friends?"

"Friends."

Before long, Jared and Lia made it to the front of the line. Just like he had practiced in his head, Jared recited the fact that he wanted a chicken sandwich with a side of fries, which was immediately brought to them. Jared then watched, mystified, as Lia inserted the small card she had in her wallet into some little gray machine that beeped obnoxiously for her to take it out just after a few buttons pressed. Lia put the card back in her wallet and then slung her backpack back over her shoulders. Jared guessed that humans paid with special cards, but how did it work? He thought that money was made of paper sheets or metal coins.

"Thank you for...you know, for buying for me," Jared expressed his gratitude.

Lia grinned and passed him his chicken sandwich and fries just before trotting off. "You're welcome."

"So...what about your friend who usually sits with you?" Jared followed after her.

"You mean Maylene?"

"Yeah, the one in the overalls. The only one you sit with?"

Lia could not decide whether to laugh or cry because of that comment. "That's her."

"Where is she?" the boy inquired as he sat down across from her at the table.

"You know...I'm actually not sure," she admitted, pulling her phone out of the middle pouch of her hoodie. "I texted her, but I'm not sure where she went. Why?"

"Oh, nothing."

Lia definitely caught the hard look in his eyes this time. She sat up stiff as a board when she realized what was going on. Lia might not have had the most common sense, but she knew obvious emotions when she saw them. No matter how hard Jared tried to hide his testing emotions, Lia eyed them as sharply as a hawk in search of prey. She contemplated mentioning it whilst taking an initial bite out of her usual peanut butter sandwich and chewing obnoxiously slow to avoid speaking to Jared, who was enamored by his generous portion of fries. Thankfully, this bought Lia some time to rehearse what she was going to say to him...if anything at all. To her own dismay, she made the decision not to use it.

"Can I ask a really weird and random question?" Lia asked without thinking twice.

Jared instantaneously looked up from his food. "What's up?"

"Is there something going on in that pretty head of yours?" Lia immediately regretted her question. *"Oh, God... Pretty?! What are you, some sort of idiot?"*

Jared could not help but smirk and shake his head. "Pretty, huh?" he asked to Lia's humiliation. "But no, nothing's going on. Why?"

"Then why do you look so serious?"

"I, uh..." Jared paused to think, knocked out of his partially egotistical demeanor. "I honestly don't know."

"Okay, cut the crap."

"...Cut the what?"

Lia could not take the obliviousness anymore and blurted out, "Do you like Maylene?"

Silence was what greeted Lia's abrupt question. At once, she hated the fact she said anything due to Jared's change in temperament. What once was a calm, composed boy who hadn't a worry in the world became someone Lia could hardly recognize. He tugged at the collar of his red varsity jacket. Lia was unsure if she was imagining it or not, but were there some droplets of sweat beading on his forehead? Before she could figure it out, Jared ran his fingers through his hair and let the fringe hang loosely just above his eyes. Prior to Jared even speaking, Lia knew the truth, and she could not let that happen.

"What makes you ask that?" he quickly questioned.

"Come on, Bud, I know when people have feelings," Lia defended her stance. "Whenever she's around, I've seen you sneak glances at her, admiring her face, her clothes…everything about her. You think she's perfect, being the shy, quiet girl that she is who only puts in her two cents when necessary. I've seen you smile at the smallest things around her. You can say you don't like her and I'll believe you, but there's something going on with you. It's none of my business, but I hope you're doing okay. Okay?"

Jared blinked at the river of words flowing from her mouth. To his own surprise, he admitted what exactly was going on in that enhanced brain of his. "I do…have feelings for her," he confessed, fiddling with a fry in his portion of food, "but I don't know what to do about them."

"So, you *like* her?" Lia wanted to confirm. "As in *like* like her?"

Jared sheepishly nodded. "Yeah…she's just so beautiful and kind and I love girls who are genuine."

"*I'm genuine! No, he's literally over a thousand years old. Don't think that way.*" Lia stuffed two pretzel sticks into her mouth and resisted the urge to pretend they were walrus tusks. "I see."

"I just don't know how to approach her," Jared continued. Lia noticed a stark contrast from her usual feel-good attitude. "I never see her when she's not with you, and the fact someone would stoop so low to bully her like yesterday makes me feel like trash."

"I'd say you were pretty cool yesterday with Declan," Lia complimented him.

"Thank you."

The brunette needed to get her act together, and fast. "I'm sorry to be nosy," she apologized. "It's just that Maylene is super shy and might not be comfortable with this whole thing. I mean, you seem pretty cool, especially after I busted my butt in the gym last week, but if you really want to get to know Maylene, it might not be…one on one."

"Really?" Jared's face fell ever so slightly.

"Yeah," she confirmed while the gears making up her mind spun on overdrive. "Maybe if you hang out with the both of us, you two can get to know each other better and then…we'll see where it goes from there."

"That might work," the boy agreed. "Would that be okay?"

"That'd be more than okay." Lia nodded with a sneakily concealed smirk.

Just then, Lia's phone vibrated with a text message on the table's surface: *"I thought I told you I was studying in the library during lunch today. Finals for this semester are coming up after Christmas and I need as much practice as I can get."*

"I told you I could help you study!" Lia vigorously texted in response. *"I'm so sorry. I completely forgot."*

"It's okay. Have fun with Jared! :)"

When Lia's gaze drifted from her phone to the boy across the table, she noticed his figure was leaning forward just a tad. "What?" she inquired.

"Was that her?"

Lia fought the urge to let her head collapse into her hands. "You are more smitten than a kitten."

"I am *not*," Jared quipped.

"Unfortunately, you are."

Lia's spontaneous plan was coming together like a jigsaw puzzle. She had found all four corners and was now moving onto the edges. She mentally sorted each three-sided piece into one box and then placed the rest in a miscellaneous pile. So far, Lia was on track to becoming closer to Jared in no time. Using deductive reasoning, Lia made the assumption that he was a Taurus, one of the three Earth signs, but right now, it did not matter. One of the fabled Mêla was in her sights and there was nothing that could get in between them.

That was at least what she thought until a soprano screech ricocheted off the propped-open double doors to the courtyard and barreled itself into every pair of ears in the open space. Upon instinct, Lia jumped out of her seat, slowly followed suit by Jared. Letting her gut take control, Lia wasted no time sprinting out of the courtyard - all of the laps from PE did her some good - and following the noise. Jared was on her tail as Lia burst through the opening and skidded to her left, pinpointing where the scream came from. At first, Lia thought she was crazy, but then she realized that with each stride she took, the gold Ring around her finger started to pulsate again. Her heartbeat accelerated as she got closer and closer. Just one more turn...and there it was.

Lia was *definitely* not expecting the scene that unfolded around the corner. Two females a little taller than average height, one with platinum blonde hair and one with black, tussled amongst each other. A lavender backpack and a maroon one were resting on either side of the hallway. Lia stopped in place to watch what looked to be a catfight go down. Both of these girls appeared to be equally strong. A fist in each hand clasped one across from it. Two pairs of arms pushed and pulled back and forth like a battering ram, or a game of tug-of-war, but with nothing in the middle. Two foreheads were touching each other - one pearly and one bronze - until the latter gained the upper hand by letting go on one side and using herself as a slingshot. The blonde was then smashed against the wall face-first but was quick to snap out of whatever trance she was out in to charge like a bull into her opponent. Lia looked over her shoulder for some sort of input from the boy who had followed her out of the courtyard...but he was gone.

"*Oh, boy...*" Lia was left alone in the hallway with these two girls pouring everything they had into each other, but in all of the wrong ways.

The girl who was much more petite than the others stood awkwardly in the middle of the tiled floor while the two females being complete opposites in appearance had it out. Lia flinched when the blonde-haired girl - Girl #1 - used both of her hands to shove the black-haired girl - Girl #2 - into the wall behind her, pinning her by the shoulders. Girl #1 gritted her teeth when Girl #2 easily kicked her in the ribs and knocked her off of the top. Girl #2 tackled Girl #1 with as much gusto as an American football player. Girl #1 spat some of her own hair out of her mouth and used all of her upper body strength to roll both of them over until she was on top. The blonde then attempted to pin Girl #2's hands above her head, but the ebony-haired woman was quicker and used her hands to push the other girl off of her. This left both of them standing again and ready to initiate another move. Lia could not take it anymore. This fight could go on forever. The smallest of the three knew she had to do something, but she was all alone. There was no brawn to back her up this time.

"Stop!" she yelled when the two girls started to charge each other.

When Lia thought that her desperate plea would get both girls to stop...she realized it did nothing. Instead, Girl #1 landed a sharp blow on Girl #2's cheek, who growled lowly and used both hands to catapult her chest backwards. Girl #1 grasped onto both of her opponent's wrists and pried them off of her, using the leverage to push her backwards. Girl #2 lurched forward and gripped onto Girl #1's collar, shaking it around.

"Stop it!" Lia could not take it anymore; she hurtled herself between the two. "This is crazy! What are you doing?"

When a palm was pushed against each girl's chest, both Girl #1 and Girl #2 broke apart from one another. The sight of another, much smaller girl who looked as if she was going to crawl into a hole and disappear, unnerved both of them. The blonde seemed relatively calm, but the girl with black hair possessed a glare behind her glasses. Lia held her arms out in surrender when both girls looked her dead in the eye. She could not run. She could not hide. Instead, she needed to be confronted by her own actions.

"...Who are you?" Girl #1 asked after a long silence.

"Oh, uh...," Lia faltered over herself; she had not rehearsed for this. "I'm Lia. I heard someone screaming from the courtyard and wanted to see if everyone was okay."

"We're fine," Girl #2 rebuked the brunette. "Just a...misunderstanding."

"A misunderstanding that ends up in a fistfight times ten? You two could get expelled for that...you do know that, right?"

Girl #1's brown eyes softened. "Yeah. It was a serious one at that."

"It was," Girl #2 surprisingly agreed. "Thanks for stopping us before it got too heated. You've got some guts."

Blood rushed to Lia's cheeks. "Thank you. I had a friend with me to back me up, but he just...up and vanished."

"I'm sorry to hear that," Girl #1 placed her hands into the small pockets of her skinny jeans topped with a purple sweater. "I'm Willow, by the way."

"And I'm Rowan." Girl #2 was the second to introduce herself, extending her arm. "It's nice to meet you, Lia."

The brunette hated the way she flinched when Rowan's hand jutted out towards her, especially after the "misunderstanding" she and Willow had. Lia smiled and shook her hand. "Nice to meet you both too."

"Sorry you had to see that," Willow emphasized on their behalf. "You witnessed the poorer half of us, which is not getting along."

"You two know each other?"

Willow and Rowan exchanged a knowing smirk in each other's direction. "You could say that," the latter replied.

Lia wanted to inquire about what they meant, but before she could, a loud, but somehow peaceful chiming echoed throughout the corridors, signaling that it was time for the fourth class sessions of the day. Part of Lia was well aware of her backpack and lunchbox abandoned in the courtyard, but the other part ignored it. Lia instinctively checked the time on her phone, as if she had not heard the bell correctly. When she looked up, though, the two girls, another example of Yin and Yang, were gone. Lia rubbed her eyes and took a double take, but her periphery was not deceiving her. Willow and Rowan had vanished.

The gentle ebbing of the gold band around her finger pieced everything together. One look at it solidified Lia's suspicion: the thumping jewelry…her gut…it was all so clear now. Lia could have smacked herself at the realization an aureate opportunity slipped through her fingers.

"What is with Mêlas and disappearing?!"

Nine

Being a teenager was hard.

Being a teenager in several Advanced Placement classes was difficult.

Being a teenager in several Advanced Placement classes as well as trying to convince three otherworldly beings to restore their realm was nothing short of *impossible*.

Two consecutive nights spent tossing and turning rather than galloping through the absurd dreams that occasionally popped up during her slumber was what led her here...to the local drugstore. Upon a relatively rare occasion, Lia would treat herself to several bags of candy to store in her nightstand drawer. Rather than significant treasures such as jewelry, Lia hoarded sugary sweets that she earned from working on chores in her free time. She occasionally offered to help around the house for free, but since school was her full-time job - as her parents said - Cheyenne and Lucas wanted to grant her the opportunity of earning pocket money.

Lia was using her pocket money for something much different than candy and snacks, though. Instead, she was holding two cacao teddy bears under her arm—one with a purple bow and one with a red bow. Each one held a fifteen-dollar gift card to *Amazon* since Lia had no clue what to buy people for gifts. The only people she would buy a gift for on a regular basis were Maylene and Yasmin–they were best friends and usually, she could get away with making her parents cards for their birthdays, Christmas, and anniversary. They would always say that her existing as their daughter was more than enough of a gift. Lia made sure to put everything she had into her parents' holiday and birthday cards. What made her feel better was that she never truly asked for anything. Whenever she wanted something, she kept it quiet, but somehow, some way...her parents and friends always knew where her heart laid.

How did Lia feel about spending her hard-earned money on buying miscellaneous gifts all of a sudden? The angel on her shoulder commended her for her kind, yet brave act, and the devil on the other continued to laugh at her. Lia had made her final decision, though. Once she reached the register at the front of the store, she placed both teddy bears on the counter. Lia could not help but look away when the cashier who appeared to be in his early twenties with a name tag reading "Daniel" gave her purchases an odd look. Lia yanked her wallet out of the middle pouch of her Oakbrooke High hoodie and produced a twenty-dollar bill as soon as the price rang up on the screen in front of her.

"...For my friends," Lia explained her gifts to the silence across the counter.

Daniel appeared to be less than interested. "Uh huh."

"Wouldn't you be happy to receive a teddy bear?" The teenager grew jokingly defensive.

"Nope," he deadpanned.

"What if you were a girl?"

"Still no."

Lia thrust the twenty-dollar bill at him and waited impatiently for her change. When he eventually got it out, down to the last penny, Lia held out her hand. Daniel deposited the five-dollar bill with several different coins into her palm along with the receipt. Then, he held out the white plastic bag, which Lia looped around her arm with a frustratingly large grin.

"Thanks." While she stepped away, Lia declared, "and don't mess with my teddy bears."

The store clerk just rolled his eyes. "Kids these days."

"You're like, what, seven years older than me?" Lia clapped back without skipping a beat. "We're in the same generation, Doofus."

"Whatever. At least I don't buy toys."

"Who says you don't? You might need one with how irritable you are."

The store clerk did not have a response for that. Instead, he shook his head and returned to whatever he was doing behind the counter.

That was the story - or a brief rundown, more likely - of how Lia got ahold of a gift for each girl she thrust herself in between earlier in the week. After standing in the hallway for at least three minutes merely staring at the spot where the two girls stood when she first encountered them. Then, before she could be any later to her class, Lia decided to get a move on before her tardiness resulted in some sort of lecture or even a punishment. Thankfully, she did not receive either of them, slinking into class just a minute late and plopping down at her desk.

Lia began to worry after not seeing a single glimpse of any of the Mêla for the past two school days. What if she had scared them off? No, that was silly. How could a sixteen-year-old girl frighten three immortal beings into submission? It was impossible, no doubt. Lia was well-aware that she could be snapped like a twig by any of these three. The Enchantress' vision to her revealed that. Being normal never concerned Lia before, but it certainly did now. Everyone had limitations, but it seemed as if the Mêla did not...at least for now.

Thus, lurching forward to the following day, Lia kept her eyes peeled for any sign of the three members of the Mêla's Earth Wing. Both teddy bears that were stuffed in her backpack seemed to mock her, being squashed beneath textbooks and notebooks somehow after her third class and lunch. Lia vigorously wrote down her notes regarding an upcoming research essay assignment for her Advanced Placement English Composition class directly after the lunch period. She had already decided what she would be writing about, which would aid her in her quest to reunite the Mêla: Zodiac signs, personalities, and how they correlate. Today was the day that she would be proofing her topic with her teacher, Mr. Walker. He had published a book regarding the concept of space and time, which correlated with the study of the star signs. Lia figured that this topic would impress him.

The diminutive professor with glasses that always seemed to fall off his nose whenever he was writing notes on the board, grading papers, or merely existing, neatly stacked his lesson plan in a manilla folder once the chime bellowed to end the block. "That concludes our lesson today," Mr. Walker finished, knotting his fingers together as he stood. "Please don't disregard your reading assignment for Monday so we can discuss it in class. For those of you still needing to meet with me about your research essay, please stay behind if you're able. If not, feel free to send me an email."

It was evident that the majority of the class either did not want to discuss their research essay topic or simply did not have the time. Students in a nearly single file line flocked out of the classroom like a herd of sheep. Lia, however, took her time slinging her full backpack on her back and approaching the teacher's desk. Mr. Walker placed the manilla folder into his black briefcase and buckled it shut. A pair of footsteps took a hold of the teacher's attention, as he lifted his gaze, pushed his thinly rimmed glasses back up his nose, and offered a warm smile.

"Afternoon, Lia," he greeted one of his most adamant students. "How can I help you? Have you decided on a topic for your research essay?"

Lia grinned widely and replied, "Hi, Mr. Walker, and yes. I was wondering if I could write about Zodiac signs and how qualities such as personalities correlate with them. I mean, how come Tauruses are always so stubborn and loyal? Is there a scientific reasoning for this? If so, what is it? Do the constellations have something to do with it? The list goes on and on."

"This seems like a highly complex paper." The teacher's eyes lit up. "You are aware that there is a five-page maximum for this assignment, correct?"

"Yes, Sir. This topic really interests me and I plan to pack as much information as I can into this paper."

Mr. Walker nodded his approval. "As long as you don't go too overboard, then this topic will be a successful one," he stated warmly. "You're a very diligent student, Lia. I'm looking forward to seeing your work. Please let me know if you need anything."

"I will. Thank you!" the teenager grinned.

"You're welcome. See you in class Monday."

"Monday it is."

Lia left the classroom feeling a little lighter that afternoon. Assignments weighed on her greatly, especially when they were worth a monumental portion of her overall grade. This was no different, being around twenty percent of her final grade. Thankfully, Mr. Walker did not believe in testing his students with a final exam, so a well-formulated essay containing an example of each concept they discussed over the semester took its place. Lia very much preferred projects that were hands-on rather than cramming material into one's head just to regurgitate it down on paper at a later date. For example, Lia's Ceramics "exam" was to create a project of her choice using the concepts learned in class. Her PE exam was to complete a certain physical exercise test...which she was not looking forward to. Advanced Placement Chemistry and Advanced Placement United States History were the only two classes that had traditional exams, and for that, Lia was grateful. She would get straight A's anyway, but a change from the normalcy she grew up in was always appreciated.

When Lia's goal was to shuffle her way down the stairs and arrive at her AP United States History class with punctuality, a glimpse of a person she was not quite familiar with caught her eye. The teenage girl halted in the middle of the hallway, which caused a group of annoyed students to dart around her as if she was a lamppost. When Lia was able to get a closer look at the girl in a maroon hoodie and ripped jeans striding down the hallway, she determined that her imagination was not playing tricks on her. Her Ring confirmed it. For the first time since the fight in the hallway, Rowan had made an appearance in the halls. Either Lia did not notice her to begin with, or the girl was a master of cloaking herself. The brunette changed course and padded hastily down the tiled floor to catch up with her acquaintance.

"Hey, Rowan!" Lia blurted once she had caught up to her.

To her dismay, Rowan hardly glanced over her shoulder and quickened her pace. "Oh, hi, Lia. What do you want?"

"I wanted to talk to you."

"Can it wait? I'm late to class."

"But class doesn't start for another five minutes," Lia made a mental note. She lengthened her strides to keep up with the taller girl. "How about I walk with you? I was hoping to catch you before your next class."

With a frustrated huff, Rowan slowed down so her black waves were not bouncing around her shoulders. "What's up?" she caved.

"I feel the need to apologize for what happened Wednesday." Lia hated how awkward walking while balancing her backpack on one shoulder and fishing through the massive unzipped compartment was. "I shouldn't have gotten wrapped up in your business, but I was worried that someone was going to be seriously hurt."

"Oh…," Rowan tripped over her words. "It's not a problem, really."

CHAPTER NINE 117

The brunette kept her eyes in her backpack so she could locate the correct item. "I know, but just in case we got off on the wrong foot, I wanted to make sure we were good. Are we, uh… are we good?" she hesitated, but asked anyway.

The taller girl did not see a problem with it. "Sure, I guess so."

"Great!" Lia's entire body lit up with anticipation; she pulled the teddy bear with a red bow out from the bottom of her bag. "I also got this for you. Consider it a peace offering."

To put it quite frankly, Rowan had no idea what to say. At this point, she had stopped completely and looked at the teddy bear as if it was something she had never seen before–a foreign entity, perhaps? The way Lia eagerly held out the gift was endearing, but unusual in Rowan's eyes. She thought high schoolers had no business with such childish things. At first, Rowan was tempted not to accept it, but then she figured if she did not, she would have appeared rude; so, she tentatively took the teddy bear from Lia's grasp, unzipped her own red backpack, and placed it on top of her textbooks.

"Thank you." Rowan zipped her bag back up and began her departure. "You didn't have to, but I really have to go now. Bye!"

Lia stood frozen like a bare tree in the middle of winter while Rowan rounded the corner. "You're…welcome?"

Around her, the chatter in the hallways diminished into almost nothing. Once again, Lia stood like a statue, left behind by one of the Mêla vanishing. This time, though, Lia knew exactly where Rowan disappeared to: anywhere away from her. Lia tried her hardest not to let Rowan's quick departure get to her head. Instead, she turned around, breathed in, exhaled, and then started for the stairwell. Prior to taking her first step, however, her Ring pulsated and a blonde whom she had only seen once startled Lia out of her shoes. Her entire body skipped a beat when the pale girl, who was a few inches taller than her and adorned in a lavender cardigan and black leggings, calculatingly gazed into her brown eyes. Her arms draped loosely at her sides, a non-hostile form of body language that Lia almost fell for. She was not going to fall victim to anyone's trickery this time.

"Uh, hey," Lia stumbled, uncertain of herself.

Willow's pupils dilated with compassion. "I saw Rowan walk away."

"...You did?"

The regal lilac-clad girl nodded solemnly.

"Oh." Lia's gaze turned towards the floor.

"There's no need to be embarrassed," Willow's soft voice echoed in the teenager's ears. "The two of us have been going through a hard time recently, and Rowan might seem a little rude or hasty at times but try not to pay it any mind. That's usually not like her…"

Lia set her backpack on the floor and unzipped it, searching for the remaining gift she had stored in there. "I'll try not to. Thank you for that. I just hope I didn't do something wrong."

"You didn't." Willow warmly smiled. "If anything, Rowan will treasure that gift like it's the most valuable thing she owns."

"Do you really think so?"

"We've known each other for a long time. I know so."

Lia wasted no time pulling the teddy bear with a purple bow out of her backpack. "In that case, I got this one for you," she revealed. "I hope you like it, but it's okay if you don't."

"I already love it." Willow's eyes sparkled at the sight of the toy being handed to her. She grasped it as delicately as such would a newborn baby and hugged it to her chest. "Thank you so much, Lia. I wonder what I should name them."

"I'm not sure," she gushed in the midst of tossing her backpack on her back. "What about some shade of purple?"

"I like Violet."

"Violet it is!"

Willow tenderly grinned towards the significantly younger Lia. "Thank you kindly. We might not have any classes together, but I hope to see you again soon."

"I hope so too," Lia genuinely agreed. "Thank you for being so kind to me."

"Kindness breeds kindness," Willow stated a well-known fact and then repeated, "Rowan will come around."

"If you say so. Good luck with your next class."

"And you as well."

The small interaction, only if it was for a matter of minutes, lifted Lia's spirits after Rowan made her quick exit. At least one of the Mêla was on her side, and all Lia really wanted was for the Three of them to get along and prosper in their world as well as our own. It seemed like she was successful with Willow, who was the easiest to speak to out of the two other members of the Earth Wing. Lia was about to stab herself in the back with a self-deprecating remark, but then realized that she was doing all she could to make the situation right. After all, the Enchantress chose her for a reason.

Lia entered her United States History class a couple minutes late that afternoon. Her teacher was not very strict on attendance policies. As long as students arrived in the first fifteen minutes of class, points were not taken off of the participation record. This was the case for Lia. She sat at the last empty desk near the front of the classroom. Her middle-aged professor with graying brown hair and a red flannel shirt offered her a polite nod. Mr. Wilkins was well aware of Lia's studious nature. He knew that she would never jeopardize her studies on purpose. She was simply…running late, caught up in something else.

The end of the school day crept up on her as silent as a mouse. Before she knew it, another day had passed and she was packing up her things for the final time. As opposed to her AP English Composition class, Lia wasted no time pushing her way out of the door and strutting down the hallway towards the front of the building. Rather than keeping herself on her guard, Lia had achieved more than she expected to today. She could not have cared less if one of the Mêla fell out of the sky. Luck was either on her side or pitting against her, since that seemed to be exactly what happened.

"Lia!"

At first, Lia thought she was simply going bonkers from the events of the past week or so, but when her name was exclaimed a second time, she slowed to a stop and peeked over her shoulder. Needless to say, she was wonderstruck when Jared, whom she had not seen since both of them rushed to the fight in the hallway, jogged up to her without breaking a sweat. Lia had no idea how long he had been running, but if he was shouting her name, then he must have been looking for her, right? After his vacancy three days prior, Lia had no idea what to think. The gears in her mind spun at a fantastic speed. Despite this, she wanted to give Jared the benefit of the doubt and offered him a smile.

"Hey, Jared," she sweetly replied. "What's up?"

"I needed to talk to you," Jared explained. How in the world was he not out of breath from running…even just a little bit? "I'm sorry about the other day."

Lia was well aware of what he meant, but she asked anyway, "What do you mean?"

This caught Jared off-guard. "I left quite abruptly, leaving you to deal with the situation," he elaborated, shifting his weight from one high-top-clad foot to the other. "How'd it go?"

"It was okay. I got them to stop and then we went our separate ways." She adjusted her crooked glasses and chewed on the inside of her cheek. "I was wondering where you went. It's none of my business, but is everything okay with you?"

A mop of black hair fell in Jared's eyes. "Oh, um, yes…everything's fine. I just needed to go get some extra work done before class. Numbers and stuff, you know? I still can't figure it out."

"I can help you if you want," Lia offered even though she knew the outcome.

"No, thank you. I can get it done on my own."

"Are you sure?"

"I'm sure."

Lia looked as if she was going to say something else, but Maylene trotted down the hallway towards them. "Hi, Lia! Hi... Jared," she fumbled over his name when she saw the boy towering over her best friend.

"Hi, Maylene!" Lia and Jared chorused. The former continued speaking: "I'll be ready to go in a minute."

"Wait," Jared called out just as Maylene turned to leave the building. "I wanted to ask you - ask you *both* - something."

Lia and Maylene stood at attention, the latter being much more closed-off than the former. "And what's that?" Lia inquired skeptically.

"Well...there's a football game tonight at seven and I was wondering if you two would like to come?" he offered. When his eyes met Maylene's downcast ones, he stumbled over his words. "I mean, if you wanted to. It would just be nice to have some moral support since I don't really know anybody that well around here."

"Uh," Lia looked at Maylene, who seemed to be unsure, but she nodded to be polite. "Sure. We'll be there."

At that, Jared's entire body lit up, his posture straightened, and he fixed the way his jacket rested on his shoulders. "You will? Awesome!" he cheered gleefully. "Gates open at six thirty. I'm sorry this is such late notice, but I'm so glad you two can make it."

"Yeah, us too," Lia bit out between a gritted grin.

"I need to go, but I'll see you two there?"

"Yep!" Lia wrapped her left arm around Maylene's right one. "See you there."

Jared was all smiles as he dashed off in the other direction. Maylene, on the other hand, was not; she eyed her best friend with wide pupils and hissed, "A football game?"

"Yeah," Lia admitted, lowering her chin just a tad. "I'm so sorry. Honestly, I felt a little pressured into saying yes, but you don't have to go. I'll go by myself."

Maylene shook her head. "You don't have to do that. I'll go with you."

"I'm the one who agreed to it," the brunette countered in a soft tone, "so I'm going to own up to it. I know loud places are not your forté, so I'll just tell him you couldn't make it."

"I'd feel bad if I didn't go."

"Don't." Lia began to lead Maylene towards the propped-open double doors at the front of Oakbrooke High's sanctuary of scholars. "It's completely up to you. If you want to come with, then go for it. If not, I'll tell him you were busy."

"I think I'll go with you," Maylene decided.

"Are you sure?"

To her surprise, the ebony-haired girl nodded, a smile tugging at her lips. "Yeah. It might be fun, and besides, there's food."

"Now, you're speaking my language!" Lia declared with triumph. "If you don't want to go for people, go for the food."

"Exactly." Despite her enthusiasm, Maylene still appeared to be conflicted. "I just have one concern, though."

The brunette frowned. "What's that?"

"How am I going to convince my mom to let me go? Yas always goes to these games, but I never do. What if she suspects something? You know how she is about boys."

"Just say you're going with Yasmin and I, which is true," Lia calmly reasoned with her. "We don't have to tell her about Jared or anything."

"What if Yas thinks something's off?"

"We'll just tell her we're here to support a friend. No big deal, and besides, if she does think that - which she shouldn't - then we'll figure it out. We always do."

Maylene certainly hoped that was true. Both of them did. They would find out tonight if that suggestion was truly possible, but for now…all they had to worry about was what to wear.

Ten

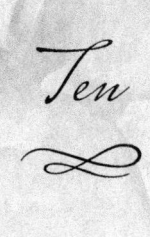

"Thanks for driving us to the game, Mom," Lia expressed once Cheyenne moved the black sedan's gear into "Park." "Sorry it was so last minute."

"Oh, you're welcome, Sweetie." Cheyenne leaned over the center console and planted a kiss between her eyes. "You guys go have fun, but be careful," she gestured to the twins in the backseat.

"We will!" the trio of teenagers echoed in unison.

Cheyenne's grin began to fall, but she tied it back. "That almost makes me more hesitant to drop you off," she teased. "What time should I pick you up?"

"I think nine thirty would be okay. What do you two think?" Lia put a number out there.

Yasmin and Maylene looked at each other and then nodded. "Sounds good to me," the former replied. "Thanks for giving us a lift."

"You're most welcome." Mrs. Hart's brown eyes shimmered behind her glasses.

"Love you, Mom!" Lia exclaimed while climbing out of the car. "Thanks again!"

"No problem!"

Maylene and Yasmin followed suit as Lia waved to her mother just prior to spinning around and trotting towards the football field to the left of the school. Oakbrooke High owned a generous plot of land which they used for their soccer fields, a baseball field, a volleyball court doubling as a tennis court, and finally, the football field, which was the largest of them all. The metal home bleachers were twice the size of the away side. The larger side was topped with an announcer's box and a painted mural writing the words "Let's go, Mustangs!" along with a portrait of the black mascot in the middle. Music blared through speakers at every corner. Maylene fought the urge to clamp a hand on each side of her head, instead playing around with the Yin and Yang earring in her right ear.

It did not take long for Yasmin to find her people. Once she spotted her usual group, she threw her arms around Lia and her blood sister. "I'll see you guys after the game," she announced her departure.

"See you later," Lia replied while Maylene nodded.

After Yasmin dashed to meet her group of friends, who were higher up on the social hierarchy, Lia and Maylene made their way to the concessions stand. Despite the long line, this area of the stadium was much more their speed. Rather than being surrounded by different cliques or individuals who thought they were better than everyone else, the concessions stand was for each their own. Everyone there was in line for one reason and one reason only: food. Lia and Maylene were no exception, ordering a hot dog and chips each. Before Maylene got the chance to pay, Lia swiped her debit card to retrieve both of their food. Maylene knew better than to resist. When she had it, Lia was generous with her money.

Despite being a fan of music in all of its genres, Lia and Maylene decided to sit as far away from the marching band as they could. Maylene was not a good friend with loud sounds and Lia understood that. The latter did not mind so much. Instead, she merely wanted to eat the food she bought at the concessions stand and watch the football game with some attractive boys - one in particular - ramming into each other on the field with a ball in the middle. Lia and Maylene made their way to an empty space in the bleachers close to the top, but away from a speaker so the only noise Maylene could truly focus on would be Lia's voice. Being a listener rather than a talker had its perks but also its disadvantages. One of the latter was overstimulation, which she avoided by paying attention to Lia and Lia only.

"So, how does this game work again?" Maylene inquired despite knowing most of the rules already. "I know you have touchdowns and field goals, but what's a safety?"

"So basically," Lia explained directly after swallowing, "you have "downs" which means you have four attempts to get a certain amount of yards. If you don't and instead go backwards into your own endzone, that's called a safety and the opposite team gets two points."

Maylene delicately plopped a Dorito chip into her mouth. "Makes sense."

"Yeah, I didn't understand them until my dad drew a picture and showed me with that," Lia giggled at her past memories. "Can't believe I was so stupid then."

"You were never stupid."

Lia shrugged at that. "I'd beg to differ. I lack a bit of common sense, so yes. I can be stupid more often than not."

"Everyone has their moments," Maylene sweetly diffused her negative mindset.

"Maybe you're right."

Ah, insecurities. These little gremlins were Lia's worst enemy. No matter what she did in life, whether it was getting a problem wrong on homework, forgetting something that her parents told her five minutes ago, or even how she looked in the mirror, there was always the little red cartoon devil on her shoulder whispering comments that were much less than kind. For some reason, Lia let her negative thoughts win, but on the contrary, she had a secret weapon. Every devil had its angel, and the glowing ethereal being on her other shoulder took the form of Maylene sitting contently next to her. Maylene was Lia's angel who only wanted sweet nothing from her. Compassion and strength growing together as two flowers in an orchard was what kept their lifelong friendship together.

At a few minutes to seven o'clock, an enthusiastic man presented several announcements regarding the school's latest events. One briefly caught Lia and Maylene's attention, being titled the Winter Formal and taking place at the end of the Fall semester in January. Neither of them planned on attending, though, and pushed it to the back of their minds. After the announcements concluded, both Lia and Maylene kept a lookout as a giant inflatable stallion blew up to its full potential, creating a tunnel at the right-hand endzone. The bleachers roared when the players in red jerseys and white helmets emerged from the tunnel. Lia kept an eye out for Jared. It would be difficult to spot him amongst all of the other nearly identical players. Then, she remembered that Oakbrooke High's academic budget was higher than the previous year's, which allowed for them to print the last names of players on the backs of their jerseys. All Lia had to do was look for a jersey with the last name "Huxley" on it.

As the players from both teams got into position, Lia kept an eye out for the six-letter name that she needed to find. Unfortunately for her, as soon as the players were ready, the marching band played a suspenseful drumroll and the game was on. The opponents had the ball first but did not go far with it. One of the Mustangs tackled the player who had caught the ball. Once more, the players took their positions and the opposing team of blue jerseys, which Lia gathered to be the Lions from across town, resumed their mission to reach the home team's endzone. After three tries, though, that did not happen and the Lions were forced to either go for the fourth down or punt. Since it was so early in the game, they chose the latter and gave the ball to the

Mustangs. Cheers rallied from the home bleachers along with the marching band playing songs they must have rehearsed hundreds of times in advance since each note was flawless. This joy soon turned to melancholy when the Mustangs punted and the ball was returned to the Lions.

This sequence continued on for an entire quarter, which was twelve minutes. It was obvious that Lia and Maylene were both getting bored, especially since the former had not been able to locate the boy she came to the game to support in the first place. She wondered why she was even there for a moment, especially since the game was scoreless and quite boring to begin with. She began a text game rivalry with Maylene during the event right in front of her consisting of pool, darts, and Connect 4. Lia won most of these games, but Maylene was the victor of a couple of them. Lia yawned dramatically and then took her occasional glance at the field.

The football had just been tossed from the quarterback to the receiver, who was running as quick as a speeding bullet towards the opponents' end zone. It seemed as if nothing was going to stop him–he was too far ahead of the rest of the players...all except for one. The entire crowd gasped and yelled out when the receiver was tackled by the most buff player on the Lions. The boy in the red jersey fell, limp as a leaf, onto the ground with this boy - no, more like a *man* - on top of him, crushing him with his weight on the grass. Even though the Lion got off of the Mustang, the receiver did not move, instead laying there like a limp fish. Lia's mouth hung agape as the team, coaches, referees, and even the team doctor ran out onto the field to check on his condition. At least one minute passed...then two...then three... until finally, the player stood up and wrapped an arm around two of his teammates who came to his side to help him off the field. As the boy hobbled towards the locker room, Lia caught a glimpse of his jersey.

Huxley.

Lia was up with a start, trying to ignore Maylene's odd

expression, "I'll be back," she rushed out breathily.

"Where are you going?" Maylene slowly chewed a chip from the bag she somehow had not finished yet.

"...To the bathroom. I *really* gotta go."

A pair of slender black eyebrows furrowed, but she nodded anyway. "Oh, okay."

Lia exploded from her seat and barreled her way down the metal stairs. Her black high tops smacked onto the cemented path that surrounded the football field and followed it towards the locker room, which was a small brick building on the opposite side of the field to the concessions stand. Lia knew there were bathrooms on both sides of the field so her change in direction would not be too suspicious. The line near the concessions was longer than the one closest to the locker room, so if Maylene asked, then she would have an excuse anyway.

The petite building containing the locker room was surprisingly vacant. Lia imagined it was because everyone else was occupied with the game that had resumed not long after the receiver was helped off the field. Lia tried the doorknob and, to her surprise, it opened. She slunk through the narrow opening she made to avoid the wooden structure from creaking. Lia pushed the door shut inch by inch and then began creeping through the hallway. While certain that her footsteps were silent, she heard a few other pairs coming from around the corner.

Without thinking twice, Lia darted into the nearest room and hid out of sight from the entrance. Lia placed a hand over her racing heart in an attempt to calm herself. Tendrils of her brown hair fell in her face and stuck to the beads of sweat forming on the creases of her forehead. As Lia tried to control her breathing, her nose scrunched at the putrid smell of gym socks and...other things she would not wish to mention entering it. Lia opened her eyes wider and realized why the stench was so distasteful that she had to lift up the collar of her shirt and stick it over the bottom half of her face. She had ended up in the boys' restroom.

The footsteps she heard just a few minutes prior were long

gone. Nevertheless, Lia poked her head out of the bathroom, and once she made sure the coast was clear, she bolted from the dumpster fire of a bathroom. The soles of her moderately-worn shoes barely made a sound against the smooth floor since Lia took much care to keep herself quiet and her presence unknown. The locker room surely could not be too far away. Lia's assumption was proved correct when a sign on the wall stating "Men's Locker Room" greeted her. The double doors were left open, so Lia peeked inside. Surrounded by tall red lockers was the lone Jared Huxley, the very boy she was looking for. He was seated on a bench on the right-hand side of the room with his helmet off and sitting next to him. All of a sudden, he looked much smaller than he was on the field because he had taken off the shoulder pads underneath of his jersey with the number "88" on both sides. He sat up straight with his head tilted downwards, a defeated look adorned on his face. By the dilation of his pupils, Lia could tell he was in pain.

As much as Lia wanted to make her way into the locker room, her gut ached for her to stay behind, which she figured was a good idea. Lia peeked around the corner as Jared began fumbling with his left shoulder, which was much less defined than his right. Jared's right hand clamped around his upper arm like a wrench. Lia bit her lip when she realized what Jared was trying to do. Popping a dislocated shoulder back into place by yourself was the exact opposite of what you were supposed to do according to what Lia learned in the Health portion of her PE class. Lia hid behind the corner as Jared's jaw clenched and his eyes screwed shut. All the common sense Lia had was begging her to lurch into the room and stop him until medical attention was given to him. Then again, what if he turned it away? Jared proved himself to be stubborn, after all.

"Come on...come *on*," Jared gritted out as he began to push with his right hand. "Holy *shit*, that hurts!" he shouted when he could not succeed the first time.

Lia flinched at his exclamation but remained quiet when

Jared tried again. This time, he did not gradually ease the ball back into place, but instead, with one foul swoop, he shoved his left arm upwards as hard as he could. When a screech of pain bellowed from him, Lia could not help but jump. In doing this, her shoes squeaked against the tile. Despite Jared's obvious agony that he just experienced, he rose to his feet at the sound.

"Who's there?" he questioned the silence.

"Oh, no… What do I do?! What am I supposed to do in this situation?!" Lia took a deep breath and made the brave decision to be honest, stepping out from behind the corner and meekly waving to him. "…Hi, Jared."

"What are you doing here?" he hissed in pure bewilderment. "You're not supposed to be in here."

"I know, but…," Lia paused to formulate an excuse that was partially true, "I saw you limp off the field and wanted to make sure you were okay. Then, I heard you scream and…well, I came down here. Did nobody want to help you or anything?"

"I turned them away," Jared replied stoically.

"*Figured.*" Lia leaned against the wall for a split second and then realized that might not have been such a good idea; she jumped away from it. "So…what happened?"

"That giant guy from the other team dislocated my shoulder," the boy explained. "So, I came down here to see what I could do to fix it."

"…You know that popping your shoulder back into place is *really* hard to do and even if you pull it off, it could damage the nerves, muscles, and blood vessels around it, right?"

Jared awkwardly scratched the back of his neck. "Um…yes?"

"How are you walking around so easily? You got *drilled.*"

"I, uh, don't know." The boy seemed to be growing a tad bit uncomfortable. "I guess the daze went away quicker than I thought. Hopefully I'll be able to play in the third quarter"

"I think you should get some rest or something," Lia diffused the suggestion. "You could have a concussion or something. Would you like me to test for the symptoms?"

Jared promptly shook his head. "I don't think that'd be necessary," he assured her. "I'm fine."

"Are you sure?"

"I'd think so?"

"I worry about you sometimes, Jared," Lia admitted with an exasperated sigh.

"So you think about me?" Jared used this confession to his advantage.

The brunette froze in place. "No?"

"I think you just said you did," he chided in a singsong tone.

"I did not," Lia argued.

"Did too."

"Did not."

"Did too."

"Did not."

In the midst of their brief banter, Jared placed a hand over her mouth and hissed, "Quiet!"

"What-" Lia's voice muffled against his palm. "Let go-"

"Listen."

For once, Lia obeyed and the locker room fell silent. In the distance, the marching band could be heard playing the beginning of what seemed to be the brief halftime show between the first and second halves of the game. That only meant one thing: the football team would be heading their way at any moment. Lia pried Jared's hand off of her mouth, which she would not have been able to do if he did not loosen his grip. That boy was the strongest human being that Lia had ever seen. It must have had something to do with his...species. No matter how much research Lia did, she always had more to learn.

"Oh, God, is that the team?" Lia hurriedly whispered.

All Jared could do was nod. "You need to get out of here."

"There's no time–they're about to round the corner."

"Um...um...," Jared stuttered out, scrambling around the room while thinking of an idea. Then, it hit him; he dashed over to his tall locker and opened the door. "Quick–get in!"

Lia stared at the open compartment incredulously. "I won't fit."

"Yes you will," the boy countered, "it's bigger than you'd think."

"I'm too fat to fit in that."

Jared fought the urge to smack his forehead. "You're not fat. Just get inside."

"It'll be dark," Lia kept protesting.

"You'll only be in there for ten minutes."

"Ten minutes is too long."

"If you don't want to get caught, it's not."

"But-"

"Just get inside!" Jared whisper-yelled.

Lia ran out of arguments. Instead, she ignored all of the red flags popping up in her mind and climbed into the locker. Jared mouthed a heartily sincere "I'm sorry" before shutting the locker. Lia had just enough room to squeeze her arms up and down in the petite metal compartment. Lia attempted to peer through one of the slots. She saw the nest of black hair atop of Jared's head since he was sitting down on the bench in front of her leaning against the door. She figured this was an alternative to locking her inside. Lia was silently thankful to him for doing so, especially when the remainder of the football team flooded the locker room.

"Yo, Huxley!" The helmetless blond quarterback greeted the receiver on the bench with a fist bump. "How's that shoulder of yours? We missed you out on the field."

Jared adjusted his posture but did not remove himself from the locker. "Shoulder's fine. Thanks for the concern, Peyton."

"Wait...it looks like it's back to normal," Peyton realized after further inspection. "Did the doctor pop it back in?"

"No, I did."

This caught the attention of a brunet nearby. "You popped it back into place *yourself*?"

"Yeah." Jared shrugged to show off his healing shoulder. "Seems like it's as good as new."

"How did you even pop it back into place? You don't even have a concussion from that guy hitting you? It's a miracle you didn't have to be carried off in a stretcher" Peyton rambled, his face lighting up when Jared just smiled and nodded. "That's like a superpower, Dude. Can you play in the third quarter?"

The girl in the locker suddenly had an epiphany. *"...A superpower? The way he pulled me up so easily, how he popped his shoulder back into place without much effort... That would explain everything!"*

"I'm not sure how smart that is, Bud," another player worriedly chimed in. "Maybe you should see the doc and make sure everything's okay."

Lia silently agreed with this one, but Jared shook his head. "I'm okay–thanks."

"Are you sure?"

"We all know Huxley's a load of horse manure," a familiar voice chortled from the entrance of the locker room. Even though Lia could not see who it was, she knew it was no one other than Declan Abner: Maylene's bully, the most annoying person in the school, and - unfortunately - the running back for the Oakbrooke Mustangs.

"If anyone's full of shit, it's you," the brunet boy defended Jared, who was still seated.

"Shut up, Clay. We all know you're the dumbest one here," Declan flat-out insulted him. "What are your grades now? D's?"

"They're C's, thank you." Clay folded his arms over his chest. "Just high enough to stay on the team."

Declan just rolled his eyes dismissively. "Anyway, Huxley here probably went and cried to his mommy to have her kiss the boo-boo and make it feel all better."

"My mom's dead," Jared deadpanned.

Silence ensued across the locker room...all except for Declan, who burst into laughter, "Wow, Hux–nobody asked you about your sob story."

"Nobody asked for your opinion either," the boy smoothly retaliated.

"Oh, ho ho!" Declan took a few steps towards Jared, who rose to his feet. Lia fought to keep the locker door from moving. "Looks like someone grew a pair."

"I've always had one. Too bad you're still waiting on yours."

Choruses of "Oohs!" and "He got you there!" filled the room. Declan stomped his foot and grabbed Jared's collar despite being several inches shorter. "You listen here and listen well-"

"No, *you* listen here."

Lia's mouth fell agape as Jared picked up Declan by the collar with one hand and hoisted him off the ground. Gasps and murmurs of shock fluttered when Declan's feet left the floor and were dangling a few inches above it. Declan was now at Jared's eye level and the latter decided he was not going to deal with the former's taunting anymore.

"I am sick and tired of your nonsense," Jared growled in his face. "You wonder why no one likes you? You're a naïve bully who knows nothing about the world and how it really works. Karma is going to bite you in the ass and when that happens, I want to be the first to hear about it so I can personally laugh in your face. Now, you can make a choice: either apologize to the team and I and you can stay here, or you can say nothing and run away with your tail between your legs."

With that, Jared released his grip on Declan's collar and the boy fell to the floor. To no one's surprise but his own, Declan took the latter portion of Jared's proposition, gathered his gear, and raced out of the locker room like a frightened puppy. As soon as the squeaking of his cleats vanished, the football team exploded into laughter and positivity around Jared, who had once again stood up for himself and the team. Jared received several smacks on the back, high fives, and what guys tended to call "bro hugs." Lia only had a limited field of vision due to her location, but when she saw the proud smirk on Jared's face, a grin rose on her face as well.

Before she knew it, the ten minutes of locker room time were up and the team began departing to play the second half of the football game. Jared lingered, though, especially since there was a spontaneous guest in his locker that was probably suffocating from the smell of countless sweaty teenage boys. Sure enough, once Jared opened the locker door, Lia hurtled out and gasped for fresh air. She straightened her glasses to view Jared offering her an apologetic frown. Maybe that was not the smartest idea in the world, but it worked.

"I'm so sorry about that," Jared sighed once he made sure his friends were out of earshot. "It was the first thing I could think of."

Instead of fuming like he expected, Lia smacked him on the back with a proud smile. "Are you kidding? You totally whooped Declan's butt and I got to see it. That was awesome!"

"Er, thanks." Jared picked up his helmet and carried it under his arm. "Are you okay?"

"I'm great," Lia grinned and began to walk next to him just after he locked his locker shut, "but I should probably get out of here. Glad to know you're alright."

"You should probably take the back door. No one walks through there."

"There's a back door?"

Jared stepped out into the hallway and pointed to his left. "Just go straight that way and you'll see a pair of doors. You can't miss it."

"Thanks, Jared." Lia began racing towards the door, but just prior to rounding the corner, she yelled a quick "See you!"

She did not see Jared wave before he put his helmet on and sprinted to catch up with his teammates. Instead, Lia focused on finding the pair of back doors, which were right where Jared said they would be. Lia shoved her way through them and ran around the building back to the bleachers. Just as she suspected, everything was in full swing. The cheerleaders were doing the same routine they did at the beginning of the game. The marching band was playing a familiar tune that Lia had heard on the radio last week. The last thing she saw, though, filled her with dread. Near the middle of the bleachers, Maylene was still seated by herself. Lia did not waste any time running up the stairs and making her way back to her seat. When she sat down, Maylene blinked her brown eyes all the way open.

"Lia?" she asked as if she was some sort of poltergeist. "Are you okay? You were gone for the whole halftime show."

"Yeah, I'm okay." Lia's lips curved upwards to hide her uneasiness. "I just *really* had to use the restroom…you know? My stomach was upset."

Maylene nodded and placed her phone back into her pocket. "Oh, I'm sorry," she genuinely sympathized. "Is it because of your cycle?"

"Yup," Lia lied straight to her best friend's face.

"That really sucks. I hope you feel better. Do you need any Tylenol? I have some."

The brunette shook her head, already feeling guilty enough. "No, thank you. Can we watch the game, though? I wonder if Jared's back out there."

"Sure. I hope he's okay."

"Me too," Lia exhaled, knowing full well that he was.

The fact that Maylene was completely oblivious to how much Lia was hiding from her clouded her senses with guilt. She hoped with the better half of her heart that Maylene would never find out about the struggle she was putting herself through in order to save an entire world. Lia was well aware that this journey was far from over, especially if her hunch in the locker room was correct. Maybe Jared was just…freakishly strong? Of course, Lia would find out if she asked him the right questions, but then, he would find out about her. Lia was unsure if she wanted that. It did not take long for a realization to hit her, though:

What if there was some way she could test her theory?

Eleven

The double doors of the library were heavier than they seemed. Gone were the crisp chills battering her face and numbing her toes underneath her mahogany pleather boots. Lia shrugged the puffy black jacket off her shoulders that was coated in rainwater. The freezing droplets fell down her cheeks. Oakbrooke Library welcomed her with open arms and humidity fogging up her glasses. With a huff, she took them off her face and wiped them off with the long sleeves of her blue snowflake shirt. When the door hesitated to close behind her, she turned around, and was startled after it shut with a *bang*. Her decrepit vision tried to focus on the blurry figure next to her until she remembered she had to put on her glasses. The silhouette morphed into Maylene's smiling face.

"So, what should we study first?" the ebony-haired girl inquired, taking off the gray puffy coat she wore around her maroon overalls and a white tee.

Lia led her friend over to the tables near the front of the library. "Not sure yet. What are some classes you need the most work in?"

"Geometry," Maylene admitted with a sigh.

"Okay." Lia sat down at the nearest table. "Let's start with that."

"You know, you really don't have to do any of this."

"I know, but I wanted to."

The grin on Lia's face was almost too big for a tutoring session. She had conjured up a plan so wonderful…so *magnificent* that there was nothing that could stand in her way this time. Lia sat adjacent to Maylene so both could see the thick Geometry textbook at the same time without having to turn it around numerous times. Maylene unzipped her backpack and took out her binder which was way too thick for its own good. She removed a sheet of graph paper from the back and clicked the lead out of a mechanical pencil, writing her header at the top. Lia flipped the pages of the textbook until she reached the chapter Maylene mentioned earlier during the lunch period.

"Oh, good…more proofs," Maylene exhaled in a derogatory manner.

Lia speed-read the chapter description. "They're not too bad."

"I just don't understand."

"What do you mean?"

Maylene was the most exasperated Lia had seen her in quite a long time. "How come you have to prove something is correct? If the answer key says it's right, it's right."

"Sometimes in life, we don't have an answer key." Lia shook her head amusedly.

"That's when you look it up."

"Touché." Lia continued reading the page. "It looks like this chapter is about circle proofs."

Maylene merely nodded. "I don't like circles."

"Me either, but you can do this," she encouraged her, pointing at the first highlighted box with her own mechanical pencil. "This first one says that the radius of a circle is always perpendicular to a chord, bisects the chord and the arc. Got that?"

"Nope," the poor girl next to her admitted.

"A chord is a line that joins two points of a curb," Lia explained as if it was second nature. "These chords are never parallel to the radius. Does that make sense?"

Maylene tentatively nodded. "I think so."

"Okay, great. How about this one? A tangent dropped to a circle is perpendicular to the radius made at the point of tangency."

"...What's a tangent?"

"A line that touches a circle with only one point."

"Oh, okay. I got it."

Lia continued onward, "How about this one? Tangent segments from a single point to a circle at-"

"For the love of God–stop talking gibberish," a deep voice that both Lia and Maylene were beginning to get to know interrupted their math lesson.

Lia and Maylene's eyes nearly fell out of their sockets when they realized who actually stepped foot in the library. There was Jared Huxley, the stubborn individual who wanted to do everything by himself was right in front of them. To put it simply, neither Lia, nor Maylene, expected him to come here. Well, it would be dishonest to say Lia was not anticipating this. She was the one who invited him to Oakbrooke Library in the first place. Except for the excess rainwater dripping from his black fringe, Jared looked as perfect as ever. Lia thought back to earlier in PE class when he came up to her to begin a conversation subsequent to their laps.

"Hey, Lia," Jared caught her attention by jogging over to her, "can I ask you something?"

Lia guzzled down a mouthful of the iced water in her canteen and swallowing before answering properly, "Sure. What's up?"

"So, uh...do you remember when I told you I liked Maylene?"

"...Yeah."

"I was wondering if you could help me get to know her some more," he proceeded with a nervous smile, much more nervous than the smirk he wore around his other friends.

Lia was caught a bit off-guard, but nodded anyway. "Sure," she replied, knowing full well that she would not let a romantic relationship between the two of them happen. "Did you have anything in mind?"

Jared shuffled his feet awkwardly. "Well, I was hoping you had any ideas. You're always around her and all...I'm honestly not even sure what she likes."

"She loves anything that has to do with art," Lia considered the request, "painting, drawing, sculpting, you name it. She also likes to read—not as much as I do, but if you give her a fantasy novel, she'll eat that right up. Right now, though, we're starting to prep for exams next month, so you're more than welcome to join us at the library sometime."

"Exams? Already?" Jared's eyebrows shot up. "Those aren't until late January, though."

"Getting into preparatory habits tends to lower the stress level that one might have while procrastinating," the brunette explained, "so, I convinced Maylene to study with me. I tried talking to Yasmin about it, but she said "Heck no" and has decided to procrastinate."

A thoughtful smile appeared on Jared's face. "The library, huh?"

"Yup."

"Any idea on when you two will be there next?"

"Probably this afternoon," responded Lia, placing her canteen back into the cupholder of her backpack. "Around this time of year, we start having study sessions there every Friday."

Jared nodded, absorbing the information. "So, right after school?"

"Yeah."

"Cool. I'll see you guys then."

That was the exact moment where the puzzle pieces of Lia's mind fell into place. This would be a golden opportunity to put her theory about Jared's "super strength" into action. While the library might not have been the ideal place, it would have to do. Lia was friends with most of the librarians there, so if any messes were made, she would clean it up and apologize to whoever was on duty without receiving any penalty. Nearly the entire faculty of both Oakbrooke High School and the library across the street knew Lia was authentic and studious. She never had ill intent when it came to her library visits, even receiving a discount on occasional books she desired to purchase for her own leisure.

Now, sitting at the table with Maylene, Lia felt like nothing short of a fraud. Here she was, pretending that Jared accompanying them in the library was purely spontaneous, but instead was a figment of her own mastermind. She had to be Machiavellian in a way–because she cared about the world beyond our own. If it fell to despair - if it became sick with the sadness and fury the Fire Wing brought it - then the guilt would rest on her shoulders. She was in a tough spot–in a house of mirrors with no way out, lost in the labyrinth of her own mind. Either way, she was sworn to secrecy–something the Enchantress said only once, but she would never forget.

"Oh, hey, Jared," Lia exclaimed just over a whisper. "What's up?"

Jared already had a Mathematics textbook cradled in his arms. "I came down here to study since I haven't been before and saw you guys at this table, so...I was wondering if I could maybe join you." From the tone of his voice, Lia could tell he was nervous.

Lia turned to Maylene, who also seemed a bit timid, but she nodded anyway. "Yeah, of course," the brunette replied once she got her friend's stamp of approval."

"Great! Thanks," Jared hastily pulled a chair out from across Maylene, which screeched against the floor.

"Shh!" the woman in her fifties hushed them from behind the receptionists' desk.

"Sorry!" Lia and Jared whisper-yelled in response.

Lia decided to change the subject once Jared got settled, "So, what are you working on?"

"Math," he sighed in response.

"Would you like some help with it?"

"No, thank you."

Lia nodded and took out her textbook for Advanced Placement Chemistry. Since Maylene and Jared were both working on Math, she figured she would join them with the most similar subject to it that she was taking currently. A sheet of silence covered the table like a tablecloth while three textbooks laid open. Maylene took Lia's advice from earlier in the semester and wrote a series of flashcards containing important formulas and proofs as well as highlighting the corresponding sections in the book. Lia had her spiral notebook opened and was scribbling down her own notes. Writing down things aided her in retaining them, so her notebooks filled up with words galore as the semester inched by. Lia's pencil drew cursive letters sloping across each line. The only individual who was not writing anything down was Jared, who rested his chin in his hands and elbows on the table pretending to study while instead, he was watching Maylene out of the corner of his eye. No matter how much Lia wanted to stop this, she needed to remain inconspicuous. Who knew what would happen if either Jared or Maylene figured out her intentions–no matter if they were inherently good or bad?

Her plan was set in stone. All she needed to do was act upon it, so that was exactly what she did. Lia rose to her feet and then pushed her chair in, which received both Maylene and Jared's attention. Prior to either of them asking about her whereabouts or if everything was okay with her, she spoke up to diminish any questions.

"I'm going to look for some books to use for my English Comp essay."

"Comp?" Jared cocked his head puzzledly.

"Composition." Lia then turned around and waltzed into the haven of books. "I'll be right back."

Once Lia was caught in the library's trance of the thousands of books that it offered, there was almost no way to escape. It was as if she was a miniscule fly caught in a spider's web, seeing no way out. Lia marched her way towards the astronomy section of the shelves, which was relatively close to the front, but happened to be high up. Lia had planned this the last time she was in the library studying a miscellaneous subject. Of course, Lia was too short to be scanning the spines of the books near the top of the first floor, which was exactly where Jared came in. It might not have been how you would think–having Jared reach a book on a higher shelf. Instead, the library invested in a mechanism that Lia adored, especially after she saw it in a childhood princess movie featuring a bookworm. That contraption was a rolling ladder.

The plan was set. Now, to get the ball rolling. Lia trotted to the table where Jared and Maylene were quietly studying and cleared her throat to get their attention. "Hey, Jared?" she spoke up. "Would you mind giving me a hand with the ladder?"

"Sure. There's a ladder in here?" Jared inquired.

"Yeah." Lia smiled along with her heart beating wildly. "It's this way."

Jared asked no questions to Lia's relief. The petite brunette led Jared towards the wall of bookshelves that appeared to be hardly touched because of the dust everywhere that she was browsing. Jared followed behind her like a lost puppy until Lia wheeled over the ladder and held it in place. Jared held back a cough from the smell of old books and yellowing pages. That gave Lia an idea. It might have not been very intelligent, but it was all she could come up with.

"Could you hold this ladder for me while I climb up and get the books I need?" Lia requested of Jared.

Obediently, he held onto one side of the ladder. "Yeah, of course. Be careful."

"I will." Lia then added on silently, *"Not."*

Lia's heart pounded against her chest as she began climbing up the creaky ladder. Once she was a few rungs up, Jared grasped onto the other side to hold it steady while she continued to climb up the unreasonably high shelf of books. The ceiling, or the floor of the second level, was at least ten to twelve feet up. Lia began to realize how high up she truly was when she reached the ninth rung of the ladder. Her brown eyes lit up the lenses of her glasses when she read the titles which were now at her reach. Just as she mentally practiced, Lia picked up one book titled *"The Constellations of the Zodiac & Their Meanings"* followed by another, *"Secrets of the Stars,"* and then a third of the same genre. The more books she piled on top of her left arm, the more uncomfortable and uneasy she felt. Lia willed herself not to look down when Jared briskly called up to her:

"Isn't that enough? Don't fall."

"Just one more-" Lia placed one last book on her stack of at least six, "-got it. Okay, coming down-"

There was a slight alteration to Lia's scheme. Instead of faking a sneeze like she first intended, once she took her first step down the ladder, a few specs of dust worked their way up her nose. Lia scrunched her face in an attempt to will it away, but it was to no avail. The teenage girl felt herself losing her balance after a ginormous *"Achoo!"* that flung her off the ladder entirely. Lia hardly had any time to process the fact she was in midair until a strong hold broke her fall - and her startled scream - all at once. The books she had collected rained over Jared - the very force that caught her easily in his arms—*one* arm in fact - but he hardly seemed to notice. With one hand holding Lia against him, Jared used the other to prevent the final hardcover book from landing directly on her head. Oxygen rushed in and out of Lia's strained lungs as she gasped for air. Her adrenaline pumped her blood a hundred miles an hour. All Lia could do was cookily fix her glasses and force out a laugh.

"...Well, that was a close one."

CHAPTER ELEVEN 145

Jared plopped her back down on the ground and shook his head in disbelief. "My God..."

"Lia!" Maylene abandoned their table and sprinted in her direction. "I heard you scream–are you okay?"

"Yeah," Lia breathed heavily. "Just took a tumble."

"A tumble?" Jared grumbled in a husky undertone. "That was more than a tumble–that was a skydive."

Lia was unsure if she should laugh, but before she could make that decision, the librarian walked as fast as her little legs could take her towards the scene. "My goodness–you all should be more careful," she exclaimed sternly, yet sweetly at the same time. "Is everyone alright?"

"Yes, Miss Lana," the brunette replied. "I'm so sorry. I must've taken too many books out at once while on the ladder, but I'm okay."

Miss Lana forced a smile on her face. "It's okay, Lia. Be more careful next time, okay?"

"I will–I promise."

"That's all I need to hear. Happy reading, everybody!"

With that, the librarian made her way back over to her desk. Lia bent down and picked up all six of the books she had chosen on the top shelf and lugged them over to the table where the three of them were studying before. Jared and Maylene sat down without much conversation at all. Lia, on the other hand, provoked a lot of questions. She opened up the page where she had started the rough draft of her essay which was not due for a long while, and flipped open the first book that she could find to the first relevant chapter. She speed-read like there was no tomorrow and jotted down quotes on a separate page that would be helpful to her later. When she finally raised her field of vision to above her workspace, she discovered four brown orbs piercing directly at her.

"What's up?" she inquired to the table.

Maylene frowned in her direction. "Are you okay, Lia? You seem stressed."

"Well, I did just fall off a ladder," Lia teased herself in a way, "but, yeah. This is a big project that I need to get started on."

"Would you like any help?"

"If you want, when I have more of an essay written, you can proofread," she offered, which made Maylene smile.

"Sounds good," she responded brightly. "I'd love to help."

Lia was more than okay with that. Even though she likely would not need help with her academic assignments, she was always willing to allow Maylene to proof her work. Her best friend thrived off of feeling helpful, which was something that Lia had learned over the years of knowing her. Lia usually received marks in the highest grade range either way, so it would not hurt anything to allow Maylene to provide a helping hand. Maylene knew that Lia would always do the same for her no matter what. Lia even acted as a tutor to her sometimes.

The three of them settled down once more to do their work, or at least this was until the library doors opened and sheltered two more individuals from the downpour. When her Ring started to throb, Lia instinctively peered towards the entrance and was taken aback when the two girls who just arrived were none other than Willow and Rowan. This time, however, they seemed to be civil towards each other. Water dripped from blonde strands and black waves alike. Rowan wiped the fog from her glasses with her oversized maroon hoodie sleeve while Willow merely patted down her lavender fluffy coat. Lia found it fascinating that the three of them always seemed to wear the same colors every day. When Lia caught the two girls' eyes, they merely looked over to her and instead focused on Jared. Both of them strode over to the table where the three of them were looking. When Lia turned back around, she realized Jared's posture was rigid and he was at attention.

"Jared," Rowan snapped in his direction which made Maylene flinch and shrink down in her seat due to the sudden company. "Come outside. We need to talk to you."

Jared took one look at the window, where the rain was still pouring down. "It's raining," he deadpanned coolly.

"Doesn't matter. We need to talk to you. Willow has an umbrella."

Sure enough, Willow held up a purple umbrella that matched her coat.

"Can it wait?" the boy sighed.

"No, it can't," Rowan clapped back. "Come on."

"Please?" Willow added on.

Jared had no choice but to stand from his seat and then begin to follow the two girls out. "I'll be right back," he notified Lia and Maylene.

Willow and Rowan led Jared towards the entrance and coaxed him out. The blonde opened her umbrella that was somehow large enough to cover all three of them. Lia could not stand to let herself remain in the unknown. She needed answers, especially since all Three of the Earth Wing were abruptly together. This was something she had never seen before. Lia stood from her chair and muttered something about needing to check on Jared before leaving. She made sure Maylene was focused on her math before she pulled the hood of her puffy jacket that she snuck with her over her head and ventured out into the blistering wind and rain. At first, Lia thought the three of them had left, but all it took was her peeking around the side of the building to find they were hiding themselves from the public eye.

"We were looking all over for you," Rowan notified him. "Why'd you leave the premises without telling us?"

Jared held his hands out in front of him in surrender. "I was just going to study with a couple friends of mine."

"We need to be careful with who we interact with," Willow gently reminded him. "We can't make strong connections with anyone or we'll risk getting hurt."

The boy's cheeks flushed crimson. "Would this be a bad time

to tell you guys I kind of like one of the girls? The one with the black hair? Like...*like* like?"

"God *damn* it, Jared!" Rowan tried to shove Jared back in frustration, but he did not budge. "How many times do we have to tell you: you *can't* do that. For one, it's pedophilia–you're hundreds of years old-"

"Twelve hundred and twenty-four to be precise," Jared corrected her.

"-whatever, and these girls are like what, *sixteen*?" the black-haired girl yelled exasperatedly. "You need to put your feelings aside and stop liking this girl. That's freaky, and besides...we need to stick together," She pointed to all three of them back and forth. "This isn't some silly game. This is important if we're going to fit in around here."

"*Fit in?*" Lia wondered; she knew that they intended to blend in, but to be a chameleon was not something to be pulled out of a magician's hat.

"Okay, hold on." Jared straightened his posture and glared at the two girls in front of him. "You're the one telling us to stick together? You and Willow were having it out in the hallway and I said nothing, but when I have a harmless crush, that's a problem? Both of you need to get your act together and stop being hypocrites. This is what got us into this mess in the first place. Do you think I want to be here? No, but starting fights with each other in the middle of a high school's hallways is just asking for trouble. I have no idea how nobody has reported it yet, but you two need to get a grip or so help me-"

Jared's ongoing rant became a muffled mumble when a sudden object clamped over his mouth that materialized out of thin air. Lia fought back a gasp when he pried a lavender flower - a massive purple iris - off of his face. With a wave of her free hand, Willow telekinetically snatched her creation from him and held the stem, beginning to twirl it around. Now, this was uncanny. From Jared's easy hold of her body in the library - with one hand - to a sudden figment of nature appearing from nothing, Lia discovered that she was right all along. The Mêla did indeed have supernatural abilities.

"Rowan's right. Actually, both of you are," Willow softly interjected as the rain poured around them. "We all need to communicate more efficiently amongst each other, but we cannot do that without trust. Are you all with me?"

Jared nodded and was all for it. "Yes."

"I'm with you," Rowan was more hesitant, but complied nonetheless.

"It's settled, then." Willow eyed Jared. "Next time, just let us know of your whereabouts." Next, she moved to Rowan. "And let's try not to spark an argument."

"Got it," Jared and Rowan agreed.

The three members of the Earth Wing had come to an eventual settlement. Unfortunately, this was not how the entirety of Kythaela worked, though. No matter how much the Earth Wing wanted their dilemmas to be resolved in an orderly fashion, at this moment in time, that was simply not possible. While the trio shared an umbrella back to the front of the library, Lia was busy answering a text from Maylene which asked where she was. We all know where this cliché goes: while her nose was buried in her phone, Jared, Willow, and Rowan rounded the corner to view her totally-not-suspicious - sarcasm - figure looming against the wall. It took a stern clearing of Rowan's throat for Lia's head to jerk upward.

"Oh, hi," Lia began to frantically ramble. "I'm sorry–I just needed some fresh air from all the dust. Phew!"

Three pairs of narrowed eyes bore in her direction. "And you think the dreary weather will provide fresh air for you?" Willow wondered aloud.

"Yeah." Lia stuffed her phone into her jacket pocket along with her hands. "Why?"

"Cut the crap. We're on to you," snarled Rowan, but lost the sneer after Jared elbowed her in the upper arm.

The brunette lowered her head and exhaled, "I'm sorry. I

wanted to check on you Three because I consider you all friends, or at least acquaintances. Is everything okay?"

"What do you think?" Jared turned the question onto her.

"What do I think? I think I'm going crazy!" Lia's mind began to spiral. "I...I'm not sure," she answered honestly. "I didn't hear any of your conversation - not that I was eavesdropping - but there was some tension from what I noticed."

Lia always knew she was a try-hard. At this moment, for instance, she was doing her very best to appear innocent while the opposite was true. The Earth Wing were not naïve to antics such as hers–they had been around for centuries longer. Lia could have deflated like a fatigued balloon when the three of them seemed to drop the subject...at least for now.

Willow smiled kindly. "We're okay. Thank you for checking on us, Lia."

"You're welcome."

Silence was never something that Lia had a good relationship with. Other than the rain pelting down on all sides, the group of four neglected to say anything else. No matter the circumstance, Lia always felt the need to fill the silence, whether it was with music, conversation, or even something in the background. This instance, however, needed something much more prevalent than the rain. That was why Lia used the first conversation starter in her mind to lessen the awkward mood.

"So, what are you guys doing for Christmas?"

All three of them looked at each other, knowing full well that no one had plans. Unsurprisingly, Jared was the one who spoke up, "I'm not sure, honestly."

"Me either," Rowan added.

Willow was third. "I guess none of us know."

"Well..." Lia barely fumbled to spit out an offer, "would you guys like to join mine and Maylene's family for Christmas dinner? We always have more than enough food to go around and if you guys aren't busy, then I'm sure you'd be welcomed with open arms."

CHAPTER ELEVEN 151

Lia's invitation did nothing but backfire on her. For a second time, Jared, Willow, and Rowan looked at each other with expressions of bewilderment, wonder, uncertainty, and maybe even a little bit of relief. Maybe the trio were not expecting a random act of kindness to be extended to them, especially in a realm that was much different than their own. The three of them seemed to converse silently which began with shrugs, then thoughtful humming, and then nods.

Rowan was the first to speak up. "Do you really mean that, Lia?"

"I do!" The girl in the puffy black jacket did not hesitate to showcase her enthusiasm. "We usually have Christmas dinner around three o'clock. My address is eighty-eight Magnolia Terrace and I can let my parents know you're coming."

"You don't have to do this," Willow protested, to which Rowan replied with a smack on the back of the head, "but we appreciate the gesture."

"We'll be there," Jared assured her. "Thank you for the invitation."

Lia was all smiles and hidden giggles. "No problem! I hope to see you then."

"Us too."

Lia returned to the library with a sopping wet coat and Three of the Mêla on her side rather than against her. Maylene had wondered where she went, and once again, Lia used the "fresh air" excuse. Now, Lia, Maylene, Jared, Willow, and Rowan all sat around the same table in the library where their brief adventure had begun. A weight lifted off of Lia's shoulders when she realized that three supernatural beings with their own talents would be attending her family's annual Christmas dinner. She knew her parents would not mind–they began sharing their tradition with the Zuíhuí family just a few years ago. You know how the traditional saying would go:

The more, the merrier.

Twelve

The city of Oakbrooke rejoiced when the clock struck midnight on December twenty-fifth. Holiday decorations filled the front lawns and trees occupied the window of every house in Elwood Manor. The entire town had been anticipating the arrival of one of the most momentous annual celebrations of the year. Christmas music played on the radio of every vehicle maneuvering through the everyday roads which were now coated in ice. White flakes fluttered from the Heavens and caked each blade of grass as far as the eye could see. The previous evening, snowplows were hard at work paving the pearly dust from the asphalt.

Number Eighty-Eight Magnolia Terrace was no different. Ever since the weekend after Mr. and Mrs. Hart's eldest's birthday, the family switched gears into the holiday spirit. A seven-and-a-half-foot faux Christmas tree adorned the space in front of the window in the Harts' living room. Garland sporting multi-colored lights flickered above the four stockings - one for a certain scaly friend - hung by the chimney with care. Mr. Hart's nutcracker collection adorned every hidden crevice of the house. At one point, his wife found one holding an alcoholic beverage in the refrigerator. Subsequent to each of the Harts turning in for

CHAPTER TWELVE   153

the night after a hard day's work, the family would cover themselves in blankets and watch a holiday film. Each of the three had their favorites. Lucas Hart had a love for A Christmas Tale. Cheyenne Hart preferred Miracle on 36th Street. Lia, on the other hand, chose a selection that blurred the lines of pure entertainment and sentimentalism: "The Cashews" Christmas Special.

Every family had its own traditions. The Harts never failed to miss a year of giving each other pajamas the night before Christmas Day. Rather than them all being the same, however, each of them would pick out a pair of pajamas for another family member by picking slips of paper from a baseball cap. Cheyenne chose Lia's name, Lia picked her father's name, and Lucas pulled his wife's name out of the hat. Lia was the only individual of the three who received a normal pair of pajamas. The expressions on the mother-father duo's faces said it all. Lucas pinched the pink bunny pajamas from his wrapped box with disdain. Lia's excuse was, "It's your favorite Christmas movie, Dad! What's wrong with it?" and left it at that. Meanwhile, Cheyenne received a play-on nightgown that read *"All I want for Christmas is wine and coffee."* along with what looked to be a tipsy flamingo on the front. Only one of the Harts went to bed satisfied that evening, but that did not mean they were full of frowns.

Waking up on Christmas morning with the mindset of a child was a rare phenomenon; so rare that it could be considered magical. Visions of sugarplums neglected to dance in the youngest Hart's head as she slept, however, but rather a dreamless sleep welcomed her with open arms. Lia's cheek pressed into her pillow as if tomorrow would never come, and for some bizarre reason, she did not want it to. There simply was too much to worry about in the little teenager's life. Along with school on her shoulders, the fate of an alternate world hung in the balance. No one should have to carry such pressure over their head...no one except for Lia, apparently.

Lia rolled out of bed that morning wearing a pair of long-sleeved red plaid pajamas. The morning was spent with all smiles and laughs. After stockings and presents were opened, the family settled in for another Christmas movie marathon. While material things were wonderful, the Harts appreciated quality time more than anything, especially on Christmas Day. That was one reason that breakfast consisted of cereal rather than making a special meal that was sporadically being prepared. The fifteen-pound turkey had been placed in the oven at around noon with Cheyenne checking on the status of it every half hour. The rest of the food was prepared in the early afternoon. Mashed potatoes, macaroni and cheese, broccoli casserole, and dinner rolls were set on the table in the dining room which was used for larger events that included the entire family coming together. Lia aided her mother and father in setting the table with silverware and napkins folded into pyramids in front of each seat–thanks to Lucas.

Rather than Christmas music being played on their home device, a black upright piano rested lovingly in one corner of the room to the right of the foyer that doubled as an office space for Mrs. Hart. Once everything was ready except for the turkey still in the oven, Lia - dressed in an ugly sweater with a llama on the front - pulled out the matching bench and sat down at a comfortable distance. She opened up one of the numerous holiday books in their repertoire and flipped to a miscellaneous page. Sightreading was one of Lia's favorite pastimes when she had nothing else going on. She still had not played all of them despite owning these books for several years. She inherited from her grandmother who neglected to play like she used to. Her Nana passed Lia the torch as soon as she discovered her granddaughter's love for music. Now, an entire bookshelf was filled with piano books from the Baroque, Classical, Romantic, and Contemporary periods alike, spanning several genres.

A rendition of an old Christmas classic - *O Holy Night* - glistened throughout the room as each key was pressed in the signature of E Flat. Lia's fingers glided across the ivory keys like skates on a freshly frozen pond, just waiting to be illustrated with swirling lines of pure tranquility and iron blades frolicking about. Ricocheting off the walls and lofting in every room of the house was the music cascading from Lia's fingertips. If there was magic in the world we could call our own, its name was "music." No matter the instrument, genre, or mood, music was what brought the world together in harmony.

An example of this was displayed when the Zuíhuí family entered the Harts' household while Lia's fingers glided away at the piano with her own rendition of *Mary, Did You Know?* in the key of A Minor. Unbeknownst to her, the twins entered the spare room with smiles on their faces and the lyrics displayed on their phones and singing along at the start of the third verse. While startled at first, Lia continued to play like her life depended on it. Her body swung with the meter and smooth chord changes through arpeggios in her left hand and the melody in her right along with some harmonic intervals. At around the third verse, Lia chimed in with her voice as smooth as butter and crisp as a cucumber–but not combined, of course. Her mezzo-soprano voice rang out over the tickling of the ivories. It was a wonder to Lia's entire circle how such a small being could sound like an entire orchestra with just her and the piano.

Once the final notes bounced from the smooth keys and faded into silence, Lia took her foot off of the damper pedal. From floating off the instrument, her hands reached to hug the twin on either side of her on the bench. Lia held her two friends close. While one had a tighter-knit relationship with Lia than the other, the girl in the middle treasured the twins like her own sisters. That was why she gave them each a tight squeeze and welcomed them into their "second home" with open arms for at least the thousandth time.

"Merry Christmas, you two!" Lia exclaimed with almost as much cheer as jolly old Saint Nicholas himself.

"Merry Christmas!" Yasmin and Maylene chorused from either side.

The brunette swung her legs back and forth since they did not quite touch the ground. "How was your morning?"

"Good," Yasmin replied for both of them. "We played some Mahjong after opening our presents. What was your favorite present that you got?"

Lia did not have to think about it. "I'd say my new flannels. Mom and Dad got me one in every color that I don't have. How about you guys?"

"I got new roller blades! I can't wait to try them out," the louder twin replied enthusiastically.

"I got some new art supplies that come in a nice briefcase," Maylene beamed brighter than the sunlight bouncing off the snowy ground. "I brought them along with a little something for you, Lia. Actually…two little somethings."

Lia's lips curved downward into a shy frown. "You didn't have to do that. I got you both something too, but you know I don't need anything."

"Of course you do!" Yasmin smacked Lia on the back as Maylene trotted out of the room to retrieve what she had brought. "Everybody deserves presents on Christmas."

"Yes, but I don't *need* them."

Maylene returned to the room along with a small, wrapped present in one hand and something that the Zuíhuí family created every December. It was a Chinese Christmas tradition to wrap apples in cellophane along with a brief message and a design in the center. In this case, a heart occupied the middle of the apple that Maylene used some white ribbon to make into an ornament. She delicately handed it to Lia, who smiled and hugged both of the twins–one with each arm. This was before Maylene even handed her the green wrapped present.

"It's from both of us," she notified her.

Yasmin just sighed. "She made it, but I claim ten percent because I meant to get you a present but forgot."

"That's okay," Lia giggled like a child. "I don't mind."

With the youthful mindset Lia awoke with that morning, Lia

yanked the ribbon off from around the box and tore open the wrapping paper as if she was four years old again without a single care in the world. Below it laid an ordinary box closed with patterned tape. Lia carefully opened it and removed the object surrounded by crumpled up newspapers and bubble wrap. There, in her hands, was the ocarina that Maylene had been working so hard on in Ceramics class. The miniature clay instrument was masterfully crafted. Flawless branches sprouting cherry blossoms crawled across the white base. Twelve holes were spaced out and sized as if a professional had made the instrument. Lia imagined that Maylene must have done a momentous amount of research to make the ocarina as perfect as it was. She cradled her new favorite instrument in her hands like it was a newborn baby and tearfully offered Maylene a tender smile.

"It's...it's beautiful," Lia spat out the only words she could think of.

Blood rushed to Maylene's cheeks. "It's the least I could do for all you've done for me."

"You don't have to do anything."

"Of course I did. You're my best friend."

Lia placed the ocarina on top of the piano and hugged the girl across from her. "Thank you so much. You have no idea how much this means to me."

"You're welcome," Maylene gushed into her shoulder, proud of herself for the gift that left her favorite person utterly wonderstruck.

Yasmin, like usual, had to interrupt the moment. "Oh, come on!" she screeched playfully. "Stop being sappy and play something!"

"But she just got it," Maylene protested, "she doesn't know how."

"She's already looking it up."

Sure enough, when two pairs of eyes looked her way, Lia was typing vigorously on her phone regarding how to play the C

Major ocarina. She pressed on the first link and skimmed the instructions. Not even ten seconds passed when she leaned her phone against the stand on the piano, sat down on the bench, and held the ocarina to her lips to play her first note. This got the attention of both girls, especially when she began playing an old classic: *Mary Had a Little Lamb* which was detailed in the instructions. Soon enough, she began playing a C Major scale up and down that consisted of one octave. Then, once she familiarized herself where the majority of the notes were, she began playing one of her favorite go-to songs on any instrument. Needless to say, Lucas hurdled into the room once he heard the introductory riff of one of his favorite songs from the 1980's. Mr. Hart was followed by his wife, and then Mr. and Mrs. Zuíhuí.

"What are we going to do with that kid?" Lucas leaned over and asked his wife.

Cheyenne shook her head and smiled. "She's too talented for her own good."

"I heard that," Lia snipped in between breaths of playing her ocarina.

"It's true, Honey," her mother assured her.

"Mom!"

Lucas nudged Cheyenne. "She gets it from me, you know."

"Oh, nonsense," Cheyenne smacked him in the back of the head.

Meanwhile, the Three Mêla whom Lia had invited on a whim stood at the foot of the Harts' driveway, taking in the sight of the two-story house in front of them. All three of them examined their situation skeptically. What if Lia was somehow trying to trick them? What if she truly knew their secret, why they were not from this world and how they could not return? None of them could risk blowing their cover, especially to adolescent teenagers with wide mouths.

"Are you sure this is a good idea?" Rowan suspiciously inquired.

"We have nowhere else to go," Willow reasoned with her, to which Jared nodded. "Besides, it's Christmas, after all."

"You're too trusting, Willow."

Jared gave Rowan a hard look. "We should give Lia a chance. Willow's right. I've known her the longest and she doesn't seem like she would turn against us."

"Oh, like last time?" Rowan antagonized with a question of her own.

"Please...," Willow exhaled with wide eyes. "It's Christmas Day. There's snow on the ground. Everyone is making merry with the time they have. Why shouldn't we do the same?"

"Willow's right," Jared agreed to the blonde's relief. "But… we need to be careful. None of us can risk a human discovering our secret."

"Well, duh." Rowan rolled her eyes.

Willow's eyes pierced into Rowan's as she retorted, "And *you* need to be a little more optimistic. None of us want to be here… in this…*place*. Don't make it a pain for everyone else."

"Fine."

Jared did not wait anymore. Instead, he climbed up the porch steps and rang the doorbell. Willow and Rowan fanned out behind him like they were some sort of frontline band. While waiting for the front door to be answered, though, all three of them were distracted by a unique noise coming from the right-hand side of the first floor. A beautiful melody of a Christmas classic that somehow none of the Mêla had ever heard glistened from some sort of flute-like instrument. All of the tension from Jared, Willow, and Rowan's bodies alike faded away into the breeze with the notes ebbing from the Harts' household. Three pairs of lips tugged upwards, especially when the front door opened to reveal a spitting image of Lia herself. Mrs. Hart's hair was loosely brushed past her shoulders and her glasses matched her daughter's. She smiled at the three guests waiting on her front porch.

"Oh, hello! You must be Lia's friends," Cheyenne exclaimed. "Come in, come in! It's freezing out here."

"Thank you, Mrs...," Willow trailed off when she realized she had no idea what Lia's last name was.

"You can call me Cheyenne," Mrs. Hart replied graciously when the three of them stepped inside and wiped their shoes off on the mat. "Could you remind me of your names? Lia told me, but I must've forgotten. That's what getting old does to you."

"We're literally over a millennium—we know," Rowan wanted to snap, but her anger lofted away when the music continued to play. "I'm Rowan," she introduced herself.

"I'm Jared," the boy reached out to shake Cheyenne's hand, who took it.

"And I'm Willow," the last of the three concluded. "It's nice to meet you."

"The pleasure's mine." Cheyenne was overtaken by their politeness. "Lia's in the room to your right. You might hear her with her new present."

Sure enough, Jared, Willow, and Rowan turned to the opened glass double doors on their right-hand side to view an enthusiastically eccentric Lia holding the handmade twelve-hole ocarina to her lips and playing the third tune she had learned in five minutes. The girl in the middle of the room, along with Yasmin who was playing Jingle Bells - the only thing she knew - on the piano and Maylene seated proudly on the couch did not even notice the three guests in the foyer watching the trio as if they were entranced by the music. It was not until the Christmas carol was over and the Three Mêla began to clap that the trio of girls looked up in unison. Lia's grin stretched from ear to ear. She delicately placed the ocarina on the top of the piano and dashed over to hug all three of them to their own surprise.

"You made it!" Lia cheered to the trio. "Thanks for coming. For a second, I didn't think you'd show."

"Well, we almost didn't, but-" Rowan started, but Jared interrupted her.

CHAPTER TWELVE

"We figured it'd be good for us. Thank you again for the invite."

Lia ignored Rowan's comment and led them into the room. "You're welcome. You guys have met Yasmin and Maylene, right?"

"Rowan and I haven't," Willow replied with a smile. "It's nice to meet you."

"I wish I could say the same," Yasmin abruptly growled to everyone's shock.

"Wait...why not?" Lia's heart dropped.

Jared protectively stepped in front of Rowan while Willow stood next to her. "Yeah, why not?" he inquired skeptically.

Yasmin rose from the piano bench. "Rowan Farago, I presume?"

"That's me." Rowan pushed Jared out from between them and folded her arms over her chest. "Why is that so distasteful?"

"Because you cheated off my sister's Geometry test last week and when she told you she noticed, you yelled at her," Yasmin accused the taller, brawnier girl.

Willow's head whisked to Rowan so quickly that her neck popped. "You did *what*?!"

"Relax," Rowan attempted to diffuse the situation. "I didn't yell. I just...raised my voice."

"Why would you do that?" Jared sternly scolded her.

"It was *one* problem!"

"That doesn't make it right."

"You shouldn't have yelled at Maylene," Willow stated.

Rowan's eyes narrowed into slits. "I didn't want to get caught, okay?"

The Earth Wing arguing was exactly what Lia wanted to avoid, but there was nothing she could do about it. Instead, she looked over at Maylene, who was sitting on the couch with her head facing her knotted hands in her lap. Yasmin was seated on her left side with an arm gently wrapped around her shoulders. Lia could tell that the louder twin was itching to get into the argument, but instead focused on her sister, who needed the attention much more than the fossils in the foyer. Lia did the same and sat on Maylene's other side.

"Why didn't you say anything?" Lia whispered to the silent Maylene.

She brushed her bangs out of her face and merely shrugged. "I guess I was tired of running to you guys for help."

"There was no excuse in what she did, and it's okay to come get us if you need help," Yasmin assured her twin. "We love you because you're our sister and shouldn't have to deal with this sort of mess."

"I guess so, but…"

"Maylene?"

The girl in question and her sisters on either side of her looked up at Rowan's voice, which was much more timid than before. "I'm sorry," she sincerely expressed. "What I did was wrong and it won't happen again. My friends and I will make sure of it."

"It's okay," Maylene was quick to utter, but Yasmin was more skeptical.

"Be sure that it doesn't," she retorted quite bluntly, "or you won't like what happens next."

Rowan swallowed back a witty remark and nodded. "Got it."

Mrs. Hart could not have picked a better time to obliviously poke her head through the doorway and announce that supper was ready. Lia led their group of six into the dining room, where a leaf needed to be added to the table in order to fit all twelve people. Just like tradition, Lia's Papa sat on one end of the table while her Nana sat on the other end. On one side in order sat Lucas, Cheyenne, Lia, Maylene, and Yasmin. On the other were Mr. and Mrs. Zuíhuí, Jared, Willow, and Rowan. Yasmin despised the fact she was sitting directly across from Rowan, but a gentle squeeze to her hand caused her to look at Maylene and smile. If anything, Yasmin was thankful for not having to hold Rowan's hand, since Nana did that for her just before grace. Just like every year before, Lia's Papa had the honor of saying the prayer.

"Most Gracious Heavenly Father, we thank you today for the food that's in front of us and that we are alive and well. Thank you for another wonderful year and for the guests amongst us. With everything going on in the world right now, we pray for safety, prosperity, and hope for the future. Please bless this food and nourish it to our bodies as we fellowship together. Amen."

Lia did not miss how the three guests all had their eyes open and looked at each other awkwardly during the prayer. She had no idea what the "God situation" was in Kythaela, but she guessed that a prayer before meals was not necessarily customary. Ever since she was little, Lia had been raised in a Christian household. So had Maylene and Yasmin. In their early childhood, the two families would attend church together. Now, though, they worshiped and prayed in their own way, most of it being subconscious. Through thick and thin, Lia never lost her faith.

While Papa cut the turkey at the end of the table and passed out plates, Mrs. Zuíhuí, the strictest of the three mothers at the table including Nana, spoke up to the Mêla, "So, do you three go to my daughters' school?"

"Yes, Ma'am," Jared replied for the three of them.

"And why are you over here for Christmas?" she inquired.

Yasmin's eyes widened and she protested, "Mama…"

"What? I'm just asking, 亲爱的," Mrs. Zuíhuí used her nickname for her daughters from her native tongue, pronounced "Qīn'ài de."

"It's alright," Willow graciously intervened. "We're new to the area and didn't really have anywhere to go, so Lia invited us over."

"Are you three…orphans?" Mr. Zuíhuí asked with concern.

"Dad-" Maylene muttered, humiliated.

Jared, Willow, and Rowan eyed each other with surprise, but then Rowan shrugged. "You could say that."

"Oh…I'm sorry I brought it up," Mr. Zuíhuí apologized to his daughters' relief.

His wife joined in. "It was rude of me to assume. I'm sorry as well."

"Don't worry about it," Willow assured the married couple. "We're used to questions like that, so it isn't really a problem."

Thankfully, by then, each plate with turkey on it had been passed around so there was no empty place at the table. Dishes began being passed around, including the mashed potatoes, macaroni and cheese, broccoli casserole, dinner rolls, cranberry sauce, and stuffing. The Zuíhuí family brought over their own signature dishes, such as roast pork, spring rolls, and jiaozi, which were Chinese dumplings. Lia put a little bit of everything on her plate…except for the cranberry sauce. She did not care very much for cranberry sauce. She noticed that the Mêla did the same with their plates but took smaller portions than the rest of the company. They did not want to overstay their welcome and take too much food despite all of it looking delicious.

"So, how did you all meet?" Cheyenne's sweet voice asked the trio.

All three of them appeared thoughtful, but Jared answered for them, "We've known each other since we were really young."

"And what brings you to Oakbrooke?"

"…We had some problems back home," Willow hesitantly replied, "but we're much happier here starting fresh."

Cheyenne smiled with the warmth of a mother. "I'm very happy to hear that."

"So, Jared, you're a football player, right?" Lucas asked the boy across the table. "What position do you play?"

"I'm a running back." Jared swallowed down his mashed potatoes.

"How long have you been playing for?"

"Just this year. I really enjoy it, though."

"And Willow, right?" Cheyenne inquired to the nearby

blonde, who nodded. "What do you like to do in your spare time?"

"Well, I love gardening. My favorite flower is the purple iris even though they become overcrowded very quickly." Willow needed a moment to consider.

"That's wonderful! And you, Rowan?"

Rowan was not expecting to be called on like she was in class. She played around with the macaroni and cheese on her plate with her fork. "Um, I love animals," she responded tentatively. "I work at the local animal shelter."

"Isn't that sweet?" Cheyenne asked herself out loud, which made Rowan crack a smile.

"You work?" Lia asked the quietest girl aside from Maylene. When she nodded and met her eye, the brunette stood from the table. "I need to show you something."

Silence ensued amongst the table for at least a minute or so. Rowan sat facing her plate and taking hesitant bites of the food that she picked from the buffet. She did not want to meet anyone's eye, instead resorting to either looking at her lap or the macaroni and cheese that took up most of her portion. Cheyenne muttered something to her husband along the lines of "If she brings that...thing downstairs, then so help me..." which was abruptly interrupted by Lia bringing the very thing that made Cheyenne screech in her seat.

"Here she is!" Lia announced proudly with Noodle the corn snake coiled loosely around her left arm.

"Ophelia Sage!" Cheyenne scolded her daughter. "What did I say about bringing your anaconda to the dinner table?"

"She's a corn snake," Rowan retorted before Lia could.

By then, Rowan quickly rose to her feet with the widest smile that Lia had ever seen on her face. She crouched down to examine the corn snake around Lia's arm. It was as if a switch was flipped from solemn to overjoyed. Lia could not help but grin when Rowan gaped at her pet in dumbstruck awe. Noodle seemed to enjoy the attention. She stuck her tongue out to assess what exactly was going on.

Rowan's brows lowered into a state of vulnerability as she asked Lia, "May I hold her?"

"Of course!" Lia extended her arm towards Rowan. "Her name's Noodle and she's really friendly."

"I don't doubt it."

As if she was an expert, Rowan held out her right hand next to Lia's arm and kept it still like it was a branch. Noodle appeared to understand Rowan's silent request. Lia coaxed her onto Rowan's arm, where the ecstatic girl watched her slither up towards her shoulder like a kid on their first day of preschool. Lia ignored the distraught face of her mother while her husband merely chuckled and fist bumped his own father next to him. Maylene wore a smile of her own, but Yasmin was not as willing to do the same. Instead, she watched Rowan with skeptical eyes as the heartfelt interaction unfolded.

Lia watched along with Jared and Willow on their side of the table. She had never seen Rowan untense her shoulders or even smile. It was obvious that the other two Mêla have, though, since they eyed their companion knowingly. Maybe this was the beginning of something new, something that Lia could use to Kythaela's advantage. Of course, she could not risk revealing the fact she knew their unworldly reality, but it was worth a shot. Maybe Christmas truly was a holiday that worked wonders and spread cheer throughout every household. Well, everyone was cheerful except for Cheyenne, who stood up and exclaimed with a sweaty smile:

"Who's up for an early dessert?"

Thirteen

It was a dark and stormy night...well, it was more of a morning...and it was not quite stormy. After Daylight Savings Time began that past November, the days had been getting shorter, which meant that when the town of Oakbrooke awoke during the first week of January, the sky transformed into an azure complexion dotted with shimmering freckles. The singular eye peering down from behind the stratus clouds outside soon was replaced by its larger twin: the Sun. Eventually, its rays burned through the frost coating the occasional blade of grass. That was how the weather had been ever since the flurries from Christmas rained down on the suburban community. While a crisp breeze still nipped at your nose and singed your ears, the Sun beamed radiantly through its territory, leaving Winter to be a time of balance rather than a bare depression.

School was back in session after a brief break during the latter half of December and a singular day in January. The first semester was still in session, but not for very long. In a matter of two weeks, new schedules would be handed out to each student, textbooks would need to be borrowed or purchased from the library across the street, and the calendars would begin to count down the days until Summer Vacation. While spirits were lifted as many students adorned the presents they received just the previous week, procrastination was also a factor. Exams were near and scholarly brains were not as studious as perceived previously. At least...it seemed as if every student was as such except for Lia, who kept up with her studies as if she was some sort of machine. A quiz needed to be done? Completed with four days to spare. An essay? Completed a week ahead of time. No matter the assignment, Lia made sure it was finished to the best of her ability as soon as possible. Whenever Lia had any free time that she needed to occupy, then she would fill it with any homework she had not yet checked off of her to-do list.

That was why she was sitting in the home bleachers of the football field with only Maylene by her side while the two of them studied to prepare for finals. It had been nearly an hour since the school day ended, but Lia had a plan that Maylene was on board with. Since they usually studied in the library, Lia decided that they should make a change and sit on the bleachers during football practice for two reasons. The first was so that there was background noise. The second, which was the most important to Lia, was to get some alone time with Jared, not for the reason you might be insinuating, but instead to get to know him better...to earn his trust. Lia had to get this mission of hers moving if it was going to be successful.

The brightness on her laptop screen was turned all the way down as she continued to type her essay for her Advanced Placement English Composition class. A list of her scholarly sources and websites were in another document directly next to the one she was vigorously typing paragraph after paragraph. The metal was cool under her dark skinny jeans that were just long enough for her legs. A pair of black and off-white checkered slip-on shoes adorned her feet and a puffy black coat swallowed the rest of her frame. With each breath, a misty fog escaped her mouth and clouded the lenses of her glasses. Every so often, she would need to wipe them off before resuming her typing session once more.

Next to her, Maylene was on her sleek tablet using a stylus pen to scroll up and down. It was split-screened–a digital copy of one of her textbooks on one side and a lined document for her to scribble down notes on. She had just completed yet another bulleted list to study for one of her upcoming exams. Once she saved the document, she closed the app and then opened another to resume a drawing of hers. An outline of a certain Shih-Tzu that lived in her residence was already made. Maylene selected a light brown from the color wheel on the side of her tablet and began shading certain aspects of the dog. Maylene leaned back against the bench above her and pulled her knees up to her chest, resting the tablet on her legs.

While Maylene sketched, Lia continued to glance up at the football field where the Oakbrooke Mustangs were in the middle of a scrimmage. Lia admired the athletic ability of each of the teenagers on the field. She knew that if she was put in the same circumstances, the results of the ordeal would be much different…huffing and puffing with her hands on her knees. She was very thankful to be on the sidelines while the team did the work along with the coach in his early forties - Mrs. Jenkins' husband - shouting commands at them. Every so often, Mr. Coach Jenkins would scream just loud enough to wreak a flinch from Maylene's frame.

"Alright, Mustangs!" the coach bellowed over the field. "Watch your back, Huxley! Abner! Quit slacking and help your teammate!"

Maylene hit the undo button to erase a mistake she had made and then fixed it. "Why exactly are we here again?" she whispered to Lia.

"I just thought Jared might like the support," Lia replied honestly. "You didn't have to come."

"I wanted to." Maylene smiled, focusing on her drawing, "and besides, it's nice to hang out with you outside of school."

"Yeah, it is. I hope you don't mind that I'm working on this essay, though."

"I don't mind. How's it going?"

Lia added yet another citation regarding the position of the stars in relation to Zodiac signs before answering, "I think it's going well. What are you drawing?"

"Oh, just another picture of Sadie." Maylene shyly tilted the tablet towards her.

"What on Earth–that's incredible!" Lia exclaimed, her arms flailing and accidentally bumping the tablet; Maylene's stylus scraped a dash of color across the drawing. "...Oops."

Maylene giggled and pressed the undo button again, "It's okay. Easy fix."

"Wish I could say the same," Lia fought against mumbling. Instead, she grinned and watched as Maylene continued to effortlessly sketch a realistic portrait of her beloved dog. "I don't get how you can draw so well."

"I don't get how you can play every instrument you try," Maylene countered.

"I can't do any of the woodwind or brass instruments. Give me a flute and I can't even get a sound out of it. Same with the French horn."

"I mean *stringed* instruments, then."

"You're good at every type of art."

"Not music."

"Oh, be quiet."

Both girls broke out into a chorus of laughter due to their miscellaneous senses of humor. Unbeknownst to either of them, practice had just ended - the scrimmage concluded along with it - and before either of them knew it, the brunet Coach Jenkins dismissed the Mustangs with his silver whistle. A herd of red jerseys and white helmets flocked towards the locker room. Lia remembered the last time she was in there with a pang. Only she and Jared knew about that circumstance, and it was a quite awkward one at that. She cringed at the memory.

Such a quest encouraged highly unorthodox decisions on her part. This time, Lia rooted herself to the spot and did not follow Jared into the locker room. He was injured last time. This time was different. Instead, she decided to wait on the bleachers with Maylene until Jared came to them. Yes, that was a much better idea.

About ten minutes or so later, Jared - along with some of the team - came sauntering out of the locker room with damp hair and a t-shirt underneath his red varsity jacket. He wore a pair of athletic shorts and gray sneakers. Once he caught her eye, Lia jumped up from her seat while Maylene had an opposing reaction. She continued to shade in her drawing without batting an eye. Lia began to hop down the bleachers, but before she made it all the way down, she turned towards Maylene and waved to retrieve her best friend's attention.

"I'm going to say hi to Jared," she elaborated. "Want to come with?"

Maylene shook her head politely. "No, thank you. I'm going to finish my drawing, but if you point him this way, I'll wave."

"Sounds good."

Lia jumped her way down the rest of the bleachers and jogged over to meet Jared halfway. She soon realized that this was a bad idea, because, just like she had thought earlier, she slumped down into a relaxed posture and swallowed as much oxygen as she could out of the cool atmosphere around her. She hated how unathletic she was, but no matter how hard she tried, she came to the realization that her body simply was not built for physical exercise, and that was okay. Some people had the capability to be more active than others.

"Hey, Jared," Lia breathed out to his amusement. "How was practice?"

One of his eyebrows raised at her fatigue. "...Are you good?" he asked instead.

"Yeah, I'm fine," she chirped and stood up straighter. "How was practice?" she repeated.

"It was alright," replied Jared with a shrug. "Well, you saw us. We were just doing the normal drills."

"Actually, I was busy watching Maylene drawing," Lia sheepishly admitted.

To her dismay, his eyes lit up. "Maylene's here too?"

"...Yes."

"Where is she?"

"Over there," She pointed to the bleachers, "but I was hoping I could talk to you first."

"What about?" Jared pushed his duffel bag further up his shoulders.

"Oh Lord...come on, Lia! Why don't you think things through!" The poor brunette struggled to string together a well-formulated sentence, so instead, she blubbered, "Oh, I mean, I was just wondering how your life is going. I mean, it's been a while since I've seen you."

"...Things are going good," he carefully answered. "Getting all of my work done has been difficult, but I'm hoping to finish it on time."

"You know, the offer still-"

"I know, but no thank you," Jared dismissed her offer to aid him. "I can do it on my own. Are you okay? You look stressed."

"Ah, and I'm fine," Lia exhaled dramatically. She then turned the conversation onto him. "So, has anything interesting been going on lately?"

The boy paused to eye Maylene, but his pupils flitted back to Lia. "Um, well...I guess there's *one* thing," he disclosed, scratching the back of his neck awkwardly.

"What's that?"

Either Lia was too enthusiastic or Jared was suddenly shy about the subject he was about to bring up. Lia waited patiently for him to reveal whatever had been going on in his mind. Surely, it must have been a lot, especially after transitioning to a new home in a short amount of time. Lia caught herself worrying about the Mêla more often than not. Did they have a place to sleep? Did they have money? If so, could they afford food? Lia's heart ached for them, wishing it could leap out of her chest and aid them with all of their hardships. Alas, Lia was only a teenager, still a child. There was only so much she could do.

"Well, uh..." Jared hesitated when Lia leaned in further once he began talking. "I was kinda hoping I could ask Maylene to the Winter Formal. I'm still working up the courage to do it."

What? No! This could not be happening! Maylene could *not* go to the Winter Formal with someone legitimately over a millennium older than her. Despite looking seventeen at the very most, she knew the truth–she heard it from his own mouth. No matter how charming or kind Jared could be, that was some sort of unintentional pedophilia. Heck, Willow and Rowan were even on her side! How could this be something within the confines of morality? Lia needed to find a stop to this, and fast. That was why she spat out the first excuse she could think of.

"I don't know if Maylene would want to go with you."

She hated the way Jared's strong build suddenly deflated before her. She could have kicked herself when he sighed and whispered, "Oh. Never mind, then."

"No, wait! I didn't mean that," Lia blocked Jared when he tried to sidestep her. "I mean, she hates going to things like dances and big parties. I just wanted to warn you because if you do ask her, she'd probably say no for that exact reason. I'm not telling you what to do, but I've known her since we were in diapers and the Winter Formal would *not* be her scene."

"...You know, I can see that," Jared agreed to her relief.

"Okay, good, because–"

"But–" Lia prevented her flurry of words from flooding the conversation when Jared continued. "I think I'll ask her this week anyway. It's worth a shot, right?"

Lia nodded nervously, not wanting to be unsupportive of her friend. She figured she would just warn Maylene later. "Yeah, it's worth a shot."

Lia crossed her fingers behind her back as she and Jared

walked towards the bleachers where Maylene had packed up her tablet and was waiting patiently for her friend to return. When she noticed Jared was next to her, she offered a polite wave. It was impossible for Lia to miss the rosy hue to Jared's cheeks just from Maylene looking in his direction. She wondered if her friend was aware of his strong feelings. While Lia wanted both of them to be happy, something did not feel right about the situation. If Jared was seventeen, just like he looked, she would not have an issue. Since he was not, though, Lia's gut screamed at her not to trust him.

If only he was not so charming when he smiled widely and waved at her friend, "Hi, Maylene!" he gushed like a hormonal middle schooler.

"Hi, Jared," Maylene kindly replied with her tablet under her arm and the stylus magnetically attached. "How was practice?"

"It was good." Jared decided to take interest in the object she was holding. "What's that?"

"My drawing tablet. I was working on something during your practice."

The boy's eyes lit up while Lia rolled hers. "Oh, really? What were you working on?"

"Oh, um…" Maylene opened the case and used her stylus to tap around until she opened her drawing app along with the sketch. "I was drawing a portrait of my dog, Sadie."

"You drew that?"

"Yeah."

"Are you sure that's not a photograph?"

"Yeah."

"Holy smokes-"

"Is it that hard to believe I drew it?" Maylene mumbled self-consciously.

Jared was all smiles as he ruffled her hair similar to how Lia had done. "Not at all. You're really talented, Maylene. I'm… genuinely blown away."

"Thank you." Lia despised the blush rising on Maylene's face.

"You're welcome." Jared's cheekbones raised, but then lowered when he looked down at the watch on his wrist and realized the time. "I need to head out, but I'll see you later?"

Maylene nodded. "Yeah, see you later."

"Bye, Jared," Lia butted her way into the conversation. "Glad you had a good practice."

"Me too. Thank you," he called back to them.

Lia watched as Jared jogged over towards the massive building that was Oakbrooke High School. She slung her backpack over her shoulders once her laptop was tucked inside and the zipper was closed all the way. Maylene closed up her tablet and attached her stylus magnetically to the side. Lia disliked the way a smile lingered on Maylene's face even after the boy had gone. This could become a disaster–a monumental...*disastrous* disaster. Lia knew she needed to take action. As the two wandered towards the main building, that was exactly what the brunette did.

"So...you and Jared, huh?" Lia inquired somewhat stoically.

"I know what you think and the answer's no," Maylene quipped before her friend could utter another word. "No, I don't like him."

Lia's eyes nearly fell out of their sockets. "How'd you know I was going to ask that?"

"We've known each other since we were practically babies," she countered, "I know what you're thinking ninety-nine percent of the time."

"*If only you knew...*" Lia swallowed down that thought to make room for optimism. "Oh," she mumbled, embarrassed.

"Why do you ask?" Ah, there was the sweet undertone to Maylene's voice again.

"I was just wondering..."

Then, Maylene's kind smile became a smirk. "Why? Do *you* like him?" she teased.

"What? No!" Lia's brows shot up as she quickly refuted the question. "You know how I feel about boys. Boys suck."

"That sounds like an excuse."

"No, it doesn't. I don't like him," Lia ignored the heat rising in her cheeks.

"Aha!" Maylene tenderly elbowed her. "You're blushing. I knew it. If you liked him, you could've just told me."

"I don't."

"Okay, I won't push you." Maylene quieted down. "I'm sorry. I didn't mean to make you uncomfortable."

Lia exhaled, half with relief, and half with exasperation. Maylene did not know any better. "It's okay," she replied authentically. "I mean, he's cute, but I wouldn't say I like him. Actually, there's something I wanted to talk to you about."

At once, Maylene was all ears. "What's that?"

"Wait…is this a good idea? I shouldn't out Jared like this…"

Lia deliberated on the subject for just a moment too long. Maylene eyed her innocently while the two walked towards the black sedan that would be taking the two of them home parked on the curb in front of the building. Once again, the white angel and the red devil appeared on her shoulders debating on which open would be the best route to take. It was a lose-lose situation: either Maylene would get involved with a boy who was freakishly older than her, or Lia would betray a friend's trust that could lead to the downfall of an alternate world. It was a heavy decision to make. The invisible figures weighed her shoulders down as if she was carrying a monumental load, but when another thought hit her, they instantaneously vanished. All Lia could do was smile and shake her head.

"Never mind. It's not important."

Maylene appeared to be puzzled, but she agreed nonetheless, "Okay."

Lia wiped her imaginary brow. Maybe making the ultimate decision to let the future handle itself was not such a bad idea… or was it?

Fourteen

Ophelia Sage Hart was an enigma...at least to Maylene Zuíhuí. At some points, her brain seemed to be that of a Stegosaurus', averaging about the size of a walnut shell. Other times, Lia was so ridiculously intelligent that Maylene wondered how she was still in high school and not in an Ivy League college at the age of sixteen. Academically, she was a natural phenomenon. Being on the Honor Roll and Principal's List ever since the very beginning of her school career, there was no doubt that Lia would go far in life. The only problem was that she had no idea what to do with the talents she had been given.

Deep down in her heart, Maylene Zuíhuí knew exactly what she was going to do with her God-given abilities. She planned on opening her own art studio that involved classes of mixed media, pottery painting, crafting, and more. She wanted to find others who had the same dream as her and band together to create the best Arts center that anyone had ever seen. Maylene's life was simple. She would receive a degree in Liberal Arts with a Minor in Business and then transfer her skills into the working world. It was the perfect plan. All she needed to do was get through high school with decent grades and get into the local community college where she could transfer to anywhere she wanted.

 A series of unfortunate events, however, had kept her eyes from being on the prize. While Maylene took her drawing tablet nearly everywhere she went, it was not a distraction from the world itself. Instead, Lia was beginning to bring the outside in with the three new friends she had made: Jared, Willow, and Rowan. While Maylene did her best to be polite, she found herself to be a bit wary regarding the trio, just like she had with other people. Jared, like other boys, made Maylene just a little uncomfortable, especially after her numerous encounters with Declan Abner. He left a bitter taste in her mouth that remained no matter which male she crossed. Jared seemed nice enough, but could she trust him? Next was Willow. Maylene had never really seen Willow around before, and she never posed a problem. Rowan, on the other hand, did the opposite. Her mind flitted back to the one-sided altercation the two of them had before Winter break. All Maylene could do was let Rowan be mad and get away with cheating off of her Geometry test. She wondered if anything was going on behind the scenes that made Rowan as...complicated as she looked. Mistakes happened, after all, and this was no exception.

 Maylene despised the way the halls always tended to close in on her every time she walked through them. With each step, more people appeared to emerge. This was expected, especially since the third block of the day had just ended and the massive groups of students were pouring into the cafeteria like a tidal wave. Maylene held her lunch box close to her chest as she weaved around the several cliques of her peers that never seemed to notice a human being trying to make her way through the flood. School was a battlefield...or was that love? Maylene pushed the 1980's song reference out of her mind and focused on reaching her destination, which was...ah! It was right in front of her! She wasted no time charging towards the courtyard doors that were propped open and prepared to wait beside them for a certain brunette who usually wore some sort of sage green or burnt red.

While a head of brown hair accompanied by a green hoodie was not visible to her, Maylene's almond-shaped eyes flitted over to another face that was beginning to become familiar. Either way, she preferred if the figure approaching her was shorter, had glasses, and was not wearing a red varsity jacket. In fact, the person was even the opposite gender than the one she wanted to be near. Instead of receiving tails like she had picked, the coin flipped over to heads. For once, Jared Huxley was approaching her without Lia by her side or even his own. Maylene had no idea why Lia and Jared had become close all of a sudden. The thought of the popularity hierarchy being altered by her best friend was almost sickening. Maylene never liked change, especially since it was walking straight towards her and she was forced to greet it with a smile.

"Hi, Maylene," Jared exclaimed with his hands in his pockets. "How's it going?"

Maylene's head was tilted downward, but she still offered him a polite grin. "Hi, Jared. It's going well. How are you?"

The boy seemed off-put by this question, as if it was not normally directed towards him. "Oh, I'm doing alright, thank you. How are your exams coming along?"

"They start next week. How about you?"

"I knew that," Jared chuckled anxiously, "that was a stupid question. Anyway, mine start then as well and I'm doing my best to study, but...it's just not working out."

"You know, Lia did offer to help with some of it," she brought up a memory. "I wouldn't be much help since I'm not very good at academics."

The boy shrugged and shook his head. "I can do it myself, but thank you. Also, I didn't want to talk about Lia–I wanted to talk about you," he revealed.

See, this was why Maylene did not like being around members of the opposite sex. For starters, they tended to be very intimidating. Take Declan Abner for example; he used his masculinity to tower over Maylene and make her a victim of bullying. Next, boys seemed to be in a whole other league entirely. She did not believe they were better than her, but they were just...different. There was no way that a boy and a girl could be compatible friends without being something more, which led her to her third point. There was no way, under any circumstance, that she, a sixteen-year-old girl, was ready for a relationship of any sort. She knew she was a pretty girl. It was only a matter of time until a boy asked her out. She dearly hoped that this would not be that instance.

"What do you mean by that?" she carefully inquired.

"Well, Maylene...," Jared faltered over his words as his confidence depleted, "I wanted to ask you something."

"Oh, no...this is it." Maylene swallowed back the anxiety building in her throat. "What is it?"

"I can do this. I can do this. God, why am I nervous about someone who's practically a kid's opinion of me?" Jared thought to himself, cleared his throat, and then confessed, "Well, you see...I like you, Maylene. I need to be honest with myself here and tell you the truth before it eats me alive. So, there it is. I have feelings for you and I want to do something about it. I know we don't know each other well, but I'm hoping to change that between us. I was wondering if there was any chance you'd like to go to the Winter Formal with me."

Just like Maylene had thought, Jared was spilling himself all over her like a misshapen glass of water tipping off the corner of a table. Rather than being the hand to catch it, Maylene was well-aware of what she had been taught all her life up to this point: "Never forget to set boundaries for yourself no matter what," her mother had said. "You and your sister are growing into beautiful young women. Don't let any boy take advantage of that. If you feel uncomfortable, the best thing to say is no."

Maylene did her best to abide by her mother's advice and put herself before any boy who might have wanted her, even if that meant letting the glass shatter on the floor subsequent to slipping through her fingers. In front of her stood Jared in the most vulnerable state she had seen him. His eyebrows knit together and tied his lips together with a hopeful smile. No matter how much she wanted to say "Yes, I'd love to go to the Winter Formal with you," to lift his spirits and make him feel better, Maylene needed to put herself first no matter what the consequence might be. Her fingers knotted together in front of her as she formulated a response that would hopefully satisfy the both of them...or at least herself despite how selfish that might have sounded.

"Jared...," her soft voice floated like a buoy out at sea that she hoped would not become a tsunami. "I'm flattered by your confession, and the offer, but I'm afraid I'm not ready for a relationship or anything of the sort right now. I'm not going to the Winter Formal anyway either. I hope you understand."

"Oh."

Maylene's heart cracked into pieces when he deflated like a balloon. "I'm sorry," she could not help but apologize, "It's not you. I just wouldn't want anything to do with a relationship in the first place. I'm not ready for something like that."

"Okay, I understand," Jared muttered under his breath, but just loud enough for her to hear. "Why should I expect someone to want to go out with me?" he added on to himself.

"That's...not what I said," she countered with a whisper.

"No, it's okay. I shouldn't have asked if it made you uncomfortable. I'm sorry for wasting your time."

Maylene fought the compassionate tears filling the backs of her eyes. "It's not a waste. I'm sorry for upsetting you."

"It's not your fault," he earnestly replied. "I respect your decision. Thanks for being honest with me."

Maylene's stomach flipped when he whirled around and briskly walked down the hallway in the opposite direction. She could only look at her fingers and fiddle around with the pink nails she had just painted that weekend, peeling off the new polish without remorse. They matched her rosy overalls perfectly, but for once, she did not care. Instead, she continued waiting by the courtyard doors...silent...motionless...until something - or someone - could bring her out of the dumps that Jared unknowingly tossed her into. When confrontations such as these occurred, Maylene often knew not of what to do, instead trusting her gut. This instance was the same. The scales weighed in her favor, but Jared was flung from it. The only emotion harboring in her swirling mind was guilt...and lots of it.

"Maylene?" Before she knew it, Lia was running up to her, concern flooding her gaze. "What's wrong? Why are you crying?"

She was crying? Maylene knew she was holding back tears, but was completely unaware that they seemed to have minds of their own while rolling down her cheeks. Hastily, she wiped them away with the sleeve of the white turtleneck underneath her pink overalls and used all of her emotional willpower to grin. Nevertheless, the remnants on her cheeks along with her quivering bottom lip were dead giveaways to how she was truly feeling on the inside. Maylene sunk into Lia's open arms that wrapped around her.

"Maylene...you can tell me," her friend coaxed her. "If Declan pulled some stunt again, so help me I'll-"

"It wasn't Declan."

"Then who was it?"

Maylene's eyes flitted around to ensure no one was listening before she exhaled, "Jared," she confessed dryly.

"What?!" Lia backpedaled as her gaze snapped to meet Maylene's. "What'd he do? I swear, if he bullied you or did anything rash, I'm going to-"

Maylene held out her hand and Lia stopped. "He asked me out," she explained, "and I said no."

Her friend's eyes bulged from behind her glasses. "He did? Just now?"

"Just now. He asked me to the Winter Formal. I told him I wasn't going anyway because I'd rather stay home."

"Are you okay?" Lia frowned despite the obvious humor in Maylene's statement.

"I just feel awful." Maylene hung her head. "He seemed really upset when he left. I did just reject him, after all."

"I'm proud of you."

"You are?"

"Of course I am." The brunette across from her smiled and wiped any lingering tears from her face. "You stood up for yourself and didn't let yourself be guilted into something you're uncomfortable doing. That makes me so happy. I bet your mom would be proud too."

Maylene returned the first gesture and popped a couple of her knuckles. "You think so?"

"I know so. Now, come on," Lia took a tender hold of her wrist, "lunch might be over by the time we sit down," she joked on the public school scheduling system.

"Right," Maylene added on.

While Lia and Maylene sat down at their usual table and their lunch period together commenced, Jared continued his search for two particular people. Neither of them were in the courtyard - or cafeteria as most students apparently called it - which was a bit of a surprise. Then again, Willow and Rowan did not like to be as social as him. Maybe they had taken their lunch elsewhere. If they left the school premises entirely, then Jared was in big trouble. He did not know the area well at all, which meant he could get lost very easily. Thankfully, though, he stumbled across them in an empty classroom on the second floor. What was not so fortunate, however, was the way he located them: through their roaring argument boiling through the walls.

"You told me that we weren't going to make this a competition," Willow gritted at Rowan, who sat casually on a desk.

"You were the one who made it a competition," Rowan blasted with her arms crossed. "All you want to do is be seen as the perfect "Queen Bee" who everybody loves because of your sugary attitude that's faker than your contact lenses."

"Are you *kidding me*?" Willow's eyes bulged. "You're the one who keeps cheating on assignments and then claiming the work is your own. At least my intelligence is honest."

"At least the only one I'm trying to please is myself."

"You know what? You're right: it's all about you, isn't it?"

"That's not what I said," Rowan retaliated. "Weren't you the one who told us to put ourselves first?"

Willow folded her arms over her chest, her eyes becoming slits. "That's not what *I* said, Smartass. Why don't you take that wit of yours and put it towards something useful?"

"Hey! I'm the only one around here who is staying under the radar."

"You weren't staying under the radar when you bullied that friend of Lia's," the blonde snapped.

"I apologized for it," Rowan began to plead. "I know it was wrong."

"Then why don't you act like it?"

"I'm just trying to get by. I'm not as smart as I thought I was."

Willow, for once, stood taller than the girl across from her. "Getting smarter does *not* mean cheating. If you want to do well, then you work for it like I am. The only reason you're the top of all of your classes is because you cheat. You know it. I know it. Soon enough, the whole school will too. I'm not going to be the one to tell them, but I suggest you get your act together and quit whatever nonsense this is."

"Fine, whatever you say," Rowan grumbled in reply.

Jared picked this time to be good enough as any to push open the door and shut it behind himself as he walked in. "Glad I found you guys before you ripped each other's heads off."

"Since when have you been here?" inquired Rowan, swinging her legs over the floor."

"It's been a few minutes," he admitted, his hands back in his pockets.

Willow noticed his slightly slumped posture. "Is something wrong?"

"Something's wrong." Rowan finally jumped off the desk and approached him. "What's up, Buttercup?"

The annoying, yet playful nickname brought a small smile to his face. "Don't you dare call me "Buttercup" again," he uttered. "Where'd you even come up with that?"

"I heard some geek say it the other day. What's wrong?"

"You don't want to know."

"Yes, we do," Willow backed up Rowan.

Jared hesitated, but made the realization that he was not going to get away with saying nothing. "I asked Maylene out... and she said no."

"What?!" Both girls were inches from a shout. Then, Rowan muttered, "Good for her."

"Excuse me?"

"I said that's good for her," Rowan shamelessly repeated.

The bow's eyebrows lowered into thin lines. "Thanks for making me feel better."

"You're welcome." If it was not any more obvious, Rowan was being sarcastic.

"Come on, guys." Willow stepped in between them. "This is exactly what we need to avoid if we're going to succeed here."

"You keep saying that, but you're the fakest out of all of us." Rowan's pupils pierced into Willow's. "At least we're trying to be like actual human beings rather than being a work machine and wasting your life here on your grades."

"Then how come you want to be the best?"

"I want to prove myself."

"Oh, *please*, you already proved yourself when you rescued that unicorn in fifty AD."

"Girls, stop it," Jared intervened. "This isn't worth it."

"You're one to talk. You're trying to date a *child* and now you're butthurt since she said no."

"That's not what I meant." Jared grew as pale as a ghost.

"Stop it—*stop it!*" Willow held a hand in front of each of them. She gave Jared most of her attention. "I'm sorry it didn't work out, but maybe it's for the best."

"I know," the boy breathed out. "I'm sorry for letting my feelings get in the way."

"I'm sorry for being an idiot," Rowan added without being provoked.

"I guess we're all idiots in this world," Willow comforted the both of them, including herself. "We'll work it out. At least we have money for food now."

"Speaking of which, why aren't we in the lunchroom?" inquired the girl in the maroon hoodie.

All three of their stomachs rumbled in harmony. All Willow could do was chuckle and lead the trio out of the classroom, "I think that speaks for all of us."

The rest of the school day passed in a much tamer fashion than what the morning brought forth. After the final period was dismissed, Lia, Maylene, and Yasmin rushed to the black sedan parked on the curb by the Oakbrooke High entrance where Cheyenne was waiting with the same motherly grin she expressed to her three "daughters" on a daily basis. When she saw the brunette and two mops of ebony approaching, she waved, ecstatic. Lia hopped into the passenger's seat while Maylene and Yasmin slid into the back through the same door.

Wind whisked against the obsidian paint covering Cheyenne's vehicle, threatening to steer it into a different lane as the four ladies spoke vaguely about their day at school. Despite keeping her eyes on the road, Cheyenne was an avid listener. In fact she did most of the talking since the events of their school routine were a tad bit out of order. It was no surprise to anyone that Maylene was the quietest one in the car, listening to the dialogue floating out of three pairs of lips and mixing with the warm air ebbing from the sedan's heating unit. She remained this way even when Mrs. Hart pulled into their driveway and Lia gave both twins a hug before they exited the vehicle. Yasmin despised the lack of a twinkle in her twin's eyes. It had been gone ever since lunch. She fought the urge to ask about Maylene's sudden drop in mood, but never got the opportunity when Lia was not around. Now was her chance, so she took it.

"Okay, what's wrong?"

Maylene blinked to her left, where a skeptical brow was raised. "What do you mean?"

"You know what I mean," Yasmin persisted somehow soothingly. "Come on, May...we have that cool twin psychic sense. What's gotten you all down in the dumps?"

"It's not important."

"If something's bothering you, then it's important." She unlocked the front door using the key in her pocket and let both of them in. "You can tell me."

Maylene's body untensed with relief when the shrilly yipping Zuíhuí's Shih Tzu slid into the foyer. The cacao and white ball of pure fluff balanced on her hind legs to greet each one of the twins, who both returned the pup's affection with scratches behind the ears, belly rubs, and finally, Maylene hoisted Sadie into her arms and allowed the dog to freely lick her face, all the while Yasmin was standing, waiting patiently for Maylene's response. It was at least a moment or two until Maylene realized she could not suck herself out of a confrontation for the second time that day.

"Jared asked me out," she told her sister, "and I said no."

Yasmin's eyes widened. She dropped her backpack by the shoe rack, and when she looked back up, a wide grin was on her face. "I'm proud of you, May!"

"But I upset him."

"It doesn't matter. You stood up for yourself and didn't let yourself get into a situation where you would be uncomfortable."

Maylene continued scratching her dog's chin. "I still hurt his feelings."

"What about *your* feelings?" Yasmin's hand under her blue hoodie ruffled Maylene's hair and strewed her bangs about. "It's like Mom always says: put yourself first and know your worth."

"I guess that's true, but-"

"Enough with the buts! Did you want to go with him?"

Maylene quickly shook her head. "No."

"Would you rather have a movie night and eat a ton of junk food during the Winter Formal?"

"Don't you want to go?"

"I'd rather spend time with you," Yasmin assured her and booped Sadie's nose, "and besides, we went to the Winter Formal last year and it was overrated."

Maylene cracked a smile. "I guess that's true." Her mind flitted back to the memory of countless freshmen running about, tossing and popping balloons every which way, and mainstream music blasting through the gymnasium which had poor acoustics due to the large volume and hard surfaces.

"I think a The Good Surgeon marathon would be appropriate for this occasion," Yasmin suggested with a wink.

Aha! There was a glimmer in her eyes! "I love that show!"

"I know." Yasmin smirked in her direction. "How does that sound?"

"That sounds good to me."

And that was how issues among the Zuíhuí twins were solved ninety-nine percent of the time. No matter the situation, whether it be boy troubles, academic struggles, or - what was most common - lowered self-esteem, Maylene and Yasmin worked it out together. Most things could be solved with quality time and good food, especially if Sadie was right in the middle of it all. While Maylene and Yasmin were like Yin and Yang, they complimented each other perfectly and knew everything about the other.

It might have seemed that the twins never experienced a

single fight, but that was far from the truth. When Maylene and Yasmin were little, they would argue about the smallest of things, whether it be a toy both of them wanted or if one of them was merely annoying the other by their existence. Both girls hastily grew out of their immaturity, though, and were developing into lovely young ladies who adored one another. Rather than being their own entity, they saw themselves as two halves of a whole...two peas in a pod...peanut butter and jelly...well, you get the picture. Either way, Maylene and Yasmin were two completely different women in unique circumstances, but always met in the middle to figure out life together.

That night, Mr. and Mrs. Zuíhuí arrived home from work to a pleasant surprise, but one that was not seldom. Curled on the living room couch into each other on the corner seat were Maylene and Yasmin, each barely awake with a cartoon flickering on the television on low volume. Sadie was snuggled right between them, snoring to her heart's content. Her belly was full of the dinner she had been provided with an hour or two prior. Dinner, which was homemade macaroni and cheese, was sitting in the oven for the family of four to enjoy together.

Just like magic, the Zuíhuí family was threaded together with invisible string, impossible to be broken...but what happened if it began to fray?

Fifteen

It was one thing to be woken up by the same alarm every morning to start the exact same day as the one before with minimal changes sprinkled throughout the usual monotonous routine. Six o'clock in the morning was not a preferable time of day for most high schoolers. Instead, they looked upon it with dread. Every day was the same: roll out of bed, go to school, go home, do homework, jump into bed. Then, the cycle repeated itself leading to the boredom of each child that eventually spiraled into at least one possible mental health dilemma. That was one thing.

The other was being woken up by something licking you all over the face, and no, it was not as weird as it sounded. The subject of said licking was curled up as snug as a bug in a rug in a pastel pink bedspread and fluffy white pillows, and the entity executing said licking was a diminutive Shih Tzu ready to begin the day with the one thing she wanted most: attention. A nest of black hair rested atop the dog's human who desperately did not want to leave her bed, but it looked like it would be inevitable. The girl begrudgingly pried open her eyes and swiped her bangs out of her face. She picked her Shih Tzu, Sadie, up and placed her by the foot of the bed, but not after planting a kiss on the top of her head.

Sadie's tail was nearly invisible as it wagged while Maylene stretched out her arms and forced herself out of bed to face the day ahead. Sadie followed her human's every move as she picked out a set of overalls to wear from her closet along with a white turtleneck, brushed her teeth, and the only thing keeping her out of the shower was the curtain. Sadie waited obediently until Maylene's hair dried with a light pink blow-dryer and she was fully dressed for the day ahead. She then sat down at her white vanity and applied her usual makeup, which was foundation, blush, concealer, bronzer, and mascara. Her straight hair that rested just above her shoulders framed her face with elegance. What was not elegant, though, was Sadie nipping at her heels at every move. Maylene was far from minding, however, she adored her built-in best friend.

Speaking of such "built-in best friends," another teenager stepped out of her half of their room that was filled with more muted colors than Maylene's pink and white. This one seemed to have literally rolled out of bed just a minute prior. Her black hair was tied in a messy bun where loose strands hung around her face. A faded blue hoodie swallowed her and her black leggings up. Other than brushing out her hair, Yasmin - the polar opposite of her twin - was prepared for the day. Maylene offered her a warm smile and a "Good morning" as Yasmin hobbled around her to reach the bathroom they shared.

"Morning!" Yasmin blubbered through a mouthful of toothpaste.

"How'd you sleep?"

"I slept like a newborn baby," her twin mumbled with a full mouth. "How about you?"

"Good until Sadie woke me up," Maylene teased the pup at her feet.

"Someone had to. Your alarm was going off for like ten minutes."

Maylene's cheeks flushed when she realized her phone was still chiming from her pocket. She quickly turned off the soothing sound. "Sorry about that."

"It's alright." Yasmin spat the toothpaste into the sink and rinsed off the brush under the running water.

Maylene hopped down the hallway and towards the kitchen. Rather than the house being filled with chatter from Mr. and Mrs. Zuíhuí, the larger, open concept portion of the building was nothing but echoes ricocheting from each step of her socked feet. A note was left on the marble countertop that Maylene did not hesitate to rush towards and read. It was placed on top of a platter of muffins wrapped in clear plastic wrap.

Hey girls!

Like normal, I had to go into work extra early today to take care of some formalities with a client. I hope these muffins make up for my absence. Chocolate chip is on the left and blueberry is on the right. Have a great day!

Love,
Mom

Maylene smiled at the note and took a pen out of the junk drawer below. She scribbled down a brief "Love you too!" note along with a smiley face and a heart at the bottom of the piece of paper her mom used just before lifting up the plastic wrap and grabbing the nearest blueberry muffin. She opened one of the cabinets near the microwave and put the muffin on a small plate from inside. Lastly, she took a fork from the silverware drawer and peeled back the muffin wrapper, throwing the latter in the trash.

Not even five seconds later, no one other than Yasmin sauntered down the stairs and entered the kitchen. "Ooh, muffins!"

Maylene watched as her sister tore open the wrapping and

grabbed a chocolate chip muffin from the top of the platter. She did not even bother getting a plate and instead ripped the muffin wrapper right off just seconds before taking a giant bite out of the side. Yasmin lazily tossed the muffin wrapper into the trash and practically consumed her muffin in three bites. On the contrary, Maylene picked through her muffin with a fork and took sensible bites rather than devouring the whole thing in less than a minute. It came to Yasmin's attention that Maylene was going through her morning routine slower than usual. Something was up and Yasmin was well aware of Maylene's nervosity.

"What's wrong, May?" Yasmin swallowed down her muffin.

Maylene continued tying her shoes. "Nothing's wrong, really. I just want to go back to bed."

"I understand that." Yasmin knelt down after sliding on her own shoes, "but you always seem like you're ready for the day in the morning. What gives?"

Maylene kept her mouth clamped shut. She finished tying a perfect bow on each of her sneakers and held up her legs to make sure they both were the same size. She then sat up straight and took another bite out of her muffin from the fork she was using. Her phone, which was sitting face-up on the kitchen table, pinged with a notification. Instinctively, she brushed her bangs out of her eyes and checked the notification. She never got tired of seeing Lia's name followed by a hug emoji and a green heart pop up on her screen. Maylene typed in her passcode and read the message waiting for her in her inbox.

"*Good morning! We'll be on our way over at the usual time. Are you still okay to go to school today?*"

Yasmin's statement reflected Lia's as she remarked, "You know, you could always play hooky if you don't want to go to school."

"I'll be alright," Maylene replied, startled by the sudden overlapping of agreement. "I just don't want to face Jared right away, you know?"

"Yeah, I know. People really suck, but if you want, I can stick by you and Lia today instead of hanging out with my friends," Yasmin offered. Despite being high up on the social ladder, she always made room for her sister right next to her who quickly shook her head.

"No, you don't have to do that."

"Jared's a regular in my group now," she informed her quieter sister. "I don't want to hang out with someone who upset you like that."

"He was just disappointed because I declined his offer."

"I know, but anybody who upsets my little sister won't get away with it."

Maylene cracked a smile. "Yas…you're only seven minutes older than me."

"So?" Yasmin grinned right back. "Still older."

"That's true."

Maylene looked down at her phone where another message had appeared on the open screen: *"I know you've read my message—are you okay?"*

"Yeah, I'm okay," Maylene typed back, her brows furrowed. *"How'd you know I read your message, though?"*

"Your read receipts were on, Silly!" Lia was quick to reply. *"Now, are you going to school or not? Totally understand if you want to stay home."*

"Is that Lia?" Yasmin inquired, to which Maylene nodded. "Figured. Is she saying exactly what I said about staying home?"

"Pretty much."

"And that's why I love that little Stinker."

"Does Lia know you call her that?" Maylene's grin increased in size.

Yasmin quickly shook her head in denial. "Oh, hell no. If she did, I'd be long dead."

"Yes, you would." Maylene typed her response to Lia and sent it before she could back down. *"I'm going. See you when you get here! :)"* Then, she gave Yasmin a wicked glance while typing something else: *"Also, did you know Yasmin calls you a little Stinker?"*

"She does what?!"

"May...what did you just do?" Yasmin tentatively asked.

Maylene just shook her head and smirked. "You'll see."

Meanwhile, at the Harts' household, Cheyenne was just handing Lia the keys as the girl was making her way outside and towards the black sedan parked in the driveway. The front door closed behind both of them to welcome a thankfully sunny, but chilly atmosphere. The breeze nipped at her nose as she put her backpack in the trunk to make room for the twins who would soon occupy the backseat. Lia climbed into the driver's seat while her mother sat anxiously in the passenger's seat. She still was not used to her daughter driving.

Lia inserted the key into the ignition, turned it sideways, and then buckled her seat belt in unison with her mother. "Ready?"

"Ready," Cheyenne replied, albeit unsteady.

Lia eased the black sedan out of the driveway subsequent to looking both ways behind her and then steered it down the familiar roadways of Elwood Manor. She steered the vehicle down the side street just like every day and pulled into what appeared to be a stony cottage but in reality, it was the Zuíhuís' home. Once she pulled into the driveway and shifted the vehicle's gear into "Park," Lia took her phone out of her pocket and sent both girls a text in the group chat the three of them shared.

"I'm here!"

It did not take very long at all for both twins to burst out the front door. Yasmin took the lead down the porch steps while Maylene locked the door behind them and kept the key in her pocket. She was regarded to be the more responsible one out of the two, so her mother instructed her to keep a hold of the spare front door key. Yasmin was prone to misplacing numerous items–the weirdest being a pair of underwear that somehow ended up on one of the blades of her ceiling fan. The only reason she found it was the fact she turned the fan on earlier in the semester and the underwear went flying towards the window. As soon as the girl in question reached the hood of the car, Lia pressed down on the horn, which blared at the top of its lungs and caused both her target and her mother to flinch, the latter out of her seat. Cheyenne was not happy with the way the seat belt locked around her body.

"Ophelia!" Mrs. Hart used the full name card on her daughter. "What was that for?"

"Just a prank," Lia grinned at her mother.

Yasmin got on one side of the back seat, followed by Maylene on the other. The former glared at her twin. "You told her, didn't you?!"

"I did," Maylene innocently grinned.

Lia turned around to face the twins, but mainly Yasmin. "That's what you get for calling me a little Stinker," she teased. "Anyways, good morning."

Now, that was one way to start a morning. What happened next would catch everyone off guard, including the girl who initiated it in the first place. Lia, Maylene, and Yasmin bid farewell to Cheyenne just before they shut each of the three doors and ventured off into Oakbrooke High School just like every weekday. Then, just like clockwork, as soon as Yasmin made sure that Maylene was okay with Lia, she spotted her group of friends and scurried after them. That left Maylene and Lia all to their "lonesome" which Maylene was not too distraught about. No matter how much she loved her sister, sometimes, but very rarely, the girl tended to get on her nerves.

Eventually, after Ceramics class - where they spent their time playing games on their phones since they had finished their final projects - Lia and Maylene parted their separate ways to their second block classes. The morning went on as usual–the mundane routine was endured without a hitch. The only possible hiccup was the possibility of encountering a certain black-haired boy in the halls or the courtyard during lunch. No matter what, though, Maylene promised herself that she was not alone, that she had Lia and Yasmin by her side to back her up if she needed it. Deep down, she knew she did the right thing by following her boundaries, but what price would she need to pay for the exchange? Everything came with some sort of a catch, and Lia was about to reel it in.

The scene began in a typical Physical Education session with Coach Jenkins–the female one, of course, who loudly announced the next course of action: "Time for laps!" she bellowed upon the class. "What are you all waiting for? Let's move!"

Begrudgingly, the large class did just as she said. Maybe they all were goodie-goodies; maybe, frankly, they were frightened of her. No matter how short in stature she was, being about as small as Lia, even the strongest of boys followed her every command, which included Jared. Unsurprisingly, he led the pack with ease. Underneath his white t-shirt, his muscles flexed as he jogged, barely breaking a sweat. Lia had to blink thrice and shake her head to turn her attention elsewhere. Well…not exactly. You see, her focus was meant to be centered on Jared in the first place. This was just for research…yeah… "Research" was undoubtedly the right word for it.

Lia never found it easy to catch up to Jared, but when the situation was dire, she knew she had the willpower in her. She used it to her advantage to pedal herself forward. While her eyes were fixated on the boy at the front of the group, Lia began to pass each student one by one, which was a feat for someone who was not athletically inclined. Ten seconds passed…then twenty…then thirty…and then an entire minute until she eventually was just a mere foot or two behind her target. Lia attempted to clear her throat to gain his attention, but while doing so, the steady flow of oxygen flooded out of her lungs and she burst into a coughing fit. While her chest ached as she struggled to catch her breath, Jared turned around mid-stride. Huh. It worked.

"Lia?" he inquired and slowed down.

Lia's legs throbbed to keep up with his pace. "The one and only," she grinned loopily.

"...Are you alright?"

"Yep." Lia forced herself along. "What's up?"

"I'm just running, I guess," Jared stated the obvious.

"Well done, Sherlock."

An eyebrow raised. "Sherlock?"

"Oops...he probably doesn't even know who that is." Lia shook her head. "Never mind. I wanted to talk to you about something if that's okay."

"Sure, I guess, but—"

Coach Jenkins' whistle blew again. "Alright, class–take five! We'll be playing a game of dodgeball after you all have caught your breath."

Jared grew silent while he and Lia walked over to a set of bleachers where they kept their water. Lia picked up her green canteen and gulped down at least two mouthfuls of water while Jared barely had to take a sip out of his plastic water bottle. Lia often caught herself wondering how in the world he could be so athletic, but - once again - it would hit her that he was literally built to exhibit feats of strength. Lia was unsure of how something like that worked, but the answer was quite literally out of this world. Once she swallowed her final gulp of water, Lia bit the bullet and initiated conversation.

"Maylene told me what happened."

Jared narrowly avoided choking on his own saliva. "She did?"

"Yeah," Lia admitted, fiddling around with the pockets in her drawstring shorts. "I don't mean to get in the middle or anything, but I know you liked her and I wanted to make sure you were okay."

"I'm fine," he replied rather stoically.

"You look a little drained if you ask me," she countered without even realizing it. When Jared's brows shot up, she corrected herself. "I mean, you look fine, but I've noticed you seem a lot less like yourself."

"I guess I'm not used to any sort of rejection."

"That's okay. Usually people my - *our* - age have already had their first date or something like that. I haven't. Maybe you have, but we can be alone together."

"Alone together?" Jared quizzically questioned. "Is that even a thing?"

"It is now." Lia wanted to stuff her head in the floor like an ostrich to avoid further embarrassment.

"Where are you going with this?"

"...*Where am I going with this?*" she asked herself, but her mouth expressed a thought she had in the middle of AP Chemistry instead, "Hey, I have an idea."

Jared lazily leaned against the bleachers. "What's that?"

"What if we went to the Winter Formal together?" Lia then realized how forward her question sounded when he lurched upright. "As friends. I mean, I know I'm not who you wanted to go with. If you don't want to, that's fine, but it might be fun... you know what I mean?"

"I guess so," he replied a bit more than half-heartedly... maybe two-thirds-heartedly, perhaps?

"The Formal is two weeks from Friday," Lia informed him of something he probably already knew. "Why don't you think about it and let me know? I do *not* want to wear a dress, though."

"Then wear a suit," he shrugged nonchalantly.

"Wait...that's not such a bad idea." Her eyes lit up at the thought.

Jared cracked a smile. "I'll let you know by Friday."

"Friday," Lia agreed. By his expression, she already knew his answer would be a yes.

With one problem being resolved came another: how in the world would Lia find something to wear? She was completely and utterly broke!

Sixteen

"Thanks again for letting me get this, Mom," Lia expressed her gratitude, "I'm still surprised you didn't ask as many questions as you usually do."

Cheyenne replied from the hallway, "You're welcome, Sweetie. I know you hate dresses, so this is a great alternative. You're still wearing your hair down, right?"

"Only because you're making me." Lia tucked a white undershirt into her dress pants. "If I had it my way, I would've put it in a ponytail."

"But your hair is so beautiful down," protested her mother. "It'll compliment your outfit."

"Or you don't want me to look like a dude."

"That too."

"Mom!" She pulled on the matching blazer and left it unbuttoned except for one in the center. "Why does it matter?"

"It doesn't, Honey. Never mind. Are you almost ready?"

Lia hastily brushed out her hair and let it flow behind her as she walked towards the door and opened it. "Yeah, I'm ready."

Mrs. Hart could not contain her smile when her daughter emerged from her room. Lia was dapper from head to toe in a pair of dark green dress pants and a matching blazer along with the white undershirt underneath. She wore opaque pantyhose underneath her pants and black flats to compliment the rims of her glasses. Her wavy hair hung loosely past her shoulders with some strands astray. The golden Ring the Enchantress had given her still rested on her left-hand ring finger. Cheyenne leaned forward and, to her daughter's dismay, began picking through her hair to fix the loose bits.

"Mom!"

"Oh, Honey, you look beautiful!" she gushed, caressing her cheek. "I do think maybe a little bit of makeup would make your face pop even more."

"No, thank you," Lia denied her request.

"Please?" Cheyenne began to beg. "I've always wanted to have an excuse to put makeup on you–not even Picture Day was good enough."

Eventually, the teenager just shook her head. "Alright, Mom. Just…don't go nuts."

That was all Cheyenne needed to hear before she darted into the master bedroom and came back with her extensive makeup kit. All Lia could do was follow her mother's lead and sit down on her desk chair while the ecstatic woman began to apply more-than minimal makeup to her daughter's face. She used foundation, concealer, bronzer, powder, blush, mascara, a brow pencil, and, for the finishing touch, delicately winged eyeliner. Despite not wanting too much on her face, Lia sucked up her complaints and allowed her mom to have her moment.

"You have no idea how excited I am for you, Darling," Cheyenne beamed with pride while assessing her work. "My, you look so beautiful."

Lia hated how itchy her face was with the extra products, but smiled anyway and peered at herself in the mirror. "Thanks, Mom. You did a great job."

"Thank you, Honey." Lia's mom brushed her daughter's hair

out of her face. "Can I get a picture of you before you leave?" She yanked her phone out of her pocket. "You just look so lovely that I can't help myself..."

All she could do was agree. "Alright, Mom, you win..."

Once more, Cheyenne did, in fact, "win." She dragged Lia down the stairs and towards the Christmas tree which was somehow still up after nearly a month post-holiday and posed her in front of it. Lia stood awkwardly with her fern green suit that blended in with the faux tree branches behind her. Ornaments were strewn every which way among the tree's surface, some being memorabilia from her first few Christmases, some handmade, and others collected from different places and from family members over the years. Lia knotted her fingers together and stood up tall while her mother took several pictures with her phone camera.

"Oh, Honey, these are gorgeous!" Cheyenne exclaimed. "Turn a bit to your right and then look at me."

Lia did as she said and her mother took a few more pictures. "Perfect! Thank you."

"You're welcome," Lia exhaled with a smile.

"You ready to go, Kiddo?" Lucas slipped on his pair of checkered Vans and grabbed his keys off the rack by the front door.

"Yep!" Lia stood on her tiptoes and hugged her mother as tightly as she could. "Thank you for doing my makeup. Can you send me those pictures?"

"Of course." Cheyenne squeezed her back. "Have a great time and text if you need anything. I love you."

"Love you too!"

Lucas held the front door open for Lia, who eagerly trotted through and approached her father's vehicle, which was a small smokey gray truck just big enough for two people and a place to store belongings in the back that was directly in front of the bed. Lia was not used to riding in her father's truck, but it was always a unique experience. She would never admit it, but her father's driving made her feel safer than her mother's. As she buckled her seat belt, Lucas turned the key sideways into the ignition and let his beauty roar to life. The radio was turned to the regular 1980's station that her father always listened to except in December, when Christmas music would take the reins. Lia sat quietly with her hands folded in her lap, just waiting for her dad to begin interrogating her.

Sure enough, he did just that: "So, Maylene isn't coming tonight?"

"No," Lia replied, looking out the window.

"What about Yasmin?" Lucas put his hand on the passenger's seat and craned his neck around to see while backing out of the driveway.

"Nope."

"So, you're going alone?"

"No, I'm meeting someone there."

"Oh?" Her father was instantly suspicious. "Who is it?"

"Oh, boy... Here it goes..." Lia cracked her knuckles and dropped the bomb: "I'm meeting my friend Jared."

Silence. That was not a very good sign. She gulped down a bullet of anxiety shooting up her throat when his knuckles paled against the steering wheel. Lia bit her lip and thought she tasted blood for a moment. Simultaneously, she did and did not want her father to speak up about the decision she had made when it came to the Winter Formal. This was the first time she had ever gone somewhere with a boy...let alone being by herself.

"Lia, does this Jared boy treat you with respect?" Lucas finally spoke up.

Lia made herself look at his driving figure as the truck rounded a corner. "Of course, Dad. I wouldn't be associated with him if he didn't."

"That's my girl," he proudly smirked at the road ahead. "I trust you, but I don't trust guys your age. They're-"

"Indecent pigs," Lia butted in.

"Well, that too, but I was going to go with "Morons" instead." Lucas pulled into the parking lot and steered his truck to the curb. He spotted a certain boy in a black tuxedo and hair to match waiting by the front doors. "Is that him?"

Lia squinted and then nodded. "Yeah, that's Jared."

"I hope you know I'm going to give him a talking-to."

"Dad!"

Lucas adjusted the gear into "Park" and unlocked the doors. "I have to, Lia. You're my little girl and I'd rather be in a ditch somewhere than let my daughter get hurt by some idiot."

"Dad..."

"I'll be nice," he vowed with a grin. "Promise."

Lia merely shook her head and got out of the car. She waved to Jared, whose gaze shot up when she exclaimed, "Hey!"

"Hi, Lia," Jared replied, but then noticed her father behind her. "Hi...Lia's dad."

"Hello, Jared." Lucas stepped towards the "teenager" and shook his hand firmer than he needed to. "I trust you'll take good care of Lia tonight."

"*Dad*, we're just going as friends," Lia leaned over to him and gritted out.

Lucas elbowed her in retaliation.

"Yes, of course, Sir." Jared nodded no matter how off-kilter he was caught. "I promise she will be safe and have a wonderful time tonight."

Lia cringed at the sugar dribbling off his tongue. "So, Dad, I think the dance ends at eleven. Can you pick me up then?" she interrupted the moment.

"I'll be here at eleven. Text if you need anything." Lucas wrapped his arms around his daughter and kissed the top of her head.

"I will." Lia hugged him back with just as much enthusiasm despite the blood rushing to her cheeks. "Thanks for the ride."

"You're welcome. Love you, Kiddo."

"Love you too, Dad."

Lia was very much aware of the fact her father would not leave until she was safely in the building, so while Lucas got back into his truck, she gestured for Jared to follow her into the school where the doors were - like usual - propped open. There were signs taped on the walls leading to the gymnasium, but Lia was far from needing them. She knew this school like the back of her hand, which did not have much to remember anyway except for the fact it had five fingers as it should.

"You look very nice," Jared complimented her out of the blue to break the silence.

"Thank you." Lia smiled in his direction while the two of them walked down the hallway. "So do you. Where'd you get the tux?"

"I rented it."

"It looks brand new!"

"I got a high quality one."

A frown dotted her lips with guilt. "You didn't have to do that."

"It's a dance, isn't it?" Jared could not help but smirk as he held open the gymnasium door for her. "Besides, I hardly ever get an excuse to dress up."

"Me either, but I hate dressing up–and thanks." Lia stepped through the frame.

"You're welcome."

At once, both Lia and Jared were metaphorically teleported into a different world. It was as if they stepped through a portal from a tranquil oasis to the swirling sands of chaos that was the Winter Formal. The lights above were dimmed and instead replaced with strobe lights illuminating the room with a rainbow of hues. A disc jockey was located on the far side from the entrance playing the most relevant upbeat tunes that every individual in the room knew...everyone except for Jared. When Lia looked over, he was scrunching down in his suit. Out of instinct, Lia grasped onto his hand, which was colder than she thought it would be, and squeezed it to get his attention.

"Are you okay?" she inquired when he looked her way.

Jared nodded and fixed his collar. "Yeah, I'm fine. I've just never been to one of these…things before. What do you even do here?"

"Well, you dance." Lia then took a hold of both hands and dragged him out onto the dance floor. "Come on!"

"I guess I don't have a choice-"

Jared surely did not have a choice. Lia began tossing her arms back and forth with Jared's hands in hers as well as stepping around in random patterns. Clearly, she had no idea what she was doing during such an upbeat song. Neither did Jared, to be perfectly frank. Instead, he followed her lead and occasionally spun her around while she giggled nonstop either at herself or the situation she had put both of them in. The platonic couple was surrounded by at least a hundred teenagers doing the exact same thing: improvising. Some groups made a dance circle with different people freestyling in the middle. That was exactly where Lia took Jared next.

"What is this?" Jared had to shout over the music.

"A dance circle!" Lia yelled back while watching a boy dance way too freely for wearing a tuxedo. "People take turns making stuff up."

"Sounds like you'd be good at that."

"No, I wouldn't."

"Let's see, shall we?"

Lia had no time to respond. As soon as the center of the circle had cleared up, Jared pushed Lia into it. She whirled around to see the boy himself offer her a wide, gleeful grin at the chaos he had just caused. Lia was as still as a statue, but that did not last for long. She knew one dance move that her father taught her from an early age. With her heart pounding in her chest, Lia dashed forward, made sure her back was facing the majority of the circle, and began to flawlessly moonwalk just like Michael Jackson did in the 1980's at his concerts during a certain song. Unfortunately, that was not what was playing on the turntables, but Lia adjusted her strides to fit with the beat. She added a three hundred and sixty degree spin - which was a bit flimsy - at the end and trotted off as the circle began cheering for the girl they hardly knew. Lia could not help but smirk when Jared blankly blinked in her direction.

"Was that successful or were they just giving you moral support?" he teased despite being proven wrong.

Lia whacked him on the back of the head. "Oh, shut up."

After watching others brave the social anxiety that the dance circle brought forth, the disc jockey switched songs from being upbeat to slow. As several people around them paired into couples, Jared awkwardly offered Lia his hand, which was the opposite of what she expected. Instead of chickening out like her mind desperately wanted her to do, she accepted his offer, took his hand, and allowed him to lead her into the midst of the dancing couples and the occasional circle of girls who did not have dates. Lia, for once, had a date, and no matter whether it was platonic or not, she was having the time of her life. Lia wished she could wash away the butterflies in her stomach as Jared placed one hand around her waist and one in her hand. She had never slow danced before, but she guessed Jared had before since he led both of them along in one fluid motion.

"You know how to dance?" Lia's words echoed her thoughts.

"Of course," he shrugged as if her question was outlandish. "I was taught how when I was...little. It's been a while since I've actually been able to execute it."

"Sorry I didn't wear a dress," she laughed. "It might be a little awkward to see two people in suits dancing."

"What's awkward about that?" He cocked a brow. "I don't mind."

Lia's complexion burned red. "You know...I know we came here as friends, but I'm having a great time. Thanks for coming with me."

"You're welcome. Thank you for asking me." To her surprise, Jared smiled.

Lia thought nothing - or, at least, tried not to - of her silly crush until that moment. Right then and there, the room was empty…silent…motionless. Everything around them disappeared. Lia willed her emotions to leave her like they were demons being exorcized from her body. Out of anyone, she could not be falling head over heels for *him*. This was a mistake and she knew it, which was why she refused to act upon the drive deep down in her chest just begging for her to stand on her tiptoes and connect their lips. *No.* This was not happening. Whatever temptation floating in her mind needed to be whisked away somehow…some way…but Lia was at a loss. All she could do was remain in the moment and enjoy it as much as she could because it was not going to last between them.

Jared was an enigma of some sort because Lia had no idea in the slightest about how he was feeling. While seeming fully encaptured in their dance, his eyes would occasionally flit upwards or in different directions. Something seemed to distract him, but Lia was unaware of what. Neither did anyone around them, it seemed…at least until the object Jared was focusing on unhitched from the ceiling with a monumental creak and was hurtling straight for himself and Lia. At the sound, Lia's gaze snapped upwards to see one of the massive ventilation pipes growing larger as each second passed. Once again, Lia was frozen. Her train of thought derailed as she let go of Jared's hands and her breathing became heavier. Instead of pushing her out of the way of the falling object, amidst the screaming attendees, Jared stood over Lia and caught the pipe before it could hit anyone in the room. The dance floor was cleared. The music by the disc jockey was halted, leaving Jared - with his inhuman strength - on full display.

This time, the room was silent for real–not just in Lia's imagination. She snapped back to reality as hundreds of pairs of eyes were staring directly at the middle of the gymnasium where both of them stood. She watched sweat begin to bead on Jared's forehead. He knew he had made a ginormous mistake by revealing his abilities to the non-magical world. Jared slowly bent down and placed the pipe on the gymnasium floor since he could not make it disappear no matter how much he wanted it to. Lia hated the way his eyes widened with pure fear and how he felt the need to flee the room entirely. Lia stood, watching, as he sprinted from his spot through the double doors and away from the incident that was brought forth.

No matter how much her heart battered against her chest, trying to force her to remain put along with the rest of the student body, Lia's legs carried her forward into a brisk dash. She raced after Jared, who was several steps ahead of her, but she imagined he had gone outside. The twisting and turning halls became a labyrinth, even more so than her head had developed into. She pushed through the double doors and was met with a gust of wind smacking her in the face. Lia pried her eyes open and searched for Jared, but he was long out of sight. Lia knew he could not have gone too far, especially in such a short amount of time. Lia began rushing around the school's premises, starting at the courtyard but then working her way out. She was beginning to lose hope as her limbs ached as much as her heart did. She was surprised that no one else thought to look for Jared, especially after the display in the gymnasium.

The final spot Lia decided to search was the football field. She had no clue why she did not pick this spot first, because there he was, seated on the third bleacher from the bottom on the home side. Lia shivered from the January air nipping at her nose and bit the bullet. Within the next few steps, Jared knew she was there despite her suit blending in with the night sky above. Only one of the floodlights was on over the field since there was not a game going on. Instead, it illuminated the very spot Jared was seated, creating a hazy glow. Lia stepped into the light, but Jared did not even look at her. Instead, he picked at one of his fingernails with disdain.

"Jared?" she softly spoke up. "Are you alright?"

Jared shook his head and did not speak. Lia chose her words

carefully. How was he supposed to know she knew about his special ability unless she told him? Would notifying her of her awareness cause a rift in their friendship? There was no going back, especially since Lia had no clue what she was doing, or how a Mêla would act to their deepest secret being revealed. Then again, if Jared was this upset, he knew she knew as well as the rest of the school. He had made a mistake and now he was going to suffer the consequences.

"Jared, I know you have inhuman strength," Lia confessed before she could stop herself. "I know you're not from this world. I know you're from a realm called Kythaela and there's eleven more of you called the Mêla. I know you-"

With every word, Jared's complexion grew paler. He rose from his seat, leaped over the bleachers, hurdled towards Lia, and smacked his hand over her mouth. "How in the hell would you know that?"

"Jared, I-" her frightened voice squeaked.

"You knew this the entire time and didn't think to say anything?" Jared's hand clamped over her mouth and nose tighter, which began to obstruct her breathing. "Were you a spy? How *dare* you walk amongst us and pretend to be oblivious. You heard our conversation outside the library. I know it. You knew it all."

Lia's lungs began to burn for oxygen. With shaking hands, she reached up to try to pry her face free from Jared's grasp, all the while pleading, "No, let me explain-"

"I can't believe you did this to us!" Jared roared as she struggled against him. "You lied to us, befriended us, and for what? Your own personal gain? You are *pathetic*, Lia, thinking you can take advantage of something you know nothing about."

"*No*! I know enough. Stay away from me and my kinship, or so help me, I'll-"

Jared stopped short when from a certain angle, the light from above bounced off of the Ring on Lia's left hand. It was right in front of his face–the final piece to the puzzle. At once, he released his grip on Lia and allowed her to wrench herself away from him, resulting in her toppling on the concrete spluttering and gasping for air. Lia held a hand - her left hand - tenderly over her chest as she gradually regained her composure. Brown hair stuck to her face from sweat and the hand that caught herself was scuffed with a minimal scrape. Jared could not keep his eyes off of the girl on the ground. When he stepped forward to help her up, Lia desperately scrambled backwards, her chest heaving up and down with nothing but fear.

"I know who gave you that Ring," he breathed in shock.

Lia gulped down a wave of anxiety. "You do?" her voice wavered.

"I do. My good friend gave it to you" Jared took a step back and knelt down in shame. "My deepest apologies for mistrusting you, Lia."

"I-...It's okay, but..." Lia knew she needed to be honest, "that really scared me..."

The boy hung his head low to avoid her glistening eyes. "I know, and I understand if I can never win back your trust."

Lia sat cross-legged across from Jared, who refused to look her way. "The Enchantress gave me a mission, and that was to meet all Three of the Earth Wing. Kythaela is *dying* without the twelve of you together. You, Willow, and Rowan need to come back and help restore it. People will *die* if you don't."

"You don't understand. The Fire Wing has taken our harmony away from us and there's nothing we can do to get it back."

"Have you seriously lost all hope?"

Jared's own eyes possessed a sheen of tears overlaying his dilated pupils. "There's nothing we can do," he repeated solemnly. "Believe me... When we were abandoned, our Kingdom fell into destruction. We were forced out never to return."

"By whose orders?" Lia questioned in a firmer tone which grasped his eyes and ears. "Who says you can't go back and make things right? The Enchantress and I want to help your realm. Even though I've only heard from Her one time, I know She doesn't want Kythaela to die. I don't either, especially since I know three of my friends are from it."

"You consider us friends?"

"Is that all you got from that?" Lia joked, but nodded. "Yes, I consider you friends, but you really should think about this," she persuaded. "Without you Three, Kythaela is destined to fall."

"I know that," he whispered tentatively, "but I don't think I have the strength to do it."

It was time for more teasing. "Seriously? You don't think you're strong enough yet you almost just suffocated me to death easily?" When Jared merely stared at her, she winced. "What? Too soon?"

"Very much so."

"But seriously, you're stronger than you think you are. Can you at least consider it?"

It took a long moment for Jared to eventually nod and say, "Yes, I can consider it. What should I tell the girls, though?"

"Let me tell them on my own," Lia requested in a rush, however, she settled down quickly. "You're the first to know. I don't want them to have similar reactions."

"If you want any help, just let me know."

A wide smile developed on Lia's face. "Does this mean you're in?"

The gears turned wildly in Jared's mind. One minute, he was pretending to be a normal high schooler attending classes and receiving terrible grades but somehow managing to pass. The next, he had been found out by a girl only a mere fraction of his age but with intelligence beyond her years. Guilt had clouded Jared's view for an immeasurable amount of time, but just then, that proved to be wrong. The hourglass was running out and Jared needed to come to the terms that there was nothing he could do about it. Just like he had done on the dance floor, Lia offered him his hand, right there by the bleachers, as a symbolic gesture that she was not going to abandon him like the Fire Wing did. She knew he was afraid, and - in a way - she was too. Reluctantly, Jared leaned forward, took her hand, and looked her in the eyes with a ginger smile.

"I'm in."

Seventeen

The Saturday morning air was nothing but tranquil, only filled with the rumbling of cars against asphalt and birds chirping on power lines overhead. Mid-Winter snow sizzled and fizzed away into dew on the blades of grass throughout every yard in Elwood Manor. Only puddles surrounding minimal patches of frost every few yards remained. Misty clouds wisped around the late morning sun beaming down to shed light on the city of Oakbrooke. Being in such a state was nothing short of magical. Near the beginning, Lia never would have believed it as such, but after witnessing it firsthand, she was able to pinpoint small bits and pieces of it in her everyday life.

There, on the damp redwood deck on the top stair, sat the girl herself. She either ignored the way an occasional droplet of water would soak through her black leggings and onto her skin, or she chose not to mind it. Resting upon her lap was the white guitar previously residing on her wall, hung sturdily with a hook. Her right hand rested over the tortoise maroon pickguard adorned with a dove and floral outlines while the fingers of her left held down certain strings for her other one to pluck. A graceful melody emitted from the instrument's wooden body.

CHAPTER SEVENTEEN 215

The rosewood capo clamping the third fret pitched the original sound three half-steps up. Lia hardly found the fog clouding her glasses to be an inconvenience. She could play this instrument blindfolded. Her head hung back with ecstasy, as if each note brought her the utmost pleasure, and in a way, it was. The very concept of making an inanimate object sing was something Lia was endlessly grateful to possess the talent for.

In another type of way, nature provided the accompaniment, as if they were an orchestra of their own. Birds chirped in the distance despite the cold. In a tree in the far corner of the backyard, a squirrel carried several acorns in his mouth that he had received from his stash that he had created earlier in the year. A gray rabbit or two hopped through the grass as if their feet were too delicate to touch the snow before crawling under the fence into the next-door neighbor's lawn. Lia smiled at the swing attached to a tall branch of the very tree the squirrel disappeared up. She remembered when her father first installed it on her ninth birthday. Despite hardly using it, the wooden swing attached to the branch with rope was a fond memory of hers.

This, the world around her, was what magic was to Lia now. It was not in the extraordinary things, but rather the ordinary. The little things were what made life so grand: the animals living their lives, snow melting to make way for an eventual Spring– the very existence of it all was nothing short of impossible. Lia shifted the capo up a fret, making the strings a half step higher still, and began to play a different melody in a more upbeat key. With this improvisation, Lia began to include delicate percussion against the top - and thickest - string with her thumb. With each chord change, Lia made sure to incorporate at least some sort of meter with her right hand, which was now multitasking.

Her intricate melody weaved itself into the world around her for what seemed like an eternity, but in a harsh reality, it was not for long. Just like on the evening of her sixteenth birthday, a breeze from out of nothingness whisked in the center of the backyard, gradually creating a tornado-like funnel. Lia's attention altered from the instrument in her lap to the blinding white orb that was conjured right in the middle of the oddity in the weather pattern. This time, however, she did not scream. Instead, Lia delicately rested her guitar against one of the railing pillars at the edge of the deck, and reluctantly rose to her feet. No matter how unsettled she was, Lia knew that this had happened before, and not long ago. The wind picked up speed while the spherical object morphed itself into the figure of a Woman in white–the same Woman who appeared in her bedroom that fateful night. The light never disappeared entirely, but instead harbored itself around the woman's tall frame. She approached Lia with swanlike elegance in the strides of Her bare feet.

"Lia." Her pale lips parted to lace the teenager's name together in a greeting.

Lia resented the way her mouth opened and closed like a goldfish. Despite this happening before, déjà vu failed to influence her senses. "...Hello," she uttered out.

"I see you have embarked upon a sizable leap in your journey," the Enchantress recollected the events of the past evening.

"I guess so," replied Lia, subconsciously ensuring her posture was built upon. "How do you know that?"

The Woman's smile did not quite reach her eyes. "I've been watching you, and you have come a long way in such a short time."

"Then why do you seem so…insincere?" the girl took a step back with her suspicion.

"I suppose I've become too transparent too soon, my dear." In the Enchantress' voice resided an undertone of uncertainty… vulnerability. Whatever it was, Lia did not like it–not one bit. "I'm afraid you might be treading on ice too thin to hold your weight."

Lia joked to break the metaphorical ice in her words. "Are you calling me fat?"

"Not at all, my dear," the Woman chuckled when She noticed

her smirk, but Her demeanor became solidified. "I'm merely concerned by how you are going about with getting each of the Earth Wing to be on your side."

"...What do you mean?" Lia's face fell.

The Enchantress appeared to be uncomfortable by the abrupt information that was clouding the tension between Herself and the mere child in front of Her. Putting pressure on such a young human being was nothing but harmful, but She knew that it was something that needed to be done. She offered Lia a weak smile, which only made the brunette's nerves worsen. Did she do something wrong when communicating with three people she hardly knew? Was becoming friends with them something she was not supposed to do? She watched the Enchantress with a wary gaze, awaiting the words that were about to fall out of Her mouth.

"I admire your compassion and straightforwardness when it comes to interactions with the Earth Wing, but forming Earthly relationships with them can bring more harm than good."

Lia's mind spiraled to the Winter Formal the previous night. Had she gotten too close to Jared? Was the relationship she was forming with him too much for him to bear? "Are you talking about the dance last night?" she bravely inquired.

"Yes. Indeed I am." The Woman brushed Her alabaster hair behind Her ear.

"What did I do wrong?" The anxiety injected itself into her veins and circled around her body as if it was her blood itself. "I'm trying my best to make all Three of them feel welcome and accepted here. I don't know what else I'm supposed to do."

"That is a very noble thing, Lia, however-"

Lia began to fret wildly, "I hope I'm doing enough to help them feel like they matter. I want to be their friend–really, I do. I just don't know what I could be doing wrong to screw this entire thing up. It's hard enough that an entire world hangs in the balance, but having the scales in my hands only makes matters worse."

"Enough!" The Enchantress held up Her hand to stop her exceeding ranting.

"Sorry," Lia squeaked.

"That's quite alright." The Woman then floated up the stairs and sat down on the top plank. She patted a spot next to Her for Lia to sit down, so she did. She looked the teenager in the eyes with a sincere gaze. "Lia, I commend you for your kindness towards the Earth Wing. You are doing just that - making them feel accepted - but that is the very problem at stake."

"...Problem?"

"Yes, Lia. The compassion you are offering them might make them not want to return to Kythaela at all. Your gentleness is hitting them right where they are the most vulnerable. None of them have been on their own before. This is their chance to feel liberated–to be what they have always wanted to be, but that simply cannot happen. Not at this juncture."

Lia's eyebrows lowered as she scowled. "You know...when you say it like that, it kind of sounds like you're being a bit of a jerk. No offense."

The Enchantress once again found her statement amusing. "None taken, and I understand what you are saying, but in order for our realm to be built back to what it once was, we need their help: all Three of them."

"Okay, okay, I get it, but...," Lia wracked her brain for a way of wording. "I just don't get why each one of them can't be who they want to be in their world. If that's the truth, then - again, no offense - Kythaela sounds kind of crummy."

"It's not about the world itself–it's regarding who is in it and who has corrupted it and shaped it into what it has now become."

"Come again?"

"You remember how I informed you of the Fire Wing. Correct?"

Lia nodded.

"Their hunger for power and greed for what they thought

CHAPTER SEVENTEEN 219

they deserved was what put Kythaela over the edge. That is how it came to fail, and why it has not been restored."

"Okay, I think I understand, but I'm still a bit confused," she admitted reluctantly. "If you didn't want the Mêla to feel welcomed, then why did you choose me for this mission? If you picked me, then you must've known that I don't shut up."

The Enchantress chuckled and placed a tender hand on her shoulder. "You are a very sweet girl and I have known that because I've watched you."

"That's a bit creepy."

"I apologize for my straightforwardness." What little color that was in Her face faded. "I meant to discuss last night's events with you. You took Jared to the dance because you felt sorry for him, yes?"

Lia was caught off-kilter by her question, but nodded anyway. "I guess so," she replied with all honesty. "I mean, he really likes my best friend, Maylene. Like, he *like* likes her. I just didn't know what to do when she rejected him. No matter how polite she was, he would've been upset anyway."

"You did the right thing by showing kindness to him."

"So, what did I do wrong?"

"Lia, my dear…to put it plainly, you went too far."

The teenager sat up straighter and eyed the woman in white. "How so?"

"The emotions of a young adolescent never go unnoticed," the Enchantress explained. "I was your age once…many, many years ago. Teenagers, as you call them, possess vast hormonal instincts. If you hadn't been stopped last night during your dance with Jared, both of you might have become something far from what is needed of you."

"We didn't kiss or anything," Lia shrugged with nonchalance.

"But you had the capability of doing so." The Woman smoothed out Her pale dress. "There needed to be some sort of intervention. I needed to do something."

The final piece of the puzzle that was last night fell into place and was a perfect fit. The gears in Lia's brain stuttered and clunked until they stopped altogether. Her train of thought slid to a screeching stop on the rails–there was no need for an engine any longer since the mystery had been solved. Lia could not control the sudden rage that flooded her core. She lurched to her feet and stood in front of the Enchantress with her fists clenched at her sides. She ignored the brown strands of hair falling into her face from her unkempt ponytail. If she was some sort of cartoon character, smoke would be steaming from her ears.

"*You* did that?" she bellowed from deep in her chest. "You unlatched the pipe from the ceiling? You could've killed me–both of us as a matter of fact! If it weren't for Jared, I'd still be squashed on the gym floor like a pancake!"

"Lia."

"I can't believe you would put us in such danger," the young girl ranted onward. "You really scared me–I was afraid for my life. I thought you were supposed to be helping me."

"Lia."

"Does almost squishing the very person who's supposed to save everything help the situation, or do you think you made a mistake by picking me?"

"*Lia!*"

Lia's mouth immediately snapped shut when the Enchantress' tall figure loomed over her like a gargoyle…one of those scary ones on the exterior of haunted mansions. Lia swallowed down the sudden fear that replaced her anger. The Enchantress did not appear to be a normal Woman anymore. Instead, Her eyes became completely blue, the color of Her irises - and illuminated where Lia was standing. She slowly backed away from the Woman she had considered somewhat of a friend - an acquaintance, perhaps - and towards the tree swing on the other side of the yard. The Enchantress' feet left the ground as She hovered in the middle of the yard. Her silhouette became a piercing white light that Lia quickly decided she was afraid of.

"Your distrust of my methods angers me," Her voice boomed in a lower octave. "You are lucky my reign has not grown to be Dark due to these past misfortunes. The ear of the ignorant is in vain, but the mind of the ambitious is treacherous. You must choose which of these paths you are willing to take or your task is destined to fail."

"Um, Miss..." Lia backed away as the light grew brighter. When She did not answer, her voice grew panicked. "Miss!"

It was like a switch had been flipped. The Enchantress' eyes morphed back into their normal kind hue and all illumination Her body conjured had vanished as if it was never there. Lia watched in horror as the Woman collapsed into the grass and shook her head wildly as if she was trying to rid herself of a daze. Lia ran to aid the tall Woman by offering her hand, to which She took and allowed the teenager to hoist Her back to Her feet. The Enchantress appeared to be shaken up–as did Lia despite not being the focus of the scenario that just occurred in the middle of her own backyard. She wondered how on Earth neither her mother nor her father heard the commotion through the back door or even through the sturdy walls.

"I'm so sorry...," the Enchantress exhaled when She eventually caught Her breath. "I did not mean to frighten you."

Lia kept her distance once the Woman was steady. "...What was that?"

"My temper loses control of itself on occasion," She elaborated. "I am terribly sorry you had to see me like this. I do not like when others speak against me."

"I'll keep that in mind." Lia held a hand over her pounding heart. "Are you okay?"

"I'm okay. Thank you for your concern, but I should be asking you the same question." The Enchantress hung Her head. "I apologize for putting an immense amount of pressure upon your shoulders. No one, especially a young girl like yourself, deserves to endure such baggage."

"I want to help all of you. Really, I do. I just don't understand what I'm doing…or how my parents didn't hear a lick of whatever *that* was."

"I can use my magic to warp the senses of those around us," She explained, calmly this time. "For instance, the only one who can currently sense my presence is you."

"Really?" Lia's eyes lit up at the revelation. "That's so cool! I feel so special."

The Enchantress could not prevent a smile. "You *are* special, Dear, which is why I chose you. I know that you know what to do in such a dire situation and I trust that you will make the correct decisions as long as you're careful."

"I overthink things too much," Lia heartily confessed. "How do you know if I make the right decisions?"

"You made the right decision by ensuring your friend did not embark in a romantic relationship with Jared. By your subtle hints, I could tell you were carefully calculating how you would go about with ensuring each party's feelings remained stable."

The teenager's eyes bulged. "How did you know that?"

"I have my ways, my dear."

"Once again, creepy. *Please* tell me you don't watch me in the shower."

"Oh, *heavens* no!" The Enchantress' gaze stretched. "That is not how it works. I don't actually "see" what is occurring but rather sense it."

Lia grinned in Her direction. "Like Spiderman?"

"Who?"

"He's a superhero who can sense when people are in danger. He gets a tingling feeling at the base of his skull. Is it like that?"

The Enchantress just shook Her head and laughed, "A bit, yes. That is how I knew to come visit you. You were troubled about how last night's dance played out."

"Yeah, I guess you're right," she confessed more somberly. "I just don't get why you would do something to put me in danger. That could've put me in the hospital or worse. I could be in the morgue right now as a popsicle."

"I've known Jared for over a millennium. I knew he would step up and come to your aid if it was needed, and I was right."

"But that caused him to reveal his powers to everyone!"

"I see you've discovered his Katári."

"... His what?"

"A Katári is a special gift that each of the Mêla possesses. As you've found, Jared's Katári takes the form of immense physical strength. Willow's is a summoner of plants. As for Rowan, you have yet to discover her Katári."

"Can you tell me what it is so I can save some time and get everybody back sooner?" Lia appeared hopeful.

The pale Woman shook Her head. "I'm afraid I cannot do that."

"What?" she asked in sudden dismay. "Why not?"

"Because it is not my place to provide you with such information."

"But it would be so helpful."

"Then, it would be too easy."

"What's wrong with that?"

The Enchantress offered her a smile, but shook Her head. "This is something that you need to figure out on your own," She sternly replied. "I chose you for a reason, and that reason is because you have the proper skills to complete the assigned task."

"What skills?" questioned Lia, all the more anguished. "I don't know what skills to use if you don't tell me."

"You'll know when the time is right."

"But when's that?"

"Soon, my dear. Very soon. While you have been looking out for the Mêla just fine, you need to look out for yourself as well. Trust your instincts, and the truth will find you."

"Being in the unknown scares me," Lia suddenly disclosed. "I hate when I have no idea what's going on, especially if I can't control it."

A gentle hand rose her chin. "You *can* control which path you go down and how you embark upon it. You must choose wisely."

"How do I know what is wise?"

"You ask too many questions. You will know. I swear on Mother Nature Herself."

"Of course I ask every question but the one that's plaguing me," Lia scolded herself, however, she found it in herself to nod. "I'm sorry."

"I admire your curiosity and enthusiasm, but the answers you seek will arrive when you are ready to receive them."

"That makes sense," the teenager agreed despite feeling the exact opposite.

"I must go now, but reflect on what I said." Lia watched as the Woman began to backpedal towards the middle of the yard. "If you require my help, you know where to find me."

Lia instinctively approached Her. "No, I don't. Where?"

The Enchantress reached out and placed a cold, but tender hand upon Lia's forehead. "Right here. If you need me, I will know, and I will find you."

"Got it." She nodded to avoid further aggravation of the sorceress in front of her.

Lia did not, in fact, "get it." Instead, she stood in place as the ground under the Enchantress' bare feet began to glow a vibrant white. Her figure became translucent with the same light. Lia thought back to her first encounter with the powerhouse of a Woman and recalled…well… *nothing* regarding her departure. She had lost consciousness before that happened. Now, she was witnessing it with her very eyes. Just like She appeared, Her luminescent figure became the shape of a sphere that grew smaller until it disappeared entirely. Only mere sparkles, the remnants of the Enchantress' magic, fluttered to the ground and disappeared in the blades of grass.

Once again, the teenager was alone with her guitar, but - unlike the normality she was well acquainted with - had lost the motivation to play it that she had before the Enchantress' spontaneous visit. Instead, she gripped the instrument by the neck and held it daintily by her side as she entered the house and shut the back door behind her. Lia's initial goal was to sneak upstairs to her bedroom loft, put her guitar away, and mentally recover from the supernatural phenomenon that had just occurred in her own backyard. While it might not have been too serious, as Lia was now used to these encounters, after the Woman's outburst, Lia could not help but feel a sense of uneasiness trickling down her spine. She soon learned that her plan was going to be in vain, especially since her mother was busy typing on the desktop computer in her office that was across the hallway from the stairwell.

"Hi, Lia!" Cheyenne turned around in her wheeled chair and grinned at her daughter. "How was the outdoor guitar playing?"

Lia's socks, since she had flung her shoes off by the back door, slid to a stop on the hardwood floor. "Hey, Mom! It was good," she answered in the best way she knew how. "I got to do some improvisation with the third and fourth frets capo-ed."

"I have no idea what that means, but good job, Honey!"

"Where's Dad?" she briskly changed the subject.

All Cheyenne had to do was nod her head towards the living room where Lucas was sound asleep in his recliner with a sports game on television. Lia's lips pursed. "Oh, right. It's Saturday."

"Seems to be a weekend tradition," Mrs. Hart joked on her husband. "What are you up to next, Sweetie?"

Lia shrugged. "I was going to put my guitar away and hang out in my room."

"Well, don't let me stop you." Cheyenne stepped towards her daughter and planted a kiss on the top of her head. "Just be sure you're down in time for dinner. I'm making lasagna."

"I will," she beamed at the thought. "Thanks, Mom."

"You're welcome, Honey."

Lia wasted no time dashing up the stairs, being careful with her beloved guitar, of course. She did not rest until the door to her room was shut and her guitar was safely hanging on the wall hook. Even then, she could not relax, but instead opened up her journal–the same one she was using to research the Zodiac signs earlier in the year. Lia flipped to a new page and clicked the top of the nearest mechanical pencil on her desk. She quickly penned the phrase that the Enchantress had boomed in her face during her outburst in the yard. As soon as the final full stop was dotted, Lia leaned back in her rolling chair and assessed what she had just written in elegant cursive letters:

The ear of the ignorant is in vain, but the mind of the ambitious is treacherous. You must choose which of these paths you are willing to take or your task is destined to fail.

Lia underlined the words "ignorant," "vain," "ambitious," and "treacherous," seeing them as being the most important. While she knew what the Enchantress meant by Her words, what scenario was this warning pointing to? Lia could see the desperation leading towards last night, where she and Jared could have made the leap from being mere acquaintances to more-than-friends. Maybe that was what the Enchantress was talking about. Then again, however, what if it was regarding something completely different–something that could have correlated with the other two-thirds of the Earth Wing.

Prior to Lia's brain suffocating itself with the vast admonition placed upon her shoulders, she shut the notebook and placed the pencil on top. Lia yanked her glasses off her face and also placed them on the desk before stumbling past Noodle's vivarium, where the snake was comfortably snoozing in one of her hiding places underneath a multitude of branches. She plopped face-down on her bed and released her fountain of hair from the ponytail it was kept in. The hair tie ended up somewhere on her carpeted floor, but the teenager could not care less. Instead, all she needed was a nap until the enticing aroma of lasagna and garlic bread wafted up the stairs along with her mother's voice shouting up at her that dinner was indeed ready. Lia shoved aside the bumbling thoughts swirling around in her brain like a tornado.

Dinner was ready; the supernatural could wait.

Eighteen

No matter how long the supernatural has been within the confines of the natural world, none of them figured they would be used to Earthly concepts anytime soon. It was the beginning of yet another school day, or a school week, in fact. No...to put it in an even broader sense, it was the beginning of the Spring semester. The first day was always the hardest, seeing as new schedules were handed out, new textbooks had to be rented either online or physically, and each student needed to figure out what in the world they were doing before the day even began. That seemed to be Jared, Willow, and Rowan's problem. They were not of this world, so they had not a clue what they were supposed to be doing or how they would go about doing it.

The trio of other-worldly creatures stood in front of Oakbrooke High School like they had never seen the building before. The only way they knew that a new semester was starting was due to an announcement that Jared and Lia overheard at the Winter Formal that past Friday. None of them had a technological device other than the computers at the library across the street. To put it simply, all Three of them were - in their view - doomed.

CHAPTER EIGHTEEN

That was why they were waiting outside the school for a certain someone who was familiar with how high school worked. Lia Hart had been nothing but kind to the Earth Wing, which was why the trio allowed themselves to tentatively trust her...at least with navigating them around the school. They knew she would not purposefully steer them wrong. While Jared was a bit wary of her knowing his secret - his *Katári* - along with possibly the rest of the school, he was beckoning himself to open up, even if it was just a little bit. So far, if Lia had known about the Three of them not being of this world, and if she had bad intentions, would she have done something to undermine them already? Jared was well-aware of her intelligence, and he knew that she would not let it go to waste. So far, out of the one Mêla Lia had revealed her knowing of the truth to, one was still on her side. That left two to go, which she was uncertain of. Maybe Willow would accept the information with an open mind, but not Rowan. Rowan would take some time out of the Three.

In the meantime, Lia sat comfortably behind the wheel with Maylene and Yasmin in the back seat along with Cheyenne in the driver's seat as normal. Everyone except for the driver was using their cell phone - of course - with Cheyenne being the exception; she was using Lia's to read her daughter's class schedule. Maylene and Yasmin were doing the same. While the schedule had been sent out earlier over Christmas Break, they thought they would at least familiarize themselves with the room numbers and floors.

"So, we share our second and fourth period classes this semester, Maylene?" Lia inquired from up front.

Maylene nodded and confirmed, "Yeah–we have Creative Writing and Spanish I together."

"Woohoo!" The driver cheered and steered into the school's parking lot. Would you look at that–another rhyme. "Do we have any classes together, Yasmin?"

"I think we might share...oh no..."

Lia frowned when the usually talkative girl trailed off. "What's wrong?"

"Public Speaking. I have Public Speaking."

"That's okay," she replied as if there was nothing to it. "You're good at talking. You'll do well, and if you need help, you have me!"

"I'm good at talking *to* people, not in *front* of people," Yasmin clarified anxiously. "There's no way I can write a speech and say it to the whole class."

"How about you practice with my stuffed animals?" Maylene offered.

"Very funny, May."

The quieter twin frowned. "I was being serious."

"Seriously, though," Lia butted in kindly. "If you need help, I'd be happy to be of service. Just let me know if you need anything."

"But you've never done a Public Speaking class."

"Lia's crazy smart," assured Maylene, which made the brunette blush. "She'll figure it out soon enough and then can pass her skills onto you."

"Maylene…," Lia protested timidly.

"Let's face it," Yasmin interrupted her retort. "You're the smartest person we know. If I need help, you'd better bet I'm coming to you first."

"Sounds good, then…I guess."

Once the black sedan parked at the curb near the front of the building, Cheyenne grinned and pointed at a group of people. "Honey, look! Aren't those your friends that we had over for Christmas dinner?"

Lia followed the direction of her mother's index finger and sure enough, there was the Earth Wing in its entirety. Jared, Willow, and Rowan were talking amongst themselves standing outside the propped-open doors of Oakbrooke High. When she looked their way from inside the vehicle, somehow, some way, all three of their gazes landed on her. Lia smiled and offered them a friendly wave while Maylene averted her gaze and the former discovered that Yasmin was glaring subtly in Rowan's direction. Maylene elbowed her twin in the upper arm which made her aware of her facial expression and replaced it with a not-so genuine smile.

"It is," Lia responded to her mom and leaned towards her with a hug at the ready. "Love you, Mom! See you after school."

"I love you too, Honey!" Cheyenne then turned around to look at the twins. "Love you, girls–have a good day at school!"

"Love you too!" Maylene and Yasmin replied in unison.

As quickly as they arrived, Lia, Maylene, and Yasmin were off to their first classes of the day. This was not before Lia stopped in front of the trio awaiting her presence at the door. Maylene and Yasmin halted with her, but were not planning on staying too terribly long. Instead, they had classrooms to find as well as not wanting to seem awkward around Lia's friends.

"Hey, guys!" Lia chirped to their already-hitched attention. "How's it going?"

"It's going. How are you?" Jared was the first to speak up.

"I'm doing good." Lia scanned the trio. "Shouldn't you guys be finding your new classrooms, though?"

"That's the thing," Rowan piped up with her hands in the middle pouch of her hoodie. "We can't really figure out how the schedule works. Why are there new classrooms?"

"Because there's a new semester and we switch classes each semester," explained the brunette. "Did they not do that at… your old school?" she inquired, careful not to jeopardize the fact she knew very well indeed that this was the first school they had ever attended.

Rowan briefly forgot that very same thing and caught herself before making a similar mistake. "That's right. This concept is very new to us, so we were wondering if you could give us a little bit of assistance as to what our next steps are."

"Oh, absolutely! Do you have your schedules?"

All three of them removed a sheet of paper from their pockets almost in unison. "We wrote them down," Jared explained, unfolding his copy.

While Lia began to elaborate, Willow elegantly approached the twins behind Lia. "Maylene and Yasmin, correct?"

"Yep," Yasmin answered for both of them.

"How are you two doing? It's been a while."

"We're okay. How are you?"

"I'm doing quite well, thank you."

Maylene tentatively spoke up. "Shouldn't you be listening to the instructions?"

"Oh, it's okay," Willow declined politely. "I'll just ask either one of them. I thought you two looked a little bit left out."

"Don't worry about it," Yasmin assured her, possessing a more genuine smile than before. "We were just heading out, actually."

"We were?" asked Maylene.

"Yeah." Yasmin tapped Lia on the shoulder. "Hey, Lia… Maylene and I are going to find our classrooms. Love you."

"Oh, this soon?" Lia blinked in surprise, but hugged both of them at the same time. "Love you guys! I'll see you in Creative Writing, Maylene."

"Bye," Maylene whispered, quite confused, but agreed with her sister. Being around three people she did not know very well was getting her the slightest bit nervous.

Yasmin and Maylene began to turn away and walk through the doors, but Willow dashed up to them with a hand behind her back. "Wait, you two."

"What's up?" the former inquired.

"I found these by the sidewalk and thought you'd like them."

Both twins' eyes lit up when two identically flawless daisies with white pedals were revealed from behind Willow's slender frame. Rather than handing one to each of them, she delicately placed the flower behind their left ears. When she was finished, both twins wore matching smiles. It was clear that Willow was not hostile towards them, at least not as much as Rowan tended to be during her first encounter with Maylene.

"Wow, thank you!" Yasmin gushed while Maylene followed with a quieter, "Thank you."

"You're most welcome. I hope to see you two around sometime soon." Willow offered them both a kind smile.

"You too," the louder twin agreed. "If I'm going to be honest, you're much tamer than Rowan."

Willow leaned forward to whisper: "Rowan is one of the sweetest girls I know. Sure, she has her moments, but she regrets them afterwards. What she did to you, Maylene, was not of her nature whatsoever and I can assure with confidence that it will not happen again."

"I know," Maylene nodded timidly when Willow's eyes landed on her. "Thank you."

"You're welcome," the blonde similarly repeated to before. "Now, I must be going. I wish the both of you well."

"You too," said Yasmin with more genuinity while Maylene waved.

The twins soon disappeared into the swarm of students who were also doing their best to find their classrooms for their first day of Spring semester classes. Willow watched them vanish and then rejoined Jared, Rowan, and Lia. She removed a piece of paper like the ones Jared and Rowan were holding in their hands and watched as Lia continued to elaborate on something she must have already disclosed.

"Notice how the "two" is at the beginning? That means your classroom is on the second floor."

"Oh, that makes much more sense," Jared exclaimed, astonished. "I have no idea how I didn't think of that before."

Rowan amusedly shook her head. "That's the Jared we know and love...charming, but idiotic."

"Hey!"

"Come to think of it, how did you even find your classrooms last semester?" Lia inquired with lowered eyebrows.

"I guess I followed the crowd who were talking about the subject that I was taking and discovered the room numbers matched. I didn't think there was a connection."

"Moron," Rowan teased, for which she received a smack on the back of the head.

"If I recall, you couldn't find the courtyard, which could be found by the giant tree sticking through the roof," Willow joked on her friend.

"In my defense, I didn't know to look for the "giant tree" sticking through the roof."

"This school is called *Oak*brooke High. Get it? Oak tree?"

Rowan rolled her eyes and blew a piece of her black waves out of her face. "Whatever."

"Okay," Lia interrupted the potential argument between the two girls. "So, does everyone know where they're going?"

"I think so." Jared came to her aid and glanced down at his list. "My first class is on the first floor."

Willow leaned over to look at Rowan's paper. "Rowan and I share Anatomy & Physiology for our first class, which is on the second floor."

"We do?" Rowan peered at Willow's sheet.

"Yes, look." The blonde pointed to the top of her handwritten schedule.

"Oh."

"Do you guys need any help as to where your classrooms are?" Lia questioned…almost hopefully. "Mine, AP Government & Politics, is on the first floor."

"I think we're okay," Rowan declined politely. "It'd be very far out of your way."

The brunette seemed a little disappointed but hid it well. "Oh, okay. Well, I'll see you guys later, then, right?"

"You definitely will." Willow smiled in her direction and took Rowan along with her. "We'd better head out before we're late, but thank you for your help."

"You're welcome."

CHAPTER EIGHTEEN

When it was Willow and Rowan's turn to vanish into the crowd, Jared remained behind. "Join me," he offered, picking up on her change in mood.

"Really?" Lia's expression brightened at the thought of not having to be alone.

"You said our classrooms are close together, did you not?"

"I think so...yeah."

"Then, what are we waiting for?" Jared smirked knowingly. "Let's get a move on."

Lia trotted eagerly beside Jared while the two of them were the final duo to enter Oakbrooke High School's premises and venture towards their respective classrooms. The hallways were nearly as populated as the first day of school. Everyone had the same mission with their eyes glued to their phones to view their emailed schedules. Lia, on the other hand, had her first room number memorized and would double check her second block location on her phone once she sat down for class and possibly after. Lia could not help but wonder why no one was giving Jared their attention? After all, most of the school had seen the altercation in the gymnasium. When the hallways gradually began to thin out the further away from the front doors they got, Jared lowered his voice.

"Have you spoken to either of them yet about your knowledge of us?"

Lia shook her head, her hands in her pockets. "I haven't. I was planning on trying sometime this week."

"Sounds good to me."

"I did get a visit from the Enchantress on Saturday morning, though."

This revelation definitely caught Jared's attention. "You did?" When Lia nodded, he asked, "What'd She say?"

"She was basically warning me about the situation at hand. And she told me about the Katári. I guess yours is super strength and she clarified Willow's."

"Yep. Pretty cool, huh?" Then, Jared's expression grew

solemn as the rest of her response processed. "Warning? Is everything alright?"

"Yes, as far as I know." Jared's concern caught her off-guard, but it was not unwelcome. "She mainly told me to get a move on with my "convincing" strategy."

Jared offered her a kind smile. "You know I'm on your side, right? No matter how much I want to stay here, I know Kythaela needs our help, and I'd be honored to aid you with your "convincing" strategy."

"If I need help, I'll let you know, but I was told to do it on my own."

"The Enchantress is a gracious Woman. She would understand if you needed a little help."

Lia ignored her mind pleading for help right in front of the man who could provide it. "I will let you know," she repeated sternly. *"And I thought I was the stubborn one."*

"Oh, okay." Jared stopped in front of the door that matched the number on his paper. "I just thought…I know them best and would be willing to provide any guidance you might need."

"Oh, maybe he is." Lia was quite tickled by his persistence. "I'll keep that in mind."

The boy nodded and checked his paper before looking at the room number. "Well, this is my stop. It was nice to talk briefly."

"Yes, it was." Lia looked up at him and then nodded. "I'll see you later."

"You too."

As Lia and Jared were going their separate ways, the former could not help but think, *"Oh, for the love of God—I forgot to mention anything about the dance. Well… I guess it'll have to wait or it'll diffuse into nothingness."*

Meanwhile, Willow and Rowan were making their way to their shared classroom. The stairwell door was propped open, so the two of them pranced right up the stairs along with the rest of the flock exploring the school's premises. Both girls strode side by side without a single breath being taken out of them. Between flights, however, a bulletin board was attached to the wall at most students' eye level, which included theirs. A certain red poster caught Rowan's eye, and she tugged on the purple sleeve of Willow's blazer. Now, both pairs of eyes were reading the contents of the poster that had a goofy cartoon horse on it. That was not what grasped their attention, though. Instead, it was the bold lettering.

Do you aspire to be the top of the class?
Are you a senior this year?
Do you want to be honored for your efforts?
Aim for valedictorian!

Willow and Rowan looked at each other. A smirk hastily grew on the latter's face. "Valedictorian, huh?"

"That sounds like something worth trying," Willow agreed.

"Wait...can't there only be one, though?"

Willow looked at the poster and then at Rowan. "From what I've heard, yes."

"Oh." Rowan's lips screwed together. Then, her eyes brightened at an idea. "What if we had some sort of friendly competition for it?"

"I'm not sure if competing for something that doesn't really matter is such a good idea," Willow tentatively countered.

"If it doesn't really matter, then why did you look so interested?"

"It might be a nice goal to reach. I don't know about you, though."

An eyebrow of Rowan's shot up. "I'm the one who brought it up. I wouldn't have mentioned it if it didn't look interesting."

"Okay, okay." Willow put her hands in front of her. "I didn't mean to start anything."

"It's alright. I *do* want to go for this, though." She poked the poster.

"Me too."

"What should we do about it, then?" Rowan repeated. "After all, there *can* only be one valedictorian."

Willow took another look at the poster. "You know…a competition might be fun," she grinned at the thought. "But we need to set some ground rules."

"Oh? And what are those?"

"Well, number one would be no cheating." Willow started up the stairs.

Rowan sturdily followed behind. "That sounds fair."

"Are you sure?"

"What do you mean by that?" Rowan's tone grew a bit more defensive.

"I mean…you cheated last time you had a big test," the blonde nonchalantly brought up. "Would you be tempted to do that again?"

They reached the top of the echoey stairwell. "Just because I did it once doesn't mean I'll do it again. Are you sure *you* won't be tempted to cheat?"

"I've never cheated on any school assignment, and so far, I have straight A's."

"So do I."

"But you received one of those A's by cheating on that test."

Rowan's face contorted into a glare. "I'm not stupid. I've said it won't happen again."

"Make sure it doesn't," Willow instructed her to her dismay, "or I might not be so quiet next time."

"I'm not going to cheat!" the black-haired Mêla raised her voice. "Why are you so insistent that I would?"

Willow stopped in the hallway in front of the classroom with the corresponding number on their papers. "You just never know what stress and pressure can do to you. I don't want you to fall deeper into temptation."

"And what about you, huh?" Rowan argued by turning the tables. "There's no way that you're perfect in everything you do. How do you have straight A's if you've never been to school before? You know *none* of these concepts."

"I've studied ever since we left our world and entered this one," the blonde defended herself. "I genuinely want to learn about everything there is to know here, or especially in this area. I find Earth to be fascinating, which beckons my studies and self-education further. I take extensive notes through every class and don't leave a single detail unnoticed. It's not that hard."

"What do you mean, not *that* hard? You're just rubbing the fact you're smarter than me in my face."

"That's not what I'm saying at all." Willow frowned at Rowan's accusation. "What if we work together instead of competing against each other for the role?"

Rowan smirked at the idea. "Competitions are much more fun."

"But that's what causes more harm."

"Only if the competitor's toxic."

"So, let's agree not to be toxic towards one another," Willow offered a solution. "I know it hasn't worked out very well before, but we shouldn't let some silly competition get in the way of our friendship."

The blonde outstretched her pale hand to Rowan's copper one. The latter seemed to be unsure of Willow's proposition, but then again, a bit of a challenge was healthy in one's life as well as getting out of your comfort zone. In a way, Rowan would be doing a bit of both. While Willow and Rowan were both well-acquainted with their academics by now, being in competition with each other would be a whole different level of the playing field. At first, Rowan was merely doing her work to get by. When her C's turned into B's and B's turned into A's, though, she began to relish in the delight that being successful with something gave her.

"You know what?" Rowan gripped Willow's hand in a hearty handshake. "You're on."

Willow could not help but smile. "Let's just keep it friendly, okay? I don't want to get into any more unnecessary fights with you."

"Me either." Rowan then laughed at a memory. "Hey, remember when we were having that brawl in the hallway? That was when we first met Lia."

"Oh, yeah!" Willow chuckled with remembrance. "I forget what we were even fighting over."

"Me too, actually. Let's make sure it doesn't happen again, though."

"Sounds good to me."

Willow and Rowan were two of the last people to enter their Anatomy & Physiology classroom, but neither of them cared. There were two desks next to each other in the very front row that both took. Both of them removed a notebook from their backpacks that corresponded with the usual color that they wore - red for Rowan and purple for Willow - along with a pencil. Their older, balding professor in a plaid shirt and jeans began to welcome everyone to the class once he shut the door and it was time to begin. Willow and Rowan looked at each other with a smirk as soon as the teacher started going over the syllabus for the semester. Both of them wrote the date at the top of their new sheet of notebook paper and immediately went to work. Already, it appeared that Willow and Rowan were racing against each other to scribble down as many notes as possible. Both were thinking the same thing:

As the first Olympians from Greece would say: *let the games begin.*

Nineteen

"I'm not sure if this is such a good idea," Lia worried out loud to her company walking next to her.

Jared offered her a kind smile. "It's going to work," he assured her. "I know Willow, and if you tell her that this is for a good cause, she's bound to agree."

"This is more than a *good cause*. The fate of an entire world lies with this."

"Don't put it like that," Jared argued with her anxiety. "You got me to help you, which is not an easy feat. If you've noticed, I can be a bit…"

Lia finished his sentence: "Stubborn?"

"Yeah…wait a minute."

"I'm just teasing, you know."

"How am I supposed to talk to her and get her to do this?" Lia inquired, once again asking more questions than she probably needed to. "I mean, with you, it was kind of forced out, but with Willow, we're in a perfectly calm environment."

Jared thought and then winked. "Want me to throw something?"

"No, thank you."

"Maybe you could trip over a tree root."

"I'm not *that* clumsy," she defended herself.

"Says the girl who fell off a ladder."

"What if I told you I did it on purpose?"

Jared's thoughts skidded to a halt. "Excuse me?"

"You heard me."

After that, Lia was quiet. She continued walking beside Jared who appeared to have run out of applicable words as well. Lia kept her eyes on her shoes as they glided over the pavement of the sidewalk the two shared. She had not realized that she had gotten so straightforward with the very person she was supposed to convince to be on her side. Why was he so…*ready* to return after what had happened? Was it not traumatizing? Maybe that was exactly it, but prior to her raising the topic, Jared already seemed to dodge it.

"Do you mean to tell me you put yourself in danger just to help us?"

Lia was stunned by his tone of voice. The last time she heard him be so vulnerable, so…*guilty*…was when he revealed to her the truth. In his eyes was that same faded notion that he had somehow done something wrong. Lia would give anything to know what other individuals were truly thinking. Being empathetic was her strong suit, but she was far from a mind-reader. She made herself remain within his eye contact as she spoke.

"I couldn't think of anything else I could do that would make such an impact," Lia mumbled nearly incoherently. "I knew there was something off about you…"

"So, practically throwing yourself off a ladder is how you wanted to get our attention?" Jared raised an eyebrow at that. "What's next? Was the pipe falling at the dance your doing as well?"

What? No! If it was her doing, then why did she appear so frightened. "If you must know," Lia took a deep breath and explained, "I fell off the ladder because I wanted to test how easily you could catch me. That was when I discovered your strength. The pipe, however, was anything but my doing. In fact, it was the Enchantress."

"What?! Why would She do that?" Jared could not hide his astonishment.

"Well, she didn't want me to…you know…"

At Lia's embarrassment, the boy smirked. He caught on immediately. "No, I don't know."

"She didn't want me to "make a move" or anything," Lia grumbled.

"And the truth comes out! Do you think I'm that attractive?" Jared was clearly enjoying himself–and the conversation.

"Quit changing the subject."

"You're the one who started it." He snootily stuck his tongue out at her.

Lia's cheeks heated up. "So, where are we even going?"

"Now, who's changing the subject?"

"Shut it! This is important!"

"Okay, okay, don't catch on fire," Jared raised his voice briefly to match hers.

Lia's eyes widened. "Wait, are there people who catch on fire in Kythaela?"

"You don't know the half of it."

"…Uh oh."

"*Anyways*…we're headed to Willow's favorite place that she's discovered so far," he explained. The sidewalk was leading out of the suburbs and into the nearby park. "With all of the flowers and plants here, she could live here."

"Which can cause a problem," Lia concluded, concerned.

"Exactly."

"Aren't there flowers back home?"

All Jared had to do was give her a pointed stare before she realized.

"Oh. Right."

"After the Fire Wing expressed their vacancy, everything froze to death."

Lia knotted her fingers together. "That's horrible..."

"I know." Jared hung his head. "But, with everyone banding together, we can bring it back to its former glory."

"I wish I had your optimism."

"You did at the beginning." Jared frowned at the realization. "Where did it go?"

Lia averted her eyes. "I guess I didn't realize how difficult this would be."

"You can do it," he encouraged her, lifting her chin with his index finger. "We're here, anyways. Would you like me to stay?"

"To be honest...I don't know."

Jared suggested, "What if I wait on this bench over here?"

"You don't have to," the brunette protested.

"I'll be here if you need me," he assured her with a calmness she desired.

Lia let a smile creep onto her face. "Thanks, Jared."

"You're welcome." Jared returned the gesture. "Willow is right down the path to your left. She found an abandoned greenhouse that she's been taking care of."

"No way. That's so cool."

"That's Willow for you. Now, how about you get going before you chicken out."

"Hey!"

"Joking, joking."

Staying true to Jared's proposition, Lia started down the path to their left. Jared sat down on the nearest bench and began fiddling around with the varsity jacket he was wearing. Lia felt a bit bad for leaving him behind, but she gave him the option to leave, and he made his own choice. Now, all Lia needed to focus on was talking to Willow and gravitating her to her side. Despite one Mêla being behind her, she was still built upon a web of lies...and she was lost for a way to untie it without causing conflict.

Lia continued down the dirt path that had grown thicker with trees, moss, and weeds. The further she went, the more abandoned her surroundings became. A sense of unease trickled down her spine and dribbled down to her slip-on checkered shoes. What if she had been sent on a wild goose chase? What if Jared did not trust her after all and this was his way of getting revenge? The very thought of it plagued her until she came upon a relatively small transparent building at the end of the path. Even from the outside, vibrant flowers and a multitude of small crops illuminated the entire structure. On the inside, a certain blonde wearing a lavender sweatshirt pranced around with a silver watering can, humming a melody she must have heard on the radio as she lovingly watered each plant. It would not take a lot of brain cells to determine that this was the greenhouse Jared was talking about.

Sure enough, when Lia approached and hesitantly knocked on the door, Willow's friendly gaze met her own. The blonde placed the watering can down on a nearby wooden stool and dashed over to the door where Lia was standing. The teenager awkwardly waved from the outside. Willow did not seem to find it strange at all that there was a guest. She opened the door and let just a tad bit of the interior humidity escape.

"Hi, Lia!" she exclaimed cheerfully. "Come inside before the cold gets in."

Lia did as she said and stepped into the instantly warmer climate. "Hi, Willow," she replied with almost as much enthusiasm. "Wow! This place is beautiful."

"I'm so glad you think so! I've been taking care of the flowers ever since we moved here." Willow picked up the watering can and continued watering a small patch of strawberry plants.

"I can tell. It looks *amazing*."

"Well, thank you very much!" Willow moved on to the tomatoes that were climbing up their metal plant cages. "What brings you here?"

"*Well, that question came about fast,*" Lia silently fretted. She kept her nervosity well under wraps. "I was walking down one of the park paths and saw all of the colors, so I went to investigate. I had no idea you were behind it."

It was not a complete lie, but either way, Willow bought it. "Getting out into nature is very important for the mind. I'm so glad you were taking advantage of today's weather."

"Yeah, me too," Lia agreed. "How often do you come out here?"

"Just about every day before school and on the weekends, I tend to spend more time with these beauties. How often do you come to the park?"

"If I were honest...not often. I should bring my guitar out here sometime and play."

Willow's smile was as bright as the sun overhead. "I knew you were well-acquainted with the piano, but guitar as well? That's incredible, Lia."

"How'd you know I play the piano?" questioned Lia.

"We heard you outside on Christmas Day," she beamed a rainbow into the water sprinkling onto another set of plants. "It sounded beautiful."

The teenager's cheeks grew red. "Oh, thank you."

"You're quite welcome."

Lia looked around until she saw another watering can sitting in one of the two corners by the door. "Would you like some help watering?"

"You know what? I'd love that." Willow frollicked over and handed her the second can. "I brought this one up in case I ran out with the first, but if you water the other half, then it should go twice as fast."

"Sounds good to me." Lia began watering right near where the second watering can was placed, which was a large patch of Black-Eyed Susans.

The entire greenhouse was just as vibrant as it was on the outside...in fact, more so. Everywhere Lia looked, there was a new type of flower, crop, or vine making its way around the interior. Lia's forehead began to prickle with sweat, not just from the humidity the greenhouse used to keep the plants healthy and happy, but from her ever-growing nerves as well. Willow seemed happier than Lia had ever seen her. Of course she was– her natural habitat surrounded her. This, like the library for Lia, was Willow's happy place. Lia realized she was overwatering a set of the hydrangeas and quickly lifted her watering can, causing some of the water to spill. Luckily, Willow had not noticed...yet.

"So, how'd you get all of these plants to grow so fast?" Lia knew *exactly* how, but she wanted to give Willow a chance to tell her the truth.

Knowing her luck, that was the opposite of what happened... or was it? "Oh, I gave them all a little help," Willow nonchalantly answered.

Tentatively, Lia pressed further. "How would you do that?"

"Oh, um...," the blonde faltered. She was caught in Lia's trap, but quickly wriggled her way out of it. "Fertilizer, of course! I've been getting some at the local hardware store.

"Would fertilizer make things grow that fast? No matter, because I know that's a lie. Should I tell her that, though?" Well, it was now or never. "Are you sure it was *just* fertilizer?"

Willow whirled around to look at Lia, who had innocently moved on to water a small blueberry bush. "What do you mean by that?"

"It takes a while for some of these things to grow, especially to this magnitude. Did you use something else to make it happen quicker?"

"Well, I come by and water them every day," Willow offered lamely.

Lia pressed forward, "That doesn't cut it, though. You've been using something else."

Her face scrunched up into a suspicious frown. "What are you implying?"

"I know you can grow flowers and plants at will," the

brunette revealed, her voice growing a tad louder. "To put it in simple words, it's your Katári.."

If it was possible, Willow grew paler than she already was. The watering can fell from her hand and landed on the ground with a *clang*! Lia cringed when the rest of the water from the can spilled out into the dirt below Willow's feet. Despite her shoes slowly absorbing water, she was stock still…like some sort of a statue. Willow stared at Lia as if she was a ghost. Her chin trembled. Her eyes were wide. Her cheekbones were sunk in.

"What…what are you talking about…?" she stammered as a whisper.

"You, Jared, and Rowan are the Earth Wing from Kythaela," Lia disclosed her knowledge. "The Enchantress paid me a visit on the night of my sixteenth birthday saying I need to find all of you and bring you back before your world is completely destroyed. I've already explained this to Jared and he's with me."

Unlike Jared, Willow did not resort to anger first. Instead, she bent down, picked up the watering can, and placed it back on the stool. "Jared knows of your plight?" When Lia nodded, she inquired, "Do you have definitive proof that we can trust you?"

"I-…"

It was Lia's turn to be trapped in the web that was holding their connection together. What proof *did* she have? Then, it hit her. The realization took longer than it needed to. She took her left hand out of her pocket and splayed her palm so the gold Ring around her finger was in full display. Willow leaned forward and studied it. The precious metal glistened in the sunlight above the transparent roof and hit Willow's mind in just the right spot.

"She gave that to you," Willow realized, stunned.

Lia nodded, barely able to stand her ground without fear cowering over her senses. "She did. The Enchantress told me that whenever I'm near one of the Mêla, it will pulse and that way, I will know how to find you."

"Does it still pulse?"

"It does, but I've gotten used to it when I'm around you Three."

"...How did you know about my Katári, though?" Willow's eyebrows lowered.

"...I saw you," Lia shakily confessed. "Outside the library...in the rain...when you shoved a flower in Jared's mouth..."

"You saw that?!"

The young girl nodded again. "Yeah...I'm sorry for snooping. I just needed to find out more about you so I can continue on with the mission."

There was a disturbance in Willow's very existence. From the calm spirit relishing in the ecstasy that keeping an ecosystem alive and prosperous brought her, she had become tied to the ground with a ball and chain–that being reality itself. Lia looked upon Willow with the sorrow and guilt she had felt earlier, but magnified a thousand times. The mirror staring back at her shattered into millions of pieces into the dirt and sank under the surface. Lia hung her head, unable to keep Willow's longing stare anymore.

"I'm sorry," the teenager repeated when Willow did not respond.

The blonde took one step forward...followed by another. "It is not your fault."

"I should've told you sooner," Lia recalled her earlier doubts. "It didn't have to get to this point, and I'm very sorry."

"Stop apologizing."

Lia's eyes snapped upward to meet Willow's. Her tone was firm–something she had not quite seen from the representative of Virgo. "...Sorry." A pointed look from the blonde returned her focus. "Okay, I get it," she tried again. "So, you know why I'm here."

"I know, and I want to go with you. Truly, I do, but I'm not sure how my return would aid your premise."

Wait. This was not how it was supposed to go. Willow's

acceptance to her - and Jared's, now - cause needed to be easier than this. Sure, Jared was wary, but now Willow? This was going to be harder than she thought.

Lia got back to watering the plants like nothing ever happened. "So, why can't you?"

"If you haven't noticed already, I'm quite attached to the little family I've got going on here."

"The…plants?! *She's not leaving because of plants?!*" Lia struggled to keep her cool. "Why can't you bring the plants with you?"

"I've already thought about that." Willow picked up what was left out of her watering can and continued to water as well. "Unfortunately, the climate would be too frigid for them to survive."

"Oh, true." Then, an idea hit her–smacked her directly in the face. "Wait."

"What's that?"

"What if you made a greenhouse there too?" Lia grinned from ear to ear. "Just like this one."

Willow considered the idea. "That would be wonderful, but we don't have any materials."

"That's true, but if you come back and revive Kythaela's old glory with the other members of the Earth Wing, then you won't have to worry about a greenhouse!" the brunette declared.

"That's not such a bad idea, but it can't be that simple."

"Yes it can," Lia persisted bravely. "We don't have to figure it out right now, but I would love it if you at least consider joining Jared and I's team."

Willow was silent once again. She placed her watering can back down on the stool, likely because it had run out of water. It appeared as if she was wracking her brain for any possible loophole in Lia's proposition, but there were none to be found. Instead, her posture deflated into a weathered balloon that had been through too much. Had it popped yet? That was undetermined.

"I will consider," she finally replied.

A wide smile occupied Lia's face. She darted forward and engulfed Willow into a hug. "Oh, thank you! I can't express how much this means to me."

"You're...welcome." Willow offered a hesitant grin in response. "...But it's not even your realm, Lia. Why are you so passionate about it?"

"I can't let innocent people suffer." Lia broke apart from the embrace she initiated.

Willow patted her tenderly on the shoulder. "I can very much respect that," she agreed. "Now, I assume Jared came out here with you, so go tell him I'll be of assistance."

"How did you know that?"

"Just a hunch." Lia was unsure if it was already there or if she had just conjured it, but Willow presented one of the Black-Eyed Susans to her and placed it behind her ear. "Thank you for bringing this to my attention. You're a strong girl, Lia."

The young girl could not help but smile. "Thank you, Willow. I'll tell him."

"You're most welcome." Willow returned the gesture and opened the door for her. "Now, run along. I'm sure Jared's eagerly awaiting your arrival."

"You don't happen to have mind-reading powers too, do you?"

"I do not," chuckled Willow at that.

"Aw, man, that would be so cool!" were the last words Lia uttered before dashing out of the greenhouse.

True to her word, Lia did, in fact, "run along" as Willow had suggested she do. Unfortunately, she had forgotten about her body not quite being athletically inclined. By the time she was a matter of yards from the bench where Jared was still seated, Lia was huffing and puffing oxygen like she was drowning in an endless ocean. That was too dramatic...or was it? By the way Jared was dashing towards her, you would have thought that a bear was chasing her. He had lurched up by the time her footsteps came into earshot.

"Lia! Are you okay?" his voice boomed with preliminary terror. "You look like you've seen a ghost."

"What?" Lia skidded to a stop, but it was not quick enough. She slammed directly into Jared's chest, where she awkwardly pried herself off of him. "I'm fine."

Jared stood tall, ready to defend whatever Lia was running from. "You're exhausted, so you were clearly running for your life. Did Willow do something to hurt you? Did she stuff a flower in your mouth like she did to me? Did she tie you up with ivy? Did she-"

"Jared! Jared! Relax!" An uncontrollable bout of laughter was summoned by Lia's realization. "I wasn't running for my life– I'm just out of shape!"

Jared's face turned beet red. "Oh. My apologies."

"No worries," Lia brightly giggled. "I need to do more cardio. Seriously, though, Willow didn't do anything to hurt me. In fact, she did the opposite."

"Really?"

"She agreed to band with us."

At this, Jared's entire figure relaxed and he exhaled a sigh of relief. "I can't believe it. She's so attached to those plants of hers that I thought she'd never leave."

"I gave her the idea of making a greenhouse or something back in Kythaela, or when it's back to normal, she can plant an even bigger garden."

"I don't know…" The boy's face fell. "The temperature is too drastic for anything to grow, much less thrive."

"Where's that optimism you had earlier?" Lia elbowed him gently in the upper arm. "We'll figure it out. I know we will."

"How can you seem so sure?"

"Have we switched places or something? The good thing is that Willow is now on our side. That just leaves…," Lia gulped nervously as she began walking out of the park, "…Rowan."

Jared followed her lead back to the suburbs. "She's going to be a tough nut to crack."

"I know," she fretted. "I have no clue how I'm going to get through to her, much less how I'm going to bring her onto our side."

"I think she has even more connections to this world than Willow and I do."

"How would that be?"

"Well, for starters, she works at the local animal shelter - Claws & Paws, I think it was - every day after school," Jared explained. "She's made some wonderful friends there and is the furthest out of all three of us from coming back."

"As in the animals?"

Jared nodded.

"Great." Lia's situation just had another hole dug into it. "If Willow can't take flowers back to Kythaela, then there's no way Rowan can take all of her animals."

"You're right." Jared was thoughtful. "How are we going to get her to follow us if she has no connections or desire to return to her homeland?"

For the first time in a long time, Lia's mind was completely insecure of its own abilities. Usually, it would take her a while, but at least one idea would pop into her system that would solve the problem. Right now, however, that hope was far from becoming a reality. Instead, she stood in the middle of the sidewalk, halting from her previously slow pace. Jared kept moving forward, but after a couple of steps, he turned around and realized she was not at his side anymore. He backpedaled to her quaking frame and used both arms to steady her as she uttered out the last resort - a transparent plea for help - that came to her mind:

"I. Don't. Know…"

Twenty

Without Jared's presence by her side, Lia's surroundings were barer than she had anticipated, but there he was...still in relatively close proximity. His back was turned and his shoes were facing the other way as they walked briskly down the sidewalk in the opposite direction of her location. Her shoes were rooted to the ground as she witnessed his departure. No, it was not on improper terms, but rather the opposite. All Lia wanted to do was get a "move on" with the objective that was now pressed firmly in her grasp. The only obstacle remaining was like a bull in a china shop: obvious and destructive.

Rowan.

Now, Lia had no hard feelings towards the final Mêla other than the fact she used Maylene to cheat off of. That situation was long gone, however, and it was resolved. Every time Yasmin and Rowan were in the same room, however, the former displayed some sort of obvious resentment towards the latter, whether it be a glare, a few uttered curses, or a tapping of the foot. Sure, forgiveness was the key to the phrase "Forgive and forget," but Maylene's twin was not doing such a good job with the "forgetting" part. Instead of peace revolving around the group that Lia

CHAPTER TWENTY 255

had accidentally pulled together, there was now tension. Thankfully, if Lia's plan was going to work, then there would not be a spontaneous group to worry about.

It was all written in a metaphorical permanent ink. Right there, on the top and in bold, was the key to the lock that would open the door to the solution Kythaela needed. With the first two Mêla - Jared and Willow - Lia was straightforward and presented her intentions blatantly to their faces. It seemed to work with them, but would it do the same with the third member of the Earth Wing? Not necessarily. Instead, Lia needed to think outside the box and be discrete about the matter at hand. Instead of unlocking the door with a key, Lia figured that going about with picking it with an outside source would be the best way to lure Rowan towards a similar ideal. All Lia knew was what Rowan worked at the local animal shelter on a near-daily basis. There must have been some way to connect her Earthly ties with the world she left behind.

There must have been a denominator that Earth and Kythaela had in common.

Lia could not wrack her brain too much at that time. The sky overhead was darkening into hues of pink, orange, and purple. Jared was long gone by then. The teenager wondered how foolish she appeared to be as a lone girl standing in the middle of the sidewalk in front of her house without any motive to go inside other than the chills rattling her skin from underneath her jacket that was too thin for the weather. What point was there in standing outside in the bitter cold? She wondered just that as she walked towards her front door and fished her key out of her pocket. Lia unlocked the door and stepped inside, but prior to her shutting it, her father's voice boomed from the living room.

"Lia–who was that boy you were with?"

Lia's shoes squeaked against the hardwood floor in the foyer, which reminded her to take them off and deposit them onto the shoe rack. "Jared," she replied honestly. "Why?"

"You told your mother and I that you would be at Maylene's

house." Lucas stood from his recliner and suspiciously eyed his daughter.

"I-...um...," Lia faltered, especially when her mother's head popped through the kitchen doorway. "There was a change in plans?" She lopsidedly grinned.

"There must've been...because I texted Mrs. Zuíhuí when you never answered your phone and she said she knew nothing about you being over at their house, nor did you make plans." Lucas took a step towards her. "I'm not mad, Lia, but did you use visiting Maylene as an alibi so you could hang out with this boy?"

The brunette's eyes bulged–that was exactly what she had done. "Well...not exactly."

"Not *exactly*?" Lucas's eyebrows shifted.

"I was visiting with Jared and my other friend Willow." "*It was not a lie... It would have to do.*" "It was last minute, so I didn't want to worry you or Mom."

"Where was that third one? Isn't there a third one in that group we had over for Christmas?"

"She was working at Claws & Paws."

"Where?"

"The local animal shelter."

"Oh."

Cheyenne deeply sighed and stepped through the doorway into the foyer where her husband and daughter were. She focused her attention to the latter. "Lia, Sweetie...you can hang out with your other friends, but please don't lie to us," she softly reprimanded. "We just want you to be safe, especially around new people."

"I understand, Mom." Lia hung her head. She could have smacked herself for lying in the first place. "I'm sorry."

"It's okay, Honey, but don't lie to us next time." Cheyenne wrapped her arm around Lia's smaller frame.

"I'm sorry," Lia repeated authentically.

"I still have one question," Mr. Hart spoke up.

Oh, no... Lia truly thought she was out of the woods. "Yeah, Dad?"

"Why were you *alone* with Jared?" he questioned with emphasis.

"I forgot about that... I need to think of an excuse...and fast! Willow was in the greenhouse, so technically I was with her for quite a bit, but Jared walked me home. Yeah...walking me home is a good excuse because why? Hm... Oh! Willow was busy! Busy with what, though...?" Lia's inner voice was spitting out ideas like wildfire, but she only said one. "Jared walked me home because it was getting dark out and Willow's place was on the way." Would that work? There was only one way to find out.

Slowly, stiffly...Lucas nodded. "That makes sense. I respect him for walking you home, but at least let us know next time instead of lying to us."

"Oh, my gosh, that worked!" Lia tried to conceal the twinkle in her eyes as she apologized once more. "I'm sorry, Dad. It won't happen again."

"Thanks, Kiddo." It was obvious that her father wanted to change the subject. "Speaking of sports...the hockey game is about to start. Want to watch some with me?"

"I'd love to! Mom, want to watch with us?"

"I'll watch a little, but I also have some work to do."

"I actually do too, but I'll bring my laptop downstairs," Lia agreed.

Lucas fist-bumped his daughter. "You go do that–and bring Noodle too!" he exclaimed. "The more, the merrier."

"Oh, *please* not that anaconda-looking thing again..." Cheyenne's complexion paled.

"What's wrong with Noodle?" Lia frowned. "She wouldn't hurt a fly."

"But yet she eats those thawed mouse things..."

The young girl deadpanned, "She doesn't eat humans. Wouldn't it be cool if she was some sort of zombie snake who ate brains, though?"

"Well, your mother wouldn't have anything to worry about," Lucas teased her.

Cheyenne's eyes nearly fell out of their sockets as she smacked him upside the head. "*Lucas!*"

"Kidding!"

Lia could not resist her fits of laughter even as she bounded up the stairs to retrieve two of her most important items. The first was, of course, her best friend who happened to take the form of a corn snake. Lia ensured that Noodle was awake before opening the small door in her vivarium and allowing her to slither onto her arm.

"Hi, Noodle," she cooed as the snake found a comfortable spot on her shoulder.

Once she knew Noodle was comfortable and secure around her arm and shoulder, Lia then moved over to her desk to grab her laptop. When she saw the notebook she had been using to jot down ideas, theories, and other topics of the sort, she yanked it from its spot as well along with the mechanical pencil safely looped into the spiral. With Noodle perched on her arm, Lia bounded down the stairs and into the living room with her laptop and notebook tucked under her arm. Lia sat cross-legged on the floor and set her notebook to the side. She placed her laptop on her lap and typed in her password to unlock all of the homework that was awaiting her. Her ears, meanwhile, were focusing on the announcers on the television. Lia recognized one of them to be the announcer from the *Miracle on Ice* game in 1980: Al Michaels. His final words before the buzzer screeched throughout the Lake Placid Arena, "*Do you believe in miracles? Yes!*" still never failed to give her chills.

"Who's playing, Dad?" Lia inquired as she opened a document for yet another essay she was to write. She recalled the perfect score she received on her Zodiac essay earlier in the month; Mr. Walker had been very impressed.

"It looks like the Redhawks and Fleeters," he replied, slightly turning up the volume.

"Boo, Fleeters," Lia spat, which made her father chuckle. Each team being nowhere near the metropolis of Atlanta would normally provide a neutral playing field for viewers of that location. This, however, was not the case. Lia thought back to several incidents where players performed acts of bad sportsmanship. She despised when members of athletics would go out of their way to make the game worse for everyone. She recalled an instance in one of last week's games where a Fleeters player deliberately slammed an opposing skater headfirst into the glass. Other than a consequent five-minute major power play, it did not affect the game at all. It was pointless–utterly pointless.

When the puck dropped a few minutes later, Lia found it difficult to focus on the work that she had brought down from her room. Instead, her eyes remained on the game while she typed blindly into her document. She would fix the typos after she returned from autopilot. Unlike other individuals who would prioritize their academics, Lia treasured quality time with her parents rather than doing such a thing. Of course, she would not jeopardize her grade–there was no way that she *could*. Lia knew she had potential and took advantage of that. The first week of the Spring semester had just ended and Lia was confident that all of her teachers enjoyed her enthusiasm and work ethic.

Unfortunately for Lia, a Creative Writing assignment was not given to her quite yet. Instead, the task that loomed before her was an Advanced Placement US Government & Politics regarding each branch of the American Government and how they all contributed effectively to the good of the country. History and Government were not subjects that Lia disliked. In fact, she was quite talented when it came to these sorts of topics. All she had to do was open up her virtual textbook that was used for the class and scan the chapter discussing each branch, regurgitating the information in her own words on the document. It was quite simple, really, only being a five-hundred-word essay that was due Sunday evening before class that following morning. Lia had no need to start it, especially since it was so short and she preliminarily knew the material.

That was why most of her conscience focused on the screen directly in front of her. She was sure that despite only ten minutes had passed in the first period, her father was already sound asleep in the recliner in his *Batman* pajama pants. At the same time, her mother was working on yet another crocheted blanket - this was one of her hobbies - with an earbud in one ear. It was clear that she was watching one of her crime shows. That left Lia being the only one to watch the game that was Lucas's idea. She merely shook her head at her two parents and continued on with her essay that was already near-finished in such a brief amount of time. Meanwhile, Noodle slithered down her arm and began to weave her slim body around Lia's fingers. At once, Lia stopped what she was doing and absorbed all of the love her pet snake was giving her. Lia adored the way that Noodle displayed affection. All she wanted was Lia's attention– and lots of it. Lia moved her arm to let Noodle slide onto her lap and "assess" the work she had done. Lia could not help but smile at Noodle's inquisitiveness.

When Noodle eventually got bored of inspecting Lia's essay, she returned to her spot around Lia's arm. The teenager thought now was as good of a time as any to resume her work, so that was exactly what she did. Lia continued typing along in her essay, but eventually, other thoughts plagued her mind more than the task at hand. No matter how hard she tried, she could not get the Mêla out of her head. Instead, the less she "thought" about it, the worse her obsession got. After all, she had quite a heavy weight on her shoulders. While Jared and Willow were pretty much taken care of, it was the final member of the Earth Wing that worried her. Lia was pretty sure that Rowan was Capricorn's representative. After delving down through another rabbit hole of research, Lia discovered that Capricorns tended to be overachievers, persistent, and practical, but also sensitive. Lia had yet to see Rowan's sensitive side. So far, all Rowan seemed to act like was…a robot. That girl was nothing but a conundrum. To quote Looney Tunes' Daffy Duck, Rowan was going to be "a tough nut to crack."

Lia opened her notebook which described the facts she had just mentally gone over. When Rowan was convicted of cheating off of Maylene's test, she seemed more disappointed that she got caught than the fact she committed a poor deed. When Lia had given Rowan that apology gift a while ago, Rowan was hesitant to accept it before rushing off to her class even though it did not start for several minutes. A comment from Willow just seconds after that interaction hopped back into her mind.

Willow's pupils dilated with compassion. "I saw Rowan walk away."
"…You did?"
The regal lilac-clad girl nodded solemnly.
"Oh." Lia's gaze turned towards the floor.
"There's no need to be embarrassed," Willow's soft voice echoed in the teenager's ears. "The two of us have been going through a hard time recently, and Rowan might seem a little rude or hasty at times, but try not to pay it any mind. That's usually not like her…"
"Usually not like her?" Lia thought skeptically. *"What did Willow mean by that?"*

At that point, only one logical explanation reached Lia's mind, which was: maybe Rowan was having a hard time adjusting to her new home. That seemed to have been it, but if that truly was the case, would Willow have looked so concerned at that moment? Maybe something behind the scenes was occurring. Who knew at this point? Lia blatantly did not. Instead, she sat watching the hockey game with a clueless mind that probably contained only one working brain cell at the moment. Lia wanted to lay face-down in her bed and wrack her brain until a thought would hit her. Usually, they arrived just in time, but this time, it seemed different. She felt as if she was a defense attorney with no evidence to prove the defendant innocent. Finding a solution was near impossible...but not completely. Lia refused to give up the hope bubbling in her chest. She knew there was an answer to the endless question of Rowan's mind...but what? The whole scenario was taboo. Lia knew it. Willow knew it. Jared knew it. Everyone at this point was very much aware of the task at hand. That changed nothing.

    Lia bit back an exasperated groan and averted her eyes from the laptop and notebook that absorbed her and instead looked elsewhere. Noodle was draped around her shoulders. Whether the snake was asleep or not was questionable, but either way, the reptile was in the most comfortable place she could be. While doing her best to ignore her father's snores from the recliner and the faint noise of her mother's show that was playing on her phone, Lia's gaze drifted towards the television screen where there was one minute remaining of the first period. Her eyes followed the puck as it raced across the ice faster than she could keep up with it. It appeared to be nearly impossible for the players to as well, but somehow, they were in control. Each player that had possession over the puck masterfully maneuvered it by directing the rubber object in a certain direction with their stick. Then, it was passed to another player who did the same. For some inexplicable reason other than the factor of the game itself, Lia's eyes were locked on the puck and how each player had expert control of it. A player for the Fleeters handled the puck like it was second nature and if the stick was an extension of his body. He wound up a shot towards the Redhawks goalie, who flicked it away with his own stick. Then, the Redhawks gained possession over the puck and began hurdling in the direction of the Fleeters' goalie. With one shot from a Redhawks player wearing the number "eighty-eight" on the back of his jersey, the puck flew past the Fleeters' goalie. No matter what the outcome of that goal was, whether it was made or missed, the point was that the player had control over the puck. That was all that mattered.

"*Control...control!*"

That was it! Lia lurched to her feet with Noodle safely around her neck and shoulder and hastily gathered her things. This must have gotten the attention of Lucas, since he asked, "Did I fall asleep? Where are you off to in such a hurry?"

"Yes, you did. The Redhawks scored, by the way, and I just figured out some of my homework, so I'm going to get it done in my room."

"Okay, Lia...just don't scare me like that," he sleepily yawned.

Lia cringed–she must have been loud, but not thunderous enough to disturb her mother. "Sorry, Dad. I should be down for the second period."

Without waiting for his response, Lia sprinted towards the stairs, nearly slipping on the hardwood floor, and ran, skipping a step upwards. She shut the door behind her and threw her belongings - except for Noodle - on her bed. Instead, Lia gently placed Noodle back in her vivarium where she crawled onto a branch to take refuge. Lia, on the other hand, was far from retreating to the realm of sleep. She jumped onto her bed and pulled her laptop into her lap. She saved her essay and closed the document, making the internet browser full screen as she typed in a particularly odd search:

How to control other people.

Lia clicked search and then began to read the first result. At once, another piece of the puzzle fell into place and she practically ripped her notebook open by the way the pages clung to the spiral. She started to scribble down information like her life depended on it. Lia did not care how neat her handwriting needed to be. As long as she processed the information like she needed, that was more than enough for her. The singular brain cell that was once seeming to dominate her mind was joined by dozens. It was all coming together quicker than she could handle it. This discovery could be the keystone to solving this entire investigation that her curiosity had brought forth. There was no objection this time. Now, it was obvious.

Lia underlined a certain pair of words near the top of her page: *Coercive Control.*

This was it. Instead of wanting to smack herself, Lia patted herself on the back. This notion of hers might have been a bit far-fetched, but somehow, somewhere in her mind, it all made sense. There was no way she was wrong about this. In fact, it was unfeasible. That was how confident the teenager was in her investigative abilities. The hardest part was past her. Now, all she had to do was…well…maybe do something a little bit on the exasperating side.

She needed to play the Waiting Game.

Twenty-One

The Waiting Game was not a very amusing one of sorts to play. After being in the queue of time itself for over a full day, it was a miracle that Monday had come as quickly as it did. The previous day was spent by completing homework and doing more research on the concept of coercive control. Lia was more than certain that this was the culprit of Rowan's abnormality. How, though, was entirely a different playing field. Lia was never good at being patient, but she had to admit having extra time, no matter how minimal, got her thoughts in order.

Now, it was Monday morning, where Lia could not wait to speak to Rowan, or the other two Mêla if she happened to cross paths with them. While this could occur entirely by chance, Lia did not think that was going to happen, which was why she planned on ensuring that it did. She knew that Willow and Rowan shared their first class, Anatomy & Physiology, together on the second floor, but what about the others? Last week, she discovered that she and Jared shared PE again, which was going to be helpful to her in one way or another. She could employ him as a last resort if it was entirely necessary. She hated using the word "use" because then, she felt as if she was a manipulative person. At the time, though, maybe she was.

Lia rushed through her morning routine quicker than clockwork. In fact, she had time to make herself a couple pieces of cinnamon toast for breakfast rather than rummaging around in the pantry for a granola bar. Her lunch - still a peanut butter and no jelly sandwich - along with a couple other things she found in the kitchen, was packed. Her green canteen was squished in the cupholder of her backpack along with the rest of her supplies. Before she knew it, Lia - dressed in a green flannel with a white undershirt, black leggings, and a pair of slip-on checkered Vans - was out the door as soon as her mother got a hold of the car keys.

The teenager was closer to obtaining her driver's license–just two more months to go until she was old enough. She had already completed every requirement - a semester-long driver's education course and behind-the-wheel instruction - but now had to play the Waiting Game once again. Lia found the requirement to be a tad bit ridiculous, but what was she to do against the Georgia government? Instead, she placed that thought behind her and drove her mother to the Zuíhuí household. Lia's heart panged with guilt when she remembered using their home as an excuse to speak to Willow, plus Jared, outside of school. She hoped that Maylene and Yasmin were unaware of her actions, especially since their strict mother had answered the phone when Mr. Hart called about Lia's whereabouts. Lia bit her lip as the twins entered the back seat of the black vehicle. Either both twins seemed tired or were frustrated about something. Lia desperately hoped that the latter was not the truth.

The car ride to school was quieter than normal, but Maylene and Yasmin still shared conversation along with Cheyenne in the front seat. Lia was asked briefly why she was not talking or doing anything of the sort, but she turned Mrs. Hart's inquiry down, saying that she was simply tired and nervous for a test later in the day. In all honesty, there was no academic test, but one of wits instead. Lia had almost cracked the case–she just needed to take a few more steps before obtaining the end result.

Other than her brief question, Cheyenne acted as if nothing peculiar was occurring. When they arrived on the premises of Oakbrooke High School, she sent off the three girls just like she always did, telling them she loved them and that she hoped they all had a good day. The trio replied just like always, and Cheyenne got into the driver's seat of the sedan, satisfied. She would probably text her daughter later to check on her. At the same time, Lia accompanied both Yasmin and Maylene towards the doors. Both of the twins were walking slower than usual and - especially Maylene - had a look of worry in her eyes. Lia desperately wanted to ask them what was wrong, but she knew exactly what: herself.

"Is something going on with you, Lia?" Yasmin questioned when Lia said nothing. "I'm getting the feeling that something's wrong," she quickly concluded.

"What?" The brunette was caught off-guard resulting in a fib. "I'm just nervous for that test."

"We haven't heard from you all weekend and that's not like you. Plus, Mom told us that your dad called asking if you were over at our house. What gives?"

Lia knew this was coming, yet she somehow was not prepared. "I've been studying for that test for a long while," she carefully replied. "I got so stressed that I decided to take a long walk around the neighborhood. I guess I forgot to tell my parents where I was going and they assumed I was with you guys."

"But that doesn't make any sense," retorted Yasmin. "You're *never* this nervous for a test, and even if you were, you wouldn't spend the entire weekend studying."

Maylene pulled on her sister's sleeve and timidly countered, "It's a new semester and we're not used to our classes yet. They're getting harder, especially Lia's since she's so far ahead."

"That's what I meant," Lia added on, knowing full well that

it was a lie. "This Government & Politics class is kicking my butt. I had an essay and a ton of studying for our first test in class."

"I guess…" Yasmin was still not convinced. "I'm just confused. We'd be willing to help you if you asked us. You don't have to be doing this stuff alone."

"You have no idea…" Lia conjured a smile onto her face. "I'll keep that in mind after this test. I just needed time to study for it and make sure I knew each concept."

"Are you sure you're doing okay?" inquired Maylene with timidness.

"Yeah, I'm okay." Lia smiled although it was not quite authentic. "Thanks, you two."

"You're welcome," Yasmin replied and Maylene echoed.

And so, the trio of friends were on good terms once again. Lia had to admit to herself that making amends was much simpler than she initially thought possible, but now, she did not have to worry about it, so that satisfied her roaming focus. All Lia had to worry about in the present was the AP Government & Politics test that she ended up not lying about. It was the stress that she was making up as she went. Lia knew she was easily capable of receiving an "A" grade.

On the other end of the school, Willow and Rowan were making their way to their Anatomy & Physiology class on the second floor. It took everything in Willow's power for her not to share what she now knew with Rowan. After discovering Lia's knowledge of their homeland as well as their roles in it, Willow needed to have a conversation with Jared. She thought back to yesterday afternoon when Rowan was working at Claws & Paws.

All was still in the forest, but harmonious at the same time. Trees thickly lined every corner, providing shade that only fragments of sunlight and rainwater could ebb through. Birds chirped overhead and squirrels took refuge in their little holes of the woods. This dense under-

growth occurred on the outskirts of Oakbrooke Park. Unlike the greenhouse where Willow spent most of her time, where the Mêla had decided to call home was much more secluded. Unless you went looking for it, their temporary home would be invisible to the public eye. A cave carved into a rocky ledge was their choice of shelter...at least for a little while.

Willow sat alone in the small one-roomed burrow that the cave provided for them. To pass the time, she summoned a plethora of vines and ivy to insulate the cave from the outside in. She covered the entrance with these leafy arrangements. She ensured that the vines were not too heavy to push aside for entrance and exit, but thick to keep the heat inside and the cold air outside. This was something she did often to ensure the safety of her peers in their shelter that they could tentatively call home. She was not alone for much longer since Jared had pushed a few vines aside to let himself in. In his right hand hoisted over his shoulder was a bundle of branches to use as firewood. He placed the pile strategically in the center of the hollow.

"I need to speak with you," Willow stated something she had been considering.

Jared kept his eyes on the wood pile he was shifting around. *"What's up?"*

"Lia stopped by the greenhouse yesterday and said something quite interesting."

"Oh, really?" The boy played dumb. *"What did she say?"*

"Quit your nonsense," she firmly shot his façade down. *"I know you two have been conversing about Kythaela and the state that it's in."*

Jared sat cross-legged in front of the fire and attempted to create a spark with two rocks. *"Okay, you got me. Yes, we have discussed this."*

"And you've agreed to return."

"...Is that a bad thing?"

"Of course not," Willow assured his worried expression. *"You're following your heart, which is the most important, however, you cannot save Kythaela on your own."*

Jared hung his head and focused on the stones. *"I know."*

"Which is why I'm coming with you,"

"You are?!" The Taurus representative dropped both rocks and eyed her with bewilderment. He already knew what Lia had told him, but hearing it from Willow herself solidified his relief.

Willow's lips curved upwards. "Yes, I am."

"That just leaves Rowan…"

"I know, but I believe in Lia." The blonde's optimism was more elevated than Jared's. "She will figure out something."

Jared nodded, picking up the rocks and fighting for a spark. "I know. I just wish we could help or do something to make her life easier. I can't imagine being her age and having so much pressure."

"Remember our eighty-third birthdays when we were summoned to aid Her? We were practically kids then." Willow grinned at the memory.

"Oh, yeah… I remember that."

"We need to trust Lia. She'll figure it out."

A spark finally emitted from the two stones and lit the wood on the cave's surface. "I know."

Willow and Jared had decided to keep quiet about Lia's quest from then on and let the future handle itself. Their trust was laid in Lia to do the right thing and think of a way to persuade Rowan onto their side. Without the final member of the Earth Wing, their return to Kythaela would wholly remain hopeless… meaningless…pointless. Either way, the Mêla needed to stay together, no matter how Lia's meeting with Rowan would go. That thought alone was what plagued Willow's mind even as she and Rowan entered their classroom and sat down at their desks in the front row. Concentration was scarce for the time being.

The fog in Willow's mind did not cease when the professor on the latter half of life entered the classroom and began his lecture discussing the end of the first chapter of their textbook. Even though Willow had her notebook open and her pencil was copying down notes from the whiteboard, her entire existence was operating on autopilot. Like Lia, her head was high above the clouds in an attempt to gain a bird's eye view of the affair at hand. All she wanted was a final verdict to be proclaimed by the judge of reality, which often seemed to be against them. From the way Kythaela suffered and was still suffering, the ball was not in their court but rather a comet in outer space merely passing them by out of reach without a second glance.

The blonde's eyes wandered over to Rowan, who was diligently writing down notes of her own. She flipped to another page and began more scribbles - but with neater handwriting - on the next slide in the teacher's online presentation projected on the whiteboard. Her black eyebrows were furrowed and her hand cramped from the speed of which she was etching words onto the lined paper. Willow briefly halted with her own note-taking and watched as Rowan's body became more rigid as she hunched over her paper. Either she was very stressed about something, or she *desperately* wanted to achieve the role of valedictorian. Willow wanted the latter as well, but it was not as important to her anymore.

"Psst, Rowan," Willow whispered to her classmate and fellow Mêla. "Are you okay?"

She cringed when Rowan's body tensed and she muttered, "What's it to you?"

"My...she's certainly in a mood." Willow was certain that something about Rowan's demeanor had changed. "I'm worried about you."

"Don't be," the girl hissed. "I'm fine."

"No, you're not," Willow protested, concerned. "What's wrong?"

"I'll tell you later."

"Come on...what is it?"

"Girls," the Anatomy professor raised his voice at the two of them. "Can your conversation not wait until the end of class?"

"It can. I'm sorry," Rowan apologized for both of them.

"My apologies," Willow added on.

When the teacher continued on with his presentation, both Willow and Rowan awkwardly returned to their note-taking. By the way Rowan's face contorted into a glare, Willow could tell that her actions did not brighten her peer's spirits. Instead, Rowan tore off a sheet of notebook paper and wrote a quick statement on it. She folded it up and pushed it onto Willow's desk. At first, the blonde did not notice this gesture, but when she did, her heart dropped. She picked up the note, held it under her desk, and unfolded it.

Nice going. Do you not want me to win or something? Some self-sabotaging strategy you've got there.

Willow's stomach flipped at the blatant rudeness of Rowan's note. There was certainly something going on with Rowan, and it was an unsettling essence that plagued Willow's well-being. Willow had faith in Lia, though. She would find a way through the brushwood of Rowan's abrupt coldness towards the Virgo representative and possibly even the embodiment of Taurus as well. For now, though, Willow possessed the task of "laying low," which was much easier said than done. Passively existing was harder than she thought.

The rest of the school day was relatively quiet. Lia, Maylene, and Yasmin were still on good terms. During lunch, Yasmin branched off to meet with her usual group while Lia and Maylene sat together at their usual table. Lia appreciated the quiet throughout the rest of the day. It would be preparing her for her interaction with Rowan after school–the calm before the storm. She had already texted her parents that she was going to be walking to the local animal shelter to "hang out" with Rowan. Both of them replied along these lines: *"Have a good time!"* and *"Text when you need a ride home."* It was quite simple to guess which parent sent each message.

Only one class stood in Lia's way now, and that was Physical Education–her very favorite if sarcasm was allowed in this

CHAPTER TWENTY-ONE 273

narration. Lia had just changed into her gym clothes, once again being an old loose-fitting t-shirt and a pair of drawstring shorts along with comfortable sneakers. Lia set her backpack on the bleachers along with her other classmates' and grabbed her green water bottle to set it apart so it was easier to grab after such a vigorous exercise. It was easy to say that Lia would never get tired of Coach Jenkin's motivation, but it was the opposite reaction when her "motivation" was linked to physical exercise. Lia tied her chestnut ponytail higher and tighter on her scalp before dashing over to the rest of her peers. She ended up stopping next to Jared, who was at the rear of the pack. The only regret Lia had now was her diminutive height not allowing her to even see her professor who was barking out orders.

"Alright, everyone—you know the drill by now," Coach Jenkins' voice boomed throughout the gymnasium. "Complete your warmups and then meet back here."

Lia wished she could openly groan of frustration even though this was an everyday thing. Lia readied herself for her "warmups" as the coach called it, but the routine was really torture in disguise. Jared, on the other hand, was not at all fazed by such a daunting workout ahead. Side by side, both of them completed their twenty-five pushups, twenty sit-ups, and the grand finale of suicide sprints. By the end of it all, Lia was sweating bullets and gasping for breath through her aching chest. Meanwhile, Jared appeared as if he had not done anything at all other than the miniscule beads of sweat dotting his forehead. Still, he took a long, hearty sip from his plastic water bottle on the bleachers while Lia fought the urge to chug her own. She knew she needed to ration it throughout the rest of the class.

The teenager's gaze scanned the gymnasium and it looked like the rest of she and Jared's classmates were not even halfway through their warmups. By the way Coach Jenkins was fussing at each student, especially the new ones as of this semester, it seemed as if most of them were taking their own sweet time. She just shook her head and set her canteen back down on the metal bleachers. She sat down next to her belongings and let her legs dangle loosely above the floor. Jared, on the other hand, was ready for more. He stood eagerly awaiting his next "order," which was what he sometimes referred to a teacher's instructions as. Lia figured this would be a good opportunity to speak to him, so that was how she spent the short break both of them shared.

"I'm going to speak to Rowan after school," she notified Jared.

This clearly caught Jared's attention. "Oh, you are?"

"Yeah." Lia nodded, albeit nervously. "I'm walking to Claws & Paws after school. You did say Rowan would be working, correct?"

"That's correct. She actually leaves early since her last period is study hall…somehow. I wish I got that as well."

"Me too." The teenager knew full well that she easily could have, but she was saving that opportunity for her senior year of high school. "How is she doing, by the way?"

Jared merely shrugged. "Honestly…I don't know. She's been acting kind of weird towards Willow and I for a while."

"How so?"

"I don't know. She's just been more distant and maybe even hostile," he replied solemnly. "I'm just glad something hasn't happened to tear us apart."

"Is that foreshadowing? Please don't let that be foreshadowing…" Lia kept her courageous smile on and nodded. "Me too. I hope everything's okay with her. I'll try my best to get through to her today."

"Be careful," Jared worried out loud. "Ever since our descent into this world, Rowan hasn't been one for friend-making."

"I've guessed. I'm just worried that I'll say the wrong thing or something."

"You won't."

Lia's pupils enlarged. "How on Earth would you know that?"

"I'm not from Earth, Lia." Jared smirked at her concerned stance. "And besides, the Enchantress chose you for a reason. You'll know what to do."

"Well, that's helpful," she sarcastically frowned.

"You just need to trust me. Would I lie to you?"

"Hopefully not."

Jared shook his head. "I wouldn't. I hope you know that by now."

"...I think I do," she tentatively agreed. "I just don't have a plan, which I know is disappointing."

"Keep your chin up," Jared assured her despite being uncertain himself. "It'll come to you when you need it, and if you need help, just let Willow and I know."

"I just wish you two had phones so I could text you," sulked Lia.

"They're crazily expensive. It wouldn't be worth it if we can just see each other - and you - at school every day."

"That's true."

"Seriously, though." Jared gently squeezed her bicep. "You'll do great."

Despite the odds being stacked against her, Lia grinned at the gesture. "Thanks, Jared. I'll let you know how it goes tomorrow. Meet me outside the entrance before first block?"

"Sounds good to me."

"Alright, class! Now that you all have *finally* finished your warmups, let's meet at the center to discuss our next order of business!"

"I guess duty calls." Jared shrugged and started towards the center. "You can do it," he repeated authentically.

"Thanks, Jared."

Lia followed behind the Mêla who had become a good friend to her in such a short time. While she was still anxious over her future encounter with Rowan, her and Jared's discussion was beneficial to her mental and emotional preparation. After yet another tasking selection of instructions, all Lia had to do was make her way to the Claws & Paws animal shelter downtown once the Physical Education session would eventually come to an end. Lia cracked her knuckles and persevered anyway, clueless to the conviction that the worst was yet to come.

Twenty-Two

This was it. Lia's chance to speak with Rowan one-on-one had finally arrived. Too soon or not hastily enough was out of the question. Either way, it was here, and the weight on Lia's shoulders telling her "Don't mess this up!" only continued to get heavier with each step she took. The semi-busy streets of downtown Oakbrooke were nothing compared to the taunting that a little voice pounded upon her. She knew exactly where the animal shelter was. Heck, she had lived in this small town for years upon years.

Oh, how Lia wished she had brought Noodle when the thought surfaced. Still, she would not have been able to return home and have her mother give her a ride to the animal shelter without throwing a fit over the "anaconda-looking" thing that Lia called her best friend. Well, Maylene was technically her best friend, but in human form. Noodle put her and the rest of the people Lia surrounded herself with to shame. All Noodle needed to do was exist in Lia's presence and the teenager was brainwashed by her enamoring personality and affection. The fact that such a small living being could consider Lia her lifeblood meant the world to the girl.

As the teal Claws & Paws sign appeared over the horizon - or in reality, merely the sidewalk - warmth devoured her senses. She remembered visiting a shelter like this one who specialized in reptiles to adopt Noodle. This was basically the same scenario except for all of the adoptees having fur and loud voices rather than being near-silent scaly creatures. Lia was unsure of which she preferred, but she was certain of one important detail: she absolutely adored animals.

Such magnificent creatures were not what needed to be the focus of Lia's attention, however. Instead, she clenched and unclenched her fists rhythmically with her strides. Maybe it was her imagination hindering her tight respirations, but the proper explanation would be the slight uphill incline in the sidewalk. Cars whisked by on the road to her right; all of them seemed to have a particular destination that they were rushing towards a common goal. Lia was not one of those folks, though. Instead, she somehow managed to take her own pace while needing to move forward at the same time. So, she did just that. Lia marched onward and refused to let her preliminary fear get a hold of her. Instead, she stood tall and strode right to the front door of the Claws & Paws animal shelter. There was no turning back now, and even if she was tempted to do so, she would appear a fool.

That was why she opened the door with as much gusto as she had in her system. The front door swung open, flinging the poor gold bell off of its latch. Lia watched in horror as the small notifier clanged across the tiled floor until it eventually hit a wall which stopped it in its tracks. Her complexion became tomato red when the store clerk in his twenties watched her through his square glasses far up his nose. He wore a collared shirt, jeans, and a name tag saying "Henry," which Lia guessed was casual work apparel. All Lia could do was smile, walk over to the bell, and pick it up.

"I'm so sorry," she expressed, walking over to the counter and placing the bell on top. "I didn't think I opened the door that hard. If I broke your bell, I can pay for a replacement."

Contrary to the cashier named Henry's formerly stoic appearance, the young man smiled and waved it off. "Oh, no worries–we need a new bell anyway and were looking for an excuse."

"Are you sure?"

"Positive." Henry stuffed the bell in a compartment under the counter. "What can I help you with?"

"I was wondering if Rowan was working right now," Lia brought up her query. "I'm a friend of hers and had some questions regarding our homework."

The cashier boy smiled and gestured towards a door next to the counter. "She's feeding the pups their dinner right back there. Knock yourself out."

"Thank you! Are you sure it's okay to go back there?"

"It's fine with me. That's where all of our eligible dogs are being kept and taken care of behind the scenes. If you want to go on back, I don't see why you can't."

Lia beamed a hearty smile. "Thank you! I'll definitely leave this place a good review."

"Wow, that means a lot." Henry returned the gesture. "Thanks for your support."

"You're welcome. Bye!"

Henry offered her an awkward wave as Lia made her way to the door and steadily opened it. At once, her senses were overcome by the presence of...*dogs*. The barking filling her ears, the smell of dander and countless bowls of dry food, and a vast assortment of surprisingly generous kennels for each adoptee made it obvious. This place was like a hotel for its furry residents. Every hotel had its unique form of room service, and that was exactly what Lia was searching for. Sure enough, when she rounded the first corner that she was aware of, she spotted Rowan in a completely different state than she was used to. First of all, her hair was tied in a tight bun at the top of her head. Instead of her usual maroon hoodie or flannel, she wore a loose-fitting tee and a pair of ripped jeans. Her double-knotted black shoes were well worn. Lia guessed those were the pair she wore to work most of the time. Lia hid behind one of the kennels while Rowan cheerfully made her way to one of the dogs about halfway down the aisle.

"Alright, Vincent, here you go!" Rowan dumped some of the dog food out of the giant bag she was carrying into his bowl. "You do like that amount, don't you? Just a little extra to keep your teeth strong?"

A couple of barks later from the black and tan dachshund staring happily up at her and Rowan continued, "Oh, good–I got it right this time. Enjoy your dinner, Buddy."

Another bark from Vincent made her stop in her tracks.

"Oh, I'm so sorry. I forgot you didn't like to be called that. Am I forgiven?"

Bark!

"Okay, good."

Rowan moved on to the dog next to "Vincent" as she had called him and repeated the same process. "Hello, Ginger! I hope you're having a good day," she exclaimed while pouring the food into the Yorkshire terrier's bowl. When Ginger whined, Rowan frowned. "Oh, I'm so sorry you couldn't catch your tail. That must be really hard. You'll get it next time, though!"

At Rowan's response, Lia could not help but snicker. Dogs had the most miniscule of problems compared to humans - even *children* - in this day and age. She was unable to mask her perfectly human urges to react to such an amusing dilemma. Sure, dogs were much different than people, but this was what made them so much better, to be perfectly honest. Lia forgot where exactly she was and what she was doing there. When a small giggle emitted from her mouth due to that fact, Rowan stopped in her tracks. Her posture stiffened and her eyes narrowed into slits. Lia bit back a gasp and froze behind the kennel she was using as a shield. She pushed her glasses up her nose and instead of following the sound, she merely stated something Lia did not know.

"I know you're here."

Lia wanted to ask what she meant, or if Rowan was mistaking her for someone else, but prior to her making a move, Rowan's firm voice cut through her whirlwind of panic. "Don't shield yourself any longer, Lia. I'm already aware of your presence."

"*Uh oh...*" There was no backing out of this one. Lia rose to her feet and awkwardly revealed herself to Rowan's piercing gaze. "Um...hi," she squeaked. "I'm sorry for disrupting you."

"You aren't allowed in here," Rowan said instead of something along the lines of "It's okay."

"The guy at the front desk named Henry let me back here, so technically, I'm allowed."

Rowan rolled her eyes and continued on down the line of feeding the dogs. "Okay, whatever. Why are you here?"

"I wanted to talk to you?" Lia attempted to create an excuse.

"A better excuse than that, Ophelia."

"How do you know my full name?"

Rowan merely shrugged. "It was in the school's directory."

"Why the heck were you looking in the directory?" Lia spluttered out.

"I was curious, okay?" The girl dumping food into a dog bowl was more defensive than Lia had originally imagined. "Is that a crime?"

"...No, it's not." Aha! Here was some conversation material! "So, how are you liking it at Oakbrooke?"

"I'm quite enjoying it. It's my senior year, though, so I'll be gone before long."

"What about Jared and Willow?"

Was it Lia's imagination, or did Rowan's body ridge even more? "They're seniors too."

"I thought so," Lia shrugged. "You guys are really close and look the same age."

"Don't all teenagers in high school look the same age?"

"Huh," Lia wondered out loud. "I guess you're right."

Rowan moved on to another kennel forcing the brunette to follow her. "I know you aren't here to chit-chat," she accused her. "What are you *really* here for?"

That was quite straightforward. Then again, Rowan was one to cut to the chase. Lia certainly was not here for "chit-chat" as she called it. Instead, she was here for something much more serious. How did Rowan pick up on it so fast? Maybe it was the way Lia was stupidly hiding behind one of the kennels and "spying" on her. In reality, she was working up the courage to approach the most distant of the Earth Wing. This was it. Lia cracked her knuckles and opened her mouth to drop the bomb, but she was stopped by Rowan bending down and picking up a beagle puppy who had been barking at her and scratching at the door. When the puppy proceeded to lick her face, a giggle escaped Rowan's mouth. Lia did not want to ruin her fun.

"So, you're close with animals?" she asked instead.

Rowan was caught by surprise, but she nodded and kept her eyes on her furry friend. "Very close," she replied truthfully. "This here is Snoopy."

"Oh, named after the Cashews character?"

"...Yes."

Lia guessed the hesitation was because she had no idea what "Charlie Brown" was. "That's adorable! How old is he?"

Snoopy barked, seeming to answer the question himself, but Rowan did for him. "He's about five months old. Oh, excuse me, six months old. He's the runt," she added the last couple of sentences after a whine from the dog.

Wait a minute. Lia's train of thought skidded to a stop. It seemed as if Rowan and Snoopy had been having a full-on conversation, or at least Snoopy corrected her mid-reply. This was much more of a connection with animals than Lia had ever seen before. She thought back to just a few minutes ago when Rowan would speak to the animals. Would they speak back? How would Rowan know so much about each animal if they did not tell her directly? Then, it clicked. Everything made sense now!

"You can talk to animals," Lia breathed in disarray.

Rowan grew deathly silent. Her eyes resembled wildfire as they bore into Lia. "What do you mean by that?" she gritted out.

"Exactly what I said." The brunette bravely stood tall. "You can talk to animals, and I know why."

"This is preposterous."

"No, it's not!" Lia argued, stiff. "I know what you're hiding, Rowan. Jared and Willow hid similar secrets, but I'm on your side." She did not hesitate to reveal the Ring on her finger. "Kythaela's in danger, Rowan… We need your help."

Instead of replying with some sort of enthusiasm, all Rowan did was continue on with feeding the dogs. At first, she ignored Lia's plea for aid. She knew that Jared and Willow needed her help, but for some reason, all of the empathy that used to be in her body had completely drained. This was not what she wanted when arriving in a new place. She was comfortable here in Oakbrooke, and she was not planning on leaving it, so she expressed that with one simple word:

"No."

"*What? This isn't how it's supposed to go!*" Ignoring the roaring panic that was building in her chest, Lia began to protest, "What do you mean, *no*? We need your help…"

Rowan shook her head, barely acknowledging her presence. "I said no."

"But why?" she spluttered out, anguished. "We can't do this without you."

"Too bad, then."

"Tell me why!" Lia ignored the fact the Backstreet Boys' most popular song began playing in her head on loop.

"I've bonded with the animals here," Rowan replied, her voice becoming calmer when she began petting a golden retriever. "I cannot abandon them, and besides, why would I want to leave for that wasteland?"

"So, you can *fix* it. Don't you care about your home at all?"

"No."

Lia tried to understand, but it was to no avail. "Okay, I get it. I know you're attached to all of these animals, but why won't you look into your place of origin and want to restore it? Are you that selfish?"

"Selfish? *Selfish*?" Rowan roared, dropping the bag of dog food. Lia swore smoke blew out of her ears. "You're calling me selfish when all you want is to feel wanted. Loved. Respected. You want to be the hero but get this: it's not going to happen. Why? Because you *failed*, Lia. I'm not coming home."

"But-"

"Don't even try it." The Capricorn representative marched away from her. "I don't know how much you know about us or our Katáris or our world for Her sake. Just shut your trap about this nonsense and let me continue my duty."

Ouch… Rowan's comments were unexpectedly stinging. Lia wished tears did not threaten to spill from behind her eyes. Instead, she willed herself to be brave, and, most of all, get the job done that she was assigned. How was she going to complete such a daunting task if the cornerstone was shattered into pieces? No matter how much Lia wanted to run through the exit door with her tail between her legs, she knew she needed to stay strong and fight for what was the moral thing to do.

"Can you at least *consider* what's at stake?" Lia hated how her bottom lip trembled. "It's really important. Maybe you should talk to Jared and Willow about it…"

Rowan's eyes flashed a menacing red. "Oh, believe me, I will."

It was an understatement to say that Lia suddenly thought that Rowan was quite scary. She began to back away from the prowling tension beckoning itself over the edge. Lia was unsure of what to do now. Should she leave? Should she consult Jared and Willow for guidance? Then again, the Enchantress did swear her to secrecy. Did that count with other Mêla as well? At

CHAPTER TWENTY-TWO

the same time, Lia wanted to analyze what exactly was occurring behind the scenes with Rowan. Why was she so attached to this world? Were there no other species in Kythaela she could take care of? What about the ones that were currently suffering?

Either way, prior to Lia making any sort of assessment on Rowan's odd behavior, the entire scenario became even weirder with the flip of a switch. Henry opened the door and led a husband and wife along with a little girl into the vast array of kennels. At once, Rowan put on a smile and gave the last waiting dog their food before tucking the large bag away in a storage closet. As if it was routine, a ginormous smile appeared on Rowan's face and she dashed over to the little family, slowing to a stop in front of them. Lia was baffled by her sudden friendliness.

"Hi, there!" Rowan chirped with her best professionalism. "What can I do for you?"

"We're looking for a dog!" the little girl exclaimed.

The father chuckled, "Yes, we're looking for a dog. Are there any who need good homes?"

Rowan turned towards the vast array of dogs, but one's bark stood out from the rest. She turned on her heel and grinned. "I think I have just the dog for you." *"And I know because he just told me himself,"* she added internally.

Lia watched from the sidelines as Rowan led the family towards Vincent's kennel. She took him out and the little dachshund leapt right into the girl's arms. She could not help but smile as her parents crouched down around her and immediately showered the black and tan fluffball with all the affection they had in their hearts. Rowan stood above them with a knowing smile, especially since Vincent had said, "Let them pick me, please!" and the other dogs encouraged him, saying, "Let him go! He deserves a loving family!"

The mother looked at Rowan with a grin and proposed, "I think this is the one."

"Fantastic!" Rowan cheered, albeit bittersweetly. "Let's get started on the paperwork."

Henry, who somehow had made his way next to Lia, explained in a hushed tone, "I don't know how we survived without Rowan."

"...What do you mean?" Lia nervously inquired.

"She always seems to know which dog wants which customer." He smiled at the happy family following behind Rowan, Vincent being in the little girl's arms. "It's like she can understand what they're really saying and pairs them up with the perfect match."

Lia hesitated. She needed to be careful–she was sworn to secrecy after all. "Yeah, that's incredible. She has a talent for it."

"Oh, absolutely. I hope we can keep her on the force for as long as we can."

"*Oh, good. Now, I feel like a jerk.*" Rowan was very clearly occupied, so Lia turned to Henry and generated a smile. "Thank you for your help."

"No problem!" The cashier returned the gesture. "I hope you were able to chat with Rowan about your homework."

Lia offered him a polite nod before turning around and walking through the door that Henry promptly opened for her. She was too drained to express her gratitude any longer, so she kept her mouth shut. She surely did have some "homework" that she needed to improve on. Lia left Claws & Paws emptier than she was entering. Now, she had no idea what to do other than consult the other two members of the Earth Wing. They knew Rowan best, after all. The conversation would have to wait until tomorrow, however, since Lia had no clue where the Earth Wing was holding residence. Asking Rowan seemed like a bad idea too, so she did what she could. She walked home with her tail between her legs.

The rest of Rowan's shift passed by quicker than she would have liked, especially after the commotion that Lia brought forth. Rowan was perfectly comfortable with her job, close to earning enough money to rent a small apartment for herself, Jared, and Willow. Sure, there was quite a bit of temptation to take most of the money for herself, but she knew her closest friends needed it just as much. That was why she was slowly asking for more hours, which could also become an excuse to remain here in this world. Rowan wanted to see how far she could get in this society, especially since Kythaela was so different. She did not care for the latter anymore.

The fact that an ordinary human cared more about her homeland more than she did filled Rowan with boiling hot rage. She knew precisely how this situation came about; she was going to find the source and rip into it with her stormy tone. Nothing was going to stand in the way of something that made her feel wanted...loved...respected. Those were the same things she accused Lia of being, but did she feel a sliver of guilt? Absolutely not. This was none of Lia's business and Rowan wanted to keep it that way. Even if Jared and Willow were *miraculously* on her side, Rowan was going to walk down her own path. No one could stop her at this juncture.

She made her voice heard when she shoved the ivy doorway that Willow created out of the way so she could storm into the cave. Sure enough, there were the other two members of the Earth Wing. Jared and Willow sat around a small campfire that the former had made. Willow was focused on a textbook she had rented from the Oakbrooke Library. This only poked the bear more until its claws came out. Rowan fought the urge to stomp the fire out, but it was cold outside and she could benefit from its warmth as well. Instead, she glared at the two of them and bellowed:

"You two told Ophelia about our homeland and now you want to go *back*? What is wrong with you two?! We're making a new life here!"

Jared only cocked his head to the side. "Ophelia?"

"That's Lia," Willow whispered.

"Oh." The boy got to his feet and dusted off his jeans. "We

didn't tell her. She already knew. Didn't she show you the Ring from the Enchantress?"

"Yes, but I don't care about that," Rowan argued wildly. "I don't *want* to go back. It's pointless, and the fact that you two really believe in this puny *child* over me is ridiculous."

"Rowan, what do you have against Lia?" Jared defended his friend.

"She just barged in during my shift and tried to feed me hogwash regarding Kythaela. She doesn't know anything about us or our world. How can we expect her to know how to save it?"

"Because she's been learning about it. Wouldn't you want to save a realm of innocent people left to practically freeze to death? We can help them but not without you."

Rowan crossed her arms over her chest. "I am *not* going back and you can't make me."

Jared and Willow looked at each other in shocked silence. Neither of them knew what to do regarding Rowan's sudden ignorance and indifference towards their home's destruction. Both of them had been convinced and were already making a game plan about what to do when they returned, but Rowan... Rowan was going to be much more difficult to sway than they thought, which was completely unlike her. There must have been something going on behind the scenes, but what could it possibly be? From the way Jared and Willow possessed blank stares, neither of them were even close to discovering the truth.

"This isn't like you, Rowan...are you okay?" Willow tentatively inquired.

"I'm *wonderful*," She used sarcasm to clap back. "Once I get comfortable in our new home, you two have to pull this out of your asses and shove it in my face."

"Now, wait a minute," Jared countered rather loudly. "We're in this together and we can't go through with this without you. If you don't come along with us, then Kythaela is doomed to completely freeze over. Everyone will be *dead*, Rowan."

CHAPTER TWENTY-TWO

"Why's that my problem?"

"What is *wrong* with you?!" cried Willow in utter anguish.

"At least consider..."

"I'm happy here and I'm not going to let either of you stop me." Rowan tightened the straps of her backpack around her shoulders and gathered whatever items she had strewn about in the cave.

"Are you...*leaving*?" Jared's jaw fought to drop.

"I'm going to rent a room somewhere until you two come to your senses."

"What in the world, Rowan?" Willow was now standing. "Can't we at least talk this out before you just up and leave? We're a team."

Rowan's eyebrows lowered and her eyes became slits. "It doesn't seem like we're all working towards a common goal, though...are we?"

Just after that statement, Rowan stormed out of the cave and let the vine doorway swing shut harder than usual. Jared began to walk after her, but Willow clamped her hand around his wrist. Due to his Katári, the act of breaking free and chasing after their friend was like breaking a toothpick, but he listened to Willow's silent plea anyway. He backed away from the doorway and then sat cross-legged by the fire once again. Willow sat next to him rather than across from him. She placed a gentle, soothing arm around his shoulder.

"It's okay, Jared. Just let her go," she tried to advise him.

"How can we just "let her go" as you say?" Jared stared into the burning embers agonizingly tearing each branch apart. "We're supposed to stick together."

"I know, and she'll soon realize that," Willow replied in a softer tone than even she expected. "We just need to...give her space, I guess."

"How much space could she possibly need?"

Willow looked him in the eyes. "As much as she's going to take."

"I guess that's true," the boy exhaled through his teeth. "We need her."

"I know. We just need to trust her."

"After she got up and left us?" Jared scowled and flicked a small pebble across the cave floor. "That doesn't seem very *trustworthy* to me."

"I know, but it will work out. Remember who got us into this in the first place–we have someone else on our side."

His eyes seemed to light up a little. "That's right. Without her, we wouldn't even be here discussing this and how we can move forward. We're one step closer."

"Exactly. I hope you know what I mean by this."

Jared thought for a moment, considered it, and came back blank. "...What do you mean by this?"

"We have all of the resources we need to fix this except for one."

"Really? What's that?"

"Patience."

Patience...such a debilitating asset to every situation, but also a necessary one. Waiting was what made most individuals become destined for eventual failure. The Taurus and Virgo representatives knew that this could not happen whatsoever, or their entire plan would shatter into pieces. Patience was what their entire worldview was built upon at this very moment. Nothing could alter it. Nothing could *fix* it. They simply needed to lay low until the final piece of the puzzle fell into place.

Thus, it was not only Lia playing the Waiting Game, but the other perspective as well. Neither standpoint knew what was going to happen next...or how their next encounter would change the trajectory of reality's fabric itself.

Twenty-Three

Lia had no idea how she had gone so wrong so quickly. One minute, she thought she was going to make at least some sort of progress with Rowan. The next, she was walking out of the animal shelter knowing less than she did before. It was as if she was in some sort of blackout, but when she turned on the nearest flashlight, the batteries were dead and the sole light source flickered away like all knowledge Lia had gained over the past couple of months. It was now the beginning of February - the first, to be exact - and Lia felt no closer to the verdict of what was going to occur next. Were all of her attempts already in vain? She still had Six more to find! If only she had known of what transpired the previous evening. If Lia was aware that Rowan had booked a hotel downtown by the animal shelter merely to avoid Jared and Willow, she would be in absolute shambles. Lia would need to discover this very soon, and that was about to happen in the near future.

The new semester was aging like milk instead of fine wine. Already, most students had grown tired of their new schedules and were counting down the days to Spring Break in a couple of months or even Summer Vacation later in June. In some way or another, Lia caught herself becoming one of those students, except she was crossing off the days of her metaphorical calendar until a solution was brought to her attention. This entire quest felt like a broken record playing a loop of her least favorite song. While she adored her new friends, she knew that in order for them to succeed, she would never see them again afterwards. Her skin absorbed that sinking feeling. She needed to get over it and not be selfish as Rowan had accused her of being yesterday. She had Maylene and Yasmin after all.

The twins... Lia had nearly forgotten about their presence due to the massive weight on her shoulders that only kept adding plates leading closer to her crumpling under the increasing pounds. Sure, Lia had driven the twins to school that day with her mother and walked through the front doors with them, but each of them had classes to go to, leaving Lia alone once again. At least the three of them were on good terms with each other, as both Maylene and Yasmin offered Lia a group hug. The brunette was comforted by the gesture, filled with warmth all the way down to her toes, but it did not solve everything. What certainly did not help was the sudden appearance of both Jared and Willow directly in front of Lia as she rounded the corner consequent to bidding farewell to the twins.

"Woah...hello," Lia stammered, not expecting their arrival.

"Good morning, Lia," replied Willow in her normal ginger tone, but something undetectable was uncanny. "May we walk with you?"

"Um, sure. Is everything okay?"

Jared shook his head, but Willow nodded. "We merely need to clear up some fog."

"What do you mean by that?" Lia cocked her head to one side.

"We need to tell her," he whispered to Willow, although the teenager could hear it full well.

Lia decided to butt in. "What do you need to tell me?"

Jared and Willow looked at each other in silence. It felt a bit odd, standing in the middle of the hallway while everyone else was filing into their respective classrooms. Lia never had been late before, but there was a first time for everything. Lia hugged her notebook to her chest that she was planning on using for her first class: Advanced Placement Government & Politics. What on Earth were Jared and Willow hiding from her? Had this been occurring for a long time? Worry began to cloud her judgment. What had she done wrong?

"Did something happen?" Lia pressed on nervously.

Once more, Jared and Willow eyed each other before the latter confessed, "Yes, something has happened with Rowan."

"What?" Lia's eyes grew larger. "What happened? Is she okay?"

"None of us have that sort of information," Jared replied–it seemed as if he had lost all hope.

At this point, Lia was desperate. "What happened?" she repeated once more.

He shot Willow a pleading look. "Tell her."

"I guess there's no more avoiding it," Willow exhaled and then looked Lia in the eye. "Rowan was angry after your confrontation with her yesterday and it caused a rift between us. She moved out and is keeping her distance.

The blood running through Lia's veins grew cold. Could this be true? "What?" was all her voice could muster.

"She wants to remain here at all costs, and if that means pitting Kythaela towards destruction, then so be it."

"Oh, my God." Lia's conscience grew weaker. *"This is my fault..."*

Right there, right then, Lia's entire world came crashing down around her. All of her efforts *had* been in vain, just as she feared. Rather than bringing the Three together, she pushed them further apart. At least the Earth Wing were previously living in the same residence. That was about as "together" as one could get. Now, though, she had jeopardized it even more. Lia's knees shook and locked up as if they were holding up a crumbling statue ready to dissolve into the dust it came from.

"I'm so sorry," the teenager's tone was as broken as she felt.

At this, Willow's face fell. She lurched forward to place both hands on Lia's shoulders to steady her. "Lia... Don't blame yourself..."

"Who else is there to blame?" Lia choked out. "I was given a task and now it's ruined. I don't know where I went wrong, but I did and now lots of people are going to die."

"Lia..." Jared's solemn face only broke her heart more.

His consolation was too late. The tears building up behind Lia's eyes finally spilled onto her cheeks. "I'm...so...sorry...," she began to sob.

"No, Lia, don't..."

Before Lia could register what was going on through her teary outlook, there were two pairs of arms locked firmly, but gently around her. At first, she tensed up, only being used to receiving hugs from her parents, grandparents, and the twins. This one, though, felt different. A comforting warmth oozed through both Jared and Willow's bodies. As it ebbed into Lia's, it felt like a warm blanket was draped over her shoulders. She promptly wrapped her arms around the two taller figures who were providing her with as much peace as they harbored within their very beings.

"Lia, no matter how daunting the task may be, remember that, essentially, you're still a *kid*." Willow's right hand rubbed soothing circles upon Lia's back. "Nothing you could've done would have prevented this from eventually happening. Ever since we arrived in this world, Rowan has been - oh, how should I say it? - *off*. None of us know what it is, but it is nowhere near your doing."

"That's right," Jared agreed, his breath fading upon her ear. "You're a tough girl, Lia, and it's incredible how you've gotten this far."

Lia sniffled, trying to ignore the sudden congestion in her nose, "You think?"

"We know," both of them chorused.

Willow gave Lia one more tight squeeze before letting go, to which Jared followed her lead. "We're here to help you," the blonde reminded her. "What can we do to make your quest just a little bit easier?"

"I...don't know." Lia wiped off each side of her face with her sleeve. "I do know that I want to apologize to Rowan, though. Hearing her side of the story would be the best idea I've got."

Jared ruffled her hair with a smile. "I think that's a great idea, but be careful."

"I will."

"When are you thinking of speaking with her?" Willow inquired.

"After school." Then, a light bulb lit up in Lia's mind. "Hey... I have a great idea! What if I give her a little gift? I can skip my last block, stop by a store and find something to give to her before she...wait." Another light bulb! Yes! "What kinds of things does Rowan like?"

"That's very generous of you," Jared admired her sudden optimism.

Willow thought for a moment and then smiled. "She loves anything that has to do with nature."

"Well, that narrows it down," Lia thought sarcastically, but grinned instead. "Thank you both. I really appreciate your help."

"Let us know if there's anything else we can do," Jared reminded her.

"I will. Thank you."

Now, Lia had another item on her list that she needed to check off sooner rather than later, and that was Operation: Mending Ties. She was experiencing lots of "firsts" all in one day, the first of the firsts being late to class after she and two-thirds of the Earth Wing's conversation...or more like a crying session. Lia absolutely despised when she needed to cry. She could never control it, especially under deep pressure or stress. This encounter was no exception, especially when the fate of an entire world hung in the balance.

Sneaking out of school just before her final class was not exactly what Lia had in mind when she got out of bed that morning. It was another "first" of hers. She only skipped school when she was physically sick, and even then, she would provide a doctor's note to ensure that her teachers never thought illy of her. Would you look at that? A pun in that previous sentence was not intended. Rather than leaving school early being difficult, the actual process was much simpler than she thought. After sending a quick text to her parents, Maylene, and Yasmin saying that she would be hanging out with a friend after school - specifically Rowan - she gathered her belongings in her backpack and slipped out the front doors while the hallways were occupied with her peers switching classes.

No matter how silly it sounded, Lia thought that the next best course of action would be to hide behind the shrubbery lining the perimeter of the vast school building while she waited for Rowan to exit. From a previous conversation, Lia discovered that she left the school's premises early due to her having study hall as her last block of the day. That must have been very helpful with the job she picked up at Claws & Paws. With a pang, Lia wondered how difficult it would be for Rowan to explain to her boss that she needed to quit her job due to her own world being in grave danger. Of course, she probably would lie...if she left them at all. That was up to Lia's next actions to decide.

Soon enough, Rowan appeared from the double doors and began to walk in the direction of downtown. Lia was not technically following her. Instead, she was merely...*checking* to ensure she was working that day. Even though Jared and Willow told her that she was, Lia could never be too careful. When Rowan finally disappeared from earshot and from view, Lia crawled out of the bush and brushed off the stray twigs, leaves, and dirt from her frame before heading in the same direction. Now, her plan was in motion. This had to work, because she had no clue what she would do if it did not.

CHAPTER TWENTY-THREE

One good thing about Downtown Oakbrooke was the vast variety of stores. Lia thought back to when Willow notified her that Rowan liked anything that had to do with nature. There were not many stores that had to do with nature itself except for the flower shop. Lia did not want a bouquet only for it to die a week later, though. Lia desired something lasting, something that would plant a positive seed in Rowan and would hopefully allow her to see her point of view. While indeed, she was still a kid, Lia was strong-willed and did not want anything to happen to her new friends or their homeland. If only Rowan understood that notion. That was why Rowan's gift needed to be *perfect*. Lia darted into an antique shop on her left. Maybe this store had something that Rowan would like. The old man at the register smiled in her direction and Lia returned the gesture.

"Afternoon, Sweetie!" he exclaimed in a way that was not creepy whatsoever. "Is there anything I can help you with?"

"Good afternoon!" Lia approached the counter. "Actually, there is something if you don't mind."

"Not at all! What can I do for you?"

"I'm looking for a gift for my friend. She loves everything that has to do with nature and animals. Do you have anything that fits that genre?"

It did not take long for the elderly man to consider. "Right this way, Sweetheart."

Lia eagerly followed the kind old man throughout the store. She knew that she needed to be careful when speaking to strangers, but this man seemed nice enough, and he would not have a store job if he harassed his customers. The graying man led her to a section of the store close to the back wall. Gradually, Lia grew suspicious, but when the man fought back a tiny hop of joy, all of her worries faded away. He gestured towards the section in the back right-hand side of the antique store.

"Over here, we have all of our most unique items as they affiliate with nature," he explained. "Personally, it's my favorite part of our store, but no one ever comes back here anymore."

Lia could not keep her jaw from dropping at what laid in front of her. Trinkets of new and old lined the shelves along with decorative ivy and flowers. The wallpaper was a moss green covered in several small paintings depicting each of the four seasons. Once Lia composed herself, she grinned at the old man and gave him a polite nod.

"This is perfect! Thank you."

The man smiled. "You're welcome. I hope you find what you're looking for."

"*Me too...,*" she thought to herself.

As soon as the elderly man returned to his position at the register, Lia began wandering the aisles that were defined by the naturesque theme. Most items were delicate statues of different animals or glass flowers. Even miniature paintings in frames were discovered hiding behind the rest of the items. Lia was unsure about these types of items. Maybe she should move to another store? But the older gentleman was so happy to have business... Lia was sure she would find something, and she was relieved to have listened to her gut when on the last aisle on the back wall, she discovered a mahogany wooden box. It was just big enough to fit in her two hands. Mushrooms were engraved on the front along with ivy and flowers growing around them. When Lia opened it, she instantaneously knew that this was what she was going to purchase.

Lia dashed towards the register and placed the box on the counter with a wide smile. "I found something, Sir!"

"Already?" He put the magazine he was reading down on his chair and walked over to the counter where he inspected the box. "My, what a wonderful choice! Because of your interest and patronage, I'd be happy to give you a fifteen percent discount."

Lia's eyes wanted to fall out of their sockets at that. "Really? You don't have to do that, Sir."

"I want to, especially since this box comes up to fifty dollars."

Oops... Lia had not even looked at the price. She had the money, but did not particularly want to spend it. Oh, well. She

CHAPTER TWENTY-THREE

needed *something* for Rowan. "If you're sure, then thank you very much!"

"Alright, little Missy." He rang up the box. "Your total comes to forty-five dollars and eighty-two cents."

Without hesitation, Lia inserted her debit card into the chip reader and typed in her pin while the man put the wooden box in a bag. "Thank you for your help."

"You're very welcome." He placed the receipt in the bag and handed it over to her. "I sincerely hope your friend enjoys your gift."

"I hope so too."

Lia offered one more smile to the elderly man and then frollicked out of the antique store. She speed-walked to the Claws & Paws animal shelter as quickly as she could without ending up out of breath. Since the afternoon slowly waned away, rush hour was almost upon Oakbrooke, which meant a lot more traffic and pedestrians were present, especially in the downtown area. Lia tried to ignore the numerous flocks of people stampeding down the sidewalks and streets. Soon, however, she found her escape by darting into Claws & Paws.

Unlike last time, there was no one at the front desk. Lia guessed that Rowan was working alone today, or maybe the cashier was in the back along with her. In fact, the entire shelter was silent other than the numerous animals barking, meowing, and even chirping from every direction of the shelter. This type of vacancy was uncanny to Lia, as if something was wrong. Maybe she was overthinking. Maybe something serious was occurring behind the scenes. What if Lia spent nearly fifty dollars for nothing? Although money was not her primary concern, Lia still would feel more at ease if she had not taken a sizable dent from her bank account. Thankfully, it turned out that she had been merely overthinking, since seconds later, Rowan emerged from the back door while on what Lia figured was the company phone. She held the flip phone by her ear and continued to speak, not noticing Lia's presence.

"Yes, that sounds wonderful!" her oddly friendly voice gushed. "I'll get the paperwork started for you so you can pick up Ginger tomorrow. Do you have any more questions? Okay. Thank you, bye."

Still not seeing Lia, Rowan walked back behind the counter and hung up the flip phone. She set it down next to the cash register. True to her word, She began typing up something on the store's computer - also on the counter - and watched as a nearby printer began to regurgitate several sheets of paper which Lia imagined was the paperwork she was speaking of. While the sheets were printing, Lia saw her chance. She approached the desk without thinking.

"Rowan, I need to talk to you."

The last Mêla's gaze snapped up to view her spontaneous customer. Her face fell when she realized it was Lia. "Can it wait? I'm working," she blatantly shut her down.

"No. It needs to be now," the teenager demanded; even she was surprised by the strength of her tone. "I don't care if you're working. You need to hear what I have to say."

"Give it up, Lia." Rowan walked over to the printer and picked up the sheets of paper, stapling them together with a nearby stapler. "What is *so* important that you've barged in here, interrupted my shift when I could be helping a customer, and are so *rudely* barking orders?"

"What customers?" deadpanned Lia.

Rowan looked around to sheepishly come to the conclusion that the shop was currently empty. "You get my point."

"I'm still not going to leave until you hear me out."

"Then, get on with it." Rowan rolled her eyes and occupied herself with the computer.

Lia took a deep breath, eyed the store to ensure it truly was vacant, and then expressed, "I mainly came here to say I was sorry."

A long hesitation occurred from Rowan's side. "...You came all the way over here just to say that?"

CHAPTER TWENTY-THREE

"I know you're attached to your animals, and returning home wouldn't give them the best environment even if you wanted to take them with you," elaborated Lia. "Willow said something similar about her flowers-"

"Bah! Enough about Willow," Rowan scoffed to Lia's shock.

"...What's wrong with mentioning Willow?"

"She just wants to prove that she's better than me. That's all she's here for."

"What?! Why on Earth would you say that?"

"We're both seniors at Oakbrooke High, so we're eligible to earn the role of valedictorian," Rowan explained her plight. "It was my idea first, but when I mentioned it, she instantly wanted to copy me. I gave her the option to compete, and then she instigated a whole competition dedicated to becoming valedictorian by the end of the year. Snotty stuck-up bi-"

"What? *Willow never said anything to me about that...*" Lia cleared her throat from the nausea crawling up it. "There's more to school than competitions."

"I know that, but she only wants to prove that she can get higher grades than me, that she can just…win at everything."

"Why don't you two talk about the issue?"

"I would, but not after she and Jared shoved you in the middle and made you their mole to get me to go back to Kythaela with them." Rowan clicked the mouse rather hard. "You don't understand - you wouldn't - because you're a *child*."

"Nobody has any ill-intent." Lia's voice shook as Rowan's tone grew louder.

"Prove it."

"Well…" The brunette reached into the bag she was still holding and pulled out the wooden box she had just purchased. "I can prove that I don't have any ill-intent because I came here to give you a gift."

"A box?" Rowan's eyebrows furrowed. "That hardly tops the teddy bear from last time."

"You remembered!" That simple statement planted more joy

in Lia's subconscious than she initially thought. "It's more than just a box, though." She placed it on the counter just after making sure the small metal lever was wound up all the way. "Open it."

Lia waited semi-patiently, rocking back and forth on her heels. She clasped her hands together in her lap as Rowan skeptically examined the box's top before eventually lifting the lid and letting it open. At once, a crystalline melody began to play in a major key that was automatically pleasing to the ear. Lia could detect that it was in the key of D Major and the melody resembled that of Howard Shore's *Concerning Hobbits*, but had a slightly different arrangement when it came to the specific notes. Rowan was instantaneously starstruck, the tune flowing into her ears. To some, Lia's gift was merely an ordinary music box, but not to Rowan. There was something much more luminescent to the melody ebbing from it. It was as if she was floating out of her own body, or at least part of what she thought was herself had abandoned her when the music box expressed its emotions of love and compassion directly from Lia's heart. There was no doubt about it.

This gift was magical.

Rowan's knees buckled and her body had had enough, especially since some of its essence, the intention unknown, had separated itself from her being. Lia jumped in fright when the figure behind the counter collapsed onto the floor without a word. She dashed around the painted wooden desk to find Rowan slumped against the structure. Her eyes were shut and her glasses were crooked. Unsure of what else to do, Lia began shaking her shoulders.

"Rowan? Rowan!" she pleaded with her unconscious state. "Wake up!"

Oh, God… What if she had hurt her?! Lia's fear quickly grew into a panic. Should she call nine-one-one? What would the operator say if they found out someone was knocked out by a music box? Frankly, Lia did not understand it herself, and she doubted Rowan would either if and when she came to. Thankfully, there was no one else in the store to question whatever insanity had just occurred behind the counter.

Lia's nerves quieted down when Rowan began to stir. A small groan rumbled in her throat. Rowan's eyes fluttered open when she felt another hand adjust her glasses. "What...what's going on?" she feebly asked.

"Rowan!" Lia breathlessly cheered. "Are you okay? Are you hurt?"

"I don't...think so."

"What happened back there? I played that music box for you and...you fainted. How can you faint from a music box?"

There was no answer.

"Rowan?"

Once more, the Capricorn representative was silent. Lia's palms began to sweat.

"...Rowan? Are you okay?"

Only one word was uttered from Rowan's mouth. "Something's wrong."

"What?" Lia's eyebrows shot up. "What's wrong?"

Instead of answering, Rowan grabbed the music box and opened the back door. "Henry!" she yelled.

"Yes?" the cashier from the other day replied from the back.

"Cover for me!" Rowan left no room for argument. "There's an emergency!"

Henry's voice grew concerned. "Is everything okay?"

"We'll just have to find out," Rowan muttered mostly to herself as she briskly walked back behind the register and hid the music box inside. "Come on."

"What?" Lia began to fret. "What's going on?"

"Just follow me."

Without another word, Rowan leaped over the counter - since apparently walking around it was too slow for her - and clamped her hand around Lia's wrist, dragging both of them out of the premises of Claws & Paws and down the sidewalk.

Twenty-Four

"Where...are...we...going...again?"

With a frustrated groan, Rowan slowed to a jog and turned around to view a quite fatigued teenager huffing and puffing to keep up with her. The black-haired girl ruled her eyes and dashed in the opposite direction. Rowan forced herself to slow down as Lia caught her breath while still speed-walking down the brief suburbs between downtown and Oakbrooke High School. Both of them were in a hurry, and Lia knew that, but it was impossible for her to keep up.

"Don't panic, but Willow and Jared are in danger," Rowan warned her.

"*What*?!" Lia shrieked. "Why didn't you tell me this before?"

"I didn't want you to panic, but obviously you're going to, so come on!" Rowan grabbed her arm again and continued to pull her forward. "The sooner we get there, the better."

Lia struggled not to lose her breath again. "Why can't you just tell me?!"

"Because this situation is too complicated."

"Complicated? I'm good with the complicated if you haven't noticed."

"How would you be good with the complicated?"

CHAPTER TWENTY-FOUR

Lia snapped back, "I've been hanging around with three interdimensional beings for two months and you think that's not complicated?"

"Touché, but you need to listen to me!" pleaded Rowan. "I can handle this myself. I don't want you getting hurt."

"Is that in a caring or passive aggressive way?"

The female Mêla frowned deeply at that. "Why would you think I would be passive-aggressive towards you?"

"You-"

It was no use. Rowan continued dragging her along until Lia realized they were in fact in transit to Oakbrooke High. "Why are we going back to the school?" she inquired.

"Have you not been listening?!" Rowan asked in exasperation. "Willow and Jared need our help and we need to find them."

"We? How am I going to help with this?"

"I thought you were smart."

A metaphorical hand smacked Lia in the face. "I *am* smart! How would you explain my perfect grades?"

"I have nearly perfect grades as well, but that doesn't essentially mean I'm smart," Rowan retorted between long strides. "I fell for that-"

When Rowan stopped herself, Lia decided to pry a bit. "Fell for what?"

"It doesn't matter. What *does* matter is that my fellow Mêla are safe."

"Why do you care all of a sudden?"

Rowan halted abruptly, which led to Lia nearly tripping on the flat concrete. The brunette opened her mouth to say something, but when two copper hands latched themselves onto her shoulders, Lia made the wise choice to keep her mouth shut. There was still something about Rowan that she did not trust. Lia needed to keep herself on her toes before she would be knocked off of them yet again. The way Rowan's eyes bore into her own unnerved her, but when she spoke, there was nothing but truth in her hushed tone.

"Listen to me, Ophelia. When it comes to Kythaela, there is always more than what meets the eye. In a sense, I fell for the oldest trick in the book: coercive control over any individual at the first sense of doubt or dismay. Upon escaping our homeland, I did not know what to do. I was trapped...hopeless...and needed help. Instead of receiving the aid I needed, I fell under the spell of fear in its physical form. You'll understand in the future."

All Lia could do was nod her head and close her open jaw. If there was something important that Lia needed to know, she would figure it out eventually. Despite the fact that Rowan seemed to be speaking nothing but gibberish, there was something about her tone that made her able to believe, and even more...*trust*. This made Lia more prone to follow Rowan when she spoke up yet again after there was no response from the teenager.

"Now, let's hurry. If any danger truly arises from here, then you must never leave my sight."

"Noted." Lia knew better than to argue and followed behind Rowan.

Oakbrooke High was still in session, which would make pinpointing this "danger" that Rowan spoke of even harder. That meant anyone within the premises was a suspect, and Lia was not looking forward to inspecting every single possibility that could take place. Rowan never let go of Lia's wrist as she walked towards the building. There was no time to ask any more questions. Rowan clearly knew what she was doing, so Lia followed behind. That was, at least until she stopped just after walking through the doors. Everything appeared as normal. The final block classes had just let out. Students flocked the hallways and made a break for the front doors, right where Lia and Rowan were standing.

"The danger is here…but it's not regarding the Earth Wing," Rowan mumbled, at a loss.

Lia eyed her companion with worried brows. "What? What does that-"

She was cut off by a scream beckoning from down the right hallway. Lia knew that scream, although she had never truly heard it before. All at once, Lia's world came crashing down for a second time, but this time, she was actually a part of it. Her blood ran cold and her palms began to sweat. It could only have been her best friend who had made that shrill, heart-stopping screech that was desperate for aid. Terror filled every inch of her body as she hastened towards the right-hand side of the school and realized that it was indeed Maylene…being held against her will by arms that resembled chains.

Declan.

"Maylene!" Lia cried in horror.

She looked desperately in between Maylene and Rowan. The latter merely shoved her towards her best friend and yelled, "Go! I'll take it from here."

Lia did not need to be told twice. Without looking back, Lia bolted towards her best friend that the brown-haired bully - or perhaps something more now… - had now claimed for his own. Maylene continued to yell for help, but no one, at least that Lia could see, was coming to her aid. It was all up to her. Lia wondered what in the world was wrong with this school. First, Willow and Rowan had a full-on brawl in the middle of the hallway with no interference, and now a young woman was being taken against her will by someone who could cause a heaping load of damage. Anger filled Lia's conscience. How could someone be this *cruel*?

Lia's mind clouded with pure fear. She had no idea what Declan Abner was truly capable of, but if he was taking Maylene against her will, possibly on some sort of a kidnapping charge, then that could not be a good thing. When Declan noticed her presence, he roughly yanked Maylene along and began sprinting towards the back of the school. Ignoring the fatigue clouding almost all of her senses, Lia broke into an even quicker sprint. Adrenaline flooded her veins and propelled her even faster, but somehow, Declan was almost impossible to catch, even with a deadweight who tried to run in the opposite direction. Maylene was about an inch taller than Lia, but she was quite petite, making her easier to "travel" with.

"Let her go, Declan!" Lia screamed at the top of her lungs, which finally got the attention of some of the teachers.

Declan was certainly not weakening anytime soon. "Why should I?"

"Leave her alone, you son of a-"

The teenager's profanities were drowned out by the commotion in the hallway. At least one group of high schoolers ran off to grab more teachers and even the principal. Such a situation as this was not common in the premises of Oakbrooke High School. Instead, it was very rare, which implemented fear into the student body. The city outside of Atlanta was not acquainted with acts of violence, especially in the school. With the Mêla's arrival, that all seemed to change, especially on the school's grounds. Lia continued to keep long steady strides even when an individual behind her shoved through the crowd with an extraordinarily loud mouth.

"Out of the way! Move it or lose it! Scram!" Before she knew it, Yasmin was dashing alongside Lia. "What's going on?"

"Declan's got Maylene!" Lia shakily disclosed and pointed in his direction.

"Oh, my God...," Somehow, Yasmin shot ahead of Lia and began closing in on the antagonist. "Let go of my sister!"

Either Declan did not hear her or he merely ignored her as he opened the door to the nearest approaching stairwell and slammed it in the duo's face. He dragged Maylene up the stairs, his grip so tight that Maylene thought that his hand was ripping through her skin. Tears pricked behind her eyes and did not hesitate to stream down her face. When Maylene could turn around briefly, the sight of her best friend shattering in front of her broke Lia's heart.

"It'll be okay, Maylene—we'll figure this out!"

No matter how many encouraging mantras Lia spoke to herself, her outlook was not getting any better. Yasmin, who was now in front of her, climbed the stairs after her sister and the one who was holding her hostage like she was a monkey scaling a tree. Lia could barely keep up without her breath running away from her, but her adrenaline and sudden energy spikes from the situation at hand disagreed with her. Before long, Lia was stunned to see the final door after the highest flight leading to the roof of the school. Declan had already powered through it and did his best to lock it, but that attempt was in vain since it only locked from the inside. Were criminals usually this dumb, or was Declan lacking more brain cells than the average person? Lia figured the latter was the case.

There was no escaping the two furious girls now. Only a limited space occupied the roof, and pretty soon, Declan was going to run out of room to escape unless he would circle back and go right back down the stairs. That would only make it harder to catch him, which gave Lia a sacrificial idea. Without giving it another thought, Lia opened the door and locked it from the inside before shutting it, which left the group of four all stranded on the roof. When Yasmin realized what had happened, her blood ran cold.

"Lia! What in the hell did you do?!" she squealed, trying to get the door back open.

"Stop it," Lia ordered in a whisper. "If we're trapped up here, then that means…"

Yasmin quickly caught on. "Oh! Smart…"

That did not seem to faze Declan, however. He continued to lead Maylene closer to the edge as Lia and Yasmin approached them with clenched fist and an unhealthy dose of fury. It appeared as if everything was going to plan. Whatever kind of plan would involve stealing Maylene from her last class, forcing her up the stairs, and onto the roof? Lia was unsure for now, but she was going to find out, especially since the more Declan backpedaled, the more the two girls could cage him in.

"Declan, stop this," Lia pleaded with him.

All he did was tighten his grip around Maylene's frame. She opened her mouth to scream again, but he clamped a palm tightly over the lower half of her face. He shot a wicked smirk towards them and sneered, "Why should I?"

"Let go of my sister!" Yasmin lunged forward to retrieve her twin from his grasp.

Lia clamped onto Yasmin's arm when Declan backed even closer to the edge and swiveled his body so that Maylene was teetering over the margin. The group of four were easily twenty feet off the ground, and that was more than enough to cause serious harm for anyone who would fall from the roof. Lia swore her heart stopped, especially when Maylene's heels were hanging off the flat roof. The only thing keeping her upright was Declan's steady hold, and no one could trust him to keep her safe, especially after his antics throughout the whole school year.

Declan's brows lowered sadistically. "Are you *sure* you want me to let her go?"

Both Yasmin and Lia took a step back, which only made his grin wider.

"That's what I thought."

"Declan, what is the meaning of this?" Lia softly questioned him. "Why are you hurting Maylene?"

"Do you *really* have to ask me that?" he retorted, being blunt. "Have I not made it obvious all year?"

Yasmin growled in his direction, "Cut the bullshit, Declan. You've been targeting my sister all year and for what?"

"How are none of you figuring it out by now?"

"Figuring out *what?*" Lia was getting closer to figuring out the answer, but she hoped to God that it was not true. "*Please don't tell me it's what I think it is...*"

Declan shrugged with the nonchalance he should not have

had. "If I want something that I can't have, then no one can have it," he disclosed, lacking any shame in his words. "I'm making this possible right now."

All movement on the roof stopped.

"It is..." Lia's stomach plummeted down to her toes.

"Are you *shitting* me?!" Yasmin roared in pure agony. "You're abusing my poor sister because you *like* her?!"

"I always have," he confessed through gritted teeth. "She was just too selfish to see it, only focusing on her sister and her "best" friend. When she continued to express no interest towards someone who obviously wanted what's best for her, I began forcing her attention in my view."

"You...you piece of trash," snarled Lia. "Why couldn't you just *speak* to her rather than making her life a living hell? Don't you realize what you've done has made a domino effect in the opposite direction?"

"I have, and now I'm going to deal with it."

"Let. Her. Go."

Declan loosened his grip on Maylene, causing her to slip and nearly fall off before he grabbed her again. "Are you sure?" he repeated with that same malicious intent.

Both girls gasped in fright when Maylene screamed just before he placed his hand over her mouth again.

"Declan, please stop this and let her go..." Lia tried again. "You'll already be in enough trouble as it is. If you drop Maylene, then you'll be convicted of attempted murder or worse."

Yasmin was close to tears at this point as well. "Don't say that. *Please* don't say that."

"No matter how much you don't want to believe it, it's true," she whispered to the girl next to her. "Follow my lead."

"...Okay," Yasmin unsteadily agreed.

"So, Declan...may I ask you something?" Lia knew she was treading on thin ice, but it was a necessary risk for her to take.

The boy grumbled, but seemed intrigued enough to say, "What is it?"

"I think you had a good plan here, but there are a few loopholes you forgot to tie shut."

Maylene's mind panicked even more. *"What is she thinking?!"*

"Oh, yeah?" Declan's eyes became slits.

"Don't get mad, now." Lia took a tentative step towards him and placed her hands in her pockets to prove she was not being hostile; at the same time, Yasmin approached the door with a bobby pin that was formerly holding up her messy bun while Declan was distracted. "I just wanted to give you a few pointers if there is a "next time.""

"...Why are you speaking to me in this way? You're making fun of me, aren't you?"

"No, not at all. I'm just trying to share my point of view with you." The teenager shrugged innocently. "Maybe if you had thought longer and harder about this whole thing, you would've gotten away with it. Instead of, say…dragging your victim all the way up the stairs, what if you did it in an easier-to-reach place? Instead of letting your victim scream, getting the attention of everyone in the building, what if you duct-taped their mouth shut or knocked them out first?"

Declan thought about it, still wary, though. "I didn't think of that, but I still won, so you need to beat it."

"Like the Michael Jackson song?"

A low growl rumbled from Declan's throat.

Lia just shrugged her shoulders. "You're very naïve, especially for a budding criminal. I only thought you were a petty thug, but the kidnapping charge will look quite serious on your record."

"Oh? And how would I have a record if no one can catch me?"

By this time, Yasmin was back by Lia's side. The latter smirked and cracked her knuckles. "Then they'll just have to find you up here instead."

"What? Hey-!"

In one fluid motion, both Lia and Yasmin lurched forward and snatched Maylene from his grasp that had loosened while he was distracted by Lia's suggestions. Little did he know that the conversation was a part of Lia's plan all along. While Yasmin would sneak away to pick the lock on the door with one of her bobby pins, Lia would keep Declan's eyes on her and hope that his mind would subconsciously wander from Maylene and instead onto Lia's ideas. So far, the plan seemed to have worked, but the second half was in transit.

All three girls - Lia, Yasmin, and now, Maylene - made a break across the roof towards the door that Yasmin had left cracked open, including around the massive oak tree that stuck through the top of the roof. Time slowed down around the higher ground and nearly stopped. Lia felt like she was in slow motion as she sprinted down the thankfully flat roof with Declan on their heels. When the trio reached the door, not a single wrong move could be put in place or their entire plan would be in jeopardy. With the cougar behind them ready to devour its prey, Lia shoved Maylene ahead of her and let her go through the door first, followed by herself, and then Yasmin coming up the rear. The latter slammed the door shut and locked the door - including the deadbolt this time - behind them. All three heartbeats stopped when the doorknob began jiggling, but it was to no avail. Declan began pounding on the door.

"Hey! Open this door! Let me out!"

None of the girls answered, instead running down the stairs and leaving Declan behind. The quite...slow teenage boy could continue banging on the door for as long as he wanted. In fact, if Lia were to call the police, they would be directed towards the loud thumps at the top of the stairs. Lia was in the lead as the three made their descent with Maylene sniffling and fighting back sobs along with her sister behind her rubbing calming circles on her back. With every whimper and hiccup, Lia's heart cracked just a little more. She could not believe that someone who she thought was just a petty bully who would do anything in his power to make someone's day just a little worse. That target just happened to be Maylene. Lia did not think Declan was capable of doing something as reckless as threatening to push her off the roof. Would he have done it? Lia was unsure, but the risk was there. When the three of them were about to embark down the last flight, they were intercepted by a hoard of teachers and the Principal led by a small group of students who had retrieved them.

"Are you three okay?" Mr. Walker, Lia's favorite English teacher, frowned down at them.

"Nobody's hurt," Lia consoled the worried professor. "Maylene's really shaken up, but we're all okay."

"Glad to hear." It seemed as if this particular professor was the one taking orders. "Take Maylene to the nurse and make sure she's okay." Then, his normally kind brown eyes darkened underneath his glasses. "Where's Mr. Abner?"

"We locked him on the roof."

At this, Mr. Walker smirked and nodded his gratitude. He led his possé further up the stairs. "This way, folks–he's on the roof."

Once everyone was out of the way, Lia, Maylene, and Yasmin continued down the stairs and shut the door behind them. At last, there was some peace and quiet amongst the school grounds. With Lia and Yasmin on either side, they led Maylene to the nurse's office. Despite Declan's poor behavior, Maylene thankfully never had visited this place. Once they approached the room, they peered through the propped-open door. All three of them were nearly blinded by the pastel pink walls, pink desk, pink rolling chair, and pink...everything, to put it plainly. The nurse herself - "Mrs. Haisley" according to the nameplate on the door - was gathering her belongings from her desk and placing them in her tote bag until she noticed the three girls' arrival.

"Good afternoon, girls!" Mrs. Haisley greeted them cheerfully. "What can I do for you?"

CHAPTER TWENTY-FOUR 315

All Yasmin had to do was push Maylene in front of her. The pair of teary eyes flipped the nurse's mood upside down.

"What's wrong, Sweetheart? Are you hurt?"

"Shaken up," her twin explained as Maylene shuffled behind her. "Declan Abner grabbed her and took her to the roof. That piece of garbage threatened to push her off."

Mrs. Haisley's face grew solemn, as if she was fighting off tears herself. "Oh, child... Let's make you comfortable. This is a safe space for you. Is your mom coming to pick you up?"

"Usually, my mom picks us three up since we live in the same neighborhood," elaborated Lia, who had nothing else to say.

Finally, Maylene mumbled something to the nurse. "I'm going to call Mom..."

"That's okay, Sweetie. We can leave you be and go over here." Mrs. Haisley directed Yasmin and Lia towards the other side of the office.

When Maylene frowned at Yasmin's departure, the latter stated, "I'm not leaving her. We go through stuff together, thick and thin."

"My apologies, Honey." The nurse quickly understood.

Lia was neither afraid nor angry anymore. Instead, she stood in the corner of the nurse's office as still as a statue. Her eyes locked on her shoes. Even when the nurse asked of her well-being, all Lia could do was nod. How in the world had a more mediocre situation - although bullying was *never* mediocre - escalated into something like this? Lia was at a standstill, both literally and metaphorically. She sent her mother a quick text saying that Mrs. Zuíhuí would be picking up the twins and that she would be the only one in the black sedan that afternoon. She planned on notifying her mother about what happened later... when she was ready.

Lia hated the way Mrs. Zuíhuí's eyes brimmed with tears as she dashed into the nurse's office merely ten minutes after her daughter had called her. At once, Maylene wrapped her arms around her mother and let the dam break. Yasmin, who was usually the toughest, most outgoing girl in the room, had finally broken down along with her sister and joined in the family's embrace. Lia watched from the sidelines with Mrs. Haisley, who put a loving hand on her shoulder. Lia wanted to leave, feeling unneeded, but instead, she figured she would stay for Maylene's sake. She was grateful that she did, especially since once Maylene let go of her mother and sister, she held her arms out for Lia to walk into, which was exactly what she did. Lia hugged her best friend tighter than she could remember. All that was important was that she was safe. As far as she knew, Declan was taken care of. She did well not to mention the faint sirens from outside the school and the occasional police officer walking down the hallway. Karma was certainly a relaxing thought at that point. Declan was going to get what his absurd mindset deserved.

One thing that Lia did *not* notice, however, was her lack of worry for the Mêla. She had chosen Maylene and chose well. Soon, however...she would come to wonder:

Whatever happened after she ran off?

Twenty-Five

Rowan was unsure of what had possessed her to do so, but as soon as the music box transferred from Lia's possession to hers, everything about herself became... lighter. It was as if she had snapped out of some sort of trance, a deadweight that finally lifted off of her shoulders and disappeared into thin air. There was something uncanny about that scenario, however. What goes up must come down, and Rowan was terrified of where this unknown force would land next. A gut feeling raged in her stomach and made its way to her chest. Her heart pounded as it realized that its next likely target was her fellow Mêla.

Being more than emotionally attached to her peers was both a blessing and a curse. Instead of merely animals, Rowan seemed to have some sort of special connection to her fellow members of the Earth Wing. In fact, this was the case with all of the wings, but not outside of them. For example, an Earth Wing member could not have such a close connection to an Air Wing member. That, actually, could have been considered forbidden depending on the scenario. In this case, however, Rowan let her instincts run wild, almost animalistically. That was one thing about herself that Rowan enjoyed. No matter what, she could pick up on what was wrong with her two closest companions.

How come, then, was she so distant and cold from them ever since their arrival on Earth? The exact answer, a revolution, was indefinite, but one thing was for sure: Rowan did not want it to happen again. She cared about her fellow Mêla more than anything else in the world. How fear personified itself into some sort of spirit that she absorbed and let corrupt her was beyond Rowan's being. Her overachieving nature had taken over her senses and put herself before anyone else in this world, even those she held the closest. It was no matter now, however; she was going to use her ambition to her advantage and chase after the sinking feeling in her stomach that something was wrong.

Rowan was torn between aiding Lia when she heard her best friend scream for any sort of help, but she knew where her priorities needed to lie. She was confident in Lia's abilities to solve the problem herself, and - unbeknownst to her - she was exactly right. Maylene was safe and sound, surrounded by her family. That was not the case for Rowan's family, though, who still needed aid. The rock holding her stomach down became an asteroid as she ran, summoning nausea up her throat before she swallowed it down. Not a single drop of sweat dripped down Rowan's forehead that was not from the adrenaline pumping throughout her. She had no idea where she was going, but her legs took her towards Oakbrooke Park, where she and her fellow Mêla had taken shelter for the past two months. Home was where the heart is, after all.

No matter how quickly Rowan ran towards whatever sinking feeling was summoning her, it seemed as if she was somehow slowing down. Rowan soon made it to the cave that she, Jared, and Willow could call their temporary home. Rowan shoved her way past the vines that Willow used as a doorway only to find it completely vacant. The last time she had been in her own home was just prior to her storming out and making the controversial decision to rent a hotel room in order to stay away from her

CHAPTER TWENTY-FIVE 319

family. Rowan wished she could have smacked herself for such stupidity and naïvety that clouded her thoughts then. All of their belongings had been strewn across the cave's floor and nearly destroyed. Rowan's copper skin grew paler than she thought possible. Yes...her gut feeling was correct.

Jared and Willow were gone.

Rowan could not afford to panic, but her interior senses pleaded for some sort of release instead of eventually bursting from the seams. The first tear fell from Rowan's left eye. Slowly... Agonizingly... Dejectedly... Rowan sank down to her knees in the middle of the cave. Her blurry vision eyed the remnants of the branches Jared would always collect from the forest around them to keep them all warm. The numerous flowers that Willow would use to decorate the cave walls were now torn to shreds and littered all over the floor. She sat with her head pointed downward as tears never failed to relinquish streaming down her face. Rowan was at a complete loss. If Jared and Willow had somehow disappeared, just like *that*, then there was no logical way that she could catch up to them. Maybe they decided enough was enough and decided to leave her behind? What if they returned to Kythaela entirely? The thoughts were too much to bear as she sank lower to the ground in despair.

The cave was dark, ominous, and was vacant of all life. Not even a single bug crawled across the dirty floor. The only thing that occupied the grains of dust were the salty droplets falling from Rowan's eyes and soaking into the soot below. Not a single thing could strengthen her confidence and generate new life within her cracking bones. At least, that was until there truly was life revealed to be in the cave along with Rowan. A bright light summoned itself a few yards away from Rowan, which made her field of vision shift upward. It began as an orb, but it slowly grew and increased in intensity until the silhouette of a tall Woman appeared from within. Rowan immediately sat up straight, but did not rise entirely from the ground that had claimed her. There, right in front of her, was the Woman in

White, pale as the snow and as bright as the Great Star. Her bare feet sunk into the dirt, but the grime never covered them. It was as if the Enchantress was somehow immune to unclean fixtures.

Rowan had to take off her glasses, rub her eyes to wipe away some of the stray tears, and then put them on to ensure that the sight before her was truly real. "...I haven't seen you in a long, long time...," she muttered.

"Rowan, my Dear, it's wonderful to see you," the Enchantress chorused with a voice like silk.

"It's good to see you too, but..." The Mêla was perplexed. "Why are you here? You said that you wouldn't come in contact with us unless it was something dire."

A pair of crystalline blue eyes gleamed into hers. "This seems quite dire...does it not?"

"I guess it does, but didn't Jared and Willow go back home?"

"If they had, would I have come?"

That was not what Rowan was hoping to hear. "Oh."

"I'm so sorry, my Dear," the taller Woman sympathized with her. "They aren't too far gone yet, though."

"How do you know that?" Rowan sniffled. "I was too late."

The Enchantress bent down and tenderly wiped a tear from her face. "It's never too late to do the right thing."

"I guess you're right, however, how am I going to find them?"

"Something tells me that they aren't terribly far." The Enchantress visibly glowed despite the dark and drab of their surroundings.

Rowan lifted an eyebrow. "What is this "something" that you speak of?"

"The same "something" that brought you here," she mused in a gentle manner. "Throughout your journey in this realm, you've seen and learned so much, no?"

"I wish I could say that...but I was so wrapped up in my own fear that I never paid attention to anything but myself." Rowan hung her head in shame. "I'm so sorry."

CHAPTER TWENTY-FIVE

The Enchantress offered a small smile as She lifted Rowan's chin with Her finger. "It's not your fault."

"How is it *not?*"

"Do you remember back in Luthyia...who we would discover was causing havoc such as this before this adventure began?"

Rowan stopped short. How had she not seen it before?!

"Phobo!"

It was obvious now. The Enchantress summoned memories that had become distant subsequent to their transition to Earthly life. There was no such thing as a "Phobo" to worry about. At least, she thought that was true until the last piece fell into place of yet another puzzle that plagued her brain. No wonder havoc was being raised within school grounds and the Mêla themselves. There was no specific way to track where said "havoc" was coming from unless Rowan followed her instinct...and the trail of disarray that Phobo left behind.

The Enchantress only smiled. "I've detected Phobo's presence here. Now, go. Your fellow Mêla await."

"I'm on it." Rowan stood to her full height and offered a grateful upward twitch of her lips before embarking on the second portion of her journey. "Thank you!"

Whether Rowan heard the Enchantress; reply or not, the pale woman was long gone, disappearing just as she arrived. Her silhouette began to glow once more and it morphed into the bright orb that it came from before it shrank and disappeared entirely. Rowan exploded out of the cave with a new mindset. Now that she knew what she was looking for, her vision was clearer. Twigs snapped underneath her floating feet that fleeted down a path towards nowhere in particular. Just as the Enchantress had hinted, Rowan needed to follow her instinct, which was leading her throughout the depths of the forest on Oakbrooke's outskirts.

Rain began to fall from overhead, soaking her hair and causing her side-swept curtain bangs to stick to her forehead and cheeks. The lenses of her glasses fogged from the sudden humidity the change in weather brought forth. While Phobo tended to be nothing but a petite creature, Rowan figured that being prepared with at least some sort of backup would be the intelligent direction to take. Her jaw lowered and vibrated with a summon that she had not used for longer than she could remember. Her voice rang through the woods, weaving around trees and underbrush like it was a tsunami's gust. Rowan's legs pushed her forward, and in a matter of seconds, she was joined by a herd of woodland creatures - her friends, as she called them despite never meeting - by her side who had answered the call.

From the feathered birds - robins, blue jays, pigeons, chickadees, and even a hawk - to the larger animals - made up of rabbits, foxes, squirrels, racoons, and even white-tailed deer - every creature was working together in harmony at Rowan's side. Her gut drew her to the side of a steep, rocky hill. Rowan cracked her knuckles and inserted her fingers onto the nearest ledges. With all of her strength, she leapt from her knees and began to climb her way up–her possé of animals still by her side and finding different ways to the top. Rowan gritted her teeth as she climbed higher and higher, her body moving in one fluid motion...until one ledge of stone cracked and her hand slipped. Rowan's breath escaped her until the nearby hawk used its talons to grasp her shirt and pull her back up.

"Thank you, my friend," she expressed her gratitude, to which the hawk squawked.

Rowan pushed herself the rest of the way to the top. The rain pelted down harder as she approached another cave that appeared to be a bit similar to the Mêla's hideout. The only difference was that the entrance was covered in rocks of all different shapes and sizes. At first, Rowan's face fell by the number of boulders blocking the entrance, but then, she remembered who she had at her side. With one nod of her head, the entourage of forest creatures began to poke, pull, and dig at the heavy barrier with Rowan as their leader. One by one, little by little, the entire group picked away at the stones that prevented them from passing through. One of the two deer who had joined their party was a stag who used his antlers to remove a particularly big boulder from the center of the wall.

"Stay back!" Rowan warned her new friends.

Sure enough, the rocks began crashing out of the wall and all over the mossy ground beneath their feet. Rowan stood next to the two deer who were protectively in front of the smaller animals. The birds were perfectly safe, hovering over the ground with ease. A snowless avalanche was what ensued, and it took a monumental amount of time for the dust to clear. Rowan coughed and gagged at the remnants of rubble that clogged her nose. She fanned away as much of it as she could, and when it finally was washed away from the rain, there was no turning back now, especially since a faint glow emitted from the inside of the cave. This was it. Rowan had found them!

"Come on!"

And thus, Rowan led the pack into the darkness, leaving the stormy gail to their backs. The labyrinth was only decipherable by the faint shimmering that was the hue of periwinkle. Rowan was subtly reminded of the purple outfits that Willow always wore no matter the occasion. In fact, Rowan could not remember a time that Willow ever wore anything but purple. Rowan knew this purple, though. It was much different than Willow's friendly presence that she easily - and regrettably - took advantage of. Instead, this shade was more ambitious…dark…eerie…and the army of animals - plus one humanoid - were rushing straight for it.

The cave opened up into a cavern where Rowan quickly determined the light was coming from. She came to an abrupt stop in the center of the massive limestone room. Her vision trailed upward to a developing vortex just below the ceiling followed by a giddy laugh. Rowan knew that laugh, and this time, when she had seen what the little creature was capable of, her fists - despite the small cuts and scrapes the rifts in the rocky ledge gave her - clenched with fury. She had found Jared and Willow, but both of them were encapsulated in a cocoon-like sac that was attached to the ceiling. Both appeared to be unconscious and too high up for Rowan to reach. Luckily, the flying portion of the flock understood Rowan's trife without her needing to say a word and fluttered to the roof of the cavern only to be knocked away by the swirling vortex. As birds literally rained from above, Rowan's features screwed into a glare. How dare he!

"Phobo!" Rowan bellowed from the cave floor. "Quit this nonsense and let them go!"

The maniacal laugh only grew louder and higher pitched as the floating, swirling being continued to zip around as if it was a game. "But I'm having so much fun!"

Rowan whispered to two of the hawks that had joined her militia and the two of them obeyed orders almost immediately. Both of the brown, majestic birds swooped up in unison. When Phobo tried to swat one away, the other one tried to grab him with its talons. Phobo yanked his leg out of the bird's grip, but that was when the other one took advantage of his altered direction. The little sprite began getting pecked in the back of the head and he whimpered at the sensation even after he smacked the feathers - quite literally - off of it. The poor hawk screeched and swooped back down towards the ground, leaving its partner to fend for itself.

"Get off! Ow! Scram!" he squealed like a little girl.

"*Phobo!*" Rowan's voice grew louder. "I'm warning you."

From within the whirlwind that Phobo had created, his two eyes, white as the Enchantress' glowing dress, popped out. The mist concealed the rest of his miniscule figure, but Rowan could tell he was grinning playfully. "Well, okay. Fine, but have fun getting them down!"

With that, it appeared as if Phobo had vanished entirely into the lavender haze he had created. The sparkling tornado of his magic dissipated into thin air, leaving fragments of transparent crystal to shower onto the limestone and disappear as soon as it hit the ground. The only evidence that Phobo was there in the first place were the purple cocoons that he put Jared and Willow in. Now that the coast was clear, the flock of various birds tried again. This time, they were successful with floating up to the top, detaching the cocoons from the ceiling, and lowering them gently to the ground. Rowan certainly was not expecting to stand over her two equals, especially after she finally snapped out of whatever trance she was in. Now that she thought about it, that must have been the work of Phobo as well.

Along with the help of her new friends, Rowan tore open each cocoon that was holding her two fellow Earth representatives hostage. Despite the translucent goo that began to coat her fingers, Rowan continued on until each one broke open and flaked to the ground as if it was a molding tortilla. She fought the urge to cower backward at the odd, decaying stench that emitted from the interior of each sac. The two deer - the stag and the doe - aided Rowan in removing both Jared and Willow from their cocoons. Rowan shook as much of the sap-like substance off her hands before she began nudging both of them and poking their faces. When that failed to work, Rowan placed two fingers in her mouth and whistled for her companions to come to her aid. At once, the birds began squawking, bunnies and squirrels ran around the room, and the deer stomped their hooves to create as much noise as possible.

Jared was the first to awaken, and his initial reaction was to lurch to his feet and begin shaking as much as the purple goop off of himself by frolicking around the cavern and flinging his arms and legs every which way. "Oh, my God—ew ew *ew*! Gross!" he shrieked like a little girl. "What happened to me?"

Rowan could not help but giggle. "A "Thank you" for my friends and I would be nice," she joked, relieved.

"Friends? What..." Jared trailed off when he finally noticed the possé of animals of different shapes and sizes occupying every corner of the cavern. "Woah."

"Were you going to say, "What friends?"" Rowan insinuated. "That's a bit rude for someone who just saved your life, don't you think?"

"Saved my life? *Please.*"

"Was that sarcasm?"

Willow was next, and the final, Mêla to regain consciousness. She did so in a more elegant manner. "You did it, Rowan," she spoke calmly.

Two heads swung in the blonde's direction. Despite her being covered in goop, Rowan leaned towards her and embraced her in a warm, soothing hug that was much-needed for both of them. "Oh, Willow," she exhaled shakily. "I'm so glad you both are okay."

"Hey! How come I didn't get a hug?" Jared accused Rowan, to which she laughed.

"Because you were jumping around like a maniac trying to clean yourself off."

"What?" Willow was confused until she looked down at herself. "Oh."

"The rain should wash us off," Rowan advised them. "Come on. Let's go home."

"Can I just process something first?" Jared interrupted them.

Willow and Rowan stopped in their tracks. "Of course."

"Let me get this straight," he dramatically set the scene by flaying his arms. "Willow and I were about to leave class when this purple haze overcame us. I have no idea how or when we got here, but next thing we know, we're being yanked out of mucus membranes in the middle of a cave. What in the hell is going on?!"

"Okay, mucus membranes? Disgusting." Rowan's nose scrunched. "I only found you because of a visit from an old friend reminding us of how these sort of shenanigans would occur back home."

"You mean…?" Willow inquired in surprise.

The girl nodded and began to pet the deer closest to her–the stag. "Yes, She visited me, and yes, Phobo seems to have made his return."

The blonde sighed, "Not him again..."

"But, where'd all the animals come from?" asked Jared cluelessly.

"Communicating with them is her Katári, Jared. You know that." Willow elbowed him.

"Ow!"

"Okay, okay." Rowan turned towards the cave's exit. "Seriously, we should get out of here. This place is giving me the creeps and the rain should wash us off."

"Agreed," both of them determined.

With Rowan leading the way, the three Mêla accompanied by an army of woodland creatures made their departure from the cave that Jared and Willow had mysteriously been transported to. How could one little creature be capable of so much? It was nothing they had the jurisdiction to worry about now, however. Their first priority would be getting back home in one piece... despite the fact their shelter was not. Perhaps Phobo was the source of that too. He was a mischievous havoc-wreaking creature, after all.

Harmonious was the forest once again as the herd of wildlife Rowan had mysteriously accumulated over the past while began to go their separate ways and return to their places of origin. The fact each animal had its own ecosystem...its own society...its own *family* to take shelter in filled Rowan's heart with warmth. Kythaela used to be as such, where every individual would live in euphony instead of chaos. Alas, that reality was far from relevant...at least anymore. Now, the Mêla were forced to reside in the human world where they knew nothing of their peers unless they found a proper place to educate themselves, or, in this case, *be* educated. It was a wonder the Three of them stumbled upon Oakbrooke High School, which gave them some problems, such as the fictional "race" for valedictorian, but mostly conveniences. Not one of the Earth Wing knew how to operate a computer - in other words, turn it on - before their arrival here, and now, each of them had something to be proud of.

Droplets of rainwater continued to pelt somewhat gracefully from the ominous cumulonimbus clouds overhead. Mud squished underneath the three pairs of shoes and soiled the soles at least for a little while. Along with the lavender catastrophe, the Mêla's despondency were washed away as well, ready to create a new beginning on a fresh slate. As the trio walked through the forest in silence, Rowan's mind went about the unnecessary process of overthinking. While Jared and Willow appeared to be passive, especially after the literal sticky situation she got them out of, how was she to know if anger still resided within them? There was one way to find out, and she was finally more than ready to test that theory.

"Are you two upset with me?"

From next to her, Willow replied, "Absolutely not. Why would we be?"

"I was not kind during the majority of my stay here," elaborated Rowan, twiddling her thumbs as rain poured down her face.

"We all make mistakes we wish we could take back," Jared contributed. "Don't worry about it too much, okay?"

The black-haired girl's jaw lowered. "How come you all are so forgiving towards me?"

"We've been stuck together for over a millennium," Willow shook her head in amusement. "If we didn't get along, there would be a serious problem."

"...Right," Rowan chuckled hesitantly.

"Besides, once you told us about Phobo, we figured that's what your previous attitude was all about," Jared brought up, nonchalant.

"What do you mean by that?"

"Phobo is a creature of pure chaos, who feeds off of people's fear and uses it against them. For example, you didn't want to leave home, and he gave you attachment issues. Once you arrived here, you wanted to stay. He made you more afraid of change."

The concept made a bit more sense to her. "I see."

"And for us," Jared continued intelligently, "we were worried about your whereabouts ever since you moved out, so he fed off of that and put us even further away from you. He's a clever little guy if you think about it."

Willow's eyebrows narrowed. "Don't encourage him."

"Says the one who's wearing his signature color," Jared teased, which resulted in a smack upside the head. "Ow!"

Rowan began to giggle at such nonsense but was abruptly stopped by a twig snapping a few yards away. All three of the Earth Wing stopped in their tracks and scanned the perimeter of their eyes' range. The stick was too sturdy for a squirrel or a rabbit to have broken it and there was no deer in sight. A bird could not have made that noise unless one of their wings was broken and Rowan did not sense any nearby animal in jeopardy. That could only mean one thing:

They were being watched.

Standing back-to-back, Jared, Willow, and Rowan stood as still as England's Stonehenge and represented the circular shape. For a moment or two, the rain falling around them was the only sound that the three pairs of ears could pick up. After a while, the Mêla untensed and began to continue their trek, but were halted again when a patch of bushes about ten feet away began to rustle. Instinctively, Willow and Rowan merged closer together while Jared stood in front of him. He made the decision to be the brave one of the three - despite the other two being ready for anything as well - and approached the bushes that continued to rustle until, in one foul swoop, Jared tore the leaves away. He was met with a shrill shriek and a bright light that startled the daylights out of him more than the figure behind the underbrush. As the silhouette continued to scream of terror, Jared immediately recognized the tone to be none other than Lia's. Sure enough, there she was with a waterproof flashlight that had clattered to the ground, a green raincoat that blended in with the dripping leaves, and lips chapped and blue from the sheer cold. When Jared reached out to touch her, Lia only screamed more and tried to escape his clutches by kicking at the air, but he only held her tighter. Willow and Rowan approached the teenager just before Lia's adrenaline settled down and everything clicked.

"Oh...," she squeaked fearfully. "Found you guys."

"Lia!" Rowan raised her voice over the downpour. "What in the *hell* are you doing out here?"

The teenager sheepishly wiped away the frightened tears. "I was worried when I never heard back from you. I never knew if you guys were okay..."

"Wait, what?" Jared blinked, slowly releasing Lia from his grip. "How did you know about this?"

"She was with me when I figured out something was wrong," Rowan explained.

Lia then grumbled, "Yeah, and then she made me run halfway across town."

"Did she really?" chuckled the boy next to her. "You can barely run in PE."

"Hey!"

"It's true."

Willow elbowed him again. "Be nice to her, Jared. After all, she came all the way out here to search for us. How *did* you know where we were, though?"

"My Ring." Lia proudly held up her left hand. "It pulsates whenever I get close to one or all of you."

"That's actually really cool," Rowan piped up. "Did you happen to enchant that music box too?"

"Music box?" Jared questioned. "What is she talking about, Lia?"

Lia's teeth chattered when particularly large raindrops plopped down on the top of her hood. "Can I explain later? I'm *freezing*!"

CHAPTER TWENTY-FIVE

The Earth Wing collectively laughed along with Lia's plight, to which she eventually joined in. "Yes…yes you may." Willow placed a gentle hand on her back and led her forward. "Let's get you home."

"Wait!" Jared stopped them from going any further. When they turned around, his eyes lit up and he proposed, "I have a better idea."

Twenty-Six

Lia was more than thankful to hear the rain pouring down outside but not on top of her still-shivering frame. Chestnut strands stuck to her forehead and cheeks as her frame shook like a leaf. There, in the middle of an unfamiliar cave's cavern, she was sat by a pile of branches and sticks. She watched as Willow sat cross-legged creating friction between two rough - and dry, most of all - rocks she found somewhere within the cave's confines. While her attempt to make a spark was so far not successful, Lia was grateful enough to be out of the cold, especially when a warm, oversized coat was draped over her shoulders.

She offered a weak smile to the boy standing above her. "Th-Thanks, Jared," her teeth chattered relentlessly. "You know...this *was* a good idea."

"You're welcome." He sat next to her and began to draw lines in the sand. "Are you feeling any better?"

"I g-guess so..."

Rowan sat on Lia's other side. "Won't your parents be concerned about your whereabouts?"

Lia's gaze expanded at the realization. "Oh...I almost forgot."

The teenager dug into one of the pockets in her raincoat and revealed a plastic bag that she had been stowing away. She unzipped it open to reveal her phone inside. All three of the Mêla were mystified to see that it had no water damage, especially when the screen lit up and she typed out a message to her parents. When Lia eventually put her phone away, she was not expecting three pairs of wide eyes staring in her direction with nothing but amazement.

"What?" she inquired cluelessly.

Jared pointed at her phone. "I thought water made technology malfunction."

"Not if you put it in a bag," Lia determined proudly. "You see, I was smart before going out in the rain and took all precautions necessary to ensure my safety. For example, what if something happened to me in the woods? I'd need to call for help?"

"Was that what you called your screeching like a banshee earlier?" The boy smirked and raised an eyebrow.

The teenager tugged the coat around her tighter. "How was I supposed to know it was you? After all, my mom taught me that if I'm in trouble, scream."

"You surely screamed our ears off," Rowan teased the young girl.

"I just did as I was told," she defended herself.

"You scared off my friends."

"What friends?"

At this, Jared and Willow burst into a fit of uncontrollable laughter. Lia did not realize she had made such an accidentally hostile comment, but when she did, she cringed at her own words.

"Oops."

All Rowan could do was chuckle, "I meant my animal friends, Lia. You figured out that my Katári is speaking with the inhuman, so I requested their aid. Most of them had returned to their homes by the time we encountered you, though."

"Whatever happened to you two?" Lia asked when the thought arose.

"It's a long story."

The girl grinned, content. "I have all night."

Once more, Jared gestured to her phone. "No offense, but will your parents allow you to stay with us?"

"I told them I would be at your place until the rain let up, and if need be, I'd stay the night. They said for me to have fun."

"Oh. I stand corrected." Jared shrugged. "Carry on."

At this time, Willow had finally generated a spark from the two stones she was striking against each other. The strategically stacked brushwood lit at an instant and created a flame that began to gradually increase the temperature within the insulated cave. Lia instinctively huddled closer to the campfire Willow created along with the aid of her peers. Along with the teenager, Jared and Rowan scooted nearer to the flames and held out their hands to warm themselves up. By the heat, all four of their heads of hair were drying at an accelerated rate. With each moment that passed, Lia felt more at home, especially surrounded by the very people she swore to bind together with an invisible string.

"We had the most unexpected of encounters today," Willow explained to Lia, sitting down across from her.

Lia instantaneously was intrigued, nearing her gaze. "What kind of encounter?"

"Well, one minute, Jared and I were within the confines of Oakbrooke High, and the next, a sheen fell over our memories. For a while, we lost consciousness, and that was until Rowan and her allies came to rescue us."

"Rescue you? From what?"

Jared leaned towards Rowan behind Lia's back and whispered, "If she tells her that we were bested by a little sprite, then we'll never hear the end of it."

"What's this about you being bested by a little sprite?"

"She heard," Rowan muttered, shaking her head.

"In our defense, Phobo is a creature of chaos, wreaking havoc in every direction he goes," Willow elaborated to Lia's benefit. "He is a cunning enigma, one that we have yet to understand.

He feeds off of our fear and uses it in his bidding to tear us apart, but thankfully, the opposite has occurred, and that is because of you, Lia."

Lia almost fell over from the gust Willow's words brought forth prior to Jared steadying her posture. "...Me?"

"You were chosen for a reason." Rowan's eyes shimmered from more than the embers. "We might not know exactly why, but you surely pulled through for us in some way or another."

"How exactly is she connected to all of this?" questioned Jared, having not a clue.

"Have I not told you?"

Jared and Willow shook their heads.

Rowan positioned herself closer to Lia, who was now warming her hands above the fire. "The kindness of her heart and the loyalty to her task are the sole reasons we are standing here together. If she had not interrupted my shift and snapped me out of whatever Phobo was holding over my vision, I don't know where we would be now."

"It was *Phobo* who was doing that to you?" Jared incredulously snapped. "I'm gonna-"

Willow leaned over and placed a ginger hand on his shoulder. "We've been over this, Jared. He's toyed with all of us, but where we're going, he won't be able to anymore."

"...Where you're going?" Lia repeated out of curiosity. "Where *are* you going?"

"Did we not tell you yet?" Rowan turned towards her in surprise.

The teenager slowly shook her head.

All the blonde could do was smile and reveal: "We're going home, Lia."

All movement stopped. Lia's muscles were untense, but perfectly still at the same time. Even the flames from the firepit feigned to flicker in Lia's slow-motion capsule. The rain grew quieter outside when the realization of what exactly was occurring hit Lia like the dodgeball in PE class all those weeks ago.

Finally, there was a light at the end of a tunnel: the Mêla were going home. *Home.* That was where they needed to embark towards in the first place. Lia's efforts were no longer in vain, but the belief had not reached her heart quite yet.

"...You mean it?" Lia squeaked.

Rowan gently squeezed her shoulder. "We do," she confirmed to her relief. "Once all of our affairs are in order, we will be en route to Kythaela once more."

All of the anxiety released itself from Lia's aura as if she was a balloon that had been let go before it was tied and the air was sealed on the interior. She herself felt like bouncing off the walls when Rowan assured her of their current intentions. Lia willed herself to believe that her plan to guide the trio back together had worked. She made a difference without realizing it even though that was where her desires laid. Even though she was still freshly sixteen, the fact that anyone, no matter how small, can make a difference, finally hit her.

"You guys are *actually* going home?" she repeated even though they had already confirmed it.

Jared ruffled her damp hair. "Yes, we are *actually* going home. You can relax."

"I *am* relaxed." Lia's entire body was shivering not from the cold, but from excitement. "I just can't believe it's actually happening."

"And it's because of you, Lia," Willow earnestly stated.

"Me?"

"Yes, *you.*" Willow shuffled closer to her. "I know it might be hard to believe, but with your kindness, diligence, and bravery, you have inspired us to do the same and venture back into the unknown. You, Lia, are an inspiration to us."

Lia eyed Jared and Rowan in pure shock, who both nodded their heads with admiration for the girl who was only a fraction of their age. Finally, she walked on her knees to give each of the Mêla a bone-crushing hug. First was Jared, who was the closest to her. When Jared wrapped his arms around her, Lia felt as if she was being crushed by a trash compactor...but in a good way. His inhuman strength provided warmth in the depths of her heart which thought would never see the light of day upon some occasions...but also a bit of tightness in her chest. Next was Willow, who was the exact opposite of her predecessor. She hugged Lia much looser, but with her arms locked together behind the teenager's back. Rowan was the last of the three to receive Lia's embrace. There was something different about Rowan's spirit from before. This time, her optimism and desperation to fight for what was morally right shined through rather than her own desires, that Lia now knew was corrupted from the very beginning. Lia had a new respect for Rowan and what she endured here on this planet. Lia could not imagine how much pain and suffering she and the rest of the Earth Wing endured upon their path.

"That means the world coming from you Three," Lia sniffled once she and Rowan released their hold on one another.

Willow questioned somehow sadly, "Whatever do you mean by that?"

"I mean..." When the words formed at the tip of Lia's tongue, they began to carry more weight than she anticipated. "I know I'm young, and I have no idea what I want to do with my life yet. Hearing that I'm somehow an "inspiration," as you call it, especially from those who have been around so much longer than I have, is really unusual. I'm always afraid that I'm doing the wrong thing or making things worse because of the choices I make."

"That doesn't seem to be the case in this scenario, now, does it?" Rowan grinned from next to her. "You're very mature for your age, Lia, and your persistence is admirable."

Lia's cheeks grew blood red. "Stop making me blush...I'll grow an ego almost as big as Jared's."

"Hey!" the boy interjected when Willow and Rowan began laughing. "What's that supposed to mean? I don't have an ego!"

"It's just a joke," she retorted playfully. "It's just that most people in movies who have super strength or who are even on the school football team have a massive ego."

"Oh, I see."

"Wait." Rowan grew quiet. "How are we going to leave school to go home?"

Willow was on the same page. "I...don't know."

"Easy," Lia spoke up, which caused three heads to turn in her direction. "Say you're transferring schools."

"That's a good idea," Jared agreed with her.

The blonde frowned at Rowan. "I know you wanted to be valedictorian," she sympathized. "I'm sorry we can't wait to go home so you can achieve that goal."

"What?" Rowan was bewildered by her apology. "That doesn't matter to me."

"Well, it did before."

Lia quickly interrupted, "But what matters now is that it's all over."

"Exactly," beamed Jared before the two of them could argue.

At this, Willow and Rowan eyed them with suspicion. "What?" the latter inquired. "Did you think we were going to fight or something?"

"...Well, I met you two when you were having a full-on brawl in the hallway," Lia uttered out prior to Jared stopping her. "What were you even fighting about anyway?"

The two girls looked at each other, then at Jared and Lia.

Then, back at each other.

Back at them.

Back at each other.

Back at them.

Finally, the two of them erupted into laughter and Willow snorted, "We have no idea!"

"You've got to be kidding me." Jared lowered his face into his hands.

"Oh, my God." Lia found their giggling to be contagious.

The chortling quickly died down when Rowan's smile

collapsed. "Lia, I've been meaning to ask you…is your friend okay?"

"She's…shaken up, but she's alright." Lia reused Yasmin's words from earlier.

"Do you mean Maylene?" When Lia nodded, Jared grew more worried. "What happened?"

"…It's a long story."

"We have all night," Willow sweetly replied and adjusted her seating position.

"If you're sure…," the teenager trailed off.

All three of the Mêla were seated comfortably around the fire. In a way, Lia was telling a scary story that was often used at campgrounds to frighten little kids. This time, however, the tale was real, and Lia did not want to relive it. The terror in Maylene's screams…Declan's malice and indifference towards the situation at hand…it was almost too much for her to bear. Lia inhaled a deep breath and knotted her fingers together in her lap.

"Jared, do you remember that bully that you stood up to for Maylene?"

The boy nodded and swallowed nervously. "I don't like where this is going."

"Well, you really wouldn't appreciate it if I told you he practically kidnapped her, took her up on the roof, and threatened to push her off, would you?"

All at once, the Earth Wing erupted into a volcano of fury, "What?!"

The Three of them had a unique answer.

"Oh, my goodness…is she okay?"

"I'm going to kill him!"

"Did he get away?"

Lia blinked, attempting to take it all in prior to answering: "Like I said, Maylene is okay, but she's still shaken up. Yasmin and I really wanted to get back at him, but we took the smart way out. While I kept Declan distracted, Yasmin picked the lock on the roof's door that we had secured behind us. When he wasn't focusing on Maylene, Yasmin and I snatched her out of his arms and made a break for the door, locking him on the roof. At the same time, students and teachers were heading up the stairs and someone called the police."

"Well, I'll be damned," Jared breathed in admiration. "Well done."

"I'd say that was a good plan," Rowan earnestly complimented.

Willow exhaled a sigh of comfort. "I'm relieved that you all are alright."

Either Declan did not hear her or he merely ignored her as he opened the door to the nearest approaching stairwell and slammed it in the duo's face. He dragged Maylene up the stairs, his grip so tight that Maylene thought that his hand was ripping through her skin. Tears pricked behind her eyes and did not hesitate to stream down her face. When Maylene could turn around briefly, the sight of her best friend shattering in front of her broke Lia's heart.

Lia shook away the brief flashback and wished she had a fan to cool down her complexion; she was sure the fire and the jacket around her shoulders was making it worse. "Thanks, guys."

"Is Maylene safe?" Jared asked, adjusting his hair out of his face.

"As far as I know, yes." Lia scooted a tad bit away from the fire since she was beginning to sweat. "I saw police take Declan away and Maylene's parents are going to press charges as far as I know."

Rowan smirked at that. "Good. He deserves it."

The teenager was plunged into another unwanted memory.

. . .

"Let. Her. Go."

Declan loosened his grip on Maylene, causing her to slip and nearly fall off before he grabbed her again. "Are you sure?" he repeated with that same malicious intent.

Both girls gasped in fright when Maylene screamed just before he placed his hand over her mouth again.

"No one messes with my best friend and gets away with it," Lia growled at the horror that had once filled her very being for Maylene.

"Lia?" Willow snapped her out of her thoughts. "Are you okay?"

The brunette hesitantly nodded. "I'm okay. Seeing how close she was to danger really frightened me today. I don't know what I would've done if she didn't come out of it okay."

"We know how you feel," Rowan uttered, her eyes locked on a line she was etching in the soil with a stray stick.

"...What do you mean?"

"We feel that way about each other." She gestured to her kin that might not have been by blood, but by bondage. "When our village, Luthyia, was attacked, our first thoughts were each other. We thought the only way we could all make it out alive was to abandon everything we ever knew. The Air and Water Wings thought similarly, and we left together before going our separate ways. We agreed that if these Wings branched off, we would be harder to pursue."

Lia placed her hands in her pockets. "That makes sense in a very…sad way."

"We know." Willow accepted Jared's offer to place an arm around her. "Which is why returning to our place of origin should be our next step. Thank you for reminding us of that."

"You're welcome, but…"

Rowan's eyes were soft. "But what?"

"...Never mind." After a second thought, Lia regretted her words. "I need to be nicer to myself."

"Agreed." Jared patted her on the upper back. "We're proud of you."

"Yes, we are," Willow added with just as much enthusiasm.

Lia thought it was her imagination at first, but then she realized that the abrupt silence surrounding them came from outside: the rain had finally stopped. "As much as I've enjoyed this detour, I think I should be getting home now."

"Sounds good to me." Rowan was the first to rise to her feet. "Let's get you home…for real this time."

Lia was more than content with that.

Twenty-Seven

Do you ever anticipate something so much that when it finally comes, you have not a clue how to react to it? That was exactly how Lia felt as she closed up her laptop and stood from her desk. She had just finished her last assignment for the week, but the day was far from over. Her eyes drifted over to Noodle's vivarium where the petite reptile kept refuge under a faux log that Lia found one day at a pet store– probably Claws & Paws, actually. Lia's mind flitted back to the last time she walked through those doors and presented an apology gift to Rowan. Little did she know that the seemingly insignificant little box would change everything and swivel her down a different path.

Lia dashed over to Noodle's habitat and opened the small door to reach her hand inside. Since her little friend was sound asleep, coiled in a near-perfect circle, she resorted to a simple *boop* on her nose and allowed her to continue her slumber. She shut the door and double-checked that it was secure. Lia then shoved her phone into her pocket, slid on a pair of checkered shoes, and stampeded down the stairs like an elephant. She was already dressed for the weather outside since the sun shot beaming warmth over the usually frosty air during this season.

Her green hoodie nearly swallowed her whole body above her black leggings. Her brown hair was tied back in a loose braid with shorter pieces framing her face. The usual wire-framed glasses were resting on her face but slightly bounced as she hit the floor. This also grabbed the attention of her parents.

"Hi, Sweetie!" Cheyenne chirped from her usual chair, crocheting what appeared to be another blanket since she had finished one not long ago. This one was maroon. "Where are you off to in such a hurry?"

"Hi, Mom!" There was no point in lying to her parents; they knew she had friends other than the twins. "I'm going to hang out with Jared, Willow, and Rowan at the park. Is that okay?"

"Of course it's okay. Have fun!" she replied enthusiastically.

Lucas chipped in from his spot on the recliner. "Be careful, Lia."

"I will!" the teenager responded to both of them. "Love you!"

As soon as both parents echoed the same words of affection, Lia ensured that she had everything she needed on her person. She barreled through the door and locked it behind her, as that was a policy her parents had put in place ever since she was a small child. You could never be too careful with people - especially strangers - in this day and age. Lia was off with a start and a spring in her step. She relished in the sunshine illuminating every nook and cranny of Oakbrooke on this beautiful Winter day. While Lia wished she could communicate with her friends with her phone, she knew exactly where she was going. In fact, the Mêla had given her explicit instructions as to where and when she was going to meet them.

While everything was indefinitely "fine" as she would call it, anxiety lingered in the depths of Lia's mind, holding themselves hostage in a familiar place. Lia's limbs itched to change directions and return to her place of solitude within the confines of her green comforter. Peace was what she longed for, and to the dismay of her own senses, the battle was far from over. As long as her journey continued, Lia's desires would yet to be fulfilled.

All she could do was wait for the time to come when she least expected it.

Lia never understood the beauty, the pure *magic* of the world around her until she met Jared, Willow, and Rowan. All three of them seemed very much out of place as they took in every single insignificant little detail as if it was the most incredible thing in the world. In their own way, the Earth Wing's fellowship took advantage of the new opportunities they had been given. For example, Jared immersed himself amongst his fellow classmates at Oakbrooke High. The last thing he wanted to be was alone, so he did everything in his power to ensure he was not left in the dark. Willow surrounded herself with the very place she called home: her sanctuary filled with plants and crops of every shape and size. Rowan dealt with the change with a similar notion: getting a job at the nearest animal shelter. Even under Phobo's possession, her love for animals never faded and she was able to pair a countless amount with new families. Why? Because she could speak to them and they told her themselves where they wanted to go.

How the Mêla adapted so quickly to Earthly life was nothing short of stunning in Lia's view. After sixteen years of residing in this very place, she had yet to find her place, and the long journey ahead was evident. A portion of her very being was shrouded with guilt for prying each member of the trio out of the lives they had solidified themselves into. Lia was well-aware of her imperfections, and tried not to let them affect her view of herself. Life went on with or without her, and in this case, so did the Mêla. Lia needed to hurry if she was going to catch them before the sun dipped down and the moon took its place over the horizon.

By the time Lia arrived in the exact spot she was instructed to, droplets of sweat glistened on her forehead and reflected the amber hue of the setting sun. She tossed her loose braid behind her shoulder and realized she had once again ventured into the forest where she was searching for the three of them just days prior. Her complexion burdened her with maroon splotches as she remembered the embarrassment she caused herself by her piercing screech. There were certain instances where Lia wished she had kept her mouth shut, and, unmistakably, this was one of them. As soon as the three vaguely familiar – and taller – figures emerged from the sheen of fog that had developed over the past morning due to the humidity.

"Hey, guys," Lia trailed off once all three silhouettes became her friends. "You look…different."

Her revelation was more than an understatement. Rather than wearing their usual "Earthly teenager" garbs, it seemed as if they had dressed more appropriately for their realm. Jared wore a loose-fitting white cotton shirt and dark gray breeches. Willow was adorned in a plum dress that stretched to just below the knee. The sleeves were flowy and opened wide around the wrist. Finally, it appeared that Rowan refused to wear any sort of dress and instead settled on a maroon vest overtop of a shirt much like Jared's and form-fitting leggings made out of similar material to his as well. The biggest difference was the absence of Rowan's glasses. Maybe she was wearing contacts? When Lia realized that the girls' hair was tucked behind their ears, her train of thought switched tracks.

"…Since when have you had pointed ears?"

To her surprise, all three of them chortled at her obvious question.

"What's so funny?"

"Oh, Lia." Willow smiled endearingly at her unknowing companion. "You didn't think we resided in Kythaela in our Earthly forms, did you?"

Lia shrugged since she genuinely had no clue. "I didn't know you had different forms or anything. What is going on?"

Jared seemed to be even more comfortable in his pally clothes. "It's quite simple, really. When we're in Kythaela, we have our natural form, but when we're on Earth, we have to adapt to blend in with our surroundings. Thankfully for us, our

Wing's form only has one significant difference: the pointed ears."

"You guys look like elves!"

"Elves?" Rowan cocked her head to the side.

"What? Oh." Lia shook her head with the humiliation she just caused herself. "They're a species from my favorite movie trilogy, but they have pointed ears and dress kind of like you do."

Jared grinned at the connection. "Makes sense."

"It does?" Rowan inquired once again.

"If we had televisions in our realm, we would check out this *trilogy* you speak of," Willow replied thoughtfully.

Lia's jaw collapsed. "You guys don't have *any* televisions?"

"Not a single one." Willow shook her head. "We don't have televisions, cell phones, computers, or anything of the sort."

"Wow. I guess I can understand that." Lia figured that was true, but hearing it from them personally was a culture shock, especially for someone in the modern world. "It's nice to have such helpful devices, but from what I've experienced, these things don't bring us much aid. Instead, I find myself absorbed in it. I only really use my phone to text friends or play a game or something. Social media is infectious."

Rowan placed a hand on her shoulder. "This one's a smart one. Don't ever change, Lia."

"I'll try!" Lia beamed up at her. I'd love to learn more about your realm, though. What's it like? Do you guys have castles and forests and mythical creatures?"

"You ask so many questions," Willow chuckled at her enthusiasm.

"...Sorry."

The light in Jared's eyes faded. "Well, Lia, to answer your question…we used to. Hopefully that will be the case again, but everything is still in black and white."

"Not necessarily."

The spark slowly began to return. "What do you mean?"

"Do you remember me saying how I wish I had your optimism?"

Jared tentatively nodded.

"It's almost as if we switched places," Lia remarked. "No matter how awful your world may look when you return, it doesn't have to stay that way. As much as I can help it, I'm not going to give up, and neither should you."

Before she knew it, Jared engulfed her in an embrace. "I'm so glad we met."

"Me too," she squeaked from the tight grip crushing her abdomen.

"Oh, sorry." He quickly let go.

Willow and Rowan found the predicament quite amusing. "Thank you for being so persistent and patient with us–especially with me," the latter expressed. "I don't know what I would've done with you freeing me from my fear."

"You're welcome." Lia swallowed a pit of emotion that sank down to her stomach. "I don't know how I did that in the first place, though."

Jared knowingly shrugged. "It certainly is a mystery."

"He knows something, but I'm not going to press it," she thought to herself. "I guess it is."

Oakbrooke Forest was an eerily calm place. The only exception was the pouring rain searing through the top of the hood Lia wore on the night she was discovered by the very people she was searching for. Lia both cringed and relished in the memory, the very moment that relief replaced the terror flowing through her vessels. There was nothing to worry about now. It was all over. The Earth Wing would be returning to their home just like she wanted. Kythaela was one step closer to being saved.

Then, why was Lia so…*empty*?

A brilliant light shimmered from the shaded undergrowth of the woods. Lia had seen this lumosity a couple of times before, but it was not as magnificent as she recalled. She and the Mêla stood back and watched as the Enchantress emerged from the white orb of light and how it shattered into mere specks of sparkles vanishing into the grass below Her bare feet. Her ivory hair blew away from Her face as She stepped forward, at least three inches taller than her company–even Jared, who was above average height of a male on Earth. Lia was unsure of the standards in Kythaela. Apparently, everyone was taller there. Somehow, the Enchantress' smile was brighter than Her luminescent clothing. Maybe it was the joy in her azure gaze as it peered down onto the four individuals standing in front of her.

"It is wonderful to see you all here on a merry note rather than a solemn one." Her voice regally reverberated off the trees surrounding them.

"It certainly is." Ah, Willow...always the formalist of the group.

Rowan fiddled around with the sleeve of her shirt. "We were not expecting to be...back so soon."

"Neither was I," Jared admitted, "but *someone* got in the way."

Lia gasped dramatically when he looked at her. "Excuse me?"

"Well, I'm overjoyed that you are. A lot has changed since your departure."

"...Now I'm worried," Rowan gulped at the idea. "I'm guessing it's not in a good way."

The Enchantress shook Her head. "I'm afraid not, but I'm hoping that if we work together, by the time the other Wings return, we can have some aspects restored."

"It's better late than never to get started," the blonde to Lia's right stated.

"Then, what are we waiting for?" Jared cracked his knuckles and began to saunter forward. "Let's get going before more damage is done."

"...I don't know if that's such a good idea, Jared," Rowan whispered in his ear.

"What? Why's that?"

All Rowan had to do was gesture to the small brunette who had quickly averted her gaze to the dirt and moss beneath her shoes. Lia's eyes squeezed shut when a sheen of moisture built overtop of her corneas. The action caused two tears to emerge down her cheeks–the first from her left eye and the second from her right. Lia tried to wipe off her cheeks, but it was to no avail, since there were more where that came from. Right then and there, Lia felt alone despite being surrounded by three individuals whom she had grown closer to than she initially thought. Now that they were leaving, the pain was too much for her to bear. Lia took off her glasses, wiped off her face again with her sleeve, and then put them back on only for the lenses to fog over from the moisture almost instantly.

Jared could have sworn his heart snapped in two at the sight before him. "Oh, come here."

The boy beckoned her closer, but before she could make her second step, Jared lurched forward and let his strong arms swallow her up in a hug that was not too tight, but firm enough to keep her in place. Lia only began to sob harder, her chest heaving with heavy respirations into the cotton of Jared's shirt. He placed his cheek on the top of her head and a hand to the back of it while the other was around her frame. Lia remembered the very first time she met this boy. It was in the middle of gym class when a dodgeball of his smashed into the side of her head. Lia had retaliated in the same way, thinking he was a bully. Later on, she discovered he was the utter opposite of that stereotype. Instead, Lia found his heart, which - out of the blue - was attracted to Maylene as if she was metal to a magnet. While Lia's emotions were temporarily drifting towards him in a romantic sense, especially at the Winter Formal, they faded away as soon as they came. Lia had more important things to worry about. Still, she was down about how the first boy she had a small crush on turned out to be an immortal being who had been around for over a thousand years at that point. While his intentions were nothing of the sort, Lia could only think of one thing that described his scenario: pedophilia at its finest. Now, he held her in his arms with the affection a close friend or even a brother would–the brother she never had…and never will have again once he departed.

Willow was the second to take Lia into her arms. It might have been her imagination, but Lia thought she smelled of the rarest purple iris at the dawn of Spring. A nearby breeze wafted the desolate scent of scarce pollen and morning dew into Lia's nose as she breathed in the comfort that the blonde provided her with just her presence. Seeing Willow now was a stark difference from when she first encountered her: in a hallway in Oakbrooke High whilst putting everything she had into a physical altercation with Rowan. Now, she was nothing short of a princess from one of her favorite childhood movies. Gone was the naïvety that came with being a little girl and playing with her favorite princess figurines. Now, those toys were stored in her closet and the real thing was standing right in front of her. Despite the absence of a crown, Lia could tell that Willow would take the needed authority to put Kythaela's well-being back on track. Lia wondered if there were any flowers back in the mythical realm amongst the frigid temperatures that an eternal Winter brought forth. Maybe there was a diamond in the rough that sprouted beyond the ice coated rivers and frost-laden grass. Maybe Willow *was* that radiant jewel. She certainly looked the part without even trying, but her authenticity advanced all the way to her core. There was absolutely no way that the fate of Kythaela's wildlife was in jeopardy.

This was the very same case with Rowan, who was the last of the Mêla to offer her farewell condolences. It was safe to say that Lia's most fascinating journey resided within her and Rowan's interactions. The Capricorn representative was much different than the other two members of the Wing. While Rowan was closed off and sour most of the time, she was also the one who struggled the most out of the Three. Often, the quietest are the ones who are in their darkest moments. That was a lesson that

Lia learned all too well with Rowan. Unbeknownst to her, she allowed a small, but mighty personification of fear itself to take hold of the reins and steer her into a direction contradicting where she truly wanted to go. It was not until she was freed by Lia's compassion - which the teenager still did not understand - that she was able to realize the error of her ways and make things right. For instance, earlier in the week, she had approached Maylene and apologized for using her test to cheat rather than taking it honestly. Not much was spoken by the timid girl, but the glimmer in her eyes revealed how much the sentiment truly meant to her as a person. Finally, the last loose end had been tied up here in our realm and Rowan was ready to start over with a clean slate. Even though she was not entirely able to control her actions then, she still felt responsible for how she allowed herself to be corrupted by her own emotions. Little did she know that a little creature would use her fear to his advantage to instill even more vigor within him.

The Three very contradictory, but compatible, members of the Earth Wing stood before Lia as if they were royalty. There was something different about their genuinity and gratefulness for the teenage girl who barely reached their chins in height. In a way, Lia felt like one of the Shire's Hobbits, who only ranged between two and four feet tall. The average height was about three feet, six inches, and while Lia was just over a foot and a half taller than such, the magnificent creatures in front of her made her feel small. A desolate throbbing in her chest grew much more prominent when the woman in white took a step towards her kin. Lia knew what was about to come, but she was not nearly ready for it.

"Are you Three ready?" she asked the Mêla.

A deep breath emitted from Jared's mouth. This was it. "We're ready."

"Farewell, Lia," Willow acknowledged her small, but noble friend. "Thank you for all you've done for us."

"We will never forget you," Rowan echoed with a sad smile.

"I won't forget you either," Lia blubbered behind her tears. "I'll miss you."

"Likewise," the boy made known.

The Enchantress' voice was soft yet commanding. "Now, we must away. Lia, I will be returning to you when the time is right, but for now, continue your studies and embark on your path here. I cannot express enough gratitude towards you."

"Yes, Miss." Out of instinct, Lia curtsied, which made the Woman smile.

"We will meet again in time. Farewell."

The moment Lia had been dreading had finally arrived. With one more nod from the Enchantress, the woman in white turned around and began to trod across the dirt into the depths of the forest. One by one, the Mêla followed after her. First was Jared, who knew if he had stayed any longer, he would not want to leave. He offered Lia a goofy, informal smile before spinning around to follow after the Enchantress. Willow was next, dipping her head and returning Lia's curtsy with a daintier one of her own. Finally, Rowan halted just prior to following the group. She looked at Lia with her pupils dilated. Moisture started to form behind her eyes where Lia's was dripping down her cheeks. Before the teenager knew it, Rowan's legs carried her towards one last embrace. She hugged Lia with all of the fondness she had gathered for the mere *child* in front of her. As Lia continued to cry into her shoulder, Rowan stroked her hair and tucked a tendril behind her ear. Eventually, she pulled away and looked Lia in the eyes with a vibrant, alluring stare.

"Be good to yourself…okay?" Rowan's final request rang through her ears.

Lia nodded and wiped away more tears from her cheeks. "I will."

That was all Rowan needed to hear. She used her sleeve to rid the rest of Lia's face of her tears before she backed away and reluctantly joined the group behind her. Lia watched in silence as the Enchantress was the first to be absorbed into the misty woods that appeared to be thicker than before. Jared followed soon after with Willow next to them, They too disappeared from sight. Finally, it was Rowan's turn. She eyed Lia one last time and smiled just before she was the last one to fade from view.

Before she knew it, Lia was alone in the middle of the forest. What once felt safe became a rickety bridge leading to nowhere. Every one of the floorboards could have snapped under her shoes at any moment. Lia was afraid to move. Her eyes glued onto the last place she saw the Mêla before her waking eyes. It was as if they were not even there to begin with. By then, her tear ducts had run out of droplets to spare. There she stood, still as a statue with moss beginning to grow between the cracks in the stone. The weather grew colder as time went on. The shadow on the sundial grew towards a later hour. It was not until a breeze picked up around her that Lia finally returned to reality. Her eyes blinked open, but, sure enough, there was no movement other than the leaves in the trees fighting the wind. In the past, Lia would have thought nothing of it, but now, she knew better. There *was* magic that existed in our realm. The winds surrounding her very being whispered affirmations in her ears. One stuck out in particular…one that broke the roots from the girl's feet off the ground and allowed her to return to her place of solitude:

It is far from the end. This is only the beginning.

Acknowledgments

Many thanks are expressed to everyone who has stayed by my side during my writing journey. Thank you to my parents and my younger sister, Carissa, for always supporting me in everything I do. Thank you to my grandparents, Nina and Papa, for usually being the first to read my novels and leaving kind reviews on Amazon. Thank you to my many friends for sharing my progress on social media with their friends and family and supporting my journey. A huge thank you to one of my best friends, Gabriel Dandrade, for beta reading *Whispering Winds* and ensuring that it is the best it can be!

Most of all, thank You, God, for providing me with the gift of writing and telling my story. Thank You for never giving up on me just like You've always promised.

About the Author

Cassidy Stephens is a twenty-year-old author who used to focus on the Teen Fiction/YA genres, but has been experimenting with the realm of Fantasy. Whispering Winds is the first installment of her urban-to-high fantasy "The Mêla" series. When she is not writing, she can be found playing her guitar, the piano, the ukulele, singing, or teaching her musical skills to her students. She is currently in her third year at Regent University to get her Bachelor's degree in English and a Minor in Music.

Follow her writing journey on Instagram: @_casswrites.

Also by Cassidy Stephens

Indigo - An Urban Fantasy Novel

Paige O'Connell hoped for a better world.

One where she did not have to worry for her own safety. One where she could be anything as long as she put her mind to it. One where she was free to make her own choices.

One where she was *normal*.

Blessed (or cursed) with experimental superpowers, all Paige O'Connell wanted was to not be isolated from the rest of the world. After yet another incident causes her powers to be introduced to the world, the organization in charge of her has had enough. Paige proposes her idea of enrolling in nearby Azure University so she can finally receive the life she has always wanted. What she did not expect was to have to change her identity entirely in order to strike a deal with them. When Paige crosses paths with a sophomore in her History class, the two of them become inseparable…except for the fact she needs to pretend to be someone she's not. As portions of her reality seep into her façade, what was a blossoming rainbow reverted to black and white. Two halves make a whole, though, and there must be a gray area in between. Blue and purple make indigo.

Paige was the epitome of purple. What if he was her blue?

* * *

The Huntington Avenue Series

Huntington Avenue: Part One - Second Edition

Nearly perfect grades, a loving family, and being a guitar prodigy seem to be attributes of the ideal teenage life, right? In his case, there was a debilitating catch.

Zachary West - a blind teenage boy - had no clue what he was getting himself into when he stepped foot into Oceanview High School. After recently moving to the suburbs of Kitty Hawk, North Carolina, the seventeen-year-old desired a chance at the normality of being a teenager. Being homeschooled for the past eleven years after a traumatic accident caused his condition was a nightmare for an optimistic extrovert.

Soon enough, and consequent to a couple of encounters with resident hothead, Jaylen Hunt, Zach crosses paths with the bully's long-term girlfriend—Kelsey Davis. In contrast to what her peers might assume her personality to be due to her boyfriend's nature, Kelsey was a sweet soul who made the best out of every situation. Her life seemed to be perfect, but everything changed when the teenage girl noticed Zach's intriguing sight impediment. She wanted to learn more about it.

As questions, an unlikely friendship, and possibly more begin to arise, life continues to wreak havoc for the both of them. With Jaylen and his close friend, Lyla Walker, becoming a problem, Zach and Kelsey find themselves growing closer together and further apart from the people they had been familiarized with.

Would Kelsey flip her life around for the unique boy on Huntington Avenue who needed a friend, or would she remain with the people who might not have been the best for her?

Huntington Avenue: Part Two - Second Edition

Supportive friends, an eligible love interest, and an opportunity to obliterate the concept of blindness seem to be the dream of Zach's, right? Unfortunately, it was more of a nightmare.

Following an unexpected confession of lies, concealed emotions, and an unconsented first kiss from Kelsey at the airport, Zach had no idea what to think of his life crashing down upon him. He finally had the chance to regain his eyesight after eleven years of confining darkness. Kelsey had proved to be his light and guide throughout his adjustment to his new home and school. There was nothing distrustful about her...until the airport incident.

For the duration of the two teenagers spending some much-needed time apart—Zach being in Florida for his procedure and Kelsey remaining in Kitty Hawk, tensions begin to rise between the latter and her significant other: Jaylen. The relationship between Kelsey and her "so-called" best friend, Zach, caused too much insecurity in the seemingly confident teenage boy. He wanted their friendship to end as quickly as it came about, but it was easier said than done—oh, how much easier. While several attempts, lies, and pure toxicity tear Kelsey and Jaylen's "golden" relationship to pieces, Zach attempts to readjust to society. With the help of his friends, family, and trust issues, it was nearly a walk in the park. Alas, a recurring string of nightmares, confidential information becoming jeopardized, and dishonesty sprouting from Zach and Kelsey's new chapter of romance kept the situation from remaining peaceful.

Would a simple mistake drive Kelsey and Zach apart for good, or would the two of them work through their struggles side by side?

Cambridge Bound (HA Volume 3)

What could go wrong if you follow your dream? It might become a nightmare before your very eyes.

Being accepted to Harvard University had been August's dream ever since he discovered the school existed. Because Harvard was one of the most prestigious universities of the United States, August made it the "Holy Grail" of his high school experience. With a 5.0 grade point average, a perfect standardized test score, countless Advanced Placement classes, and even a published novel under his belt, August thought it would be the teeniest bit of a challenge.

Despite beginning a new life away from his annoying sister and otherwise friendly environment back in Kitty Hawk, August found his college experience to be more difficult than it seemed. With a nuisance of a roommate, a puzzling schedule, and homesickness as the icing on the disappointingly bitter cake, the eighteen-year-old began to give up hope on his goal. With his mental health on a downward spiral, there seemed to be no hope for return.

Would August continue to hold up and commit to his lifelong dream, or would he leave everything behind for a second time?

Being The Bystander (HA Volume 4)

Being in middle school was tough to begin with. When his only three friends abandoned him and he was left on the verge of academically plummeting, Mason had no idea what to do.

Mason Cooper was the epitome of a middle-class middle schooler on the brink of his teenage years. Friends come and go, but in Mason's world, the latter seemed to be the only applicable aspect of his social life. Despite not being the sharpest knife in the drawer, Mason's attempts to end up on top were nothing short of honest work. His trio of "friends," though, did not appreciate his company, leaving Mason alone on a dying oasis of low self-esteem.

After a good deed sends him into a battle between two of his classmates, the bullets of self-hatred continue to ricochet, but not in the direction he hoped. Mason's desperation for friends left him in one of the most difficult spots imaginable. Despite wanting to do the right thing, the first person Mason could consider a true friend led him down the wrong path, resulting in a sticky situation that Mason had no capacity to know how to get out of.

Would Mason do the right thing and discover who authentically cares about him, or would he succumb to the peer pressure egging him on?

* * *

The Behind Series

Behind The Lens

Nobody knows what happened to Abigail Bartley. Ever since one fateful day near the end of her junior year, paranoia clawed its way up her throat, latched onto the crevices of her mind, and didn't let go. Joined by her best friends, Keagan, Jade, and Brielle, along with her supportive parents, she is tasked with yet another challenge: navigating through her final year of high school with a brave face.

When an innocent dare leads Abigail to reluctantly attempt to steal an unusual pair of glasses right off the face of Hillwell High School's "new boy," she and Noah Howell cross paths that she thought would forever run parallel. That notion was quickly proven wrong when the very person Abigail fears returns to where she thought she was safe. Her only choice to get away from him is to enlist Noah's help. As one situation snowballs into another, Abigail starts to crumble and slide into the decrepit avalanche she was before.

Will a silly pair of glasses, her friends, and a spontaneous request save Abigail from flying through the free fall of her flashbacks, or will her already-cracked resolve shatter to pieces?

Behind The Motive

Ever since a restraining order was placed against her abuser, Abigail Bartley has been thriving. She graduated high school with flying colors, just turned eighteen, and was planning to attend Hillwell University with two of her friends: Keagan Lopez and Noah Howell–the latter gradually becoming just a little bit more. Her other friends, Brielle, Jade, and Ryder all had successful futures ahead of them. What could be better than that?

Life, however, was not perfect. When Abigail begins receiving mysterious letters from the person she fought to avoid, she willingly seeks help from those closest to her for the first time. Meanwhile, her friends are all struggling with their own difficulties. Noah's family is still grieving the loss of his father. Keagan begins craving attention from her adulterous mother, causing her to rebel. Brielle and Ryder's family is struggling with money and hiding behind their walls. The latter's best friend tries to help in a controversial way. With everyone else falling apart around her, how will Abigail possibly manage to stay afloat herself?

Will Abigail and Noah piece back each of their friends like a jigsaw puzzle, seeing the beauty within the fractures, or will everybody eventually go their separate, broken ways?

Printed in Great Britain
by Amazon